Published by David J Publishing 2017

First David J Publishing edition 2017
www.davidjpublishing.com

Cover Design: Copyright © Jacqueline Stokes
www.yannadesignstudio.co.uk

Author's photograph by Annie Given

A CIP catalogue record for this book is available from the British Library
ISBN: 978-0-9957057-0-8

GW00584849

Dedication

For
Robin Leslie Graham 1937 – 2013
With all my heart and soul

Also for Henry and Patrick, their Claires,
our grandsons Oliver, Lloyd and Ben
and, of course, Roberta.

Acknowledgements

I would have never contemplated writing this book without the encouragement and support given to me in buckets by Lynda Tavakoli and her wonderful writing group. My sincere and deepest thanks to you all.

My gratitude must also go to Peter White, Shirley Bork and Don Fey for each doing the onerous job of ploughing through my manuscript and giving me the invaluable benefit of their wise and constructive criticism.

The pals who read the first chapters and egged me on to write more must have a mention – Mary Lee Jackson, Isabel Westhead, Jill Drennan, Sally Phillpott, Lisa McCausland, Anne Butler, Pat Hunt, Annie Given, Mayo Walters, Bobbie Graham, Bill Jeffrey, my brother and sister-in-law Tim and Babs Carryer, and Welby and Sheelagh Henry – without whose love, friendship and enthusiasm in those dark days . . .

And, not least, the publishers, David and Jackie Stokes who came into my kitchen one morning and made me feel like a writer – words fail me.

Days of Wine & Wardrobes

by

Felicity Graham

DAVID J
PUBLISHING

One

'And what is all this in aid of, young man?' asked Edwina Turkington after climbing out of her Jaguar trying to avoid stepping into three inches of mud. Twelve year old James Daniels had just directed her to drive into a field generously lent by a neighbouring farmer, William Shortall, as a car park for the forthcoming event.

'Oh,' replied James with a grimace, his eyes raised heavenwards. 'Mummy's overdraft.'

Edwina's large, beige, amber-beaded bosom heaved up and down as she chuckled and patted James on the head. 'I like a chap with a sense of humour,' she said and plodded through the mud to the gate and on to the lane which led to the barn with a sign outside saying:

AUCTION TODAY

Commences at 11 am precisely

Madelaine, James's mum, known to one and all as Maddy, was standing at the door of the barn watching as car after car came up the lane. She was praying none of the Shortalls, with whom they shared the lane, would want to travel down it because it was a quarter of a mile long with no pull-in places.

As well as this her mind was racing with many things – mainly panic. What on earth had she done? How was it going to work? Had she thought of everything? How could she possibly have thought of every eventuality? She had never run anything like this – nothing remotely like this, ever. Neither had her husband who, up until a few minutes ago, had seemed quite confident that he knew exactly what to do. Now, minutes before start time, he was nowhere to be seen.

Tom, Maddy's husband, was in fact in the loo doing what a man does when a man is extremely scared. He too had seen all the cars – and not only cars – but masses of people walking up the long lane from the road to their house. They must have come by bus all the way from Belfast or Ballynahinch or, perish the thought, even further. And what had he and Maddy got to offer them? A barn load of unwanted rubbish from their attic, likewise from his sister's attic, a friend's garden shed and the back of a leaking hay loft. They were going to kill him!

All of a sudden he didn't want to be an auctioneer. What the hell had his crazy wife got him into now?

And still they came, much to young James's annoyance, as the field/car park he had been put in charge of was becoming chaotic. James didn't like chaos, except in his bedroom which frequently appeared to have been stirred with a large stick. His mother would simply moan to herself nowadays when she passed his door and gently close it.

James was thinking that, before this rotten recession his father kept banging on about, they had been a normal family. Dad had gone to his job every day which was something to do with textiles and Mum had worked part time for a vet.

They had recently moved to this house in the country with fields all around and masses of space to skateboard and ride their motorbikes. He, his older brother and his sister, all had rooms of their own, and they had a cat and a springer spaniel; Dad drove a Porsche. What more could a family want? And why he had to spend a Saturday directing people and their silly cars to park in a muddy, slithery field he couldn't think.

His grumpy musings were interrupted when a car appeared with a trailer. Hah! That was not at all neat. It would stick out far too far and wreck all the lines he had so meticulously ordered – it would just have to go away.

'Sorry sir, no trailers!' That was that sorted!

'You did WHAT?' his mother had yelled at him later.

'I sent him home, Mum. His trailer wouldn't fit into the line.'

'Didn't you realise that he had brought a trailer because he was intending to BUY stuff? And he caused havoc on the lane trying to get down it when everybody else was trying to get up!'

James began to think his mother's obsession with 'stuff' and people buying it had gone way too far and he slunk off to watch their one remaining television.

Tom and Maddy's daughter, Carol, now 18, had not approved of the move to the country. It was even further away from boys than their previous house. She had inherited her mother's auburn curls which had regained their luxurious sheen after two or three years of her attempts to make them look like straw. Her 'goth' eyes had more or less returned to normal and in spite of her slouching, uncaring demeanour, she was becoming a fun human being again.

Underneath it all, she was quite enthusiastic about the forthcoming sale. She had contributed what she could from her possessions – namely two dolls she had never liked and a Wallace and Grommit clock that had seen better days. She couldn't bear to part with any of the toy animals piled on her bed but felt she had grown out of the china horses a fond aunt had given her regularly when she would rather have had money. Waiting for 'A' level results was a pain and she was dreaming of a 'year out'. Out of what exactly her mother couldn't quite pin down. Life? There was a lot of it going on, that was for sure.

Life had taken a whopping great turn as far as Maddy was concerned and she was now doing the only thing she could think of to make it a bit better. Had it all happened by default? Had she just gone along with it? It almost seemed so as she watched all these strangers walk into their barn, take a catalogue and proceed to view the things she and her sister-in-law had arranged and stuck numbers on. It was beginning to feel like a mad dream and she would wake up any minute in her and Tom's cosy bed; they would be going sailing for the day in Strangford Lough and the recession and redundancy and having no money would disappear like mist in the morning sun.

All this was happening because Maddy had decided to have a garage sale. She had seen one while visiting her parents who lived in California. A neighbour had gathered her unwanted possessions, put them in her garage and placed a sign with the time and date of the sale on her gate at the road. People had come in droves and by the end of the day she had made enough money to take her and her husband on a trip to Palm Springs. Maddy had been impressed.

Tom and Maddy were broke. It was the end of the 1970s when cheap imports from the Far East were having a ruinous effect on the textile industry in Britain. Like so many others, Tom was forced to close his innovative and once famous yarn factories and make his workers and himself redundant. He had found another job but at a greatly reduced salary which just about paid for the mortgage and food, but absolutely nothing else. He had sold their boat and his beloved Porsche and had even put the house on the market but due to the recession there was as yet no serious interest.

Maddy's heart broke every time she saw the For Sale sign which was still at the end of their lane. After years of searching she and Tom had fallen in love with the old house instantly. Now that they may have to sell up and leave so soon after moving in was almost more than she could bear, but she knew she had to face the facts.

Their two boys were sprouting in different directions and each required a new school uniform for the September term. Maddy reckoned she needed at least £200. So, in the absence of winning the pools, she decided there was nothing else for it - she would have a garage sale. After all, their house was full of things they didn't really need.

Beginning in the attic she extracted redundant picture frames, lamps, cushions, rugs, old cameras, Christmas decorations, ornaments, curtains, blankets, sheets and anything else lying around she felt they could live without.

As she worked her way through the house she became more and more ruthless, like a looter, finishing in the kitchen with any gadget she didn't absolutely need then pots, pans and tea sets. At the Georgian corner cupboard they had bought on their honeymoon

12

and their inherited antique dining furniture she drew a line, but nearly everything else went straight out of the house into the big barn in their yard.

It was odd but she felt no pangs of sentiment whatsoever. All their possessions meant to her now were rugby boots, blazers and grey school pullovers. She was also soon to find that, without clutter, the house was amazingly easy to clean and having extracted all her magazines – antiques, collectables, Horse and Hound - she could even get the vacuum cleaner under their bed.

She was hauling things across the yard for the umpteenth time when Tom's sister, Mary, appeared; she thought a garage sale was a great idea and sped off home to bring two trailer loads of her own unwanted things. Then her friend, Jane, who was American and knew all about garage sales, arrived. (Jane knew a lot about everything in fact) and she went off to get some of her own bits and pieces to sell.

By five thirty in the evening the barn was filled nearly to the rafters. Myriad gizmos, gadgets, objects and commodities such as prams, toys, plants, bits of carpet, underfelt, bed heads, odd doors, chairs, prints, paintings, bicycles, old suitcases, picnic baskets, tools, trays, tiles, television sets, bundles of magazines, vacuum cleaners, fire guards, boxes of kitchen ware, crockery and china, had been arranged as artfully as possible by the three hopeful vendors who were now sitting on the wall in the yard in a neat row of exhaustion each clutching what was considered to be a well earned glass of wine when Tom returned from his daily toil.

'Now you're for it,' hissed his sister who knew him very well and took off with Jane hot on her heels.

Just like rats leaving a sinking ship, thought Maddy. She knew explaining to Tom what they were doing was not going to be easy. His morale had taken quite a beating and he was not going to like the idea of local folk riffling through his possessions and haggling over them. The response to Maddy's announcement was much as she expected.

'I suppose this is some crazy AMERICAN idea?' he fumed through gritted teeth.

It wasn't that he had anything against things American or

13

against America personally, it was simply that his mother-in-law lived there and it could not be said that they had ever warmed to one another.

He then began to deliver a fairly eloquent speech about limits to a man's tolerance, asked why did Maddy NEVER discuss anything with him first and then, mid tirade, he stopped and looked at the assembled mountain of 'effects' as if for the first time. A strange look came into his eyes and, after what, in hindsight Maddy could only describe as a 'pregnant' pause, he said quietly and firmly, 'We won't have a garage sale, we'll have an auction, I've always wanted to do an auction.' As far as Maddy knew he had never been near an auction in his life.

Delighted with his happy change of humour, Maddy agreed with alacrity and enquired as to how an auction was organised.

'Oh, just arrange things into lots, stick numbers on them and leave the rest to me!' said Tom, The Auctioneer.

Maddy swiftly realised that it was not quite as simple as Tom had made it sound, especially with other people's things involved.

How were they going to work out whose possessions had made what at the end? How were they going to keep track of everything if anyone was to buy anything?

While Maddy and Mary were sticking on numbers, making lists and pondering this problem, Tom was busy building the rostrum from which he would conduct the auction. It consisted of a number of wooden pallets piled on top of each other at one end of the barn. It was a sturdy enough construction provided one stood dead centre. Slight movement to either side caused the whole affair to tip.

'You will be my clerk,' he announced.

'What's that?' Maddy asked.

'You will sit by me during the auction and ....'

'On THAT thing?'

'It's perfectly alright if you don't jiggle about.'

'Yes, dear,' Maddy said, as she handed him a list of items for sale which she had typed in the small hours.

'Hmmm,' he replied, perusing the list. 'That's fine – of

course you'll need another one for yourself, with much bigger spacing.'

'Oh. Why?' Her face fell.

'Well – because – you just do; now hand me that hammer.'

The following morning Jane bustled in. 'You've got to advertise it you know,' she announced.

'But that's expensive and I don't have any money,' Maddy moaned.

'A small ad in the local paper is all you need and that will cost you three pounds – come on!'

Maddy knew from her past experience it did not do to argue with Jane so off she went with the advert that Jane had written, to put in the local newspaper. It read:

AUCTION on Saturday 14th August at
123 Cross Road, Killybane, Co Antrim.
Begins 11 a.m.
Viewing from 10.00 a.m.

She was convinced that no one would see it or bother.

'And you'll have to type a catalogue,' Jane decreed.

'Yes, Jane,' said Maddy as she advanced wearily once again to her typewriter.

'When you have it ready I'll go and get it photocopied – I have a friend who'll do it for nothing.'

I'll bet you have, thought Maddy.

'I'll get fifty copies – bye.'

Fifty copies! Maddy found it hard to believe fifty people would actually come.

Now the auction day had dawned. The catalogues were neatly stacked by the door of the barn under a sign saying, 'Catalogues 20p each'. Tom had spent the previous night writing a witty comment beside each lot on his copy of the list – he was going to be the funniest Auctioneer in Ireland.

He finally appeared wearing his best suit looking extremely smart. He clambered up onto the rostrum and sat behind a small table to which he had attached a microphone. The gavel he had decided to use was a parting gift from one of his mill workers - an

15

antique bobbin made into a pen. It was placed in front of him at the ready.

Maddy joined him and they smiled nervously at each other as folk drifted in, bought catalogues and went about looking at the lots.

While James was busy with his car park, Harry, their fifteen year old son was trying to psyche himself up to doing the job of porter. He had been designated to hold each item aloft as it came up for sale or point to it if it was too heavy to lift.

'Mum, I can't believe you have put our Lego in the sale – I just can't,' he'd said at breakfast.

'But you don't play with it any more – it was just gathering dust.'

'I know Mum, but it was nice to know it was there – just in case.'

'Look, Harry, do you want those Nike trainers or not?'

'Huh?'

'For the last time, I DON'T HAVE ANY MONEY and I have got to get some from somewhere. I am selling most of the things I have – I have sold all my shares, I have sold my grandmother's pearls, I have sold my favourite evening bag to Jane and all so I can buy you and James some new uniforms, so DON'T complain to me about a few bits of plastic!'

'Sorry Mum.' Harry slurped his cornflakes and said no more. Maddy felt awful but resisted the temptation to sneak out to the barn and remove the Lego from the sale.

By 11.00 o'clock the barn held a truly eclectic assortment of people from the genteel, elderly 'Jaguar' lady to every farmer in the townland of Killybane and maybe beyond. A most distinguished looking gentleman with a fine head of thick white hair, wearing a beautiful suit, gave Maddy a smile and in a soft Irish brogue said, 'It's a lovely little auction you have here, Ma'am.'

She suddenly felt much better. She had begun to feel (as Tom had) that they had got everybody here under false pretences, who when they saw all the junk, would growl and go home.

The next person to come in was a large lady with dyed black hair and a mouth that Maddy swore could catch rats. The coat she wore on that hot August day seemed incongruous, not to say unsavoury and her eyes flitted from item to item in a greedy fashion as she strolled round the barn. Maddy felt anxious as she'd had experience at charity jumble sales where 'ladies', wearing large coats with interior pockets could, with skilful sleight of hand, swiftly denude a stand of its choice items and slip away. She made a mental note to watch this one.

Young people, old people, some with baskets of sandwiches and thermos flasks came and looked around and found a perch. No one complained about anything and, by the looks of it, were all going to stay.

Carol was in charge of selling the catalogues and keeping an 'eye on things' whatever that meant, and, shortly before 11 o'clock, an expectant hush descended upon the motley throng. Maddy, with pen poised, waited for Tom to begin.

'Good morning ladies and gentlemen,' he said into the microphone and, without warning, stood up. He'd been an actor before he'd decided to go into business and, perhaps, on facing an audience again, he'd felt the urge to bow or something. The rostrum tipped and table, Tom and Maddy began to slide toward the edge. In the nick of time he sat down again and they managed to inch their way back to the centre of the quivering contraption and relative safety.

'You jiggled it,' giggled Maddy.

'Shuddup,' snarled the Auctioneer, too tense to see the funny side. At the back of the barn amid a crowd of people, Harry held up a large, heavy, black frying pan.

'Lot number one,' Tom said into the microphone, commencing the sale and, unwittingly, a whole new life for the pair of them.

Two

The night before, it had been agreed that as the auction progressed Maddy, being the auctioneer's clerk, would record each lot Tom sold with the name of the purchaser and the price. Mary and Jane, standing in the crowd trying to control their mirth at the near disaster on the rostrum, were each clutching a list of their own lots so they could keep track of what their things made.

Tom had acted in many radio plays and was therefore no stranger to the microphone. He slipped into the Auctioneer mode as if he'd been doing it all his life. *The role he's been waiting for,* thought Maddy, remembering his comment about always wanting to 'do' an auction.

His voice was quiet and clear. There were no amateur whistles or shrieks from the loud speakers and he really did seem to know what he was doing. For the briefest of moments Maddy was almost overwhelmed with pride and admiration – maybe he should have stayed with acting.

He had made the decision to give it up before he had met her – but what if he hadn't? She might now be married to a famous star of stage and screen and not sitting on a wobbly pile of pallets in a barn full of...

A dig from Tom's elbow brought her fantasy to an abrupt halt and she hastily noted what he had knocked down Lot Number 10 for – 50p to a Mr Smith who was now the proud owner of several lampshades and a book rest. Subsequent lots were knocked down to quite a few different 'Smiths' and the gentleman with the Irish brogue was 'Brown'.

Hmmm, she thought, and decided that she would have to distinguish between each bidder with a note like 'Smith – funny hat' or 'Smith – bushy eyebrows' or 'Smith – yellow anorak'. Fortunately Tom's auctioneering was slow enough to allow her to do this. His comments about each lot took time and Maddy's previous admiration swiftly diminished as these ranged from the absurd to the cringe-worthy.   Lot 27, for instance - one of Jane's - the delivery of which had been quite a performance in itself.

'I am bringing a piano!' Jane had earlier announced on the telephone.

'I didn't know you played – do you think it's a good idea during an auction?' Maddy asked.

'NO! Not to play, to SELL.'

'How are you going to get it here? I don't think it would be a good idea in our old trailer.'

'I've organised a horse box and some guys from the rugby club, see you in twenty, bye.'

Sure enough, twenty minutes later, Jane had appeared with a horse box in tow and four massive chaps who unfolded themselves from her car limb by limb. After stretching and flexing their impressive, rippling collective musculature, they strode manfully round to the back of the horse box and stood awaiting orders.

Maddy dashed into the barn to make a suitable space and came out again to see Jane issuing instructions as the rugby players began to heft the piano.

There was much grunting from inside the horse box and sucked-in remarks like 'Up your end a bit, Joe' and 'Watch yer feet everyone' and then, 'One, two, three – lift.' Had the four of them been in sync, they and the instrument might have come out unscathed but, as it was, someone decided to suddenly change his grip and things, quite literally, got out of hand. Castors caught, corners got knocked, toes got squashed, knees got bashed and, only after what seemed like endless boinging, twanging, ouching and cursing did the piano end up in the yard.

After a rest and yet more flexing and stretching, they grabbed it again and, with two of them either side, they did a sort of soft shoe shuffle with it into the barn. They each received a can of beer for their trouble from Jane before she took them home, probably via their nearest physiotherapist.

'Lot 27,' the auctioneer announced. 'An upright piano by Crane of Belfast on castors and complete with stool – every note works and I want a few notes from you for this lot.'

Just as well he never wrote his own scripts, Maddy groaned to herself.

Tom knocked it down to Mr Brown for £16.00 who explained later that he had only bought the lot for the stool as the piano was riddled with woodworm and thus, worth virtually nothing.

A few minutes later Tom came to Lot 29, saying, 'Thought of a new hobby or an inexpensive Christmas present? An enamelling kit could keep you amused throughout the winter – very decorative results too!'

This Maddy had bought years ago and, after several disastrous attempts to make brooches and belt buckles, filling the house with the acrid smell of hot enamel and singeing the cat, she had given up on it, much to the family's relief.

What a plausible so and so he is, she thought when it made the grand sum of £18.00.

Lot 31 really took her to the fair,

'For the gourmet,' announced her newly discovered plausible so and so of a husband, 'a wine rack, a spice rack and a knife rack – you supply the condiments and a nice piece of steak. Add to the kitchen for your convenience.'

Maddy hoped she had been able to conceal her astonishment as she knew he could not so much as boil an egg. And then came Lot 35.

'Even if the chrome isn't up to Royal Coach Standards, this is an excellent pram. Carrier lifts out and frame folds up. Perfect for the car. Waterproof cover.'

He was excelling himself – he had never pushed a pram in his life let alone folded one up or put it into a car. And he had never

20

worried about his babies or anyone else's getting wet. Bidding was almost nonexistent and he had to knock it down for £2.00 when he had been expecting £25.00 but, totally undeterred, he continued happily on to Lot 40.

'Three Spanish water colour paintings. Dramatic light effect, unusual and nice in a set.'

Oh blimey, thought Maddy, *now he's an art expert!* And then, when she thought it couldn't get any worse, he came to lot 41, a painting thick with impasto.

'Now from water to oils. I think this was done when oil was cheaper.'

Maddy noticed that on his list he had added a dash after this comment. Did this mean he felt he would have to pause while people fell over laughing? They certainly weren't. They were gawping with astonished disbelief.

'Colourful and original and could brighten up a wall very nicely,' he ended with a grin.

Oh dear, Maddy thought. *The art expert is on a roll. Where is this going to end?* Lot 43 nearly finished her.

'An attractive print of a Poodle,' Tom announced and then added, 'A nice present for someone you know who has one or can't be bothered with the real thing.'

If 'losing the will to live' had been an expression in those days, Maddy would have coined it herself but all she could do was smile bravely and soldier on. At the same time, she couldn't help noticing, in spite of the rhetoric which seemed to have the bidders quite baffled, they were bidding and things were being sold, albeit for way below the prices the Auctioneer had notionally written on his list. It was all being taken very seriously and people appeared to be really pleased when a lot was - eventually - knocked down to them.

Then, on gazing round the room, she realised it would be quite easy for anyone to lift anything and walk off with it. Harry was busy waiting for and holding up each item and Carol was sitting at the door conversing with a tall, dark haired fellow wearing a cap perched jauntily at the back of his head. The door Carol sat beside was wide open and people were wandering in and out. The

Jaguar lady was in animated conversation with the Rat Catcher, Mr Brown was sharing coffee with a gnome-like little woman wearing a bobble hat and others were drinking tea from flasks, chatting as if they had known each other for ever and those who weren't interested in the lot currently being sold were generally milling about. *For all the world like a Hogarth etching*, Maddy thought.

She tried to catch Carol's eye but, to her consternation, the chap in the cap had her daughter's more than full and undivided attention. Mary and Jane were looking pleased with the proceedings and had been giving her what they thought were discreet thumbs up signals until the Auctioneer pointed his gavel at them and demanded to know if they were bidding – or NOT! Red faced they melted into the crowd just when Maddy had been hoping they would notice the risky situation and do something about it. She couldn't leave her clerk's perch so decided things would just have to take their course. What would be would be, she crossed fingers and hoped everybody was honest.

Five and a half hours later Tom finally came to the end of his list of one hundred and one lots and he and his 'clerk' took it in turns to climb gingerly off the rostrum making sure it stayed balanced as they did so. Tom looked exhausted and said he was going into the house for a drink – a large one.

Almost immediately Maddy was confronted with a growing line of people wanting to pay for and take their purchases home. She had not prepared for this moment. She had been unable to envisage this part of the proceedings and had no system in place whereby she could work out who had bought what and for how much. She asked Harry to unplug the microphone and help her lift the small table and a chair off the rostrum and place them in the yard. She sat down with her and Tom's auction lists in front of her, praying she could work things out on a spiral bound jotter that would have to do as a receipt book.

She was more than conscious of everyone staring at her as she asked for names and checked through the hundred and one lots to see what was allocated to each of them. She realised it was going to take ages and Smith – yellow anorak - had taken it off which didn't help.

Meanwhile, chaos was reigning in the barn. People were grabbing things and demanding boxes to put their purchases in. Of course, none were available as no one had thought to provide any. Carol had finally torn herself away from the fellow in the jaunty cap to referee a vicious tug of war with one of her dolls that was taking place between the Rat Catcher and the gnome in the bobble hat both of whom were convinced they'd bought it. Cars were now cramming into the yard ready for loading and causing a major gridlock. Where was James? This wasn't neat at all!

Maddy smiled wanly at the queue but, apart from the contretemps between Rat Catcher and Bobble Hat, still echoing from the barn, everyone was cheerful, enjoying the sunny afternoon and didn't seem to mind hanging around at all. There was, in fact, a party atmosphere and Maddy was sure that, apart from those she knew were neighbours, a good few attending knew each other quite well – was there such a thing as an auction-going crowd?

When she eventually worked out the first bill she discovered she had also overlooked organising a float so that she could give buyers change.

Harry came to the rescue with the contents of a large whiskey bottle he kept by his bed for saving twenty pence pieces and pound coins. James, who had finally appeared, ran into the house to raid his father's pockets.

As the crowd began to disappear and the gridlock undid itself, Mr Brown came into the yard in a van driven by his friend and assistant, Alfie.

Neither man was large in stature. Alfie was tiny and thin but extremely agile. The two of them went into the barn and came out carrying the piano as if it were as light as a feather. Neither of them grunted, cursed or said 'to you' or anything.

Smiling benignly, they placed it behind the van and tipped it up lengthwise onto the point of balance. Alfie left Mr Brown to keep it steady while he gently reversed the van with the back doors open until it was just touching the underneath of the piano's tipped end. Alfie then put the hand brake on, leapt out of the cab, joined Mr Brown at the other end of the piano, which they lifted together and, hay presto, it slid into the van.

'Wow,' said Harry, 'did you see that? And none of that fancy flexing or stretching!'

Maddy was still working her way through the queue when Edwina Turkington came up and introduced herself. 'That was great!' she said, beaming at Maddy. 'Now I am retired I have time to go to auctions. When is the next one?'

'I beg your pardon?' Maddy said, taken aback, noticing Rat Catcher, Bobble Hat and others were waiting for her reply. 'We weren't actually planning on having another one.'

'But you must,' Edwina said emphatically. 'Such a lovely place – it's ideal!' She turned to the others. 'Don't you think there should be another one - soon?' They all nodded and agreed. Maddy didn't know what to say. There were at least six more bills to be worked out and she had to concentrate.

'Ah – we'll have to think about it,' she said as she tore a page from her 'receipt' book and handed it over. 'Your receipt, Mrs Turkington.'

'It's 'Miss', dear.'

'Oh! I am so sorry.'

'So am I, dear – so am I.' Everybody laughed and Maddy warmed to this plainspoken lady.

Finally everyone had gone, the barn was empty and Maddy was in a state of shock sitting in front of a whole pile of money. Her 'looting' job had made her £250 exactly, Mary £300 and Jane £70. Carol had been delighted with the prices her Beswick china horses had made and the Wallace and Grommit clock that had nearly caused fisticuffs between two bidders, had sold for £20 – the highest price of the sale. The Lego, though, had made very little, much to Harry's disgust but he knew his mum had made enough to buy him some new trainers so he didn't complain.

Mary and Jane were also delighted with the cumulative amounts their items had made, even if one or two had gone for much less than they had expected.

To Maddy's relief, no one had gone off with anything they hadn't paid for and she, thankfully, had sorted out the 'war of the doll'. Bobble Hat and Rat Catcher had to agree that on both the clerk's and the auctioneer's lists it was clearly shown it had been knocked down to a Mr. McKeown. Neither of them had got it and, much to her amazement, they went off the best of friends.

Considering how well the day had gone and what they had made, Maddy couldn't help wondering why they shouldn't have another one. She felt sure that there must be other people out there who would like to make some extra cash and had houses full of things they didn't really need...

Three

Barely a month after their first auction the following advertisement was placed in four local newspapers:

WANT TO REALISE SOME CASH?
Collectively your junk could be worth
more than you think!
Gather up all your unwanted items and
we will collect and auction them for you.
Our last auction of 100 lots for two clients
realised over £500.00

If interested telephone:
KILLYBANE AUCTIONS
Killybane 777
Between 2 and 4 pm
Monday – Friday

Maddy hadn't found it hard to convince Tom that they should give it a go. He had thoroughly enjoyed taking five and a half hours to auction a hundred and one lots and, even when Harry told him the auction goers did not appreciate his jokes or comments, he seemed to relish the idea of doing it all again.

Carol had been a bit dreamy eyed after the sale and had gone pink when her mother asked her who the chap with the jaunty cap was.

'Oh, – him,' she tried to sound casual. 'He has an antique shop in Donegal Pass in Belfast. He said his name was Sean McFarland.'

'He didn't seem interested in bidding for anything.'

'No, well, he really only buys antiques and we didn't have any in the sale.'

'He stayed for long enough!' said Harry, who could never resist having a dig at his elder sister. Carol threw him a savage look and Maddy tactfully changed the subject.

'I suppose I had better get in a bit of practice towing that trailer if I am going to be collecting other people's things to sell.'

James began to laugh. 'Oh Mum, you will never be able to do that! You can hardly tow the bin down the lane without it falling off or stuff flying out of it! And, what about reversing? I don't think so!' He shook his cynical twelve year old head.

It was Maddy's turn to go pink – with fury! 'I would remind you I did quite a few car rallies in my youth and even mastered hand brake turns. Surely any bloody fool can learn to tow a trailer!'

Tom said he would give her lessons the following evening when he came home from work – from his 'proper' job.

Fizz, their Springer spaniel, scraped at the back door and barked. It was time for her daily walk to which Maddy looked forward almost as eagerly as the dog.

Their house was surrounded by fields and they could ramble for miles without seeing another soul in a countryside blessed with a natural beauty that changed day by day and season by season.

With her pocket camera Maddy caught the light on newly mown hay, the corduroy ridges of ploughed earth, the first primroses and violets. Fizz, with her tail wagging nineteen to the dozen, would crisscross the ground at dizzying speed, following her nose telling her of rabbits, stoats, birds, foxes and other delightful scents that only springers know about.

The ever present possibility of the house being sold and their having to leave made these daily excursions even more precious. Maddy had to work hard at putting it all to the back of her mind and yet, she thought, *if this auction thing happens to work, if we could make a go of it – maybe – perhaps...*

She stopped herself even daring to dream and resolutely

waded through a stream to take a photograph of some wild violets she had spied nodding at her from the far bank.

From now on these walks would have to take place either before two or after four o'clock as Maddy had to be by the phone in case it rang. When she saw the advertisement actually in print she felt scared but also excited and, not for the first time in her life, wondered what on earth had she done now?

She sat by the phone the first day and it didn't ring once. She used the time to try to work out a system for payments after the sale. During the auction she had been conscious of people not liking to call out their names – hence all the 'Smiths' and other unlikely names. Northern Ireland was going through troubled times and, even when she had worked for the vet, people were loathe to tell her their names if there was any one else in the waiting room. Could she work out some sort of number system? Maybe when people bought a catalogue they could be given a number as well and when a lot was knocked down to them, all they would have to do was hold it up.

She decided to discuss this with Tom and filled in the rest of the time writing large numbers on plain post cards with a black felt tip pen.

It was disappointing to greet him that evening with the news that they hadn't had so much as one phone call. 'It's early days,' Tom said. 'The papers only came out this morning and perhaps people haven't had time to read them yet.'

The next day was much the same until, on the dot of four o'clock the phone rang and Maddy picked it up with a shaking hand 'Killybane Auctions,' she announced in an uncontrollable high pitched squeak.

A gruff man's voice said, 'Who?'

'K – Killybane Auctions,' Maddy said, suddenly feeling quite daft.

'Oh!' he said. 'I must have got the wrong number.'

Deflated and fed up she replaced the receiver but almost immediately, it rang again. This time it was a real enquiry. Her emotions soared as she began to take in what the lady was saying about a holiday home in Newcastle on the coast road to Annalong and would they like to go and clear the contents? This was more like it!

Maddy took directions, arranged a date and time for the collection - it would have to be a Saturday as Tom was working during the week – and, yes, we'll see you then, madam, thank you and goodbye!

Oh! Happy Days. She couldn't wait for Tom to come home from work to tell him.

Saturday came and they sallied forth with the trailer in tow. The sun shone, their hopes were high – a whole house full of furniture and goodness knew what else awaited them.

The drive down to Newcastle always lifted Maddy's heart and the sight of the Mourne Mountains 'sweeping down to the sea' brought back happy memories of childhood holidays spent there before her parents had gone to live in America.

The iconic seaside town with its ice cream parlours, gift shops, honky-tonk amusement arcade and boating pond was always much the same as she remembered. They drove through the main street full of dawdling traffic and promenading holiday makers then on to the coast road that wound round a landscape dotted with holiday cottages and bungalows. The sea glinted far below on one side and swathes of purple heather, feathery green bracken and bright yellow gorse swept up the rocky mountainside on the other. The address the owner had given them was not hard to find as there was a number on the gate.

The 'holiday home' was in a wonderful position with a panoramic view of the Irish Sea right round to the lighthouse at St John's Point and it probably had been a pleasant little timber cabin – once. It was now almost non-existent as the roof had caved in and it appeared to have been totally vandalised. Brambles and weeds were crawling round the once quite fine Victorian wardrobes, pine wash stands and bedsteads – none of which had a set of legs between them. What the vandals had left the woodworm had eaten and even the dear little cast iron stove had been smashed to smithereens.

The owner, who had been waiting for them, must have seen the horror on their faces and before they could say anything she said, 'Ye jist take what yiz want. Here's my new address fer yiz to send the cheque til. I've to go now, bye!' and she disappeared.

'Cheque?' said Tom, 'for this?' He glared at Maddy as if she were to blame for the whole thing.

When she could speak she said, 'Look, we are here now, so let's hoke about - there just might be something….'

Tom was familiar with Maddy's 'hoking'. The last time they had been to the dump together he had to physically restrain her from diving into a skip when she had seen a man toss in what she described as a 'perfectly okay spindle-back chair'. He had also been too slow to stop her from accosting another man who was about to dispose of a coffee table.

'What's wrong with that table?' she'd said.

'What's it to you, missus?' He glared at her as he lifted it over his head.

'Well it doesn't look bad enough to dump!'

'That's none of your interferin' business, – is it?' he said grinning manically, chucking it in the air as high as he could so it crashed down on the other things in the skip where, in an instant, it became eminently dumpable.

'There y' go! It's all yours if you still want it!'

Tom had to grab Maddy and bundle her into the car before she started World War Three.

Now, obviously determined to seek out something from the ruined pile, she dived into what had been the kitchen and began scrabbling about. Tom was about to put his foot down when she whooped with delight and unearthed a surprisingly undamaged cast iron and brass fender.

'These are really fashionable at the moment in front of Victorian fireplaces with pretty tiles.'

Tom grudgingly took it from her, put it in the trailer and had to admit that it was quite attractive with its moulded decoration and curlicue rests either end for fire irons. 'This will hardly pay for the petrol – let alone our time,' he muttered.

'Oh don't be such a misery guts – come and give me a hand with this wardrobe – I know it's got woodworm but someone might want to restore it.'

So Tom helped her. They took what they could wrench from the tendrils of convolvulus and that which did not disintegrate beneath their eager hands. As Tom deftly roped it all together in the trailer he decided they were both barking mad and anyone buying any of it, with the exception of the fender, would be barking mad as well.

On their way home Tom began to laugh so much he had to stop the car. He had caught a glimpse of their reflection in a shop window. With their trailer load of furniture that had definitely seen better days they looked like tinkers or Steptoe and Son. Was it only a few months since he had been strutting through airports and executive lounges in a pin striped suit?

Maddy realised with a shock she hadn't heard Tom's chortling, infectious laugh for a long time and soon she was laughing too. 'What is it?' she eventually managed to ask. 'What is so funny?'

'Do you know, Maddy,' he said, gathering his breath, 'your grandfather was absolutely right.'

'About what?'

'When he said if you stick your backside up in the air – someone will come along and kick it for you!'

'How do you mean?'

'I should have realised that if you advertise for junk you'll darned well get it!'

Four

The calls kept coming in and, on looking back some months later, Maddy didn't think she was flattering herself when she decided that Killybane and surrounding areas hadn't seen such an attractive and charming refuse collector in a long time.

In her somewhat battered blue Chrysler Estate car with trailer attached and Fizz beside her in the passenger seat she took almost anything anybody had to give her. Rusty iron bedsteads, plastic baths with holes in them not only for the plug, bicycles with one wheel, mugs with no handles, bed ends without beds, boilers, chicken feeders and black plastic covered chesterfield suites - they could always be re-covered couldn't they?

She was returning home one day with one of the latter, the chair of which she hadn't tied on very well. On rounding the last bend into their lane the trailer hit a bump and the chair bounced out and fell into the ditch. As she was struggling to retrieve the chair she was convinced everyone she knew in the whole of Northern Ireland passed by wondering had the Daniels sunk so low they were now rootling for things in ditches?

The driving-with-trailer lessons hadn't gone too badly and Tom had only lost his temper once when Maddy misjudged the distance between two gateposts and the mudguard of the trailer wheels tore the gate off its hinges. It hadn't done the mudguard any favours either. She was getting better at reversing but had to admit that James had been right, it was more difficult than she had imagined and, when doing collections, she generally would unhook the trailer and turn it and the car separately. Going in circles with it hooked on was infinitely preferable but that wasn't always possible without driving for miles.

She ended up in some strange places. One morning she had agreed to meet a Mr Duggan at a certain road junction whereupon she would follow him to his house. Mr Duggan had said this would be easiest as the directions were too complicated. By the time she realised Mr Duggan was somewhat the worse for drink it was too late to turn back.

She had made contact, as agreed, and obeying a languid hand signal from the window of his ancient, rusty, brown Ford Prefect, had followed him over several miles of winding lanes, and down a rough track through three fields which had ended up at the back of an exceedingly run down farmhouse.

By now her car and trailer were firmly embedded in two feet of mud behind his car which was likewise trapped. On opening her car door she gingerly placed her foot on a tuft of grass sticking out of the mud, cursing herself for not having brought her wellies.

Mr Duggan opened his door and, hanging on to it, began climbing out. She noticed he was wearing his wellies but on feet attached to legs which were gently buckling. His grip on the door slackened and he crumpled to the soggy ground.

'Mr Duggan!' she shouted.'Are you alright?' She desperately looked for another clump of grass to leap to.

'Ah haa!' spluttered Mr Duggan grabbing at the door again half pulling himself up, ''s the bloody rain – 's always the same – muck – Himself'll have to get the tractor an – ha – ha – get us bloody out! – tha'll teach him! Ha ha, ha, haaah!'

Wondering who 'Himself' might be Maddy gave up trying to save her feet and went to Mr Duggan's aid. He gazed ponderously at her muddy shoes and ankles, blasted her with whisky laden breath and whispered in a conspiratorial tone, 'I should a tole ye t'wear yer boots –ha ha, ha --- oops!' and crumpled again.

Maddy pulled him upright once more and, blessing the fact that he was slight and light, they set off towards the farm.

''S over there,' he said, pointing to a group of outbuildings.

He seemed to be steadier on his feet so Maddy let him go and picked her way to drier ground.

'Here?' she turned round. Mr Duggan had disappeared. 'Mr Duggan!' she shouted, retracing her steps, beginning to feel a little anxious. She found him, crumpled again, on a pile of rotting planks and potato sacks, smiling benignly and covered in mud. 'Mr Duggan – maybe I should just go home and forget about the furniture for today?' she hopefully suggested.

'Hmph!' a voice came from behind them. 'Ye may jist leave him lyin' there – I suppose you'd be the wumman what's come for the furniture.' Maddy turned to face a small, elderly, black clad lady with a potato sack tied round her waist. 'Ye'll have to forgive me,' the lady said, indicating her soiled hands and wiping them on the sack, 'I'm sortin' spuds.' As Maddy was now nearly as mud spattered as Mr Duggan she couldn't think why this lady should be apologising to her for her appearance. 'Ye should have worn yer boots.'

'Yes – I'm sorry – it was stupid of me – um – could you give me a hand – Mr Duggan appears to be stuck.'

'Mister Duggan can lie there and rot for all I care!' She glared past Maddy at him. 'Will ye get up out a' that ye drunken SCUTT,' she yelled. Mr Duggan flinched, came to life, beamed and pulled himself up.

'Sadie, darling, yer a great wee wumman – there's none to touch ye. Wud ye just show this lady me stuff – God help her – she's no boots – her feet are boggin.'

Maddy was beginning to feel like a social outcast and made up her mind to never go anywhere ever again without her boots.

Sadie looked at her, twitched her head sideways, said, 'C'mon' and plodded off.

Maddy followed dumbly with Mr Duggan laughing to himself and squelshing unsteadily behind.

It did not take long to rip the corrugated iron which acted as a door to the lean-to (which was also leaning sideways) from its grass encrusted roots to reveal the 'furniture in store', as Mr Duggan had described it on the telephone. What met Maddy's eyes was: a cracked lavatory, a box for a chicken to 'clock' in, more corrugated iron, a large mushroom thing, a rotting hall table, a roll of sheep wire, two broken sash windows and, dimly lit in the back, a sideboard with brass handles. On spying the sideboard, Maddy's sinking heart rose and she leaned forward for a better look.

'Oh no!' said Sadie at once. 'That belongs to Himself – it's not going.'

'Well I don't think we could sell any of this,' Maddy said indicating the rest. Even with her imagination working overtime she could think of no restoration or 'other use' possibilities for any of it. 'I'm sorry,' she said, trying to be polite.

'If I had a shillin' for every chicken wha's clocked in that box – I'd be a rish man,' Mr Duggan announced. 'An' tha' toilet – they don't make 'em like tha' any more – if I had a shillin for ......'

'That's enough of that!' snapped Sadie. 'If she says she can't take it – she can't take it!'

Maddy was beginning to feel she couldn't take one wee bit more of this 'Cold Comfort Farm', especially now she knew exactly what was lurking in the woodshed.

'There's more – this way.' Sadie jerked her head again and they followed her to a large open barn. Huge mounds of potatoes were everywhere and, standing in the middle, next to a set of potato scales, stood a magnificent large deal kitchen table. Maddy mentally valued it at several hundred pounds.

The woman read her mind again. 'Oh no – yer not getting that! Sure, what would I sort the spuds on?'

In a dank corner sat a three piece suite. It was a rather strange affair upholstered in mauve leatherette, patched in places, sporting long wooden legs. Sadie and Mr Duggan dragged it out and placed in the yard for further inspection. The legs gave it a duck-like appearance and Maddy hoped it would waddle away.

'Are those legs original?' she queried.

'Oh no,' said Mr Duggan proudly, 'put them on myself – t'was too low – couldn't get out of it – so I put them long legs on it – look!' He plonked himself on the sofa and tried to get up, but the crumbling syndrome set in again and he flailed about like an ailing sheep stranded on its back.

Sadie insisted he was left to get on with it and retreated into the barn where she unearthed what once had been quite a respectable Edwardian mahogany extending dining table before someone had used it to saw wood on and, of course, there was no leaf.

'Himself needed it,' Maddy was informed, 'used it to fix a hole in one of the sheds.'

Desperation was setting in with Maddy. What if she refused to take anything and, if she did, would she get any help to get her car out of the mud? She began to feel doomed, destined to spend eternity in this spud bound hell.

A wardrobe lay on its side in another corner with potato sacks draped over it. Sadie, with help from Maddy, was attempting to unearth this when a huge shadow cast itself over their exertions. Maddy turned to see the most enormous man – the giant from Jack and the Beanstalk came to mind – belt round his ample girth and all. She swore the ground trembled at his approach.

It was Himself!

'Why did ye not bring yer boots, missus?' he boomed. 'Gawd wumman yer mud to yer oxters!'

'How do you do Mr er....er..?'

'Duggan! – call me Jim. Where's that brother of mine?'

'I think he's sitting on a sofa in the yard.'

'Well – did he gi' ye the furniture?'

'I'm really frightfully sorry but I don't think .....'

'Hah! I suppose you're stuck in the muck – don't you worry dear, I'll have you out in no time – just you wait here.'

He thundered off and Sadie returned to pulling out the wardrobe which Maddy could already see was modern, mouldy and falling apart. She heard a tractor starting up and someone shouting but Sadie was intent on getting the wardrobe out of hiding and Maddy felt she couldn't leave her to her own devices. They eventually had most of it upright but bits, including its cracked mirror, kept falling off.

Rain was now beating on the barn roof and Maddy thought about the suite and Mr Duggan outside.

After a while she heard the tractor again and looked out to see it with her car and trailer in tow. Not only that – her trailer was loaded with the now rain sodden suite, the lavatory, the chicken clocking box, the sash windows – everything.

'A wee girl like you shouldn't be doin' the like o' this!' Jim bellowed. 'I've it all loaded – do ye know how to do a farmer's hay knot?' He produced the rope from the back of the trailer and was busy tying everything on. 'If ye loop it round like this and pull this through here and up and round and pull tight – see – ye can just give a tug when ye get home and it'll all come loose.'

At his insistence, Maddy tried. It didn't work. Knots, in Maddy's book, were similar to maths, she had never been very good at them. She'd been a lousy girl guide. The rain was now pelting down and she was soaked to the skin. Regardless, he made her try again and again until she finally got it right and the load was all roped on. Maddy was gazing at the suite which, having been covered in dust from the potatoes and then rained on, was a very sorry sight.

Mr Duggan Number One must have crumpled again as he was nowhere to be seen. She prayed he wasn't in the trailer. How was she going to get through the mud again? How was she going to explain this load of awful stuff to the Auctioneer? How was she going to explain no sale cheque to Mr Crumply Duggan and Himself?

'What about the wardrobe?' Sadie shouted from the barn.

'I'll have to come back for it, Mrs Duggan,' Maddy shouted through the rain knowing she didn't mean one word. 'I'll give you a ring.'

'I'm NOT Mrs Duggan!'

'I'm sorry – I assumed – you .....'

'D'you think I'm mad in the head?'

'No – I think I'm the one who's mad in the head. If you ever need a hand sorting spuds, give me a shout – it must be easier than sorting furniture!'

Her words were fortunately lost in the squall and Sadie had gone back into the barn anyway. Himself pointed to a drive that sat slightly above the mud at the front of the house and Maddy set off for home not entirely sure she would ever extract herself from the sopping, decaying place.

'You look a bit wet,' said The Auctioneer on her return. 'Look at your feet – why didn't you wear your boots? And what the hell have you got there – you don't surely think we could sell ANY of THAT? And, oh, what kind of a tie-up job have we got here? Have we been 'knitting' again?'

'Just pull the end of that rope; give it a quick jerk,' Maddy said with the sweetest smile she could muster (restraining herself from repeating the last word she had uttered) and decided that watching a soggy, odd legged sofa fall on one's husband was only second in the world to the comfort of a deep, hot, foaming bath.

Five

It was only a few weeks after their first sale with their own things that it began to dawn on Tom and Maddy that Killybane Auctions was inexorably taking over their lives. The advertisements were continuing in the local papers and the telephone was ringing non-stop with people wanting to book them to call and collect or even make deliveries of items they wanted to sell.

Maddy needed to source boxes for herself now, to pack things in. Local vegetable shops were glad to get rid of them and a local paper recycling plant sold huge bundles of unsold newspapers for wrapping for a pound each.

After several glasses of wine and much discussion late into the night, a collection form was designed on which items collected or delivered would be listed. Tom had cribbed it from a Belfast auction room where he had gone to have a look round in his lunch hour.

They decided (with one whole auction under their belts) to make a couple of amendments they thought would be more appropriate to the way an auction business should be run:

KILLYBANE AUCTIONS
Telephone:Killybane777
123 Cross Road
Killybane
Antrim

TERMS AND CONDITIONS

1. By signing the Collection Form the Seller warrants that the Goods listed thereon are the property of the Seller or that he has Rights from the owner/s of such Goods to dispose of same.

2. Buyers will be offered Goods as seen and examined by them and no Warranty is implied or given but where there exists a major defect rendering the Goods unsuitable for their intended use resulting in a claim on Killybane Auctions this claim will be recoverable from the Seller.

3. Killybane Auctions will offer the Goods for Auction and remit to the Seller within three days of such Auction the proceeds less their Commission of 15%

4. Except where the Seller indicates a Reserve Price in writing on the Collection Form all Goods will be disposed of at the highest offer received on the day of the Auction. The Seller will be informed of all goods failing to make the Reserve Price and such Goods must be removed within one week of being so informed. Failure to remove such Goods will result in Killybane Auctions disposing of same at a subsequent Auction to the highest bidder.

5. Goods for Auction will be collected free of charge within a 10 miles radius of our premises. Outside this area a minimum charge of £5 will be made and deducted from the proceeds of any sale of such Goods.

6. All reasonable care will be taken in the Storage and Handling of Goods but Killybane Auctions will entertain no responsibility for and Loss or Damage to Sellers Goods.

LOT No   ITEM   RESERVE   SALE

Name and Address:

Seller's Signature:

Date:

'What exactly is a "reserve"?' enquired Maddy of Tom.

'Well, if someone were to give us something really valuable to sell they may want to protect it from going for very little by putting a reserve price on it below which I wouldn't be able to sell it.'

'And then, if it didn't make that price, what would happen to it after we had lugged it all the way here?'

'I suppose we would just have to bring it back, or the owner could come and collect it. Or we could maybe try it again in the next sale.'

Maddy didn't like the sound of reserves. 'Just as well none of what we have at the moment is "reserved",' she commented, thinking of the not exactly quality furniture presently piling up in the barn.

They had also realised that now they were selling things for other people, they would have to charge commission. Tom upped this from the going rate of 10% to 15%. He had done his sums and couldn't believe the other auction rooms had not increased their commission for years. It would have to be 15% or they couldn't continue.

He was also determined cheques would be sent to the sellers as soon as possible. Both he and Maddy reckoned, like themselves, people sold things because they wanted money and the quicker they got it the better.

Thinking of the forthcoming sale, Tom had listened to Maddy's observations about bidders calling out their names and had devised a system whereby buyers could bid with Maddy's numbered cards instead.

Each of these bidding numbers would be written above a column on a sheet of paper so that Tom's father, Geoffrey, who had agreed to come and help on sale days, could keep a note of which buyer had bought what.

Before retiring he had been a bank manager and was able to tot numbers quicker than any calculator. They were sure he would be ideal for the job.

Mary, Tom's sister, had continued to be involved and often went along with Maddy on collections to lend a hand. She enjoyed the jaunts round the countryside but didn't always share Maddy's unbounded optimism about what would sell.

'Maddy, why did you take that awful plastic bath?'

'Someone could buy it and put plants in it – it has drainage holes already!'

'And the chicken feeders?'

'They would look really pretty painted black with some flowers stencilled over them – great for feeding wild birds.'

Mary kept quiet and thought to herself that the first 'real' auction was going to be a steep learning curve. Not everyone had Maddy's creative imagination and, perhaps, painted chicken feeders weren't to everyone's taste – that's if they could be bothered to clean off the chicken poo and paint them in the first place.

By the end of September, Tom estimated they had collected at least a hundred and fifty lots. Bearing in mind how long it had taken him to sell a hundred and five, it was time to call a halt to collections and have a sale. All they had to do now was sort out what they had collected and make it look presentable.

'That's going to be easier said than done,' said Mary, looking at the assembled collection of worm eaten pine wardrobes, rusty bedsteads, the bath, wooden headboards, black pretend-leather suites, the chicken feeders, a very old pram - all, to her mind, completely unsalable.

'I will need a list for the advert,' said Tom.

'What advert?' asked Maddy.

'The advertisement for the sale, of course - a list of what we have to sell - dates, times of viewing - things like that.'

'Oh, right.'

It was becoming real and scary again. Maddy donned her rubber gloves and prepared to clean, sort and polish. The assembled artefacts weren't going to sell for anything left in the state they were in.

AUCTION
Saturday, 10th October At 12 noon
To be held at
KILLYBANE AUCTIONS
KILLYBANE

Two miles from Harry's Hill roundabout on main Belfast Road
On right hand side. Sign will be on gate.
Viewing from 10 a.m. on Day of Sale
Included in Auction:
Oak Hall Stand, Pine for restoring, Mahogany beds, Tables, Chairs,
Victorian Cast Iron Fender, Fridge Freezer, Kitchen utensils,
Oak Kitchen Chairs, Mirrors, Radiogram, Jackson Electric Cooker,
Dimplex Heater, Gas iron, Electric Geyser, Sideboards,
Blow lamp, Pedigree Pram, Fish Tank and many other items.

COFFEE AND SANDWICHES AVAILABLE
KILLYBANE AUCTIONS
Tel. No: Killybane 777

This advertisement appeared in four local newspapers two days before the sale. Tom cut them out and stapled them to his original draft. He was a stickler for organisation and even wrote down the names of the girls in the advertising departments that he had contacted to place the ads. Maddy had teased him about this but was to find out later what an invaluable habit it would turn out to be.

Maddy's friend Jennifer and her daughter, Helen, a trained cook, had been coerced into making a small café in a barn adjoining what was now called the 'saleroom'. They were hoping to serve refreshments to the sale-goers on sale day and had placed tables therein covered with gingham cloths and flowers in little vases.

Another rudimentary car park had been cleared behind the Saleroom to save imposing on William Shortall for his field again as it had been pretty well churned up at the last auction. This involved knocking down various walls and flattening some stony ground with a JCB digger operated and owned by another neighbour. When Maddy discovered he had two strong teenage sons, John and Richard, they were swiftly engaged to become porters for Sale Day. They could assist Harry with holding lots up during the auction, help people load their purchases into their cars and they could all pay more attention to the security she realised had been extremely lax last time. Thinking of that, she was glad she had sourced the boxes and newspapers to be made available for people to pack small things bought at the forthcoming sale.

Daughter, Carol, was more than pleased to be asked to sit at the door again and sell catalogues but she would have to be more alert and under no circumstances was she to let anyone take anything out of that door without a receipt for it.

'Do we have any antiques in this sale, Mum?' she asked in as casual manner as she could muster.

'We have a lovely Victorian cast iron fender, some pine for restoration and - um - a beautiful antique chicken clocking box!' Maddy replied.

Carol tried hard not to look pleased at this news and disappeared to make a phone call. *Oh oh!* Maddy thought, *Jaunty Cap is probably going to appear again – I wonder if he has ever heard of an antique chicken clocking box.*

Six

On the morning of their first public sale, Maddy took Fizz for a run over the fields. Moisture from the damp, foggy air was hanging in long drops from thorns in the hedgerows and the sun came up, unnoticed, behind heavy grey clouds. She was glad they had organised an office space in a loft above another barn that would be a dry place for buyers to go and pay their dues after the sale, instead of in the yard like last time.

It was furnished with a few chairs, a desk for Geoffrey to sit behind and a heater to keep him warm. He had seemed to be really pleased to be asked to help and came up with the suggestion that Maddy should send him her clerk's sheet, each one a list of fifteen lots, as soon as Tom had finished selling them.

This way he could keep running totals for each buyer and thus avoid a long queue at the end of the sale. Harry had agreed to help with this and would bring over the sheets as they were completed. James, in charge of the car park once more, scowled when he was asked not to send away anyone with a trailer ever again – please.

Cleaning, sorting and making up lots of what they had collected took much longer than Maddy had imagined it would. When the potato dust had been brushed off the mahogany table from the Duggans, Maddy could see it hadn't been as damaged as she first thought but no amount of stain or polish could hide the rough saw cuts round the edge. It looked like it had been gnawed by a giant beaver.

She had been horrified on opening a fridge she had collected. It contained such an horrendous fermentation of multitudinous organisms she felt sure that, had the door been closed much longer, they would have burst out as a living thing - similar to the creature that sprang out of John Hurt's stomach in the film, 'Alien'.

Only after an hour of scrubbing with bleach and various household cleaners and the adept use of an old toothbrush, did it pass muster. She vowed to always check them in future. It had been waiting for her to collect with the door strapped – she should have known!

Pictures, mirrors and glass fronted cupboards she sprayed and polished. They had probably never been cleaner in their lives. Brillo pads came and went as she shone up boilers, kettles and saucepans.

A bearded, shifty looking gentleman with long greasy hair and driving a beaten up van delivered two Dimplex heaters he swore were in perfect working order – or they had been the last time he had used them. Tom was suspicious and, after blowing the trip switch twice when testing them, he knew precisely why that had been the last time the man had used them. Killybane Auctions was going to have to be careful about electrical goods so he tested all the others that had been put in the sale and, thankfully, they turned out to be in working order.

The paperwork also took hours longer than Maddy had anticipated but everything had to be correct and carefully done so that no seller was allocated something that wasn't theirs. Two days before the auction, having finally arranged everything to her satisfaction, she found herself sticking the lot numbers on at midnight. After this she had to walk round with the sellers' lists and write all the lot numbers against the items listed. The catalogue, which was required at the printers first thing in the morning, had then to be typed from these lists and she had finally collapsed into bed at about three a.m.

Tom was still under the impression that a merry quip about each lot was in order and stayed up late writing those. The comments were slightly shorter this time but a quick glance made

Maddy groan again. Yet she couldn't bring herself to criticise as he seemed to be so enjoying it all. Since their first auction she'd noticed the gradual return of a spring in his step and more enthusiasm for life. He never complained, even when, after a day's work, he came home to a quick meal and then, with trailer hooked on, they were off to some out of the way place to do a collection.

The rostrum had been made slightly more stable and, once again, in his good suit, Tom sat aloft as people arrived to view the sale. He had put a sign on the rostrum (also cribbed from the town auction room) which read:

CONDITIONS OF SALE
1. All goods must be paid for on day of sale
2. CAVEAT EMPTOR – All articles are sold
as seen and examined by the purchaser
3. Buyers Premium is 15%
4. All goods must be removed before 4 o'clock today
unless agreed otherwise

'Hey!' Maddy said when she saw him put it up. 'Where did that fancy Latin term come from?'

'I read about it in a book once. The translation is 'Let the Buyer Beware'. Evidently it is displayed somewhere in most auction rooms. It will save arguments after the sale if the buyer suddenly notices the thing he has bid for and bought has only got three legs instead of four – or something like that. People have to view each lot properly and 'tough' if it isn't what they thought it was.'

'Oh, right,' Maddy said, not totally convinced but kept her doubts to herself.

Jennifer and Helen, presiding over sandwiches, soup and tray bakes, were ensconced in the next door barn where Tom had rigged up another speaker so that the auction-goers could hear what was going on while they ate.

Many of the faces that had come to the first sale reappeared: Bobble Hat, Mr Brown, Rat Catcher, Yellow Anorak, Edwina Turkington and, as Maddy had expected, Jaunty Cap. She had been right, there was indeed an auction going crowd as they all greeted each other like long lost friends and everyone seemed to be pleased with the bidding number idea

'This auction is a bit different from the last,' Bobble Hat said, somewhat crisply, having done a swift round of the lots.

'Yes, it is not our own stuff this time,' Maddy said. 'We decided to advertise and this is what we got.'

'Hmm,' said Bobble Hat. 'You've a lot to learn, girl.'

Maddy's heart sank. She found out later, Bobble Hat was a retired doctor, loved antiques and knew about auctions. She frequented all the other salerooms and even had a 'minder' who drove her around, did her shopping and generally cared for her. She deliberately wore shabby clothes so that the auctioneers would think she was penury stricken and wouldn't 'bid her up'. Her name was Dr Annie Walker and she had been greatly respected in the medical profession in her day. Her minder, John, a small friendly man of about forty who obviously adored his charge, had told Maddy all about her.

Mr Brown, who was looking as smart as ever, bade her good morning but this time did not comment on the sale. Maddy was beginning to feel apprehensive as well as extremely nervous but putting on a bright smile she joined Tom on the rostrum and at 11 a.m. precisely, he commenced their next sale.

'Lot No. 1: A substantial oak sideboard – fitted cutlery drawer. Good wood.' Not one bid.

'Lot No. 2: An amazing selection of pots, pans, plates, kettles, tea pots – and all useful!' This made one pound and was bought by Mrs Shortall, the wife of the neighbour who had provided the car parking field for the last sale.

'Lot No. 3: A large overmantle, 2 small, 1 large mirror in good condition. Woodwork needs a re-tread!' 50 pence.

'Lot No. 4: Fine upstanding wardrobe – large mirror. This separates into 4 pieces for easy moving.' 50 pence.

'Lot No. 5: Surely a good buy for someone to strip – hardly the weather!! Mahogany wash stand.' Wonder of wonders! £6.00.

'Lot No. 6: Nice little bentwood chair – good condition.' 50 pence.

'Lot No. 7: Rather nice chromed brass oil lamp. Needs a

new wick and globe – still available if you know where to look!'
One pound and fifty pence.

'Lot No. 8: Small iron bedstead. Could be prettied up. You notice it has a starting handle.' (This was the spanner that came with all iron bedsteads with which to tighten the nuts that held it together.) 20 pence.

Has nobody got any imagination? Maddy thought. *That bed could look gorgeous painted white and covered with a patchwork quilt.*

'Lot No. 9: Two road lamps. Possible collector's items from a red light district!! Could be useful if you are planning a big Christmas tree!'

Oh pleeeeese! Maddy screamed silently to herself. Then the Duggans' three piece suite came up for sale.

'Lot No. 10: A three piece suite – think of this with pretty stretch covers – it's all there!' It might have been all there but bids there were none.

And so the day went on - and on - way past the four o'clock 'removal of items' time - with the prices ranging from one penny for a kitchen chair to the highest bid of sixteen pounds for the fender from the cottage near Annalong. The chicken feeders made a pound (Maddy found out later they had been bought to actually feed chickens) and nobody wanted the bath. It didn't take a genius to see Killybane Auctions was not exactly a money spinner in spite of all the hard work. Maddy reckoned Dr Walker was right. They had a lot to learn.

And yet again, Maddy observed, everyone stayed, they all seemed to enjoy themselves and even though the prices were risible, nearly everything was sold. The small café Jennifer and Helen had organised had not been a great success as no one wanted to leave the auction room. Some people wandered in to grab a coffee and a sandwich to go but nobody sat at the pretty tables and a lot of people had brought their own food like last time.

When the sale had finished Maddy went up the steps in the yard to the office to see how Geoffrey was getting on to find him announcing to Rat Catcher, 'Madam! You are on THAT side of the desk and I am on THIS side and when I am on THIS side I am always right!' What they had been arguing about Maddy didn't want to know. She fled.

'Tom, your father has just been awfully um, kind of, um abrupt with Rat Catcher. She's probably creating merry hell up there.'

Tom went up to the office to find everyone in the queue in fits of laughter. They had, seemingly, found Mr Daniels senior, a great character, and had almost given him a round of applause for standing up to Rat Catcher, whose name turned out to be Mrs Hawthorne. 'Suits her,' said Tom. 'She's a prickly one!'

'Will you STOP all these terrible puns, and jokes,' Maddy finally blurted out. 'It's not like you at all!'

Tom gave her a rueful grin and went to over to the house to take Fizz out for a run on the lawn.

'It's gone – it's gone,' a loud voice was heard wailing from the saleroom.

Maddy ran in to see a large man in a brown boiler suit waving his hands in horror in front of the stand the fish tank had been on. The tank was very definitely not there. He thrust his receipt at her and bashed it with a huge hairy finger, 'Look, I paid five pounds for it and it's gone!'

'Carol, did you see the fish tank?' Maddy asked her daughter who was looking fraught.

'No, Mum, but people were piling out of here so quickly – it was hard to check everyone.'

'A friggin' great FISH TANK!' said the aggrieved buyer. 'How could someone just walk off with that?' And he glared at Maddy and Carol as if they had gone off with it.

'I am sure it has just been a mistake,' Maddy said, placatingly. 'If we can't find it I will see that you get your money back.'

'I don't want my money back,' he yelled at her retreating form. 'I want my friggin' fish tank.'

Everyone was oohing and aahing at the terrible occurrence and Maddy prayed the ground would open up and swallow the lot of them. What an awful thing to have happened. She ran round to the car park to see if James had seen anything.

'Oh yes, Mum, a fish tank. Yes, a wee man in a van – I helped him load it.'

'I suppose he's gone now?' Maddy said.

'Oh yes. About ten minutes ago. Why?'

'It was nicked!'

'How could he have got out past Carol with a fish tank, Mum? It was huge!'

In spite of his mother's desperation, he couldn't hide his amusement and began to grin.

'It's not funny!' Maddy snapped. Then, as so often happens in a crisis, a giggle bubbled up and she began to laugh.

'Your father's description of that lot was unbelievable. You should have heard him,' she spluttered, mimicking the auctioneer. '"Tropical fish tank – a manageable size this one – nice Christmas present – keeps the smoked trout fresh – or start your own 'Jaws' farm." Can you believe that's what your father actually said? And if he uses the word "nice" one more time I will kill him! Oh my goodness, I had better go and sort this out.'

She pulled herself together, wiped her eyes and returned to the fray.

The man was refunded and no, he didn't want the friggin' stand. He stumped away mumbling that he'd waited for friggin' ages to bid for the friggin' thing and now it was friggin' gone, he would never darken the doors of Killyfrigginbane Auctions a friggin' gain, ever!

Maddy had never been as grateful for rain as the heavens opened and it came down in unremitting torrents. The assembled buyers, forced to forget the dramatic end to the sale, speedily gathered up their purchases. She prayed the fish tank nicker's car had been stopped by a flood and he was being swept away never to be seen again. She couldn't wait to close up shop and slink into the comfort of her kitchen where a stew was on the simmer and they could huddle together and sort out 'the day'.

The boys and Carol were as upset as she was about the theft of the fish tank as they had all been exceptionally conscious of the vulnerability of the lots. The JCB digger owner's boys, John and

Richard, had held the lots up beautifully and had been most attentive and helpful with the buyers during and after the sale.

The melee afterwards was the difficult bit and it was virtually impossible to monitor everything as everyone was packing and putting their lots into their cars that crowded into the yard. The fact that Maddy had totally forgotten about a second door they never used – an ancient one that led directly from the saleroom onto the car park – that had not been secured and was discovered to be lying wide open after the sale had finished, made her feel like a complete idiot. Partly hidden by the rostrum she hadn't given it a thought. Ah well, what's done is done, she said to herself, and served up the stew.

'Carol, I'm dishing up,' Maddy called upstairs.

'Oh Mum, I thought I had told you, I'm going out for dinner. Sean wants me to deliver the fender – did you know he bought it? He's only got a motorbike, okay if I borrow the car?

An antique dealer without a car? thought Maddy to herself and then said, 'Okay darling – the keys are on the shelf. Have a good time.'

'Aha,' said Tom. 'Jaunty Cap's charm seems to be working.'

'His name is SEAN,' Carol shouted as she came down the stairs. 'Will you please both stop calling him that, Mum. You are impossible!'

'Watch it, you are taking my car.'

'Well, don't be late,' Tom said. 'Be back at twelve or I will be on the warpath.'

Carol knew her dad would be in bed sound asleep by then but had finally found the sense to acquiesce on these occasions, didn't argue, gave him a kiss and sped off.

'I worry about that Sean person,' Maddy said after her daughter had driven away.

'So do I, Mum,' said Harry, surprisingly, who usually never bothered about his sister's acquaintances. 'I think he is a bit of a slime ball and I have a funny feeling he would sell his granny if it meant closing a deal.'

Now, I really am worried, thought Maddy.

Geoffrey had been delighted with the sale.

'Thought it all went very well,' he announced on coming into the kitchen and sitting down for some stew. 'Everybody paid and apart from having to give the money back for the fish tank, the system worked. I was even able to let people go before the sale had ended – thanks to Harry here getting the sheets to me every fifteen lots.'

Thank God something worked, Maddy said to herself.

'The new car park was great,' James contributed. 'Nobody got stuck in mud and there was more than enough room.' Again, Maddy thanked the Almighty for something else that had not gone wrong. Just then there was a tapping on the French window. Mrs Shortall was standing outside clutching a large stainless steel kettle, waving it up and down. Maddy let her in.

'Hello Mrs Shortall, what can I do for you?'

'Mrs Daniels, I bought this kettle in your auction today and I filled it full of water and it leaked all over my new stove.'

Maddy remembered cleaning it until it shone like new but had failed to test it for leaks – another lesson learned, she reckoned, as she went to get some cash for a refund.

The lot had gone for one whole pound and had included lots of other things as well as the kettle. What about the 'All articles are sold as seen and examined by the purchaser' condition written clearly on the rostrum?

She didn't dare mention this as Mrs Shortall's normally pretty, smiley mouth was set in a determined line and it was clear there was no give or take there. If you sold your neighbour a kettle with a hole in it you had to return her money, conditions or no conditions.

Yet another lesson well and truly learned. It had been some day.

After the meal, Tom got out his calculator, scribbled a few numbers on a sheet of paper and announced, 'Would you believe it – we made a profit!'

Maddy nearly dropped a plate on the floor.

'How much?'

'Eighty five pence! Look! See!'

The figures spoke for themselves:

Sale total	£360.00
Sellers' cheques	£274.05
Gross Profit	£ 85.95
Less Advertising/ collection	£ 48.00
Less Advertising for Sale	£ 37.10
Surplus	*£ 0.85*

'I didn't take into account the time we spent going to Newcastle or the time it took you to clean and polish and type or the cost of the petrol you used or to do other collections but if we can make even a tiny profit with that – sorry darling – rubbish – what could we do if we had better things to sell? I think we have a business here. We sold forty five catalogues and had twenty three buyers. That was nearly double what we had last time.'

Maddy was taking this in when Fizz did her 'someone at the door' bark and Maddy went to answer it. It was Doctor Walker.

'I hope you don't think I am being intrusive but I have come to collect that funny box thing I bought in your sale and while I was here I was hoping to have a word with you – is your husband here? I want to talk to you both.'

'Please come in, Doctor Walker,' said Maddy, taken aback. 'You are very welcome – would you like a glass of wine?'

'I would love a glass of wine – thank you very much.'

Maddy peered into the yard at Dr Walker's car where John was sitting in the driver's seat. 'What about John? Would he like to come in too?'

'That would be kind. He'd probably like a cup of coffee. He's been driving me round all day.'

'We also have a stew on the go – would you like a wee bowl of that?'

'Well, if you are sure .....'

So John came in too. The good doctor, having removed her grotty coat and bobble hat to reveal a beautiful silk blouse and a pair of Armani trousers, sat down to help demolish a bottle of Rioja and, along with John, polished off the rest of the stew. She then began to explain how she thought Killybane Auctions should work and, tired as Tom and Maddy both were, they listened.

Seven

'One pound and nineteen pence for doing that dreadful collection,' Maddy said to Tom over her typewriter. 'And we have to pay eighteen pence of that to the VAT man.'

Killybane Auctions
23 Cross Road
Killybane
Antrim
12th October 1981

Dear Mr Duggan,
At our recent sale your various articles realised the value stated below and we have pleasure in enclosing your cheque.

By Sale	*£7.90*
To Commission @ 15%	*£1.19*
V.A.T.	*£0.18*
Total Due	*£6.53*

Yours sincerely

Tom Daniels
(for) Killybane Auctions

'Just look on it as a learning experience," replied Tom. "In fact, the whole thing is a learning experience at the moment. It's not as if we really know what we are doing yet, do we?'

'Dr Walker was really keen that we go ahead with it – she seemed to think we had potential - although some of her criticisms were a bit blunt.'

'Yeah,' agreed Tom. 'She was pretty clear that my auctioneering needs to be speeded up and I should cut the chat.'

Well, I did try and hint that may be the case a while ago – but then, what did I know?' Maddy grinned.

'Do you know what I think I will do?' said Tom

'No – tell me.'

'I think I will go to see how the London salerooms do it. I reckon it will be an investment. The auction rooms I have seen here looked awful.'

'That's a great idea, Tom. You could stay with Stephanie – you know how she is always asking us – well, you particularly.'

Tom had the grace to blush. He was not unaware that he was, with his shock of brown hair, now going slightly grey, and his extremely mischievous smile, still quite attractive to ladies.

Maddy continued to type the statements, smiling quietly. She thought she could trust Tom but she wasn't too sure about her dear friend, Stephanie.

Tom wrote the cheques and they were duly posted the next morning.

Thinking about it all they realised they had learned a fair bit about what was saleable and what wasn't and decided they were going to have to be a little bit choosy about what they would accept for sale in future; no wood-wormed wardrobes for a start – in fact woodworm in anything seemed to represent the devil incarnate; no prams for another. Leatherette covered suites were definitely a 'no' and they now knew for certain, people did not want bed ends, not even for the wood.

Tom booked his flight to London for the following week and they continued to venture forth when he came home from work collecting things together.

They were asked to go one evening to a remote farmstead up in the hills beyond Dromore. The road became narrow and twisted and they were beginning to think they were getting lost when the lane they were looking for was exactly where the owner had described it. They bumped up the steep, stony track and found themselves in a tiny farmyard with hardly any room for turning. At its edge was a festering silage pit and Maddy was glad Tom was there to turn the car and trailer as she would not have been able to do it without serious risk of the car or trailer falling into the pit.

Mr Logan, a large jocular gent, met them at the door of the farmhouse and invited them into the kitchen. An old fashioned range was burning away merrily and the lady of the house was propped up on a chair with her feet in the oven.

'It's an awful cold night,' she said. 'Would youse like a wee cup o tea?' She didn't get up and looked so comfortable where she was Tom and Maddy declined and said they would like to see the furniture Mr Logan wanted to sell.

'Well, this table for a start,' said Mr Logan, patting a well used drop-leaf, oak dining table with not much going for it and worse, it had woodworm holes all over the top.

'Ah, Mr Logan, we wouldn't be able to take that, I am afraid, the woodworm seems to have been making itself at home in it,' Tom said, as tactfully as he could.

'Oh! Ha ha, yes I know,' said Mr Logan. 'It's all HER fault,' he announced, indicating his spouse who was fondly beaming up at him. 'She left the window open last Spring and the little buggers got in and went whirly, whirly, whirly all over the top of the table and now look at it!'

There was little they could find to say to that so Tom and Maddy kept quiet as they were shown the rest of the equally 'whirlied' furniture Mr Logan had been hoping they would sell for him. He seemed to be neither put out by their refusals nor surprised, and they wondered why they had been asked to come in the first place.

They were taken from room to room and eventually an adjoining barn where he had an ancient trunk to show them that was similarly afflicted – the lid almost disintegrated as he lifted it.

That was when Maddy spied a pine corner cupboard stacked with pots of paint, jars of nails, brushes solidifying in tins and cans of oil. It was splattered with paint but its arched pediment seemed to be intact over three shaped shelves above a cupboard with double panelled doors. It was beautiful – or would be when cleaned and waxed. Mr Logan didn't seem to be aware of its existence.

'Um – Mr Logan – er, you wouldn't want to part with that old corner cupboard would you?' Maddy asked tentatively.

'What? That aul thing? Yer jokin', sure it's covered in paint an' tar an' all.'

'Yes, but I think it would sell quite well. It's the sort of thing people are looking for these days – and it doesn't appear to have any woodworm.'

Mr Logan was instantly in front of it, flinging off the paint tins as fast as he could. One burst open as it hit the floor but he cared not a jot. He was overjoyed they had finally found something to sell.

'Wait till I tell her – ha ha – wait till I tell her!' he kept saying to himself, chuckling the while. Perhaps Mrs Logan had told him he was mad to call them out and he was finally feeling justified in doing so.

It was a clear frosty night and driving home, with the cupboard tied safely in the trailer, a bright shooting star streaked across the sky high above them.

'That's lucky,' said Maddy.

'Yes,' said Tom, smiling at her, 'I do believe it is.'

Their next call could not have been described as lucky. It came from a housekeeper who had been asked to arrange for a stuffed-over sofa to be collected from the house she cared for in Holywood, just outside Belfast.

Reposing in an upstairs room off a narrow landing, the sofa was not so much stuffed-over as over-stuffed. It was plain to see its welcome to a bottom could be nothing but hard, lumpy and uncomfortable. Its dark red velvet covering was not attractive. It glowered a dire Victorian challenge: *sit on me and be damned.*

'Oh God! Velvet,' said Tom.

'What's wrong with velvet?' asked Maddy.

'It sets my teeth on edge. I can't stand it. I hate touching it!'

She had a distant memory of knowing this once but had forgotten.

'Well, I won't be able to move that thing on my own. It is probably really heavy. Grit your teeth and let's see.'

Tom closed his eyes and grabbed the base at one side and Maddy the other. They both heaved. It was heavy – very, but they could just manage it. Tom dropped his end. 'I really can't touch it.'

'Look,' said Maddy, taking off her sweater under which she was fortunately wearing a T shirt. 'Put your hands down the sleeves and use them like mittens.'

Tom grudgingly obeyed.

'I can still sense it – it's sort of scrinchy and ergh!' he said, recoiling.

And this man skippers boats in force ten gales, Maddy thought to herself.

'That door looks really narrow,' she said, hoping to get him to concentrate on something other than the velvet. 'Do you think we'll have to upend the thing to get it through?'

'I guess so,' said Tom, flapping his now be-sleeved hands and grimacing again as he grabbed the sofa and tipped it up. Maddy at the other end pulled with difficulty as the tight stuffing made it hard to grip. Halfway through the door the sofa met the opposite wall on the landing and the top of the door prevented further progress. The situation needed to be assessed.

'Maybe if we turned it the other way round?'

'Maybe if the castors could come off?'

They pulled it back into the room. Gesticulating with his arms, Tom now looked as though he was wearing long, mad oven gloves.

'If we tip it up and angle it and turn it the other way it may just work – let's try that.'

Amazingly, this worked and the sofa was now on the landing. All they had to do was get it down the stairs. The paint work on the door had taken a bit of a beating but that couldn't have been helped, the sofa was a brute.

They pushed it to the top of the stairs and decided the best way to get it down was to put it on its side, slide it down to the return, tip it up, turn it round and slide it down on its other side. This seemed successful until just before the return it became resolutely stuck with a castor digging into the plaster of the wall on one side and the back wedged firmly against the banisters on the other. Maddy had somehow become trapped underneath at the lower end.

'Lift it, lift it!' instructed Tom.

'I can't Tom. I simply can't. How did they get this thing up there? It's just too big to budge.'

At this juncture the housekeeper appeared and offered the information that the house had been renovated after the sofa had been moved upstairs. The staircase had been altered to make room for a cloakroom on the ground floor. Maddy knew Tom was on the verge of saying something extremely rude and from under the sofa she began twittering about the advantages of a downstairs cloakroom – that it was something she would love to have, eventually, and maybe even incorporating a shower and perhaps even a…

'Will you shut up and get out of there,' hissed Tom.

'I can't. I'm stuck. You are going to have to lift your end.'

'I can't, the castor is jammed in the wall and if I move it up I am going to make a hole and if I move it down I am going to squash you.'

'Would you like a cup of tea or coffee?' interjected the housekeeper who did not seem to be put out at all by the destruction of the wall, the jammed sofa or the about-to-be-squashed Maddy.

'A cup of tea would be lovely,' said Maddy, peering through the banisters wondering if a cup and saucer would fit between them. 'Neither of us takes sugar – just milk – thank you very much.' At least she was going to get sustenance in her captivity.

'For God's sake will you stop wittering and PUSH,' Tom snapped.

Thinking her husband was beginning to sound a bit like a midwife Maddy grunted and managed to grab a chunk of the fabric. With all her might she pulled it and pushed up with her back at the same time. The sofa gave enough to let her escape but then …

'Oh, well done!' said Tom. 'You have made a huge hole in the wall.'

'I have!?' She was always getting the blame! 'Well, at least I am out. What are we going to do?'

She was dreading the return of the owners of the house to find not only a huge hole in their wall but a blocked staircase to boot.

'Just as well they have a downstairs loo now!' she whispered to Tom.

'Bastards!' exploded Tom. 'They must have known this would happen – do you think they called us because we don't charge for collections? We are damned well charging from now on! There is only one way to get this thing down. We will have to heave it over the banisters and we will need the boys to help us with that.'

The housekeeper said it would be fine for them to return later with help and, to their relief, told them that the owners of the house were on holiday and not due to return for several weeks.

Maddy and Tom were quiet on the way home. There had been something odd about the whole thing. Why had the housekeeper not been remotely put out about the plaster? Why did she not seem surprised to find Maddy trapped under the sofa? Maybe Tom was right. Maybe others with more experience had been asked to remove it and had either quoted a huge price for removal or had possessed the wit to walk away.

'I suppose it's another wee bit of our learning about the job – on the job, as it were,' Maddy said.

'It could have been worse,' Tom said. 'The owners could have been there watching us – at least the housekeeper kept out of the way.'

'We'll have to pay James and Harry for helping and find someone to go and fix that wall,' Maddy said. 'I think we'll lose on this one.'

'What do you think that sofa will make?' asked Tom.

'Haven't a clue, fifty - a hundred and twenty? As long as nobody tries to sit on it – we wouldn't get a single bid then!'

In the end it made three hundred pounds which meant a total of forty five for Killybane Auctions. The plasterer charged fifty pounds and they had given the boys five pounds each.

'Oh, by the way,' said the plasterer as he departed after

collecting his money, 'do you see that there wall? Well, it's had more than one hole punched in it! I did as good as I could but I told that wee woman it would look a lot better now covered with some nice new paper – and she didn't even offer me a cup of tea!'

The pine corner cupboard was indeed lucky as it made two hundred and forty five pounds. Maddy had cleaned off most of the paint and could see it didn't require much more work in the way of restoration. Two bidders fell in love with it and wanted it badly. Tom was in heaven as they bid against each other with ferocious determination.

'Well done, Mads,' he said after the sale. 'I wouldn't have spotted it. I was so fed up with all that woodworm, by the time we reached that idiot Logan's garage, all I wanted to do was go home.'

'I expect that's auctions, Tom; we win some, we lose some! And it made up for that horrible sofa.'

Tom's praise meant a lot to Maddy. At that moment she felt she might be beginning to enjoy this business – and maybe she could dare hope that damned For Sale sign at the end of their lane would eventually be taken down.

Eight

Within two months of their second sale, Killybane Auctions was collecting enough 'goods and chattels' to have an auction every two weeks. Maddy's days now were almost entirely taken up with answering the 'phone, going out on collections or coping in the yard with deliveries, many of which were made by the ubiquitous Mr Casey.

Mr Casey was a gentleman of some eighty years or so, who didn't exactly drive around the country in his elderly car but lurched, scouring every dump, tip and skip for items to sell at Killybane Auctions. Maddy's and Tom's first encounter with him had been one frosty morning when his car groaned and creaked to a skidding halt in front of them in the yard. He got out, bowed low to Maddy and ceremoniously shook Tom by the hand saying how proud he was to meet them as he had heard great things about Killybane Auctions.

'Now!' he said, walking round and opening the boot of his car with a flourish, 'have I got something for the two of you!' He dived into the squalorous hole and produced not one but four saucepan lids of graduated size. He flung each one on the ground with a flick of the wrist, struck a pose with his thumbs tucked behind the braces of his dungarees, gazed proudly at the lids as they slid over the yard and, when they finally came to a halt said, 'Look at them! Surely you've got something those'll fit?'

Before they could think of a suitable reply Mr Casey had departed on his cheerful, clanking way.

Out of sheer curiosity, Maddy cleaned the lids and put them in the next sale. They sold for a pound so obviously, somebody, somewhere did have something they would fit.

Two weeks later Mr Casey trundled into the yard again, this time with three what he described as 'auld prints' which he was pleased to tell them he had found in a skip in Crossgar. Later, Maddy discovered one of them was not a print but an original watercolour painting of tall sailing ships in a harbour, signed by the Victorian artist, Frank Scarborough, and, on the back, in writing, 'The Pool of London'.

She replaced the cracked and dirty glass, Tom made specific mention of the painting in the auction advertisement and, after phoning an eminent art expert who reckoned its auction value was around three hundred pounds, it was reserved at that.

Tom was delighted when he knocked it down for three hundred and fifty. It was the most expensive and classy thing they had sold to date. Thinking Mr Casey would be thrilled with the discovery and the price, they were not a little taken aback when he glowered and told them, in no uncertain terms, it would have made twice as much if it had 'gone to London' and they shouldn't have sold it.

As it happened, it did subsequently go to London and the buyer, having hoped to make a profit, had the grace to tell Maddy that it had only made £300; he'd had to pay 20% commission and an insurance fee for transportation.

This made them realise that a middle-of-the-road item can shine at a provincial auction whereas in a specialist London Sale, among hundreds of others similar, it could become run-of-the-mill. In spite of this, Tom could see now that they should have discussed their 'discovery' with Mr Casey before putting it in the sale.

'Then we wouldn't have got it to sell,' said Maddy. 'I don't feel one bit bad for doing it, we should have charged him for that new glass and the time it took me to clean that grotty frame. If I hadn't done that we never would have seen the signature or the writing on the back - to say nothing of his beastly saucepan lids.'

Tom could only agree.

As auction followed auction, people began to bring better

things to sell but they still weren't bringing things the town auctions were regularly reported to be selling - antiques, jewellery and paintings. 'And they have sales once a week,' moaned Maddy.

Geoffrey, Tom's dad, would roll up from time to time and, in spite of his help on auction days, was not, with his usual blunt manner, very encouraging. With comments like, 'Well, how many more tons of rubbish have you collected today?' or 'You'll never make any real money doing this – the other auction rooms have it all sewn up you know – you would have needed to have been doing this from BIRTH.'

By their fifth sale they were still taking in almost anything anyone gave them but were learning fast what would or would not sell. Tom had decided to cease the advertisements for 'junk' and simply put 'Call Us – We Collect' below the sales advertisements which were now going into the main newspapers as well as the local weeklies.

Maddy was gaining confidence in being able to turn away or refuse things she knew were not going to get one bid, but she and Tom were still desperately racking their brains as to how they could improve the quality of what they had to sell.

Sale number five was the first to gross over a thousand pounds but after all the expenditure, where Tom was now including advertising, heating, porters' pay, postage, telephone, petrol and printing of catalogues, they had made a grand profit of ten pounds.

'But it was a profit,' Tom said, 'and if we could only get better stuff we'd be alright.'

After visiting the London Salerooms under the guidance of Stephanie who loved auctions and seemed to know everybody in the business, his auctioneering had improved beyond measure and he was aiming for the magic target of being able to sell a hundred lots an hour. Much to Maddy's heartfelt relief and, she suspected, that of the entire auction going crowd, this ambition had eliminated the jokes and lengthy descriptions.

Most Auction Houses don't let a trainee near a rostrum for several years or until he or she has acquired the necessary skills of the trade by clerking, portering and being mentored by a senior auctioneer. After their first auction Tom could see there was considerably more to it than taking bids from a crowd of people and banging a gavel but knew he was simply going to have to learn about it as he went along. He was more than ever grateful to his father for drumming his times tables into him when he was young as his mental arithmetic was quick and good and he could advance bids accurately.

After only a few sales they had taken notice of people asking could they possibly 'view' the sale on a Friday before the Saturday sale. So Killybane Auctions began to open for viewing the evenings before their sales between 6.0 pm and 9.0 pm.

Viewers could now leave bids if they were not able to come to the auction the next day. Tom made a note of these on his auction list and, when he came to the lot on sale day, would begin the bidding with the 'absent' bid. Then, someone who had left a bid on view night, decided to come to the sale and saw him doing this.

'That's not fair,' the aggrieved absent bidder said. 'It means there's no point in leaving bids because the lot is nearly always going to go for more and there is no chance of getting it cheaper. I was hoping you were going to bid for me.'

On thinking about it, Tom could see his point but knew he had to work for the person who was selling the item. He also had to think about commission on which their livelihood was probably going to depend and decided that being Solomon was what an auctioneer really had to be.

From then on, however, he would always start the bidding with a figure below the absent bid and when, as happened quite often, the lot went for less than the sum the person had given him, this made for a happy customer and one that would trust him and return.

Maddy had also become aware that many of the private people who attended, unlike the dealers who were used to the cut and thrust of the auction room, had many hang ups about the whole auction process, the classic one being that they were scared of the auctioneer taking a bid from them when they were scratching their nose or waving to a friend. Maddy remembered the incident with Joan and Mary at the first sale and put this to Tom. He became quite cross.

'Do they think I am completely stupid? Tommy McLarnon picks his nose the entire auction and I don't take bids off him – bloody hell – I mean – when people bid they bid for goodness sake – do you really think by now I can't tell the difference between a scratch, a wave and a bid!'

Maddy hoped so, but could see clearly they had to work at making their auctions more people friendly. Many were terrified of being 'bid up' by the auctioneer. 'Taking bids from the light bulb' was a common expression to describe a dodgy auctioneer who did the 'bidding up' thing. Anyone who knows about auctions knows this is a dangerous game; an auctioneer who does it runs the risk of being left with the item - unless, of course, he owns it and, even then, it is a pretty pointless thing to do. There are occasions when the auctioneer has to take bids off light bulbs. Such as when a lot has been reserved and there are no bids from the people in the saleroom. The auctioneer has to begin the bidding himself and therefore it is necessary to take bids from light bulbs, the ceiling, the man with his back to him at the end of the room – anywhere – until someone starts to bid. When there are no bids at all the auctioneer has to withdraw the lot from the sale. Now, here is where the auctioneer, or the auctioneer's wife, feels completely stupid to have agreed a price – a reserve – which is too high for the item to sell.

With their limited experience of the sale value of almost anything, Maddy and Tom had no option but to accept things for sale, trust the owners' reserves were reasonable and try them.

It soon became obvious the word was out – there were two nut cases at Killybane who would take in items you wanted to sell, clean them, make them look nice, advertise them and you could put any price you liked on them. Thus, the horsey fraternity descended with bridles, saddles, traps, carts and harness. These were duly processed through an auction including much work with saddle soap, making stands and racks for it all and, of course, expensive advertising. All any of the lots got was an airing. Everything was reserved to the hilt and Tom had to withdraw virtually the entire sale which was humiliating. The only thing that sold was a donkey cart because the two donkey owners who were bidding couldn't bear the thought of the other one getting it. An auctioneer's dream one would think. The room fell silent as, with steely determination, they bid and bid until the rickety old cart reached 'the price of a prince's gig' to quote an observer.

The successful bidder strode off with a triumphant smirk to get his trailer to collect it but as soon as his back was turned his opponent began cackling like a turkey cock. It had been his cart. He had persuaded his son to put it in the auction for him as he knew he wouldn't be allowed to bid for it if the auctioneer had known it was his. Needless to say when the new owner found out he assumed Tom knew all about it and swore he would never darken the doors of Killybane Auctions again. But Maddy now knew, like the fish tank man, he would come back; he wouldn't be able to resist it.

The only good to come out of the debacle was that Tom had the sense to write down where the bidding had stopped on all the overvalued saddlery. From now on they would have a fair idea of what a second hand bridle or saddle was worth and woe betide anyone trying to put 'as new' prices on them again.

They also made friends with a newcomer, Jake Wright, a tall, beamy, gentle, chatty man who was very knowledgeable about anything equestrian and kindly offered his assistance in the future if they needed advice about values or catalogue descriptions. They were pleased to accept when he invited them to his house to see his vast collection of antique equestrian paraphernalia, numerous adorable donkeys and miniature ponies. Like most collectors he was happy to share his knowledge and Maddy and Tom were grateful for his generosity.

They also soon discovered that putting an item that hasn't sold (i.e. not reached reserve) into a subsequent sale was not a good idea. Those who go to auctions on a regular basis, as most people do, want to see fresh things each view day. A piece that has been seen in a previous auction becomes 'tired' and no one will bid for it. The same applies to pieces tried in other auction rooms and viewers were always delighted to be able to tell Maddy or Tom that they had seen such and such in so and so's auction room the previous week.

There was so much to learn and buyers and sellers were more than pleased to offer them advice but always from their own standpoints which, were, of course, totally opposing. Sellers wanted to get high prices, buyers wanted bargains.

'What you need, missus,' said one customer, a gangly farmer with tousled black hair, hands like hams and wearing a tweed jacket that had seen better days, 'is someone to bid things up fer ye.'

'What do you mean, Mr Dolan?' asked Maddy in all innocence.

'Well, I could come and pretend to bid for things and that would make the other bidders go more and youse would git better prices.'

'I don't think that would be entirely honest, do you? I mean, how would you like it to happen to you if you were bidding on something you wanted?'

'Hah! Don't you worry luv, I know what I'm doing – been to auctions all my life.'

Maddy chose to pursue the conversation no further and continued to list the items he was leaving in for sale. She handed him his copy and he went home. Other people came into the yard with deliveries and she soon forgot the uneasy feeling Mr Dolan had left her with.

Halfway through the next sale she noticed Mr Dolan bidding away like fury for all sorts of things, including his own, many of which were knocked down to him. When Tom stopped the auction for a break she went in search of Mr D.

'It's great, Mrs Daniels,' he said before she could get a word in. 'My stuff is goin' really well.'

'But, Mr Dolan, you are buying your own things back.'

'Niver ye worry, luv. Sure we'll sort it all out later.'

'But are you going to take it all home again? And you've bought lots of other things.'

'I've bought nothin', luv, I was jist biddin it up, like we agreed. And, sure ye can let the chap who was biddin against me take it.'

'But that's not possible,' stammered Maddy, beginning to panic, not knowing what to do next, except go back to Tom to explain what was happening.

69

'Okay,' said Tom, 'point him out to me – subtly – and I'll show him who's in charge here.'

The auction re-commenced and each time Mr Dolan bid, Tom ignored him. Maddy was dreading ructions, fist shaking at least but Tom was extremely polite as Mr Dolan raised and fluttered his catalogue each time his bids were missed.

'Sorry Sir, there was someone in front of you and I didn't see your bid.' And, 'Sorry Sir, someone here at the door was bidding after you.' And, 'Sorry Sir, the sun was in my eyes.'

Maddy, from her eyrie beside the auctioneer, noticed some people among the bidders beginning to grin at each other and giggle behind their catalogues.

Hah! Mr Dolan obviously had form they knew about. After a while he slunk away.

'Well done!' Dr Walker said later. 'He tries that on everywhere. I expect those were his own lots he was bidding for. He certainly won't try that here again. Good for you.'

What Dr Walker hadn't thought about was Killybane Auctions was now lumbered with all the things Mr Dolan had 'bought'. It was not likely that he would return to collect and pay for them but the sellers would have to be paid. There were probably going to be quite a few 'tired' pieces in the next sale.

For the first time since it had all started, Maddy was beginning to feel she was, perhaps, crazy to even dream it could become a viable way of earning their living.

'Do you know, Tom, I sometimes feel as if I have been thrown in at the deep end of a huge black pool and can only go round and round doing the dog paddle. Maybe your dad was correct when he said we should have been doing this from birth.'

'Oh, come on now, Mads,' said Tom, putting his arm round her drooping shoulders and squeezing. 'I just know we are doing the right thing. So many people at viewing said to me how much they appreciate their cheques coming through the door two days after the sale and they are going to give us more things to sell. And, you know, you have a gift for making rubbish look great. I could see the viewers take note of that last night. Do you see those brass candlesticks you polished? They wouldn't have made half of what they did if you hadn't. Cheer up, it's going to be alright, just you wait and see.'

Maddy couldn't see. She turned away quickly so Tom wouldn't notice the tears that, without any warning, had begun to fill her eyes.

She was exhausted. Keeping house, organising the auctions, school runs in between, shopping, making meals, the heaving and hauling of collections, answering the telephone and constantly making mistakes was taking its toll.

Sean, the one who would sell his granny, came to her rescue. She had come into the kitchen to find the spuds already on and Sean was laying the table.

'Ah, Mrs Daniels – I hope you don't mind. Carol asked me for dinner.'

'Oh, Sean, of course I don't mind, you are more than welcome.'

He noticed her tears.

'Are you alright?'

'I am sorry but I am feeling a bit hopeless at the moment. I am stupid to think this is ever going to be a worthwhile business. I love antiques as you know.' She gestured round the kitchen at their 18th Century dining table and chairs, corner cupboard and dresser, covered in her collection of early ceramics – those pieces she was glad she had not been able to bring herself to sell in the first auction. 'But I know nothing about selling the things - or anything else. People are running rings round us.'

She sank into the dog's chair and let the tears flow. Fizz jumped up beside her and licked her face.

Sean didn't seem to be overly put out about her crying and went on laying the table.

'Do y' know, Mrs D, my mother was a bit like yourself.'

'Oh?' Taken aback, Maddy looked up. Was she finally going to get to hear about his parents?

'Well, we never realised how wonderful she was until she died.'

'What?' Her tears stopped in their long, black, mascara stained tracks. He was bending down now in front of her offering a box of tissues, grinning, knowing he'd shocked her out of her despondency.

'Mrs D. What you and your husband are doing here is fantastic. You are honest, straightforward and…'

'No. Stupid and naïve.' The tears began again.

'No, honestly, what you are doing is great – it is – I promise. Everyone I meet in the trade is beginning to talk about you and they are not saying you are stupid – not at all.'

'Really, Sean? Oh, thank you.' She reached for a tissue and began to think about the meal. 'My goodness! There's no pudding – only fruit.'

'Would you like me to make a pudding, Mrs. D?'

'Only if you want one. I've got eggs and things.' She then realised what he'd said. 'You can make a pudding?'

'I'm a trained chef, Mrs D – did Carol not tell you?'

'You are a what?'

'A chef – I trained – Darina Allen's.'

'And what are you doing selling antiques?'

'I love the business.'

'Good for you – I hate it.'

'Ah, now Mrs D, you're only saying that – you know that's not true.'

Maddy went to the mirror to fix her make-up. She managed a weak smile at Sean and said, 'Go on then, make a pudding – prove you're a chef.'

Sean made an apple sponge to die for and custard to go with it.

Nine

'You have the buyers coming now,' Dr Walker said to Maddy at the next viewing, 'and you seem to be getting better stuff. Do you see that chap over there? He's one of the biggest dealers in Ireland and what he doesn't know about antiques isn't worth knowing. You are beginning to get there, girl.'

'But we haven't had any decent antiques yet,' Maddy said.

'Oh, there's one or two in this sale that aren't too bad.'

Maddy looked at the man in question and didn't much like what she saw. She had noticed him earlier driving his car into their yard, not the car park, having opened the gate which they normally kept closed on view day. *Cheeky so and so*, she'd thought.

The radio in his car was blaring Wagner's Ring in mega decibels into the ether. He was wearing a British Warm coat of some vintage but no tie. His slightly porcine features, she learned later, had earned him the nickname 'Porky' in the Antique Trade and she was not surprised when she gleaned that most of them were afraid of him. He was viewing the auction in double quick time, strutting round looking at everything with a patronising sneer.

'I'm Hennessy Bergman,' he announced when his perambulations brought him to where Maddy was standing. She felt he was expecting her to fall over in a faint of ecstasy.

'How do you do, Mr Bergman. I'm Maddy Daniels and that's my husband, Tom, the auctioneer, over there.'

'The "auctioneer", is he?' he said, as if this were the most amusing thing he had heard all day.

73

'Well, he's trying, anyway,' said Maddy with the sweetest smile. 'Perhaps you might be able to give him some advice – we both can do with all we can get.'

This had the effect Maddy was hoping for. It kind of took the wind out of his sails but not for long.

'Now I know where you are, I'll come and see you later in the week,' he pontificated. 'I certainly won't be coming to the auction – I never go to auctions.'

With that, he swept away, and drove off leaving the yard gate open. Maddy could hear the Wagner even when he'd reached the end of their lane.

The contents of two houses had turned up some interesting pieces that had helped to make this auction, number eight, come slightly more up to the mark that Dr Walker was insisting on. There was a grandfather clock for the first time, albeit in pieces. It had come apart as they carried it down the stairs. The house, long vacated, was extremely damp. The glue attaching the component parts of the clock had dissolved and now it was mostly being displayed in bits in a box.

There was also an Albert bed – a large Victorian mahogany affair with turned finials and a padded, ceiling-height headboard, an Edwardian chest of drawers and some quality china and ornaments.

Dealers of collectors' items were beginning to use Killybane Auctions. One of these was known to one and all as Billy Bottle, who scoured ancient dumps for old pottery and glass ink pots, poison jars, cream jars and such. He also dealt in odd things and had given them a 1930s electric shock machine to sell. Maddy wasn't too sure what it did but it looked quite sinister and she considered buying it herself to lie in wait with for the pending visit of Mr Bergman.

What had been most encouraging, apart from Sean's remarks, was that Westbury's Northern Ireland agent, Jonathan Plunkett-Smythe, had been in touch with them. He had phoned to see if Tom would be happy to give him a 4% commission in return for referring any clients of his that had things to sell that were not quite up to London standard.

Unbeknown to Maddy and Tom, Jonathan's wife, using her

maiden name, had been sending things to Killybane almost since the beginning and was very impressed with the efficiency of the service she had received. Maddy vaguely remembered gardening gloves she had very nearly rejected and some old books.

'I told you it was going to be alright, didn't I!' said Tom

'Yes,' Maddy agreed and had to admit she was feeling more optimistic now.

However, there was another problem brewing.

The second hand furniture dealers who were coming to Killybane had grown in number and had taken to walking away after the sale without paying for or removing their purchases which were mostly the larger pieces like wardrobes, dressing tables and dining furniture. So much for Sale Conditions numbers One and Four about goods being paid for and collected on the day of sale! It was sometimes a week or more before they returned to pick up and pay their dues.

In view of Killybane's policy of paying the sellers immediately, this had to be sorted out. It was also an absolute nuisance to have to move all their stuff to another barn to make way for new deliveries on the Monday after an auction.

Maddy finally became cross enough to accost one of them about it. He told her blithely that the town salerooms accommodated them, gave them a month's credit and stored their stuff for nothing.

'Right!' said Maddy. The dealer concerned didn't realise that a 'right' from Maddy meant trouble.

Harry, for whom the memory of his mother's method of admonishment still lingered, was standing nearby at the time and said to the dealer, 'It looks like she has gone to get the wooden spoon – I think I would leg it if I were you while you still have one to stand on.'

The wooden spoon turned out to be Tom who confronted each of them, explained the system and told them if they refused to comply he simply wouldn't accept their bids in future and that would be that. Killybane Auctions didn't have the staff to move everything twice and as for credit – forget it – he ran an auction room not a bank.

'My God,' one of the dealers said, 'Youse ones is serious.'
'Yes,' said Tom. 'We are.'

The first time Killybane Auctions was featured in 'Round the Auction Rooms', a regular newspaper column reporting auction prices of anything interesting that had been sold during the week, Maddy and Tom were overjoyed. The items mentioned – a World War II framed silk printed map/handkerchief, issued to RAF pilots had sold for £28 and a Japanese sword had made £42 – were only tiny compared with those of the other salerooms, but it was a mention nevertheless and a great morale booster.

Maddy began to find bits of paper around the kitchen with the total of the latest sale multiplied by twenty three written on them. It eventually dawned on her that Tom had worked out that they would probably be having twenty three sales a year and he was trying to project how much they could expect to make over that time. She knew then he was beginning to seriously think about giving up what he called his 'proper' job. A decision was going to have to be made soon. He was working almost round the clock and that couldn't continue.

It wasn't going to be easy to choose between employment (albeit extremely boring) with a reliable income and, well, whatever Killybane Auctions was - or might become. It certainly wasn't bringing in enough yet to live on but it was definitely growing. The average price per lot had increased from two pounds to six after only eight sales and the number of lots was growing exponentially. Almost overnight it had become a question of not 'if' but 'when?'

Maddy's mother, Iris, came to stay. She had some difficulty at first coming to terms with what Tom and Maddy were up to and was heard on the telephone to a friend saying, 'Maddy – oh yes – she's fine dear. What's she doing now? Well – ah – she's become a kind of – of – up-market rag and bone man.'

One morning Fizz barked and Iris opened the back door. There on the step, stood the huge form of Mr Porter, surrounded by the pong of pig manure which was part of his persona even when dressed in his Sunday best. Pig manure is second only to silage effluent when it comes to magnitude of pong and Maddy's hot-house flower of a mother found it hard to smile in her usual sweet way as she reeled backwards. Mr Porter – not in his Sunday best – was passing by on his tractor in full farming regalia – pong and all.

Iris left him on the doorstep and, holding her nose, fled into the kitchen where Maddy was cooking breakfast.

'Der's a gendleman in de porch who says you gob someding to show 'im,' she said and, to her dismay, Mr Porter, oblivious of his aroma, was invited in and offered a cup of tea. He was very eager to see the things Maddy had telephoned him about.

The tinier and more intricate they were the more they pleased him. His massive farmer's hands caressed them gently and his eyes shone with delight. It didn't matter what they would sell for, he had to have them.

'Buy them for me girl,' he said. 'I don't mind what they go for – I want 'em.'

'He collects WHAT?' exclaimed her incredulous mother after Mr Porter had gone and she had reappeared to open all the windows. A shaft of early morning sunshine made the coloured glass of the little silver mounted Victorian scent bottles glow like jewels and Maddy grinned as she packed them away in their silk lined boxes and wrote a note for the auctioneer to buy them for Mr. Porter.

Their kitchen, having been cleared of all unnecessary clutter for their first auction, had now become similar to the inside of a pawn broker's shop. The house was the most secure storage they had for valuable 'smalls' as they had learned they are called in the Trade. Nearly every surface downstairs was covered in them. Vases, ornaments, books, pictures and boxes were piled on the floor. People called at all hours with things they wanted to sell and more often than not ended up staying for coffee or a drink and frequently a party brewed. Suddenly they were in another world which, for Tom, was as far from the textile industry as the Silk Road is from Ballymena.

A frequent 'after tea' dealer was Jack Murphy who had worked in the shipyard in Belfast since leaving school at the age of 14. Along with other school leavers he had been told to queue up to be allocated a job.

'There were hundreds of us,' he told Maddy and Tom over a glass of wine one evening, 'I joined the shortest queue and it happened to be for the turning shop.'

It was a lucky shot for Jack as turning and metal work suited his artistic, creative and imaginative mind. His ingenious use of the lathe, over the years, led to many items of interest for the auction world.

The first pieces he produced for Killybane Auctions were magnifying glasses with antique silver handles. He had always been an auction-goer and could spot things that others had no use for. A box of mismatched silver forks with bent prongs provided excellent handles for the said magnifying glasses, complete with assay marks, and who could argue with those? The stainless steel turned collars were so beautifully made that one could not at a glance discern the marriage of the old and new. They sold like hot cakes – excellent presents for the elderly or short sighted.

A box of antique ivory billiard balls provided knob handles for walking canes and cut glass scent bottles soon reappeared with silver mounts from broken bottles. His repertoire was endless and, as he produced each item to be listed, he would say, 'With a bit of luck it should make ...' and the prices he mentioned Maddy wrote down as reserves. They were never unreasonable and on sale days frequently surpassed expectation. He soon became known in the Daniels' household as, 'With a Bit of Luck' Murphy.

Jack had acquired a vast amount of knowledge about silver which he was more than pleased to share. Over time and glasses of wine he introduced Tom and Maddy to its history and marketing. He explained the importance of weight and how one needed special Troy scales as an ounce of silver is slightly less than a 'kitchen' ounce; how silver is a commodity with a fluctuating market value with its scrap (melted down) value listed daily in the papers. He told them about assay marks that began in the 14th Century to guarantee silver content. He showed them his pocket book of silver marks and suggested other reference books that collectors use. It wasn't long before Maddy and Tom had acquired the necessary scales and the books.

The auctioneering world was unfolding before them and,

not knowing who or what was going to land on their doorstep next, they were learning something new every day.

One cold winter afternoon Maddy, with frozen toes and fingers, came back with Fizz from their walk to find a huge well worn, unmarked, dark maroon van parked in the yard. It had 'RAG 300' on its number plate and had been driven in by Francis Maloney. His fedora hat was as worn and grubby as his van and his dark grey coat a tad too long but he leapt out of the cab with a litheness that belied his age and his ice blue eyes had the wickedest twinkle Maddy had ever encountered.

He smiled, introduced himself in a deep, soft, southern Irish lilt and explained he was in the 'fornicking' business. Thinking she couldn't have heard correctly, Maddy smiled nervously and introduced herself. She noticed a grey vest beneath his open necked shirt and, as his warm, nicotine stained hand shook her freezing cold one, holding it a bit too long, curious foreboding shivered through her.

This man was trouble, she was sure, but couldn't stop herself thinking *interesting* trouble. She didn't know then that he told fortunes, kids loved him – he had eight of his own – he did magic tricks, he could dance like an angel and his wife hated him in a kind of mythological way. Her legendary spade wielding tirades were the talk of the town and he frequently appeared with cuts and bruises and damage to his van that only an inspired virago could have inflicted. Maddy decided he was like a street-wise, slightly evil, naughty small boy. It didn't stop her being drawn to him as he did not have the shades of perfidy of many of the other dealers – he was an openly honest, outrageous rogue.

The pronunciation of 'furniture' in a Southern Irish accent can sometimes sound like 'forniture' and the word that Francis had used at his introduction, while sounding vaguely crude, really meant the buying and selling of furniture. At least that was what Maddy decided it meant and she was sticking to it.

Francis knew everybody and if he didn't, soon did. He bought anything that was going for less than ten pounds and frequently bid against a fellow dealer with an arm round his shoulders, pretending to talk to him but bidding with a slight raise of the finger of the hand that was on the shoulder which the fellow dealer couldn't see. But the auctioneer could. When the item was knocked down, the friend would whirl round to see who had been successful to be met with Francis's innocent blue eyes.

Francis befriended ladies who came to the sales and could be seen often holding their hands, palms up, telling them what the future held for them. His charm was magnetic. Maddy didn't know, until some weeks after the event, he had told one lady that her husband was going to die and she would be a widow within a month. And the husband did and she was. He also told her she was going to die shortly herself. Maddy formed him up after another customer had told her about this and begged him not to tell people such outrageous things.

'Och alright,' he said. 'I'll tell her she's just going to be seriously ill – will that do? Here, give me your hand. I know you would love to know what's going to happen to yourself.'

'I'll tell you what's going to happen, Francis Maloney. I am going to get the porters – the big strong ones – to remove you from this room and not let you in again. If you don't stop this nonsense we are not going to have any customers left!'

'Ah, now, y'wouldn't do the like o that. Come here and give us a bit of a dance.'

With that he grabbed her and proceeded to waltz round the yard, humming tunelessly. She had to admit she hadn't waltzed for years and he was very good at it.

Unable to keep her face straight she untangled herself and tried to retain her composure.

'Now Francis! Please try and behave. Please, if you have to read palms, tell people the good things – that's what the professionals do.'

He gave her a cheeky American salute, slowly winked one eye and sauntered away.

Maddy had to admit to herself he was right about one thing – she would love to have him read her hand. She was still worried about the future of Killybane Auctions and he might be able to give her good news. She then berated herself for being a silly fool knowing this would only encourage him to further outrageous behaviour.

With every sale came the foreboding of the next caper Francis would get up to or any of the other punters for that matter. The tricks of the trade were now being visited upon them regularly. Little things were being taken at viewing such as bobbins from sewing machines, lids from teapots, handles and needles from old gramophones, keys and pendulums from clocks, small ornaments and even paper and soap from the ladies loo. Never the gents, Maddy noted with some asperity.

'Bloody kleptomaniacs,' Tom muttered after watching an elderly lady coming out of the loos shoving not one but two rolls of Andrex toilet paper down the front of her coat.

On being accosted about this she announced that her grandchild had been sick in the car and she needed the paper to clean up. This resulted in the installation of two gadgets that only deliver one thin, useless sheet at a time and soap dispensers screwed to the wall. So much for this part of Maddy's 'user friendly' auction room. *To hell with Caveat Emptor,* Maddy thought, *it's more like Caveat Venditori (let the shop keeper beware).*

None of the removed things had a value of their own but if they were missing, the lot was rendered of little value. Thus, if a bobbin had been removed from a sewing machine it made a very poor price. Ergo the person who had 'nicked' it got the machine for a lot less than if it had been 'entire'.

Book dealers and collectors were shamelessly in the habit of taking one book from a lot and placing it in another hoping to end up with only one lot to bid for. This caused mayhem the first time it happened.

A large bid had been left on a lot because it contained a particularly collectable book. Then another dealer at viewing removed the book and slipped it into another lot he was keen on. When the absent bidder was phoned and told his bid had been successful and he came to pick up the lot to discover the book wasn't there, he was quite rightly furious and refused to pay for the remaining books. Killybane had to pay – as usual. Very soon it was decided that every item in a lot would have to have a number on it. Maddy acquired a supermarket numbering machine and, once the auction was organised, she had to go round and number every item in each lot. Anything important that was removable had to be tagged and placed on the rostrum with the auctioneer and a note to say so was placed on the item concerned and also printed in the catalogue. Lids were taped onto teapots – Killybane was getting wise. It all meant more work but helped minimise the pilfering along with a large sign saying: 'There is a reward of fifty pounds for any information leading to the arrest of any person or persons removing or taking anything from this saleroom without a receipt.'

'Let the buggers watch each other,' Tom grunted as he screwed it on the wall.

Ten

As the number of people attending the auctions and the number of calls increased, so the infrastructure had to be improved. The buildings, which were originally those of a working farm, were gradually being adapted, changed and updated. The large square yard with the house on one side was surrounded on the other three sides with stone built, slate roofed outhouses and stables. Some were in a better condition than others but all afforded considerable space for Killybane Auctions to function and grow.

Most of the farm land had been sold off long before Maddy and Tom had bought the house leaving them with about six acres. Out of this, one field behind the saleroom held the car park. This had been increased in size twice and, as a result of Maddy spying two men relieving themselves among her rhododendrons, gents' and ladies' conveniences had swiftly been installed in one of the old stables.

The rostrum Tom had made from wooden pallets was now a sturdier construction made from Dexion (the grown man's Meccano) with hardboard panels. He had placed it at the other end of the saleroom which gave him a better view of the whole room and it was accessed by the bottom half of a Slingsby ladder, surplus to requirements after a loft conversion. A bar/counter was made at the other end of the room near the fireplace where Jennifer and Helen now served soup, coffee and sandwiches during the sales without people having to leave the auction, and their trade had improved a hundred fold. The bar also doubled as a reception desk for deliveries on non-auction days.

A panelled desk was also placed at the entrance so the person selling catalogues was partly protected from the icy blast that prevailed in winter when anyone came through the door. Tom also installed a massive gas heater that roared from under his rostrum in an attempt to heat the cold, damp, un-insulated, ancient barn. It made more noise than heat and gave the impression that Tom, atop his rostrum, was about to take off into space.

They had discovered an old fireplace in a stone wall at the other end of the room where on view nights they lit a log fire. Tom had also fashioned a mantel out of an old piano lid which Maddy found useful for displaying ornaments.

'You are making this place too nice,' a dealer grumbled to her one view night. 'And why do you have to clean everything? There'll be no more bargains for us.'

Sean and Carol helped when they could and Carol still manned the door on sale days. Having decided to have her year out at home she had persuaded Theobald Twinem, an antiquarian book seller, to give her a job which she was thoroughly enjoying - not entirely because she was mad about history – Theobald's shop was not a million miles from Sean's tiny antique shop.

She would soon have to start thinking about moving to Newcastle University where she had been given a place. Maddy was not looking forward to bringing the subject up with her as it was obvious for all to see that she and Sean were now an item. After the apple sponge, as far as Maddy was concerned, Sean could do no wrong. His charm and patter with the ladies caused many a cynical raised eyebrow from James and Harry but no one complained when he rolled up his sleeves and helped heave and haul furniture. His knowledge of antiques was a great help when they were compiling the catalogue or came across anything unusual and he was now joining them frequently for dinner which he would help to cook. Try as she could though, Maddy had never quite pinned down where he or his family came from.

'Mum, stop digging!' Carol said to her one night. 'Oh, God, it's so obvious when you start.' She parodied her mother,

'Well, Sean, what did your father think about you wanting to become a chef?' and 'What is such and such like in your part of the world? Mum, it doesn't matter where he's from and what his parents do – or don't do!'

'Carol, there were bombs in Belfast last night – or hadn't you noticed? You can't blame me for being anxious about you and, well, he does have a Southern accent.'

'Yes, Mum, but the IRA always give a warning and you can't believe Sean could possibly be involved in any way. Mum, he's a big softee – look at the way even Fizz adores him.'

Of course, I should have known. Fizz, the MI5 dog, knows instinctively if she sees a 'wrong un'. Nothing to do with the little bits of dried liver Sean keeps in his pocket!

Maddy did not share her thoughts with Carol. She had used the dried liver trick often when attempting to train Springer spaniels in the old days when Tom could afford to go to driven shoots. She would let the matter rest for the time being because she knew to do otherwise would cause her daughter to stop bringing Sean home and then they wouldn't have a clue what she was up to. Maddy was also more than conscious of the fact that Carol was soon going to be away altogether and, as a mother, she was going to have to learn to 'let go'. She'd heard the expression often but only now did it hit her heart with a whacking great blow.

Tom's opinion on the subject was much the same as usual, 'Stop worrying, woman, you worry too much. It'll be fine, things will work out – they usually do.'

It had been decided, in view of the ever present possibility of rain in Northern Ireland, a horse box would be more suitable than the open trailer for most collections.

Tom had somehow persuaded The Northern Ireland Bank that Killybane Auctions was now a viable concern and had acquired an overdraft to pay for the alterations and new acquisitions.

He'd had the horse box constructed with its wheel arches inside so that it would be more manoeuvrable in narrow entrances and the driver would know that if the car could get through a gateway so could the box. In spite of this Maddy declined to use it.

She had only just got the hang of the open trailer and that was enough.

One Saturday they set off to do three collections, the first two of which took much longer than anticipated. People had a habit of remembering extra things they wanted to sell at the last minute, just after Tom had finished packing and was about to go home. He would then have to unpack and rearrange everything to make room to get the last thing or things in.

This stretched his patience somewhat and Maddy would have to engage the client in loud conversation to cover the hissed expletives and curses being rained down upon the forgetful so and so from inside the box.

After the second collection it was way past time for the evening meal and they were both wilting with hunger. As well as having to go home and empty the horse box they had to have something to eat.

Maddy phoned the lady at the last appointment who had a dining room suite she wanted to sell - a table, a sideboard and six chairs - and explained they were running behind schedule and would she mind if they arrived with her later than planned?

'Not at all dear,' the lady had said. 'You take your time. I don't go to bed until late and you just come whenever you can.'

'That is very kind of you, Mrs Williams. We should be with you at about seven thirty.'

At seven fifteen as it was getting dark, they spied the white gate posts Mrs Williams had told them to look out for at the end of her lane. Tom turned off the road between them and drove up a track until they arrived at a two story farm house.

He grabbed his clip board and the small torch he used for examining furniture and Maddy knocked on the door which was opened quite quickly by a youngish lady who gave them a grim glare but showed them in.

An older lady was standing silhouetted in the doorway of a back room in the hall with arms akimbo.

'Hmf,' she said. 'We'd near given youse up. We was expectin yiz at five. But now yer here.' She gestured to a room. 'Ye may as well come in and take a chair.'

Maddy, nonplussed at the attitude, mumbled words of apology but didn't mention the phone call.

Tom, never one to hang about, walked into the room and said, 'Is this the sideboard?' pointing to an oak 1930s style sideboard which stood against one wall.

'Yes, it is,' the lady said, looking slightly confused.

Maddy went over to a chair, lifted it up and turned it over to look underneath the seat. She had learned this is the best and quickest way to spot the dreaded woodworm that renders non-antique furniture unsalable.

Tom in the meantime, having removed the ornaments that had been on top of the sideboard and placing them on the floor, was now crouched low behind it shining his torch at the back. At this point Maddy heard two sharp intakes of breath and looked up to see the young girl and the lady standing rigid, clutching each other with looks of horror on their ashen, open-mouthed faces, frozen, resembling two waxwork figures in Madam Tusaud's.

Before she could say anything, Tom, from under the sideboard, proclaimed, 'I'm sorry but this sideboard is badly infested with woodworm, madam – I am afraid we couldn't sell it.'

It began to dawn on Maddy that something was horribly amiss. 'You are Mrs Williams, aren't you?' she asked.

'No!' squeaked the lady. 'She lives next door.'

Maddy replaced the chair and went over to where Tom was standing up now brushing woodworm dust off his jacket.

'I am so sorry,' Maddy said. 'We seem to be - ah - in the wrong house.'

'What?' said Tom, who hadn't quite grasped the situation.

A large man, clad in a singlet and what looked like hastily pulled on trousers, had now appeared behind the ladies and he didn't look one bit pleased.

'Sorry, awfully sorry,' Maddy said, grabbing Tom and making for the door. 'You say Mrs Williams lives next door? Yes, well, um, she'll be expecting us. Sorry, goodbye.'

They sidestepped round the dumbfounded trio and managed to get out before anyone called the police or threatened to shoot them.

When they finally arrived at Mrs Williams' house she told them that her neighbours had been preparing all day for visitors from Canada, relatives they had never met before.

Eleven

On returning from the school run one morning, Maddy noticed the little red light blinking to say there was a recorded message on their phone. 'Jonathan Plunkett-Smythe here,' he said in what Maddy had decided was a rather delicious, plumy drawl. ' I have a client in Ballygannon and think he may have quite a number of things that would suit your rooms rather than Westbury's, would you like to come up with me sometime this week to have a look? Ring me if you are interested.'

Maddy's reaction was not one of unsullied joy as his previous referrals had been disastrous. He had taken all the good things for London leaving pretty valueless pieces for Killybane, but not without putting values on all of them.

The owners were subsequently extremely hard to deal with as their expectations had been raised to a ridiculous extent. It was infuriating and quite obvious Mr Plunkett-Smythe had no inkling of how local auctions worked or of how, once told a value, people kept that value in their heads as if carved on stone.

To most people he was a walking, talking one man Antiques Road Show and they hung on his every word. 'But Mr Westbury said that was worth…' would be the usual reply to a valuation given by Maddy or Tom following one of his visits. The auction prices Killybane would get for them could only be disappointing and they had been hoping Mr. Jonathan Plunkett-Smythe would not refer them again. He was, nevertheless, a charming, attractive and amusing man, and Maddy was prepared to have a few disappointed customers if it meant a trip to Ballygannon – a two hour drive – with him.

'Do try to use the time to get it through to him about reserving rubbish,' Tom said and Maddy, putting on her smartest jacket and fixing her hair, promised she would.

The drive was indeed entertaining as Jonathan kept her much amused about himself, from the time of his boyhood, running wild on his family's estate in County Westmeath. After boarding school he became a soldier, then ADC to a mad general and after many adventures in civvy street, he took up opera singing. How did opera singing qualify him to be Westbury's agent in Northern Ireland? Sifting through the threads of his life he had been regaling her with, none of which included working in an auction room, Maddy could see that one word alone described the requirement, 'contacts'.

His social standing in elite society (the Irishtocracy as Maddy nicknamed it) was all that was needed to be allowed into their homes and given carte blanche to discreetly send anything away to London to be sold – provided the price was right, of course. And thus, Maddy mused, it has been for centuries. Since Roman times, there has always been someone to take advantage of the impecunious aristocrat – the auctioneer. Maddy found comfort in the realisation that she had joined the second oldest profession in the world, even though it was on a slightly lower level than that of Westbury's.

The client they were going to see was a direct descendant of one of the most notorious and swash-buckling Admirals in the British Navy who, in the mid 18th Century, swept the Southern Seas in the manner of C.S. Forester's Captain Hornblower, pillaging, battling and generally making quite a name for himself. His final domicile had been a mansion in the more peaceful environs of County Fermanagh which like many old houses in Ireland was now in a sorry state of disrepair as successive generations had struggled vainly with its upkeep. Now, finally sold, Westbury's had been called in to advise about the disposal of what was left of the contents.

The last remaining member of the family, Mr Goodfellow,

had originally decided to try to sort it out himself, mostly in a small, damp back room with very poor lighting. He stood in a distracted fashion, wearing an ancient, drooping cardigan in front of a desk piled high with papers and old letters. Antiquated, peeling, leather bound ships logs filled the floor-to-ceiling book shelves, while others were piled, some open, some not, all round the room - on the floor, spread over a table and several chairs. Trunks, overflowing with miscellaneous bits and pieces, crockery, china, and glassware, were sitting amongst stacks of yet more documents. There were ships instruments – sextants, time pieces and telescopes balanced here and there along with naval swords, tricorn hats and other regalia. It was hard for Maddy not to stand and gape with her mouth open. Jonathan had seen it before but there was no way he could have prepared her for the chaos that confronted them.

She could tell almost immediately that Mr. Goodfellow, who was picking things up and putting them down, was incapable of making any decisions and obviously totally overwhelmed with what, she was sure, was one of the most valuable archives any naval historian could wish for. She sneaked a look at one of the logs and read the beautiful, hand written script: *'11th March, 1786. Chile. Off the coast. Hove to just outside the harbour as there are reports of Cholera ashore. Two more crew buried overboard this morning. Stores are low and scurvy is rife.'*

She would have loved to have stayed reading all day, but could see Jonathan was having a difficult time persuading Mr Goodfellow to make a decision to part with anything. Maddy's heart went out to the distressed old gentleman, who looked shrunk and dishevelled beside the tall, distinguished, Jonathan. There was no sign of a Mrs Goodfellow or children to help and she could tell what a wrench it was for him to be parting with the remnants of what had belonged to his once famous and illustrious family. As the rest of the house appeared to be virtually empty of furniture she had the distinct feeling she and Jonathan were the end of a long line of people he'd called in to advise or buy and was now unable to bring himself to trust anyone.

'You know, Mr Goodfellow,' she said, sitting down beside him and not quite holding his hand, 'Westbury's have a special department for this kind of thing. They will notify everyone in the world who collects maritime memorabilia including the Maritime Museum in Greenwich (for all she knew he had already done that) and they will sort it out for you. You need experts, you can't do it all yourself.' What she really wanted to say was, 'For God's sake, stop stirring it all – it will soon be an impossible mess for even the keenest expert.'

Jonathan looked at her gratefully and gently picked up the sextant that Mr Goodfellow was sure had a case - somewhere ...

'I am confident this will make between two and three thousand pounds at auction,' he said and began to look for the case.

Mr Goodfellow's eyes lit up slightly and Maddy could sense the price had triggered a positive response somewhere at the back of his befuddled mind. 'As much as that?' he said.

'Maybe even more, Mr Goodfellow. It is old and rare enough. I checked with our Maritime department yesterday and they seem very sure. Its provenance is perfect and it has the admiral's name engraved on it – couldn't be better.'

'Can it be reserved at two thousand?' Mr G was not so befuddled now.

'Of course,' Jonathan assured him and quickly began to write it down on his collection form. Maddy hoped he was sure of his valuations or he would be in trouble with London.

Gradually, slowly but surely, as Jonathan listed and put prices beside the instruments, the cutlasses and telescopes, they could see Mr Goodfellow adding up a running total and becoming a little more trustful of them and less confused. He agreed Maddy could take the trunks if she would promise to itemise the contents when she got them home and send him duplicate lists just in case there was something he'd missed and wanted to keep. It was plain to see from the jumbled mess he had unpacked and gone through the contents many times.

Mr Goodfellow finally agreed to allow Westbury's marine archivists and experts to come over to sort and package the logs and documents. Jonathan was able to take all the other items in the back of his estate car but Maddy had to arrange to come back the next day to collect the trunks. She prayed Mr Goodfellow would be of the same mind when she returned as it was going to be a long drive for Tom and the horse box.

He was and, to her amazement, met them with coffee and biscuits. He no longer had that 'little boy lost' look and seemed genuinely relieved to have made up his mind at last.

There were five trunks. She was sure they must have dated from the admiral's days. Once upon a time they had been handsome, their dome-top lids bound with studded hide and fine curved oak ribs. The interiors she could see had once been fitted with drawers and compartments and were lined with an ageing, floral patterned fabric. They were things of beauty on their own but, sadly, falling apart now with woodworm. She couldn't help imagining them waiting on docks to be carried aboard some tall ship destined for the seven seas. How many ships holds had they been in? How many battles with thundering canon and clashing sabres had they endured? Did they miss the toss and sway of the oceans?

These age old containers, retired from their sea faring days, had become receptacles for generations of flotsam and jetsam the family had been unable to throw away. The contents of each one reminded her of pictures she had seen of the tomb of Tutankhamun when it was first opened by the archaeologist, Howard Carter. A complete jumble of pre-plundered things. But interesting things, lots and lots of them and she was in heaven as she settled down to sort and list them. She had agreed with Jonathan that if she found something of any great value such as silver or gold or historical naval memorabilia, she would keep it for him to send to London but the rest Killybane Auctions could sell without reserves. She had explained to him about putting values on 'lower end' items that really had to take their chance at auction. Some would go for more than expected and some less. If everything in an auction had a price on it below which it could not sell, it wouldn't be an auction anymore it would be a shop and people would lose interest. She thought he finally understood.

Maddy found the 'goodies' coming out of the chests were proving to be old and interesting. Parts of this and parts of that that been squirreled away over the years such as glass chimneys for oil lamps, burners and old shades. All eminently saleable, she knew, as collectors and restorers of old paraffin oil lamps were now coming to Killybane. For collectors of kitchenalia there were ancient utensils, wooden butter prints, glass and china jelly moulds, a cheese press, ceramic egg crocks and an old copper stock pot with a tap. There were several Victorian china wash jugs and basins printed with flowers, part of a crested ironstone dinner service and numerous hand painted ceramic plates, cups, saucers and jugs: Coalport, Minton, Worcester, Belleek, Crown Derby, two Newhall tea bowls and a broken tin glazed enamelled earthenware charger in three pieces, carefully wrapped in cloth – kept waiting, perhaps, for the itinerant pottery stitcher that never came?

Most of the ceramic pieces were damaged but still too beautiful to be thrown away. When Maddy unearthed a Wedgwood stoneware game-pie dish she held her breath until she found the cover and, to her relief, it was intact. She couldn't remember being so delighted. Another chest contained glassware amongst which were several early Waterford crystal decanters, Victorian custard cups, numerous fine engraved goblets and glasses and an epergne which had been splendid before two of its glass 'trumpets' had gone missing. Even so, Maddy reckoned it would make a lot on its own – somebody might have some glass trumpets that would fit the embossed silver-plated stand. Then, at the very bottom of the trunk, under a linen 'envelope' of handmade lace pieces, five little 19th Century scent bottles (another phone call to Mr Porter) one of which was painted with beautiful gold decoration. Did that count as 'gold'? Would she have to give it to Jonathan for London? She hoped not. She'd better show it to him anyway and see what he thought.

Intriguing items emerged such as an old tin full of 19th Century medicaments; jars of weird looking dried-out liniments, blue glass medicine bottles, bandages, lidded cardboard boxes of pills and a thermometer in an impressive leather case. She found old silver backs for hair brushes and mirrors ('With a bit of Luck' Murphy could do something with those she was sure), ivory glove stretchers, a hunting horn, old letter scales, carved oriental frames, glass fishing net floats, wooden Mauchline Ware souvenir boxes, part carved wood and ivory chess sets. There was a battered wooden cigar box with a hand written label stuck on the lid 'Relics of the Easter Rising, 1916' with a spent bullet and bits of broken brick nestling inside on some cotton wool; a sealed truffle jar with, a Fortnum & Mason list dated 1882.

The strangest thing of all was one Mr Goodfellow had pointed out to her before they had taken the trunks away, a large, hard, blackened slab of 'bog' butter wrapped in what looked like extremely dirty greaseproof paper. He explained that in the 17th and 18th Centuries in Ireland, folk wrapped perishable food such as butter in greased paper and plunged it into a nearby bog to keep it cool and fresh but, if forgotten about and left there for a hundred years or so, it became preserved, almost fossilised. Maddy remembered doing this with bottles of white wine – tying them to a rope and dangling them in the Irish Sea from their boat to keep them cool. The only difference being there was never a chance they would be left there long enough to become preserved. To Maddy's relief Mr Goodfellow had thought this was funny and she loved seeing him laugh.

When she'd listed over two hundred lots it became obvious to Maddy this collection could almost be an auction all on its own.

Her mind was now churning with what they were going to have to do. They would have to get tables from somewhere to display it all. Keeping watch over all these small things was going to be a nightmare. Checking them out after the sale was going to be another and the lots couldn't be displayed too close to one another in case they got muddled up. Viewers, she had noticed, had a habit of picking things up to examine them and setting them back in the wrong place, sometimes into another lot. All the glassware needed to be washed and, crikey, they only had a week to do it.

Other calls had been booked for that week too and Maddy began to wish there were six of her. Washing and sorting smalls was not Tom's 'bag' and Mary was busy with other things. Help was required but where from? Who would want to do the kind of work they were doing? Tom and Maddy were discussing this when an enormous van drove into the yard. 'Is this Killybane Auctions?' the driver asked them through the cab window.

'Yes,' said Tom. 'Can we help you?'

'Got a delivery, mate. Where do you want it?'

'What is it?'

'Pine – the fill of this van. From Danny Taylor, a whole load of the stuff.'

He got out of the cab and walked round to the back of the van and opened the door. It was jammed to the roof with pine furniture – tables, chairs, beds, chests of drawers, wardrobes and much more.

'But we weren't expecting this,' Maddy said. 'Are you sure it's for us?'

'Have a note here from the boss – look – it's your address. Are you Mr Daniels?' he said to Tom, ignoring Maddy.

'Yes, I am. Can you hang on a minute? We are going to have to work out where to put all this.'

The saleroom was nearly full of large furniture, the house was full of smalls and the barn they normally used for storage was full of dealers' stuff waiting for collection. Some of them still hadn't got the message about lifting their things.

'I am going to kill them,' Maddy said. 'They can't do this to us, it's just not on.'

'There's only one thing for it,' said Tom. 'We'll have to use the garage – I'll go and take the cars out.'

Maddy remembered her mother telling her to be careful what she prayed for and went to get a clipboard to list the pine from the van.

'We are going to be constipated with furniture and how and when, with the collections we still have to do, we are going to have the time to organise it into an auction, I just don't know.' She felt on the verge of tears again.

The pine was offloaded into the garage and duly labelled with the owner's code and listed. Tom said, 'Look, the children have eaten, let's go to the pub and have a drink and a meal. We'll sort out what we are going to do then. I am sure you would rather do that than cook again.'

'I sure would,' Maddy said and had to admit she was whacked.

'You look worn out, Mrs Daniels.' Billy McConnell, the barman, gave her a piercing look as she climbed onto a stool to wait for Tom who was parking the car.

'I must confess I am, Billy. Our business seems to be growing like Topsy and we have begun to wonder how we can go on doing it without another pair of hands. Do you know though, the funny thing is, I think we need another female. Apart from the heaving and hauling of furniture, it's mostly girl's work, you know, cleaning and polishing and arranging things.'

'I've a niece who's looking for work. She's in Tate's garage at the moment and she hates it.'

'But, Billy, our work is in all weathers and there is a lot of lifting to do. It is hard sometimes. Would your niece mind that sort of thing?'

'She was reared in the yard, Mrs Daniels, reared in the yard.' Maddy took this as the 'country' way of saying she was a tough working girl and could cope with most things. 'Do you want me to send her round to you?'

'Well, if you think she would be interested, yes, Billy, do that.' Tom climbed onto the other bar stool and Maddy informed him that they had just acquired an assistant.

'Bloody hell, you don't hang about, do you?'

'The chances of her fancying the job when she sees what's involved are not very likely,' said Maddy and took a large glug of Liebraumilch.

'By the way, Mrs Daniels,' Billy said as they were leaving, 'what's Topsy?'

The next evening it was blowing a full gale and the wind was pushing rain in through every crevice in the old buildings. Tom and Maddy were struggling in the freezing cold to make sense of the furniture piled in the saleroom when a car drove into the yard. A tiny person got out of the back and came over to the door.

'I'm Emma,' she said. 'Uncle Billy sent me.'

'Oh yes, Emma, come in, shut the door, don't get wet,' said Maddy, climbing out from under a table she had been crawling beneath to get to something else. Emma stood at the door in a grey tweed coat buttoned up to the neck and gazed round at the piles of furniture, the frazzled Tom and Maddy and the enquiring Fizz who had gone up to her to say 'hello'. Her solemn face gave not a clue as to what she was thinking. Maddy broke the silence. 'Did your uncle give you any idea of what was involved here?'

'No.'

'Well, as you can see, all this furniture needs to be arranged, some of it requires cleaning and then we will have to put the small things out. Have you ever been to one of our auctions?'

'No.'

'Have you ever been to any kind of auction?'

'No.'

'Well, um, do you think you'd like to come and help us?'

'Yes.'

'When can you start?'

'Tomorrow.'

'That would be great. We'll see you then. Would nine o' clock be alright?' Emma nodded, turned and went out of the door without another word.

They stared after her and felt they should have maybe said more, asked her more questions or even gone over to speak to whom they presumed were her parents waiting for her in the car. If it hadn't been such a dreadful night they would have done.

'That went well,' said Tom. 'You have the interviewing technique down to a fine art.'

'I wasn't too sure who was interviewing who,' said Maddy and then, 'How on earth could that child possibly want to come and work here? I mean, Tom, it's bitterly cold, damp and totally chaotic. She must be off her head. Oh, God, you don't suppose …?'

'Absolutely not! Billy wouldn't send us a half wit – he's known us for years. He wouldn't do that.' He didn't look as sure as he sounded.

The following morning there was a tap on the back door and there stood Emma. She looked as if a puff of wind would blow her away. She was wearing jeans and trainers and loads of sweaters under a sensible anorak. Her grey-green eyes had long lashes and she wore a knitted, striped football hat squashed over her curly blonde hair.

'Mornin,'' she said with a smile that lit up and transformed her tiny pixie face. When Maddy thought of the work they had to get through that day, she didn't think this little waif would last that long.

By lunch time they had discovered the waif had the strength of two men and the heart of a lion. She also understood from the start what they were all about. She didn't have to be told twice about their system of taking in deliveries - the labelling and listing. She didn't seem remotely put out about carting and moving furniture or cleaning it. Maddy began to feel a great weight was lifting off her shoulders. Emma was still extremely quiet and never used two words when one would do but Maddy was sure she would come round. Lunch, however, was a silent affair and a conversation-free zone no matter how hard they tried.

'Do you feel you could answer the telephone, Emma?' asked Maddy afterwards.

'Yes.'

'Would you mind if I went off to do a collection and left you here to cope?'

'No.'

'I have to go and do a very quick one this afternoon. Is there anything you are worried about?'

'No.'

'Well, if anyone asks you anything you don't know the answer to, tell them you have just started here and you will get me to ring them when I get back.'

'Alright.' *Great,* thought Maddy, *two syllables.*

When Maddy returned from her call, Emma had written three telephone messages comprehensively on the notepad by the phone (which was more than Maddy ever did) and had taken in a delivery.

'Did you mind being on your own, Emma?'

'No, Mrs Daniels, in fact, I quite enjoyed it.'

Maddy nearly fell over. A whole sentence. They were getting places at last.

Tom sorted out the wages side of things, prayed the bank was still of a supportive frame of mind and Emma became

Killybane Auctions' first employee. She couldn't have started at a more frantic time.

As well as Mr Goodfellow's smalls they had to fit in the pine furniture, some of which was in poor condition. The dealer who had delivered it had obviously had a clear-out discarding pieces he'd been unable to sell from his shop and it was all pretty 'tired'. There was an old disused stable at one side of the yard underneath the loft they used for the sale day office and Tom had the idea that they might sell damaged furniture from there and call it the 'Restorers' Room.' It was poorly lit and extremely damp, but the furniture couldn't come to much more harm than it was already suffering from and it would only be in there for a few days. This arrangement would leave the saleroom freer for the better things.

With Emma's help, washing the glassware was done in double quick time and, to Maddy's relief, she could see the girl was as particular as she was and clearly enjoying both laying out the sale and keeping track of everything.

Jonathan called by to see how things were coming on and, before long, he and Emma were chatting nineteen to the dozen. *Boy is he a charmer*, Maddy thought, *no wonder Westbury's took him on.*

He was more than pleased with the way the sale was shaping up and didn't think the gold scent bottle was important enough to go to London. He did, however, retrieve several Irish silver spoons and a small jug Maddy had found wrapped up in a felt cloth. She felt sorry because, she knew 'With a bit of Luck' Murphy would have loved to have bought them.

Still, thanks to Jonathan, Killybane was going to have the best and most interesting sale to date and she would be eternally grateful to him.

Twelve

Right, where do you want it?' Jeremy Brixton, an old friend of Tom's, had pulled into the yard in the latest model from BMW with a trailer in tow carrying a large duplicating machine securely tied down with rope. It put Maddy in mind of a captured Dalek from 'Dr. Who'.

'Do you want to sell it?' asked Maddy, gazing at it, not having a clue what it might be worth or where on earth they were going to display it. It looked extremely heavy.

Jeremy, wearing a Ferrari parka over his Gieves and Hawkes suit, had a large, beefy companion with him who Maddy assumed correctly had been brought along to help.

'No, you silly thing, I am giving it to you. Didn't Tom tell you?'

'He may have done,' said Maddy, 'but we have been so busy I must be honest and say I had forgotten.'

'Well, where do you want it?' Maddy decided there was no room in the house so it would have to go in the loft they now used as the auction office on sale days. The steps were steep and she hoped the helper was strong.

He was, extremely, and he and Jeremy made light work of heaving it up the steps and installed it in a corner.

Now if I only had two people like you as well as Emma, thought Maddy wistfully, *all I'd have to do all day would be delegate.*

Pushing this dream from her mind she remembered having

101

used a 'Roneo' a long time ago and knew it involved typing stencils, filling compartments with ink and the turning of a handle a bit like a milk churn.

'We have upgraded,' explained Jeremy who owned a posh car saleroom in the middle of Belfast, 'to a more fancy affair but Tom agreed with me this would save you the expense of using the printer in town. So you are very welcome to it.'

She thanked him profusely. Their friends had been extremely supportive and this was yet another gesture of kindness. Maddy gave him a huge hug. Jeremy gave her a pile of stencils, the necessary correction fluid and several bottles of ink.

'Oh dear, Emma,' she said after Jeremy had gone. 'Yet another thing to cope with along with this auction – I don't suppose you can type, can you?'

'Sorry, no, Mrs Daniels - never fancied it.'

'Sensible lady. Look at all the boring work you have got out of doing!'

Emma grinned wryly and gave Maddy a look as if to say 'more fool you'. This sent Maddy's mind back to her secretarial college days and the choices girls had then – nursing, teaching, secretarial. Now that she thought about it she had never seen a boy there. Boys didn't go to secretarial schools. Men didn't type. Women did it for them. *Mmmmm. . . don't go there, Maddy. Back to work.*

The pine delivery had provided several tables that would look more or less acceptable with things on them and someone had delivered a china cabinet with a lock and a key that was ideal for displaying tiny items such as the scent bottles and the pieces of scrap silver found in Mr Goodfellow's trunks.

Maddy had explained to Emma the way they laid the auctions out: First the large pieces of furniture had to be arranged, then, after they were cleaned and polished, the smalls would be placed on and around them as attractively as possible. Everything still had a label or sticker on it with the owner's code and, when a piece was put out, a note of where it was in the room was written beside it on the collection form. For example: 'A pair of Victorian brass candlesticks' (2nd table from end – the 'end' being the last table and items on it to be sold at the sale. These were always the best pieces in full view of Tom from his rostrum). Maddy hoped Emma would understand the importance of the system she had evolved to avoid anything being allocated to the wrong owner. It was fiddly but it worked.

Again, Emma had seemed to twig straight away.

When everything was in its place the lot numbers were stuck on. Auctions and exhibitions where the numbers were all over the place always annoyed Maddy and she insisted that anyone coming to Killybane could walk round the sale with a catalogue (provided they walked the right way round, of course, which some of them didn't) the lot numbers would be consecutive.

There would be no flicking backwards and forwards through the catalogue to find the numbers and descriptions of what was being looked at.

Killybane Saleroom was organised so that viewers could come in, purchase a catalogue and walk round looking at items and pictures placed by and on the left hand wall. They could walk down, round and up the opposite wall, to where Tom had his rostrum and then continue with items arranged on tables down the middle of the room with lot numbers tallying with the catalogue. This created virtually two 'avenues' in the form of a U which were kept wide enough for two or three people to negotiate. There was plenty of space at the bottom of the U where the fireplace was and at the top where the rostrum was, to allow people room to stand and bid when the auction took place the next day.

The lot numbers that had been stuck on then had to be written beside the items on the collection forms. This took time but, again, it made sure there were no allocation muddles, especially when two sellers had submitted identical pieces which wasn't very often but it did happen.

'Have you got nice long finger nails, Emma?' asked Maddy when they had finished, glancing sideways and grinning wryly now, herself.

'Yes, well they aren't great but I don't bite my nails, if that's what you mean.'

'Good. Well, you now have to go round and peel off all the

code stickers while I go and take Fizz for her walk and after that I'll start making the list for the catalogue.'

Emma gave her an 'okay, quits' look and they laughed. Maddy knew then, that things between her and Emma, as Tom would say, were going to be just fine.

Maddy insisted that Fizz still had to have her walk every day. She didn't realise for a long time that it was as much for her as for the dog. It gave her brain and body the break necessary to keep up with the relentless demands that were now required of them. Sometimes she would have to drag herself to get into her wellies and head for the fields but always on her return she felt better, a problem had been solved or, if neither of these two happened, Fizz had had her walk and that's all a dog asks for.

Writing the list of the lots for the catalogue was becoming more arduous with the increasing number of lots they were given to sell. Maddy had a blank sheet with numbers one to whatever the final number was. She then went through each seller's list and copied descriptions of the lots beside the relevant number on her master list. It was a question of laying all the collection forms out on her kitchen work surface which was now extended by her ironing board which was angled round to the kitchen table. As she listed she would mark each item off with a felt tip pen, to avoid duplicates. Before the arrival of the 'Dalek' she would then type out the master list, give it to Tom and he would take it into town and get it printed into as many copies as they thought they would need. They had to be collated when he brought them home and stapled together with a bidding number. This would now be a job for Emma, Maddy thought thankfully, as it would allow her more time to get food organised for the family for sale weekend. Everyone was ravenous after an auction and there were always extra mouths to feed.

Earlier in the week, 'With a bit of Luck Murphy' had come up with some interesting letter openers to sell. These were made from old silver knife handles sporting new metal blades. They were pretty enough to grace any desk. Noticing the pieces they had for the Goodfellow auction spread all over the kitchen he realised the next sale was going to be an interesting one.

He returned the following evening with some Georgian silver spoons – real, unaltered, undamaged antique silver – something they had never had to sell before which more than made up for the pieces Jonathan had removed to send to London.

Maddy made sure she had the correct catalogue descriptions: two Irish Silver serving spoons, dated 1810, stamped SN, each weighing 4 oz; two Irish Silver serving spoons, dated 1779 &1796, stamped JP, each weighing 4.5 oz; and a pair of London Silver Berry Spoons, dated 1794 weighing 3 oz.

With a great feeling of satisfaction she added them to the list Tom needed for the advertisement for the sale. She wished she had the 'bible' of silver marks by Sir Charles J. Jackson that 'With a bit of Luck' had told her about. It listed the names of the silver makers and she could probably have found out who SN and JP were but it was a very expensive book. They would have to be selling a lot more silver before she suggested they add it to their growing number of reference books.

It was midnight when the catalogue list was completed. Maddy now had to cut the stencil and she would print the catalogue first thing in the morning. She had three hundred and twenty four lots to type in. Tom had gone to bed. Fizz was snoring at his feet but Spike, their little tabby cat, jumped up onto her lap as she fed the waxed sheet of paper into the typewriter. She began to type and a paw reached out and tapped one of the keys.

'Oh, Spike, you stinker. That was supposed to be an 'a' and you have typed an 'x'.'

She reached for the correction fluid and dropped a blob on the offending letter. A paw curled round and thumped her hand which dropped the bottle and fluid dribbled into the electric typewriter. All she could do was laugh as she realised her beloved cat had not had much of her attention for quite a while. She sighed. Her life was changing. The things that had always meant so much to her – her home, her animals, her children, the garden, her friends – maybe in that order, or maybe not – were all becoming secondary to Killybane Auctions. It really was taking over her life.

But she couldn't think about that now, this bloody catalogue stencil had to be typed. Spike, bribed with a bit of chicken, was now curled up on his cushion by the Aga and she got on with it. The correction fluid didn't appear to have done any damage to the typewriter and, crawling into bed at about three o'clock again, she thought, *will I ever be able to live a normal life?* She was asleep before any conclusion had been reached.

In spite of her late night, Maddy felt fine the next day and was beginning to feel quite excited about the sale. All she had to do now was print the catalogues.

After climbing the steps and entering the office she hesitated for a moment when not-so-fond memories of the duplicating machine she had used aeons before came back to her. She was unable to get the evil Dalek impression out of her head as she approached it. It looked as if it was crouching with malevolent intent. Banishing these thoughts she attached the stencil and rolled it round the drum. She placed the paper in correctly and checked the ink. Everything seemed to be fine until she began to turn the handle. The first print came out so faintly she decided to give the ink thingy a bit of a pump. She pressed the button that made the machine turn the drum automatically but as the copies began to issue forth, black ink began to ooze and then shoot from several places where it shouldn't.

Maddy pressed as many buttons as she could see but the darned thing wouldn't stop. She grabbed the handle but it nearly tore her arm off. Unable to arrest the process, stemming the ink flow became a matter of priority.

Yelling for Emma to fetch kitchen roll, loo roll – anything - she desperately tried to avoid the ink splattering the lists. By the time the menacing space alien had finished printing she looked like the man who delivered the coal and her arm felt as if it had crank started twenty vintage cars. It had, though, produced perfectly readable catalogues and thus must have saved a bit of money. She did, however, have serious concerns for her sanity.

Thirteen

Emma arrived for her first auction view night to do duty on the door where she was to sell catalogues and meet the auction-going fraternity. She looked extremely smart, quite transformed in a pencil skirt, plaid jacket and high heeled shoes. She had also applied a little lipstick and eye shadow which accented the colour of her eyes.

Maddy began to introduce her to the first few people who came in but soon realised she was more than capable of coping on her own, smiling and chatting to everyone as if she had been part of the Auction scene all her life. Maddy couldn't believe what a week of sorting furniture, cleaning, listing, sticking on lot numbers, frequently getting drenched with rain and becoming quite hysterical with laughter about her boss's relationship with a duplicating machine had done for the girl.

She and Tom had been delighted to see she was getting on really well with Carol who was probably glad to have her catalogue duties taken over on a Friday night so she could go out with Sean. Harry and James too had accepted her inclusion in the team and had swiftly become on teasing terms calling her 'Mighty Mouse' due to her ability to lift and shift furniture with such apparent ease.

'Furniture doesn't wriggle or kick like calves,' she'd told them.

Tom noticed quite a few people who came to view the Sale were clutching Killybane's advertisement cut out from the newspaper. He had obtained permission to mention the late

Admiral's Estate in the adverts for this sale and viewers were pouring in as never before.

'Where's the Belleek?' he was asked by one and to his delight Emma immediately shot over and showed the viewer where it was. *Boy, she's learning fast,* he thought.

He, in turn, was learning the importance of the detailed lists of lots he put in the advertisements and began to wonder if the local weekly papers could be dropped and should he just stick with the two main Northern Irish newspapers. Advertising was their biggest spend and it was hard to know when and where was best. People were obviously looking out for Killybane advertisements on a Thursday night which was great. He remembered Henry Ford's dictum that only half of advertising worked but no one ever knew which half. Well, one half was working tonight, the car park was full and viewers had no option but to park on the road and trudge up the lane.

Emma was enjoying the evening. She felt pleased she could remember where everything was when asked, particularly by sellers who had stuff in the sale and she knew she'd really impressed Edwina Turkington by knowing the lot numbers of things she had been interested in. Emma had always liked numbers, so had her dad. He'd made them fun when she was little. He'd counted the cows with her when they came in for milking and the warm eggs they had collected in the mornings. If she had dropped one and it had broken, he would laugh and they would have to count them again. She never had any trouble with arithmetic at school. Now, she realised, she had an almost photographic memory of the sale.

In slack periods she made herself busy fixing lots viewers had muddled and made sure logs were on the fire and it was still burning. On noticing this, Maddy sent up a heartfelt 'thank you' to whichever or whatever deity had sent this clever little gem to Killybane.

Quite a number of new viewers were appearing. Maddy recognised a friend, Sally Duncan, who worked in the Belfast Museum and wondered what she was interested in. She wasn't going to ask. Some people played the auction game very close to their chests. Two book dealers introduced themselves and said they were keen to buy a box of old die stamped business receipts and would Maddy make sure they were kept safe. She put them in the china cabinet and would tell a porter in the morning where to find them when they came up for sale. A doctor from Newry, Philip Medway, who collected old medical instruments also introduced himself and gave Maddy his phone number to call if they ever had anything in that line again. Lynda Sedge, who dealt in linen and lace did likewise and also a Scottish gentleman, Angus Firth, who collected Mauchline Ware 'Treen' (polished wood) pieces.

Maddy decided she would acquire an indexed book to list these collectors and their details and again silently blessed Jonathan Plunkett-Smythe for trusting and recommending them. They were definitely stepping up another notch on the Dr Annie Walker Scale of Auctions. She was there, too, clad in an even grottier coat than usual and, after viewing the sale, she gave Maddy's arm a discreet squeeze along with a whispered, 'Well done, girl.'

Tom rang Mr Shortall later to see if they could borrow his field again if the car park began to overflow the next day at the auction which seemed likely. Mr S said that would be fine as the field was lying fallow at the moment. Tom dreaded to think what James would have to say and groaned at the thought of having to increase the size of their car park yet again but couldn't help but be pleased at the implications.

The busiest viewing ever had given both of them a tremendous boost and for the first time they were looking forward to the sale without quite so many forebodings. Surely to God they were getting things right at last?

Fourteen

Emma woke up on sale morning feeling anxious about what to wear. She wished she'd asked Mrs Daniels last night, then giggled when she thought of her with remnants of ink from the duplicator machine still evident under her fingernails and a smudge behind her ear. Should she have told her? Mr Daniels obviously hadn't noticed. But then, what did men notice? Not much as far as Emma could see.

When she thought about her week and her new job - it was something else again compared with being a garage attendant. She hoped and prayed it would work out. It was obvious to her the Daniels were new to the auction game but that made it all the more exciting. What was more, they listened when she made suggestions – like with the buying numbers. She had worked it out that it would be better if they were stapled on the right hand side of the back page of the catalogue instead of on the front. It would make it easier for the bidders to fold over and hold up. Nobody had listened to her at the garage when she'd had an idea but the Daniels did.

She wasn't going to wear her heels again. Her feet had been killing her after viewing, with all that running about on the concrete floor. She had a pair of fairly smart flatties which would have to do and opted for good trousers and a warm quilted jacket, not sure what or where her role would be for her first auction.

She knew Carol was still going to man the door. Mrs Daniels had said to come and get the feel of it, maybe help people to pack things or give Carol a break from time to time. It was pretty obvious Mrs Daniels wasn't sure either. She would just have to go and muck in – use her head!

The little she had heard about auctions was vague. She knew her dad went to farm auctions occasionally and would come back with bits of this and that, convinced they were wonderful bargains, but she'd never seen him use any of them and they had just lain about the farm. He went to cattle auctions with cattle and came back with other cattle and that was about that. Having always thought it was a man's world she had been surprised to see women turning up to view.

Emma's thoughts were interrupted by her dad who was giving her a lift and was now shouting from the kitchen. He knew she wanted to be there on time and he had things to do himself today – did she not know that?

She suspected he was as keen as she was to find out about a Killybane Auction.

People began to arrive almost as soon as Tom and Maddy unlocked the saleroom door and Tom was glad he had organised the extra field for parking.

Mr Goodfellow appeared looking chirpy and dapper. As he came through the door, taking off his brown felt hat, Maddy glimpsed a natty gold coloured waistcoat beneath his tweed jacket. Jonathan was with him and they were both plainly pleased to see the gathering crowd. They looked up at the rostrum where Maddy and Tom were sitting, waved 'hello' and smiled.

Maddy watched the pair of them as they walked round taking note of everything - the ironstone service laid out as if for dinner on the 'end' table (a good, fairly immaculate mahogany one that had been delivered at the last minute), the clean and sparkling glassware, the game pie dish and soup tureens placed in the centre along with individual pieces like the part-epergne that looked impressive in spite of its missing trumpets and the better pieces of porcelain.

They also didn't miss the scrap silver that had been polished within an inch of its life displayed in the china cabinet alongside the scent bottles and other smaller, more valuable pieces.

Maddy knew then she didn't give a damn what the dealers thought. They were doing it well.

Harry had drafted in some of his friends to help with portering and generally keeping an eye on the lots as they were all concerned about the numerous vulnerable small items displayed. After the fish tank episode Maddy realised anything could happen and they had to be seen to be taking every precaution against pilfering. She was worried this would all appear a bit paranoid and tried hard to make it seem friendly and casual. But no one seemed to mind and a couple of people even said they could appreciate the care they were taking as none of the other auctions bothered, and good for them.

Maddy was glad to see Emma arriving much earlier than expected and beckoned to her.

'Emma, would you mind getting Mr Goodfellow and Jonathan Plunkett-Smythe a cup of coffee? I would have done but people keep asking me for estimates of the prices of things and giving me bids and I just can't get down to the coffee bar.'

Emma was delighted and zipped off to do what she had been asked. She really fancied Jonathan and was hoping for a chat. This was rudely (or so Emma thought) interrupted by Edwina Turkington who, having taken quite a shine to her on view night, had rushed up, given her a massive thump on the back and said, 'Good morning, young lady, this is going to be a whole new world for you! I just know you are going to enjoy it here.'

Emma was glad she had already handed the coffee to Jonathan at the time otherwise it would have gone all over both him and Mr Goodfellow. She politely excused herself, deciding to go up to the office to see if she could help Mr Daniels Senior, or at least find out what his function was in the scheme of things.

He was standing, looking very similar to Mr Daniels Junior with maybe a bit less hair but looking equally smart in a dark grey suit, contemplating the ink smeared duplicating machine.

'My goodness, that looks a bit of a mess. I remember we had one of those in the bank and the girls were scared to death of it. That looks like it has given someone a nightmare.'

'Oh, you have no idea, Mr Daniels,' Emma laughed. 'It

near killed Mrs Daniels the other day. Don't go near it – it will extremynate you with ink.'

Taking a wide berth they both sat down and Geoffrey began to explain to Emma how his side of the auction day worked. Before she knew it the auction had begun and she was taking in the first sheet from Harry and filling in the lot numbers and prices on the forms – numbers, it was all numbers - her favourite things. The speed of her grasp of the system and numeracy impressed Geoffrey and he gave one of his satisfied 'hrmphs'.

No one was ready yet to come up to the office to pay so Emma returned to the saleroom to watch what was going on. It was a tight squeeze and she found herself squished up beside a huge man who had viewed very quickly the night before and hadn't bought a catalogue.

'You'd be wee Emma,' he said looking down at her.

'I am,' said Emma, blushing; she wasn't sure why.

'I'm Hector. I'd be a bit of a dealer – the boys call me Big Heck.'

A bit of a dealer was a massive understatement but Emma wasn't to find that out until later. She turned her attention to the auctioneer who was now moving on to the inside lots after selling the lots in the yard as he usually did at the beginning of each sale. They had included pots of plants, garden tools, bits of old farm machinery, the sort of things people liked to put in their gardens. Thank God Mr D had a microphone because those not interested were chatting away, drinking coffee and eating Helen's homemade biscuits.

Mr Daniels didn't sound remotely like one of the auctioneers you saw on television or in the films. You could hear everything he said. He made it very clear to everyone who he was taking bids from and how much things were going for. Even when something didn't reach reserve he said so and told everyone it was being withdrawn from sale and if anyone wanted it later they could come and see him. She was mesmerised and inadvertently scratched her nose.

'Are you bidding, madam?' asked the auctioneer and pointed his gavel at her. When Maddy saw him do this from her clerk's seat she felt like killing him. What was he doing? The girl would be mortified.

'No, I'm not,' Emma said glaring right back at him. 'I'm scratching my nose!'

The entire saleroom erupted in laughter and Mr Brown, who was standing on her other side, put a fatherly arm round her, making her feel all at once she belonged in this strange place. Mr Daniels was laughing too. She realised he had been pulling her leg and, because of everyone's reaction to her repost, she almost felt grateful to him. Mrs Daniels looked as though she was going to push her husband off the rostrum and wouldn't mind if he died. Very satisfying, she thought, and felt even more at home.

The crowd of people, the bidding and the prices and the speed of it almost overwhelmed her. She could hardly take it all in as the day progressed. Some of the things she thought would make a lot of money made very little and others, like that rubbish lot with a battered bullet and bits of broken brick - the 'Relics of the Easter Rising' (whatever that was) - had made nearly fifty pounds. The awful, brown delph pot with dead rabbits on the top had made eighty pounds and she wouldn't have given five pence for it. The lovely cut glass decanters made only a few pounds but a perfectly plain large glass tumbler thing with a bit of a pattern of a harp on it and a really rough bottom that would have cut the hand off you, made a hundred and twenty pounds.

It would be a while before she would recognise antique Irish glass but this was the day she began to learn.

The auction had gone well. Tom had been holding over fifty absent bids from the night before, including some from Mr Porter for the scent bottles, which gave him a great confidence boost before the sale had even begun. It was also a relief to know Mr Porter would not be attending. Such was his aromatic presence it would have more than likely cleared the room.

And thanks to the scent bottles Tom had learned another important auction rule and that was to never accept a 'buy' bid from someone who couldn't come to the sale. Always get an upper limit. Mr Porter, on view night had, as usual, told him to just buy the scent bottles for whatever they were going for. Shortly after he had left these instructions, a lady, Mildred Lintel, came to view and asked Tom to do the same thing. Tom could see he was in trouble.

Fortunately Maddy knew Mr Porter's phone number and called him to explain the situation. She was very sorry but they now realised that, when taking absent bids, they should always be told a maximum bid price. She was terrified he would say he (and his pong) would come to the auction to see what the scent bottles were going for but he said he had to go to a funeral and couldn't be there. With enough pondering he reluctantly told her the maximum he would pay, finishing with, 'And don't miss them for a pound or two!'

Maddy wondered what he meant by that exactly and reckoned they had to be mind readers now as well as Solomons.

She found Mildred Lintel who was still viewing the sale and told her that Tom was very sorry, he couldn't accept a 'buy' bid and he would have to be told a maximum price.

Grinning knowingly, this other collector of Victorian scent bottles was a seasoned auction-goer and it was obvious she knew Tom, in his naivety, had done the wrong thing. Maddy had the impression she even knew the identity of the other perfume bottle collector she was going to be bidding against. To their relief she said she'd changed her mind and was going to come to the auction the next day and bid herself. It had ended up with her buying one of them and Mr Porter got the rest.

Tom had indeed gone a few more pounds for Mr P and hoped this would be acceptable. Time would tell and he hoped he wasn't now the proud owner of two Victorian scent bottles.

He felt pleased when he worked out that he had rattled through the sale at about seventy lots an hour − nearly up to the ultimate of one hundred. Thanks to the diligence of Harry and his mates, nothing went missing and the prices although not astronomical (bearing in mind that most of the pieces they were selling were either incomplete or damaged), the total figure for the contents of Mr Goodfellow's trunks was over two thousand pounds. He would receive his cheque the following Wednesday and Maddy bet her life he wouldn't get paid as quickly by Westbury's.

Jennifer and Helen, having been told about the super viewing, had doubled up on sandwiches, soup and traybakes and were doing a roaring trade even before the auction began. The delicious aroma of coffee gave Maddy the idea of maybe providing hot drinks and biscuits for viewing. That would annoy the dealers again - it would make the place even more people friendly.

She'd also had the idea of sending Emma a note of the absent bids that had been successful as the sale progressed so they could be swiftly wrapped and kept safe for the buyers. The boxes and papers were piled in another stable which was now known as the 'Box House'. This, unfortunately, had to be kept under lock and key to avoid a vicious box-grabbing war towards the end of the day which had occurred at the previous sale. Harry and the porters had had to intervene before serious injuries had been inflicted to say nothing of the boxes that ended up in shreds.

Emma packed the absent bid lots discreetly and efficiently and while doing so could hear some of the comments the bidders made to each other. Like Mrs Hawthorne (aka The Rat Catcher who never had a good word to say about anything) to the lady who was standing beside her, 'If you didn't know where this place was you'd never find it.' Emma got the feeling she was a bit miffed that so many other people had discovered Killybane Auctions and this was the most off-putting thing she could think of to say.

'This place is much better than the town auctions,' another person said. 'You don't have to clean the stuff when you get it home.' Emma had laughed later on recounting it to Maddy over their post auction stew and glass of wine. 'And I won't tell you what one of them said about you, Mrs Daniels.'

'Oh?' said Maddy, cross that she should be curious. Emma started to giggle.

'It was one of them dealers, Dickey Burns, y'know the one with the limp. He said he really fancied you and Big Heck told him to watch out, he'd seen you lift a chest of drawers and reckoned you'd be more than well able to defend yourself!' This was said in front of Tom and she wondered was Emma getting her own back after the nose scratching incident. She wouldn't have put it past her.

Maddy then remembered at one point in the sale she had noticed Francis Maloney sidle up to Emma and ingratiate himself with the usual success. Before a minute passed he had had her hand in his and she was gazing up at him with intense curiosity.

'And what, Emma,' Maddy asked, 'was Francis Maloney telling you about your future?'

Emma, blushing a deep pink, gave what she thought was a cynical laugh, followed by an embarrassed smile.

'He said in a few weeks I would meet a tall, thin chap with blue eyes who had something to do with soil. He could see him pushing a wheelbarrow. Have you ever heard such rubbish! I wouldn't trust that man as far as I could give him a jam sandwich.'

Emma's metaphors, if that is what one could call them, were sometimes quite baffling. She then brought everyone down with a bump when she asked what was going to be in the next auction. They had to confess to their new keen recruit that, to date, they had not booked a single call and they had nothing. So Tom opened another bottle of wine...

Fifteen

Auction number ten was looming and although they had collected little or nothing for it Tom realised that decision time had come regarding his job. Before he could do anything about it himself his boss decided for him by arranging a conference that was essential he attended on what was scheduled to be an Auction weekend.

Maddy was horrified.

'Oh my God, Tom – I can't do an auction – I couldn't do it to save my life! You know what my mathematics are like. What are we going to do without you?'

Tom grinned and felt quite pleased. 'That's a first! You have never said that before.'

Maddy wasn't an ardent women's-libber but was definitely of an independent frame of mind. He supposed that's what had attracted him in the first place apart from the fact that he found her funny. Like when he'd first met her.

She had been giving away her entire collection of teddy bears and cuddly toy animals to everybody she met in the street who wanted one. He was passing by the Grand Hotel just after she had thrust one into the arms of the commissionaire who was standing on the steps in his uniform, beaming from ear to ear, clutching a large panda bear.

She did weird things, like the time she took off for Belfast with their dustbin attached to the back of her car having forgotten to take it off at the end of their lane. He'd had a hard time keeping his face straight when explaining the wheel-less, bottomless bin to the man from the Council.

Tom's boss was an old friend who had found a place for him in his organisation after the textile factories closed. He knew very well what he was doing. He had attended several of their auctions and often stayed for supper afterwards. He could see Killybane Auctions was becoming a legitimate business and had assumed, wrongly, that it was beginning to make serious money. Threatening to send Tom to the conference had been what he had thought was a tactful way of helping him to make the decision to leave.

Tom ran his hand through his hair and declared, 'That's it. It's time I gave in my notice.'

This was going to be a huge step of faith. The auctions were not yet making enough money to make up for the salary he would lose. The quality and quantity of what they were selling would have to improve or they wouldn't be able to afford the mortgage, to say nothing of the recently acquired overdraft and expenses of running the business. Just how they were going to do this remained a mystery.

There had been a fair amount of publicity in the wake of the Goodfellow auction and a lot more enquiries but nothing substantial. Their list to the newspapers of notable things sold in the 'Around the Auctions' column was beginning to look better these days but it still wasn't nearly as grand as those of the other local auction rooms.

Tom decided it was time to pay the opposition a visit.

'We have had nine auctions,' he declared. 'Why haven't we gone to have a look at the others before this?'

'We have been kind of busy,' Maddy pointed out. 'And you are doing two jobs at the moment, in case you hadn't noticed.'

Tom had to agree. Life had been extremely hectic. But now he had made up his mind, he, Maddy and Emma would go together and have a look to see what the other auction rooms were doing that Killybane was not.

Maddy, being a born rummager, had been to the town auction rooms in the past when furnishing their first home. She had left bids with porters if she'd wanted anything but had never been to an actual auction. All she could remember was that they were mostly full of junk and a porter had pinched her bottom as she'd bent over to look at a chair. She much preferred the second hand shops in the old Smithfield Market and had found it hard to sell the treasures she had acquired there in their first auction.

From her mother and grandmother she had inherited the ability to spot a 'find'. A nice old thing, maybe long neglected, that could be bought for nothing and with a bit of cleaning and restoring be brought back to life. She hadn't been able to part with the beautiful old hand beaten copper and brass kettle with a lid adorned with an acorn she'd bought for two shillings. It had been so black it had looked like an ordinary iron kettle. It had taken weeks of elbow grease to restore it to its original gleaming state.

The first auction room they visited was on the ground floor of a building that appeared to have once been a car show room. The large floor-to-ceiling windows at the front might have let in welcome light had they been cleaned after the turn of the century. Battered sofas and chairs that gave the appearance of having taken root in the un-swept floor formed the base layer of the 'lots' for sale. Piled upon, and beside, these were tables, cupboards, filthy cookers, dining chairs, mirrors, ornaments, lamps and pictures scattered willy nilly, many with lot numbers stuck crookedly over old lot numbers and nearly everything had visible chalk identification letters and numbers scrawled somewhere on them. A person sat in a glass walled cubicle at the rear of the room talking into a phone but there was no one else in attendance and certainly no catalogues for sale.

Maddy and Emma looked at each other in dismayed astonishment. Was this the auction room that was getting those amazing prices? Surely not, yet, 'Around the Auction Rooms' said it was.

'They are having an auction once a week,' Tom pointed out to Maddy seeing the disgust on her face. 'So I suppose they don't have time to be too fussy.'

Maddy grunted and said, 'I'd rather have an auction once a month than run one like this. How can they keep track of things with all those numbers and – oh!' She paused on noticing a man sound asleep, snoring gently on one of the chairs.

She supposed a town auction had the advantage of a larger footfall than one in the country. People could come to view during their lunch hour or while shopping. Mind you, she couldn't see a smart shopper wanting to browse round this awful place – but there was also the disadvantage of some people deciding it was somewhere warm and dry for a mid-day snooze.

She remembered the dealer saying to her about not having a chance of getting a bargain if she cleaned everything. This was what he was talking about and, thinking about herself as a rummager, she could understand that. But, who, in their right minds, would give anything to a place like this to sell?

Puzzled and depressed they continued to the other, longer established saleroom in town. It was busier with more porters, some of them moving furniture into a lift. The ground floor was obviously the department for things at the lower end of the market and looked similar to where they had just come from.

Upon climbing what must have once been an impressive flight of stairs with a double balustrade they came upon a grander room which was certainly better organised and contained a good number of interesting antiques; furniture, paintings and ornaments but again, lot numbers stuck over old numbers on things that were obviously being put through the sales again and again until they sold. Nothing had been cleaned or even dusted.

'Wouldn't you just love to get yer hands on this lot?' Emma whispered to Maddy who was standing in front of a cabinet contemplating a shelf crammed with tarnished silver.

'Oh boy, Emma, would I what? We could make everything here look fantastic.'

They drove home in a pall of gloom, each wondering how on earth they were going to attract the sellers who could give them better stuff. Maddy rang Dr Walker and asked her outright if she knew where the town auctions were getting the contents of their sales from.

'From dealers and house clearances,' Dr Walker said immediately. 'You have got to get solicitors and the banks' executor departments on your side. You need dead people with houses full of contents to be disposed of. But be careful with the dealers, they will demand a cut in commission and run rings round you if you are not careful. They will try to use you like a shop.' She finished with, 'And don't worry so much, you are doing really well. Keep going as you are and you'll get there.'

'We owe you another glass or two of wine, Dr W, thank you.' Maddy put the phone down. She hadn't told Dr Walker that they were getting slightly desperate and she might have to bring her own wine next time.

Sixteen

Jim Gillanders, who owned a popular nursery and garden centre a few miles from Killybane, had come to the conclusion that his successful propagation techniques had out-stripped his greenhouse and display space. He had hundreds if not thousands of surplus plants, trees and shrubs he needed to get rid of and phoned to see if Tom would consider having an auction for him on site.

With nothing to lose and not one call in the pipeline, Maddy and Tom went to meet him to investigate the situation. Maddy had been to the garden centre many times over the years and Jim, a small, chatty man with bright blue eyes had shown Maddy how to propagate pelargoniums or geraniums, as they are commonly called.

He loved to exchange local gossip and Maddy had stood entranced, listening to his various tales about this person and that, watching him cutting sections from the mother plant, trimming them with his sharp pocket knife and leaving them with others in a row to harden off prior to pushing them into a little pots of compost. In the balmy warmth of his greenhouse that smelled of soil and the lemony scent of geraniums, Maddy had become addicted and like him, she had a greenhouse overflowing with cuttings every year. Unlike him she did not have heat in her greenhouse and many of her plants succumbed to the winter cold. She reckoned it was just as well as she would have ended up in the same pickle as Jim with far too many.

On their arrival, Tom and Maddy were confronted with about half an acre of greenhouses full to their ventilators with plants.

Mr Gillanders still had to keep his nursery customers coming but it was obvious he needed what people in Northern Ireland call a 'good red out'.

Outside, there was at least an acre of heathers, azaleas and small trees that had thrived in pots. These, like the surplus greenhouse plants, all needed to be potted on and Jim reckoned it would be more profitable to sell them as they were before investing in the time and expense of re potting them.

It was hard to know where to begin. Should they be sold in groups and if so, how many in each group? The whole place was going to have to be rearranged and the lots displayed in rows for people to walk round. It was going to be back-breaking work, but they decided to do it.

The auction advertisement read: *Over 12,000 containerised conifers, plants, shrubs, garden equipment, machinery and sundries.*

Once again Maddy wondered if they were right in the head. Emma didn't think so and was happy to hold the fort at Killybane while Maddy and Tom spent three long days at the nursery arranging the plants into lots, tying on lot numbers (stickers wouldn't do in the damp weather) and making the catalogue which was probably the most boring one Maddy had ever typed – 20 Leylandii, 20 mixed heathers, 20 Leylandii, 20 mixed heathers and so on, lot after lot. She could only pray they were doing it right.

Maddy could see Jim was becoming anxious about it, especially when he brought up the dreaded 'reserve' word.

'I am bloody well not withdrawing a lot of twenty perishing 8 inch high Leylandii,' muttered Tom, who was nearing the end of his gardening tether. 'If he mentions reserves to me I will …'

'Alright, Tom. I'll have a word.'

Maddy explained to Jim that, apart from working at the market garden for days, they had spent time and money advertising the sale which involved a good deal more than putting a poster up in the local post office. They had written about the auction to 80 other market gardens, to say nothing of masses of phone calls to friends who were keen on gardening and would spread the news about the sale. They had done everything they could to make sure he would have a good auction and an auction was what it had to be. He would just have to bite the bullet and accept that he would get more for some things and less for others etc etc… and he did want a clear-out, didn't he?

He dug his heels in about some garden troughs and was allowed to reserve those but he eventually agreed the plants could go for whatever price they were making on the day.

The weather had been mizzly and cold all week so Tom decided one of the greenhouses would be a good place to hold the sale and had made a small platform at one end as a rostrum.

Auction day dawned bright and sunny. Within five minutes of the sale beginning they were sweltering. A large crowd of bidders came but they were all timing their entry into the baking greenhouse to bid and shoot out immediately. It was becoming hard to even breathe in there and, even though Jim opened as many windows as he could, it made little difference. Tom tromped on with the auction, instructing Maddy to 'look cool – and don't take your jacket off.' He eventually couldn't stand the heat any longer and took his off.

Maddy wished she'd worn a bikini. Somebody suggested that they move outside to continue the sale but the microphone and speakers were rigged up and it would have taken too long to reconnect them - they didn't want the bidders losing interest.

Geoffrey, taking care of the bills was ensconced comfortably in a cool shed with a potting bench as his desk, and buyers were paying him in there. The porters were helpful and carted trays of plants to cars for people and Emma and Carol took turns standing at the exit checking invoices as the plants were carried out.

Jim's son, Wallace, a tall, gangly, pleasant looking lad, decided to be of assistance too and Emma was not averse to him 'helping' her at the gate. He had lovely bright blue eyes just like his dad.

After four hours, when Tom knocked down the final lot, he

and Maddy melted off their platform and staggered into the fresh air. 'Well, that all seemed to go quite well – didn't it?' Tom said to Jim, gratefully accepting one of the tumblers of lemonade Mrs Gillanders had brought out for them.

Jim didn't look too sure. 'I thought those concrete tubs would have made more. I could have probably got more if I'd just sold them in the ordinary way – and did you see that last box of 20 Leylandii went for a pound ...' and, shaking his head, he disappeared into one of his now empty greenhouses.

A shriek came from the gate, 'That's my azalea!' An irate lady in brown corduroy trousers and green wellies, who they found out later was Lady Nadine Saunders, came charging up to Maddy who had been setting a plant upright that had fallen over. 'I was just coming back to pick it up!' The woman waved a receipt in Maddy's face, picked up the plant and waved that in Maddy's face as well. 'Just because you did the auction – it doesn't give you the right to take what you want.' And she stomped back to her car.

'There's nothing like being appreciated, is there?' said Tom.

After the nursery sale people began bringing plants to the general sales to be auctioned. They never made much money and were hardly worth the bother.

One of their regular contributors was Mr Turnbull, a quietly spoken man who drove an ancient but spotless, shining BMW and who brought boxes of house plants his wife grew in a greenhouse. These made so little Maddy was continually surprised when he came back with more.

Using odd saucers and plates she found in house clearances to put the pots on they made an attractive addition to displays of china and ornaments that were in the sales but rarely made more than fifty pence each. Tom moaned about writing cheques for two pounds or similar small sums and then having to pay to post them. Maddy tried to explain to Mr T that if something was going to sell for only fifty pence it was actually costing Killybane Auctions money. In reply he would simply smile and say, 'Well, no matter.' And return the following week with more plants.

He also had a pedal organ he wanted to sell. In a carved wooden frame, it was working and everything, he assured Maddy.

He had shown it to Mr 'Westbury' who had actually played it and said it was worth about five hundred pounds. Westbury's, however, didn't want to sell it but they thought Killbane Auctions could.

Fortunately, Killybane Auctions had tried to sell pedal organs before and they knew nobody wanted them – not even for the carved wood. Tom tried to explain this to Mr Turnbull when he'd been persuaded to go to his house and see it for himself. Mr T stood and looked at the organ for a long while, heaved a sigh, smiled at Tom and said, 'Isn't it a pity it isn't a gun, Mr Daniels? Mr Westbury said guns sell really well.'

'Nice little organ – goes bang bang!' Tom said, recalling the conversation over lunch. They all agreed there was no accounting for the way people's minds worked sometimes.

Seventeen

As soon as Tom and Maddy became busy with preparations for the plant auction, Emma began to be run off her tiny feet at Killybane. By some 'sod's law' the number of deliveries began to increase and when they came home for lunch or in the evenings they found her almost buried among boxes of smalls and pieces of furniture. This didn't seem to faze her at all and she appeared to thoroughly enjoy being in charge. Everything was listed and labelled perfectly with notes of who to contact about reserves if there were any.

'Somebody up there is looking after us,' said Tom as he took stock. The next sale after Jim Gillanders' nursery was beginning to look good and what was really great was that it was coming from a number of sellers, not just one out of the blue, like Mr Goodfellow. Maddy almost didn't dare to hope that, maybe, perhaps, oh please God, fingers crossed, they were finally on their way to halfway decent auctions on a regular basis.

Bookings to go to peoples' homes to give valuations were mounting up as well. Tom and Maddy knew that most of these were in the wake of the other auctioneers but they were beginning to win with some who were phoning back to arrange to have their goods collected. In spite of this they were both aware they still had a lot to learn about the market value of many things.

Conscious of their lack of expertise, they had begun to read as many antiques magazines as they could lay their hands on and had acquired back copies and the current edition of Millers'

Antiques Guide. First printed in 1979, in response to the boom in the antiques trade, Judith and Martin Miller had compiled this most comprehensive reference book. It contained hundreds of photographs of antiques with valuations of pieces from every aspect of the business – ceramics, furniture, collectables, musical instruments, arms and armour and so on.

It also contained the names of dealers and shops specialising in their fields and masses of information, tips and pointers of what to look out for when valuing anything from all periods including Art Nouveau and Art Deco.

Maddy devoured them along with as many other books on antiques as she could find. She felt guilty if she bought a new dress but never when she bought a book. They also subscribed to the Antiques Trade Gazette, a weekly newspaper covering the whole of the UK that provided the latest in market information such as auction reports, previews, news and analysis for professionals and collectors.

Reading about all the wonderful sales across the water was sick-making and only made them realise how much further they had to go – if they could. There was much catching up to do but they were hooked and loved learning about each and every aspect of their new trade.

Maddy particularly liked ceramics, going to bed most nights with Geoffrey Godden's encyclopaedia of pottery and porcelain marks. Tom usually did likewise with some tome or other about clocks which appealed to his leanings towards all things mechanical.

When Tom finally decided to throw in his lot with Killybane Auctions it was almost like déjà vu. They had been here before - facing an unknown future. Only slightly different this time because they at least had something they could work at and, although the sums were adding up to very little at the moment, they had few doubts that what they were doing was right.

They never articulated this feeling but it was there and they each had a certainty, somewhere inside, that things were going to work out in the end.

To Maddy's overwhelming relief they had also decided it

was time to take the house off the market and the hated For Sale sign had been removed. She could allow herself to dream again.

That night they had a quiet meal and a glass or two of wine to toast Tom's decision. The house was unusually quiet as the boys were both at 'sleepovers' and Carol was out with Sean. After settling into bed with their various books Tom suddenly reached over and took Maddy's out of her hands, saying, 'I am becoming a bit jealous of Geoffrey Godden – you go to bed with him every night!'

'Well,' replied Maddy, picking up the magazine of the Antiquarian Horological Society that Tom had been reading, 'that's not as bad as playing second fiddle to "The Varieties of the French 'oignon' Watch".'

She started to laugh and put on a posh, nasal, specs-at-the-end-of-nose voice. 'I see 'their balances are protected by pierced and engraved cocks and their regulation is achieved by means of an endless screw'.'

Further observations were denied her and their reading matter ended up on the floor.

Interior décor at this time favoured the aesthetically provincial 'country' look. Laura Ashley was championing chintz for every room on anything from four poster beds to winged arm chairs and chaises longues. Dado rails, dried flowers in antique pottery jugs, wicker furniture and cleverly arranged antique bottles prevailed.

Wooden floor boards, lace trimmed cloths draped over occasional circular tables topped with electrified old paraffin lamps and bric a brac were featuring prominently in all the decorating magazines, as were Victorian tiled iron fireplaces beneath gilt or carved wood-framed overmantels. Stripped pine dressers, cupboards and chests of drawers were ubiquitous and quirky old pieces such as Edwardian brass mounted coal buckets and fire screens with embroidered panels were finding new niches for themselves. Even ordinary old blue banded kitchen crockery and earthenware storage jars were becoming fashionable.

In 1977, the BBC ran a programme called 'Going for a Song' presented by the well known antique dealer, Arthur Negus, which became so popular it was turned into 'The Antiques Road Show' and rapidly became obligatory Sunday night viewing throughout the land. Killybane Auctions couldn't have started at a better time. Now all they needed was better stuff.

Not only were most of the dealers of second hand furniture now attending the sales at Killybane but the antique dealers had begun to filter in.

As promised, Hennessy Bergman reappeared. With his hands in the pockets of his British Warm, he sauntered into the kitchen one morning while Maddy was clearing up after breakfast. She couldn't believe his audacity especially when he announced, 'Black – without sugar,' before he was even asked would he like a cup of coffee.

'And where is the Lord and Master?' he demanded, looking around.

'If you mean Tom, he's gone to work,' Maddy replied nearly biting off her tongue. This man didn't need to know any of their business let alone the fact that Tom had another job, albeit not for much longer.

'Hmm - nice dining chairs – English, 18th Century oak and probably a bit of fruit wood – not appreciated here as much as in England.'

'That's where they came from. They were my mother's. She brought them with her when she and my father came to live here after the war. She loved oak and consequently I do too.'

'The Irish are terrified of it – they think it's more prone to woodworm – except, of course, the stuff that comes out of a bog.'

Maddy handed him his coffee wishing he was in a bog and asked, 'Would you like some toast?' She couldn't believe she had just offered this rude person toast.

'No. I never eat before eleven o'clock.'

Maddy could think of nothing to say to this so asked him did he want to see what they had for the next sale and would he like to bring his coffee with him. She wanted him out of her house. His Geiger counter eyes were scanning her furniture like a licentious old man mentally stripping a pretty girl. She felt the corner cupboard, the dresser and dining furniture were being filed somewhere for some sort of unknown future use in his devious little brain.

She was yet to learn this is what all antique dealers do. It's in their bones.

'Lead on, Madam,' he said in an imperious tone as Maddy grabbed the saleroom key and they went outside.

Maddy hated anyone seeing it like this but it did not deter Hennessy who zoned in on the few halfway decent antiques they had.

'How much is this going to make?' he asked, pulling out a mahogany carver dining chair.

'I don't know really. I haven't had much of a chance to look at it. I think it is quite an old one but um ...' At this point her knowledge and courage failed her.

'Alright, you silly girl,' he said and raised his eyes heavenward as if dealing with a half wit. 'Here is how you look at a chair for starters.'

He took the seat pad out and upended the chair. Maddy noticed his shoes for the first time, framed in the square of the padless seat. Pierced brogues, polished to an incredible sheen and she wondered if he had polished the insteps like her father did who used to say you could always tell a man by his shoes. *Not this one, Daddy,* she thought to herself.

Hennessey gestured to the construction of the chair. 'Look at how the corners are joined. Are they jointed or screwed? If a joint is damaged it affects the value as it is a very expensive repair. How are the legs and stretchers attached? Have the legs been cut down? If it has woodworm it will be more noticeable in the un-polished wood here – see?'

He took her through the inspection in great detail and in spite of her antipathy towards him she realised no amount of books would ever give her this kind of information.

Her rapt attention seemed to inspire him to embellish his discourse with fascinating snippets about chairs in general; Queen Victoria never looked round before she sat. She just plonked herself down and a trusty servant was always on hand to place a chair beneath her.

Maddy considered the terrible temptations that must have daily beset that poor chap. Chairs, more than any other piece of furniture reflected the fashions of the day such as woven cane and upholstery which first came from France – for comfort – trust the French - and 'Barley Sugar' twist turning on stretchers and backs had originally came from Holland. The 'Ball-and-Claw' foot came from the Orient and represented a dragon's foot clutching a pearl.

He finished by pointing out that by the very nature of its function, the chair is a much abused soul. Not only is it constantly sat on, it is pulled, pushed, dragged and frequently stood on so not too many of great age have survived to be used as anything but ornament. Mostly late 18th and 19th century chairs are found on the market today. The number of chairs in a set is important because the price compounds itself as the number increases. A set of twelve original, matching, 18th Century dining chairs was a rare and desirable acquisition. These, dealers would come to blows for.

His lecture abruptly came to a halt. Was he regretting his generosity of knowledge? Maddy offered him another cup of coffee.

'That would be acceptable, thank you.' For a second or two he seemed to be slightly embarrassed and continued to studiously examine the chair. When she returned so had his bombast, 'I want this chair will you sell it to me now?'

Maddy and Tom had discussed the business of selling 'out of auction' as they had been asked to do so before and they had agreed that it must never happen. They were an auction room not a shop and people gave them things to be auctioned. What if an owner came to a sale to watch whatever he or she had given them to sell being sold and it wasn't there? The repercussions were too horrible to contemplate. Selling out of sale was not a viable option.

'Sorry, Hennessy, no.'

'Hah! Thought you would say that – just testing you! But, I promise, I will corrupt you the same way all the other Rooms are corrupted. Just wait and see.'

With that, he got into his car and, simultaneously turning on the ignition and his radio, drove away to the full blast strains of 'The Ride of the Valkyries'.

What suitable music, she thought, *but what a strange man. Utterly objectionable one minute, really nice the next and then horrible again.* She had yet to learn about the vicissitudes of the average antique dealer and the not so average Hennessey Bergman.

Eighteen

Although Maddy dreamed that Killybane Auctions would one day be selling nothing but antiques and beautiful things, she knew in her heart of hearts that their auctions would always be a mixture of old and modern stuff and a fair amount of junk.

It was doubtful that Northern Ireland had a large enough population to specialise on a regular basis and as Tom frequently pointed out, '15% of a washing machine that sells for twenty pounds is the same as 15% of a Victorian chair that sells for the same price. Anyway, people who collect antiques also need washing machines.'

Tom's logic depressed her slighty sometimes.

The days marched on and Tom had nearly worked his notice. Maddy was alone in the yard one morning as Emma had to go to the dentist. A Ford Cortina drove into the yard towing a trailer. She walked over as the driver got out.

'Well now. What do you think of that?'

Small, shiny Mr. Tomelty stood proudly back with one hand in his immaculate white overall pocket and the other gesticulating. Maddy peered into his trailer.

'It's – um – very nice – it's an anvil isn't it?'

'It certainly is – you don't see the like of that every day of the week!'

'No, I'm sure you don't. Do you want to sell it? Put it in the auction?'

'I certainly do.' He then peered all around and over Maddy's shoulder. 'Is there nobody about?'

Maddy found herself peering about as well, before her feminist side stepped in. 'Yes,' she said. 'Me!'

'Ah, well, I've brought a plank.'

'Do you want to sell that too?'

'No, no, no – it's to slide the anvil down – out of the trailer.'

'Oh.'

'Now,' he said, patting his stomach gingerly, 'I'm just out of hospital after a hernia – are you sure there's not a man about to give you a hand?'

'No, don't worry, I'm stronger than I look,' Maddy said. 'I can do it.'

Looking unconvinced, Mr. Tomelty lifted the plank out of the trailer, dropped it on both of their feet, bent double, groaned and clutched his middle. Two biros fell out of his breast pocket and his spectacles slid to the end of his nose.

'It's probably just some stitches settling,' said Maddy in what she thought was a comforting fashion. 'It happened all the time to my husband when he had his,' she added brightly.

'Mine's a DOUBLE one!' he hissed, obviously miffed that she could possibly compare his hernia with anyone else's.

She removed the tail gate, picked up the plank and placed one end of it on the back of the trailer and the other on the ground. The anvil squatted there, threatening orthopaedic mayhem. She glared at its pointy snout.

'Ole!' she said quietly.

'Old what?' Mr Tomelty was upright again but a bit green.

'If I put a rope through that hole in its nose I could pull it – could you give it just a tiny push?'

'Absolutely not. My doctor said I wasn't to lift so much as my wee finger for six months. I should never have lifted that plank.'

'Forgive me for asking,' Maddy ventured, 'but how did you get the thing on the trailer in the first place?'

'How do you think I got this hernia?'

'Oh,' Maddy said as she threaded the rope through the hole

and pulled with all her might wondering the while how Hannibal would have approached the situation.

'The lucky sod had elephants,' she grunted to herself as she tugged

'Well, I may have had a half'un or two at the time, and the wife helped – she shoved it up the plank – you can surely pull it down!'

'I didn't say you were "elephants", Mr. Tomelty. I was talking about Hannibal – he moved all sorts of rocks and things.'

'Great! Is he local? Could you give him a ring and get him over here?'

'Sadly no, Mr Tomelty, but oh how I wish.' The anvil refused to budge.

'If you had a bit of a broom handle you could put it underneath and then it would roll to the edge,' he suggested.

Maddy, ready to try anything, duly found a bit of handle in the workshop and handed it to him. 'You can lift this, I hope,' she said. 'And maybe slide it under when I lift the anvil?' She climbed into the trailer, straddled the beast and heaved. It rose just enough for him to slip in the piece of wood.

'Now we're flying,' he declared.

Maddy clambered out and pulled the rope again. Miraculously, the half ton of iron trundled to the back of the trailer but, of course, stopped in front of the plank. Mr Tomelty now rushed round to behind the trailer and with one foot either side of the plank issued further instructions.

'If you could just get the front up onto the plank, we'll be able to shift it down – no problem!'

Maddy climbed back into the trailer, put a hammerlock on the anvil and briefly lifted it. It fell with a slap onto the end of the plank causing it and Mr Tomelty to rise sharply at the other end. Mr Tomelty was now flying - round and round the yard, clutching a certain portion of his anatomy, mouthing silent, anguished oaths.

'Gosh!' said Maddy. 'Sorry!'

'That bloody thing will be the death of me,' he gasped, passing the trailer, the plank and the anvil for the fourth time. 'The wife said it would be and she was bloody right!'

Feeling somewhat helpless in the face of what was a case for some sort of First Aid, Maddy asked if she could get him a packet of frozen peas.

'What the hell would I want with a packet of effing frozen peas?'

'Well, when applied to ah – an injured - er – area – they can help prevent bruising and um – swelling.'

She was relieved when her offer was dismissed with a flapping hand and after some minutes his equilibrium returned.

'Now,' he ordered, 'lift the arse of her, push a bit, get her going, the plank will fall and she'll slide down.'

Funny, Maddy thought, how, after inflicting him with near mortal injury, the anvil had suddenly become female and had acquired an arse.

She heaved again, the anvil tipped and began to slide down the plank. The only thing they hadn't accounted for was momentum. It slid faster and faster and all they could do was watch from a safe distance as it careered down the plank, twisted and fell off. It came to rest on its side but unharmed and wonder of wonders, out of the trailer.

'Hah!' said Mr Tomelty triumphantly, 'who needs yer man Hanna ..... Hanna ......'

'Ball,' Maddy said sweetly. He winced.

'Right, now,' he said firmly as she was ineffectually trying to right the anvil with a crowbar. 'What about the reserve?'

'THE WHAT?' Maddy nearly fell over to join the anvil. 'And if it doesn't make the reserve you put on it do you really want to come back and collect it?'

'I certainly do.'

'Well, I hope you bring your wife with you so I have the pleasure of watching her shove the darned thing back up that plank.'

'Now, now love, you'll be surprised what that anvil will make. It'll really surprise you.'

Maddy said she thought it had done enough of that already.

'Oh yes – ha ha. Would you mind putting the plank back on the trailer again, dear, and the tailgate?'

She was ready to wallop him with them.

'I'll not take a penny less than £60.' He was adamant. Maddy was too weak to argue and wrote down his reserve.

When it sold for £150 the following week she had to admit she was surprised.

The day after the sale she was busy in the yard tidying up when the new owner came to collect it – on his own.

'Hay, Missus!' he called, 'you wouldn't have such a thing as a bit of a plank, would you?'

Nineteen

rs Daniels?' Emma asked one Friday morning as they were beginning to unpack some boxes of china they had collected from a large house in North Antrim. 'Yes, Emma?' Maddy replied.

'D'you think I could go home a wee bit early today?'

'Of course you can, Emma,' Maddy said and then, her curiosity getting the better of her, she enquired, 'Are you going out tonight?'

Emma dropped her eyes and gave slightly embarrassed smile. 'Yes.'

'Aha,' said Maddy, 'and who is the lucky man?'

'Wally Gillanders,' Emma replied, unable to suppress a small, self satisfied grin. 'He's got tickets for the Country and Western concert in the King's Hall and we'd like to get there early. It's first there first served and we want to get good seats.'

'Well, I hope you have a great time,' Maddy said. 'Be sure to leave here early enough to get yourself dickied up and ...' She gave a sudden gasp and looked at Emma with gleeful shock. 'Oh! Oh, my goodness.'

'What?' said Emma, alarmed at the tone of Maddy's voice.

'Emma, Wallace - Wally Gillanders is tall, isn't he?'

'Yes.'

'And he's slim.'

'Yes.'

'And he has blue eyes.'

'Yes,' Emma said. She began to blush.

'And it's only a few weeks since the garden centre auction where I definitely saw him pushing a wheelbarrow. . .'

'Oh my God, Mrs Daniels – Francis – he told me...'

'Yes, Emma, it looks like Francis Maloney's fortune telling is ever so slightly - accurate.'

Emma sat down with her hand over her mouth, staring at Maddy in disbelief. After a few seconds she pulled herself together and got up, announcing firmly, 'Sure it's just coincidence – that's all it is.' Then, looking over at Maddy again, she said in a whisper, 'Isn't it?'

'Well, he was right about that poor woman's husband.'

'So you think he's sidekick then, do you?'

'I think,' said Maddy, 'there is a distinct possibility that he just might be – er – sidekick.' She didn't want to embarrass Emma by correcting her malapropism and added, 'It might be interesting to see what else he has to tell you.'

'No! He might tell me something I don't want to hear. That man's a menace. And yet...' Emma's words gave way to unspoken thoughts as she and Maddy began to unpack the boxes.

After a while Maddy noticed Emma observing a large blue and white printed platter she had just unwrapped. 'Mrs Daniels?' she asked again.

'Yes, Emma?'

'D'you see this pattern?'

'Yes Emma, the Willow Pattern.'

'Well, what's it all about? Them wee birds and them people on that bridge and the wee person with the stick thing with a bit of string attached.'

'There is a story there – my grandmother told it to me. Would you like to hear it?'

'Yes, I would.'

Maddy lifted the platter and, pointing at various parts of the pattern, began.

'Once upon a time there was a beautiful young girl called Koong Shee. She lived with her very important and rich Mandarin father by a lake in a grand house with arched doorways and tiered curly roofs, all set in an exotic garden with orange and peach trees. Koong Shee's father had arranged a marriage for her to a wealthy old man she did not like. One day, shortly before the wedding, she met and fell deeply in love with her father's new secretary, Chang. Knowing this would not meet with her father's approval, Koong Shee gathered up her jewel box and distaff (that's a spindle on which wool is wound for spinning) and fled with Chang over the bridge by the willow tree. Her father saw them and followed in hot pursuit, wielding his whip – that's the stick you can see with the bit of string. The lovers jumped into a boat and escaped to Chang's house where they were married. The disappointed wealthy suitor followed and set their house on fire. Just as the lovers were about to perish in the inferno, the gods took pity and turned them into two turtle doves who flew out of the flames and into the sky to be together for all time.'

'That's so sad, Mrs Daniels,' Emma said and, after some thought, added, 'I can understand her taking her jewels with her but why would she be bothered to take that wool winding thing – must have been hard to run with? Maybe she was thinking she could make a bit of money later, knitting and stuff?'

'Perhaps,' Maddy said, smiling at Emma's practical side which, she was learning, invariably came to the fore and began to wonder how Wally was going to fare in the romance stakes that evening.

Twenty

The Restorers' Room was proving to be a good idea. Emma overheard one viewer saying to another who hadn't been to Killybane Auctions before, 'This is the "worm" room. Lots of damaged stuff in here but it's great – you never know what you will find.'

It was providing the rummagers and dealers with a more exciting space, like the town auctions. The whole psychology of selling by auction was becoming clearer now and Tom and Maddy were learning by trial and error, sale by sale.

Maddy had made it her business to find out about woodworm once and for all. Daily, she and Tom could see it was rife and, in view of the horrendous damage it could sometimes inflict, most people were terrified of it and wouldn't even consider letting a piece of furniture with one tiny hole into their homes.

Maddy contacted an old school friend, Penny Entwhistle, who now worked in the entomology department at Queen's University, who told her that the woodworm, furniture beetle, moth or, to use its Latin name, Anobium Punctatum, doesn't have to come in with furniture, it can just as easily fly in through a window.

As enthusiastic as ever about her subject, Penny seemed to be really fond of this little fellow.

'He has been with us since the Ark - he is reputed to have been the last to leave - and is likely to be with us for a long time to come.'

She went on to explain that he was part of the ecosystem

helping in the Great Outdoors to break down dead wood, such as fallen trees, enabling them to rot speedily into the vegetation and form compost for new growth.

'But why doesn't he just stick to dead trees?' asked Maddy. 'Why does he attack furniture?'

'What is furniture made of, silly?' Penny asked, laughing.

'Of course – stupid me – dead trees!'

'There you go!'

'Well, why isn't every house in the land with windows that open, crumbling away to fine dust? I have furniture that belonged to my mother with woodworm holes in it and it hasn't got any worse in all the years I have had it and, as far as I know, our roof rafters are okay.'

'Do you have central heating?'

'You know we do.'

'Well, there you are. Anobium Punctatum hates being warm. What he loves best is cold and damp. No wonder he loves Northern Ireland! He actually cannot survive for long in a warm, dry atmosphere.'

'So, if I buy a piece of furniture with a few holes in it and I bring it home, it won't get any worse? In fact the woodworm in it will die?'

'Well, not exactly. They start out as tiny eggs that are laid onto any un-polished wood. They then turn into grubs that burrow into the wood and can munch their way making little tunnels through the soft wood for up to five years!'

'Oh. That's not good.'

'For a piece of furniture, no, but you should see how they can demolish a dead tree – amazing!'

'Is there any sure way of stopping them?'

'They make those holes as they emerge from the wood – that's when they turn into beetles and fly about trying to find a mate and start the whole cycle off again. But, if they emerge into a warm dry house they will die and cause no further trouble.'

Penny sounded quite sad about this. Maddy felt sadder for her imaginary chair that was full of tunnels and about to collapse.

'The answer to that is, yes. You can inject the holes with

woodworm killer fluid and it should seep through eventually. Some people do it with paraffin. . .' Penny broke off at this moment and Maddy wondered if she was reaching for her handkerchief. 'It takes time and...' she said, pausing again. She took a deep breath and sighed, before adding, 'Kills them off for good.'

'So, if a piece of antique furniture is not too badly infested it is worth buying and treating?'

'Yes, if you really have to. But if your house is warm and well ventilated they won't come back.'

When Maddy met Hennessey a few weeks later she tentatively asked him about restoring a piece of furniture with woodworm holes. He was, again, surprisingly erudite on the subject.

'Yes, some people make a really good job of restoring the holes left by the beetle. They ream them out along the grain of the wood and fill them. They are invisible after they are stained and polished although it has to be done by a good polisher or it looks awful. In America they love what they call termite holes in antiques – makes pieces look genuine - I knew a fellow there once who used to blast his reproductions with a twelve bore shot gun. He got too enthusiastic a couple of times and shot the things to pieces!'

In spite of Maddy's new found woodworm knowledge, it didn't seem to make much difference to the attitude of the buyers and she remained diligent in cataloguing, making sure woodworm damage was always mentioned.

If they missed it there was always hell to pay and the buyer had to be refunded every time.

The Restorers' Room, however, was exempt from this – it was definitely a Caveat Emptor place – and serious auction-goers and dealers loved it. Those of a more cautious nature avoided it like the plague.

It was a great place to put broken pieces of furniture, often found in house clearances, things people had never got round to mending. These were most commonly chairs with detached legs and occasional tables that had parted company with their tripod bases. The legs or bases had to be firmly strapped or tied to the 'parent' piece or it was more than likely they would go 'walkies' during viewing, never to return and what was left would sell for nothing. Again, the nicker would get a bargain.

One day a lady booked Maddy and Tom to go to see the contents of the annexe of her house where her father had lived. The place was brimming with antiques he had acquired over the years. He had collected everything from books to bronzes, but mostly furniture. At first glance it seemed like an Aladdin's Cave, but on further inspection every single piece needed some form of restoration. Most of it, though, had been really good – once.

'I have been selling through several auction houses,' the lady said when they arrived, looking down her nose, 'and you are the last. You may take one piece and we will see how you do with it.'

Maddy, yearning to have the chance to take the lot, suddenly wanted to tell her to shove her father's furniture where the 'sun don't shine'. Much of it she could see would benefit from a simple clean and polish and, when restored, would be worth quite a bit. Tom had also taken an instant dislike to the lady and gave Maddy a look that said, *Let's choose something quickly and get out of here.*

Maddy frantically scanned the furniture, some of which was piled up in corners or lying around haphazardly. Others had obviously been before them. It was clear the lady, with a smirky look on her face, had been having fun with the trade. Was she getting some sort of revenge for her father's obsession with old furniture? Had she despaired as, piece by piece, he had filled her annexe with it?

Silly woman, thought Maddy. She would make a fortune if she were to make this a special auction. But she knew there was, as they say in Ireland, no talking to her. So, feeling she was being timed, she ran from room to room before they were told time was up and they had to leave.

Upstairs she found what she had been hoping for, an eighteenth Century cabriole leg armchair. Typically Irish and very desirable at the moment, it had shell and leaf carving and glorious hairy paw feet. And yes, it had shaped flat under-stretchers which did not occur in English chairs! *God bless Hennessey!* Maddy said to herself, not quite believing she'd thought it! The fact that both the Hogarth shaped seat rails, an arm rest and one of its front legs were detached and lying on the floor did not deter her decision. It was all there. She called to Tom for help and, gathering up the pieces, they bundled it into the car and bade goodbye to 'Mrs Charm'.

The chair's patina was deep and glowing under the grime and spoke of years of loving care. Maddy's special cleaner and wax polish had brought it and its parts back to life.

Few people understood the meaning of the word 'patina' and, on obtaining a scruffy antique, couldn't wait to strip it and give it a good dose of French polish that brought it up 'as new'. Like the woodworm thing, Maddy knew no-one would listen and would have loved the chair for herself. She had quite fallen in love with it. She hoped it would do well and end up restored and appreciated again.

It was nearing the end of viewing and Emma, looking worried, came into the saleroom and grabbed Maddy by the arm.

'A leg has gone!'

'Sorry, Emma, what leg?'

'Your chair – in the Restorer's Room – someone must have come with a knife and cut the string the leg was tied on with.'

'Oh no, Emma! Are you sure? Have you had a look around? You know how sometimes people hide a bit in the room and come and retrieve it after they have bought the lot.'

'I know that, but I've looked everywhere, Mrs D!'

Maddy was beside herself. She was sure they had secured all the pieces to the main frame of the chair. They had even used fishing line as well as string. The legs were large. How could someone have sneaked off with one? The place had been really crowded all evening.

She was heartbroken, not only for the chair but, now it was missing a leg, it wouldn't make half as much as they were expecting and that would scupper their chances of getting any more pieces for sale from whence it came. They could have put it in the saleroom and kept a better eye on it, but they knew it would make more if it was sold from the Restorers' Room.

Viewing was over and Emma went to switch the outside lights off. She came bursting through the kitchen door a few minutes later clutching the missing leg.

'Wow! Emma. You found it! Where?'

'You know that aul drop leaf-table with the cupboard in the middle?'

'Yes – the one we put those chipped urns on.'

'Yes, well, it was in the cupboard.'

'Hah!' Maddy said with glee and paused. 'What are we going to do now, Emma?'

'Well, won't we know who did it when we see who buys the table?'

'Yes, Emma, but we can't leave the leg in the table, can we?'

Then they both began to laugh when they realised they were going to have some fun with the perpetrator of this heinous crime.

Sale morning arrived and the leg was now residing in Maddy's kitchen wrapped in a rug. It must have been removed pretty late on at viewing as no-one else had noticed it was missing from the lot.

The chair sold for fifty pounds, which was a good price considering the lack of leg. It was knocked down to buyer number 67 who, Maddy saw from the register, with not a little irony, was a Mr Smith.

The table with the cupboard came up for sale about half an hour later. If this kind of table made a pound or more it was a miracle, so a shocked silence prevailed as it was bid up by two people one of whom, by some strange chance, happened to be a friend of Emma's. The successful bidder was, (surprise, surprise) number 67/ Mr Smith who had to bid the table up to nearly the price of the chair.

Emma waited in the office beside Geoffrey and Pam to see who would come up to pay.

Shortly, a flustered gentleman in a brimmed hat appeared. He was small and wore a belted coat round his rotund form. They didn't think they had seen him before. His small eyes shifted uneasily in their sockets as he approached the desk and Geoffrey. He coughed, took his hat off and began turning it round and round by the brim.

'Excuse me, sir, but I have just bought a table and I don't want it anymore.'

'Was it knocked down to you?' Geoffrey asked in his stern bank manager's voice that stood no nonsense.

'Yes, but I thought I was bidding on something else.'

'Well, I'm sorry sir, but that's your look out – you have a catalogue and you can read, I take it?'

'Oh yes, sir, I can read.'

Number 67/ Smith began to shuffle uncomfortably.

'Well, I can see from the auctioneer's sheets it has been knocked down to number 67, so I am afraid that table is yours. Here is your bill.' Geoffrey handed it over the counter.

'I, er – do you see that chair I bought as well and I was wondering, um, did you have the other leg? It had two last night and it only has the one now.'

Geoffrey, not knowing about the leg, looked enquiringly at Emma and began to wonder why she was hovering in the office.

'Leg?' said Emma, 'what leg?.'

Her eyes were wide with innocence. Number 67/Smith knew when he was beaten, paid and retreated.

From the steps of the office, hidden by the wall of the barn, Emma watched as he, and a dealer rejoicing in the name of Willie O'Hanlon and Hector Livingstone, (Big Heck) had altercations of no small measure in a corner of the yard.

Money eventually changed hands and Mr Smith scuttled away.

No more was said until later when Geoffrey was collecting his coat from the house to go home.

'You see that Livingstone fellow? He came up to pay his bill and kept going on about the leg of a chair. Did I know what had happened to it? How could I know about a leg of a chair when I am up in the office all day – I told him I didn't know what he was going on about. Then that O'Hanlon fellow – the one that jigs about – he came up and asked me the same thing. Kept going on about a leg! I told him all I knew about was money. Chair legs had passed me by.'

When getting ready for the next sale Maddy and Emma had great delight in placing lot number 105 in pride of place in the saleroom on what they called the Long Table, a place where various miscellaneous items went that weren't ornaments but more, items of interest like boxes of old records, old cameras, kitchenalia and such.

The catalogue description read: 'A carved mahogany cabriole leg from an eighteenth century Irish armchair.'

The reserve was extortionate but, with a wry and slightly sheepish grin, Big Heck bought it.

Twenty-One

Up until now pianos had always been delivered by the seller but the day came when a client asked them to collect one. According to him, it was an iron frame, very heavy and upstairs - up three flights of stairs to be precise. Strong as Emma was, it would not be fair to expect her to be involved with an iron frame piano.

On making a few enquiries from professional removal firms Tom discovered they were probably going to charge more than the piano would make at auction.

'What about that piano tuning chap from 'Twang Pianos', Dad?' Harry suggested. 'He's got a little sign just up the road. He might be able to help or advise about collection.'

Tim Jackson and his wife, Wendy, had been to their auctions and Tom knew them by sight. Tim was a piano tuner who restored and sold old pianos but had never bought one from Killybane.

He had explained to Tom at a recent sale that if a piano had only one woodworm hole it was worth nothing. It was impossible to know how far the monsters had tunnelled through the works – the hammers and other parts – rendering it useless as a musical instrument and not worth the time and trouble it would take to restore it.

Tom decided to call with them to see what they advised. Tim's workshop was in an old farm building next to the house they lived in. Keyboards and piano innards were stacked everywhere.

Tools of every kind were hung on the wall and when Tom walked in, Tim was underneath an instrument stripped of its casing, tightening strings.

'With you in a minute,' he said and then shouted, 'Wendy, how's about a cup of coffee for Mr Daniels?'

By the time Tim had extracted himself from the piano, Wendy was handing Tom a steaming cup of frothy coffee. Coffee, as well as pianos, was a passion of Tim's.

He reckoned he'd bought the first espresso machine in Northern Ireland.

'Hah! Of course you'll be charged an arm and a leg for piano collection,' he explained to Tom. 'They have to pay for insurance, not only for what they collect but for any damage that may happen to both property and their employees. It's quite a risky business, collecting pianos.'

'Well, what do you suggest? This one is up three flights of stairs.'

'You'll need a sledge.'

'A what?'

'You are going to have to slide it down the stairs. And for that you will need this,' he said and went to the back of his workshop. He produced a long flat piece of wood with sliders underneath and loops of thick strong rope at either end: a sledge.

'You mean, we get it to the top of the stairs, put it on that thing – that sledge – and slide it down?'

'Yep! That's it.'

'I don't suppose, for remuneration of course, you would come and help us do it? Our son, Harry, will come and help too. That would be five of us.'

'Have you examined the piano? Is it woodworm free? Because if it's not, you can just walk away.'

'I could go to examine it, but I am not sure how or where to look – could you show me?'

'Tell you what: I will come with you – it will have to be an evening – and we will look at it and, if it is a saleable proposition, I'll give you a hand to get it down. Wendy will come too. She'll bring some coffee.'

The building was a badly converted terrace house in Eglantine Avenue and had been empty for some time. After the removal of the piano it would be ready for re-converting into more habitable flats.

'Thank God they have left the carpet on the stairs,' Tim said. 'Makes it much easier for the sliding.'

Carrying the sledge and a four wheeled piano trolley, they climbed up to the third floor – Tim, Wendy, Maddy, Tom, and Harry. The lighting was dim as most of the light bulbs had been removed but Tim had brought his torch and when they found the piano in a topmost room he removed the lid from over the keys and the panels covering the strings and innards. Yes, it was an iron frame Rudi-Iback, a good German make and no woodworm. It was worth taking. He also explained the difference between full iron frame and part iron frame pianos and why wood frame pianos were worth very little today because central heating caused them to go out of tune in weeks. *Although*, thought Maddy, *they won't get woodworm!*

Tim now showed them how to use a piano trolley. He and Wendy, both dab hands at moving pianos, tipped the piano up to a point of balance on one end and placed the trolley underneath in the middle. When lowered onto it the instrument could be pushed and turned with ease.

They got it to the top of the stairs and on a count of three they all lifted it off the trolley and onto the waiting sledge which had a stop at one end so the piano couldn't slide off. Maddy held her breath as they grabbed the rope loop, leaned backwards to take the weight, inched the sledge to the edge of the top stair and allowed it to tip over.

Slowly the piano began to descend and, holding on to the rope for dear life, the five of them crowded on the stairs behind it. They got to the first return of the stairs, a narrow enough space but just wide enough to tip the piano up, place its side on the trolley, manoeuvre it to the top of the next flight of stairs and put it on the sledge again. Two more flights to go.

They began the second flight as easily as the first until the carpet caught on a bit of the sledge and began to loosen itself from the stairs. Tom stepped down, his feet slipped on the now taught carpet and he ended up on his bottom. At the same time Tim did likewise the other side. The piano moved faster and faster and although Maddy, Wendy and Harry held onto the rope with all their might, they had to let go because Tom and Tim were in their way.

The piano hurtled down the last few steps, crashed through a door and eventually came to rest in a bathroom. No one was hurt and neither was the piano but Tim thought it best to 'test' it to see if it was still working.

Sitting on the edge of the bath he proceeded to play a Rachmaninoff concerto with a kind of blues beat. Wendy went out to the car and brought back not only coffee but some buns and in between consuming these, Tim gave a splendid rendition of 'The Sting'.

They were immersed in Tim's playing, totally oblivious of the owner of the building standing in the shattered doorway observing their little party. Tom had forgotten he had said he would come to retrieve the key. Fortunately, Wendy had an extra cup and lots more coffee and the owner decided that there was no harm in making a perilous undertaking fun; he was going to rip out the bathroom and the door to it anyway and could Tom play something from The Beatles!

A week later they knew a lot more about pianos and that wood frame pianos simply weren't worth the required heaving and hauling to get them to the saleroom.

They tried to explain this to a pleasant and charming lady who was begging them to take her ancient upright for their next sale. She didn't care if it only made a pound and she would pay them to take it away. Tom succumbed to her charms so, using their own newly acquired piano trolley and thanking their lucky stars there were no steps or stairs involved, it ended up in their next sale.

The system of bidding with numbers appeared to be popular and was working well. Bidders were much happier holding up the numbers they had bought with their catalogues rather than calling out their names. It also speeded up payments and saved the auctioneer having to remember everyone's name.

The sale got under way and Tom knocked down the piano to a regular customer, part-time farmer and sometimes dealer, Samuel McGrogan, who, standing directly in front of the rostrum, was holding up buying number thirty eight, but as Tom took a note of this he failed to see another card with thirty eight on it at the far end of the room.

This was being held up by none other than the husband of the lady who had given them the piano!

While it was being auctioned he could see it was not making nearly the value he had been expecting and began to bid for it, hoping to raise the price. When he saw the hammer come down and heard the auctioneer announce it had been sold to buyer number thirty eight, he realised with horror he had bought his own piano from himself.

As the auction continued, Francis Maloney sidled up to Samuel and said, 'I think that piano went for nothing. I saw what you paid for it. Would you take a profit?'

A deal was swiftly done and, because Francis hadn't brought his van, Samuel agreed to take the piano back to his house for Francis to collect next day along with pieces he had bought for him at other auctions.

Meanwhile, a lady entered the saleroom all out of puff and said to the man standing next to her, 'I got here too late to bid for the piano. Did you see what it went for? I desperately wanted to buy it for my daughter.'

Not believing his luck, the piano owner, who had been racking his brains to think of an explanation to give his wife as to why he'd bought their piano back, said to the lady, 'Actually, I bought it, and would happily sell it to you - for a tiny profit, of course.'

Sighing with relief, she handed him twice what it had been knocked down for, and then left to make arrangements to pick it up later.

After the sale, Samuel, helped by Francis and James, loaded the piano onto the pig trailer attached to his green Ford Marina and he drove away. Shortly after his departure the lady who had bought the piano from the owner came into the yard with a borrowed trailer and, finding the instrument wasn't there, approached Maddy for an explanation.

All Maddy could ascertain was that, yes, it had gone away on Samuel McGrogan's trailer and yes, James had checked his receipt – all paid for and correct. Tom and Harry now got involved and, convinced of skulduggery of the fish tank kind, decided to hook on the horsebox and give chase to Samuel McGrogan, leaving the confused lady and a bewildered Maddy standing in the yard.

James said Samuel had mentioned he was going home so, knowing roughly where he lived, Tom headed in that direction and, on reaching the main road, put his foot down.

'Cor! It was fantastic, Mum,' Harry said later. 'Dad flew!'

The back of the pig trailer and the piano wending its way soon came in sight. Frantic to stop it, Tom began flashing lights and tooting the horn. If he hadn't been tired and anxious, he would probably have worked out what was going to happen next.

Samuel McGrogan accelerated and took off like a rocket. Tom was still quite far behind and even though his car was newer than Samuel's ancient Marina, the horsebox was a good deal heavier than the pig trailer so they were quite evenly matched.

After a mile or so, without any warning, the Marina turned right onto a by-road and headed for the hills. The chase was becoming serious with the bumpy, winding road taking its toll on the piano as it was hurled this way and that and Tom, swearing, in hot pursuit was oblivious of the wheels of the horsebox being more often off the ground than on it. Harry prayed they wouldn't meet anything coming the other way. A 'T' junction saved the day and Tom managed to pull up alongside the now petrified Samuel McGrogan.

'My God, Mr Daniels, it's you! I thought it was the devil himself after me – my rear view mirror's broke and I didn't dare look round for fear I'd drive into the ditch and wreck Francis's piano.'

'Who's piano?'

'Och, it was going so cheap I bought it, but pianos aren't my style, so I sold it to Francis. I am taking it home for him to collect tomorrow.'

To keep the peace and save Killybane Auctions' reputation, more money changed hands and Tom and Harry returned to the yard with the piano.

It wasn't until the next day, when the paper work had been sorted that it dawned on Maddy and Tom what had happened.

At the following sale, when Samuel McGrogan appeared they watched him carefully as he came through the door and, ignoring the pile of catalogues with a fresh batch of attached bidding numbers, began to search the pockets of his perennial boiler suit.

Sure enough, he eventually produced a crumpled and well used bidding card – number thirty eight...

Twenty-Two

Maddy was anxious about Carol. They had gone together to have a look at Newcastle University and had loved it at first sight. The friendliness of all the people they'd met, the beautiful buildings in the city, the underground railway and the modern campus had all come as a delightful surprise.

In spite of the pending separation from Sean, Carol had seemed enthusiastic and keen to get there. However, shortly after their return, she had become quiet, no smiles, heavy sighs, not her usual bright self. She hadn't been going out much in the evenings and Sean had been noticeable by his absence.

'Everything alright, Carol?' Maddy ventured to ask after supper one evening when they were alone.

'No, Mum, it's not. I …' she burst into tears.

'Okay, tell me.'

'Oh, Mum. Sean's gone.'

'Gone? Gone where?'

'I don't know, Mum. He just disappeared without saying anything to me – or anyone. His shop is locked up and nobody knows where he is. It's rotten of him. How could he just go and not say he was going and not tell me or anything?'

'When? How long has he been gone?'

'Nearly two weeks.'

'Surely, his friends in the trade must know? Maybe he's gone to a sale somewhere – maybe in England or Scotland.'

'No. He would have told me about it. If anyone knows,

they're not telling me. I believe they are as mystified as I am.'

'So, I don't suppose you found out where his parents live – or where he comes from?'

'I knew you'd say that – that's why I didn't tell you in the first place.'

Maddy realised she would have to tread carefully or it would all be her fault. This news had really surprised Maddy. She had been so sure Sean had more to him than most of Carol's previous admirers – especially when she remembered the apple sponge…

'Look, darling, we are living in funny times. I find it hard to believe he would just bunk off like that. He had me fooled too. I thought he was lovely.'

'Oh, Muuuuum.'

The sobs returned, breaking Maddy's heart. She did her best to console her daughter but found it hard to be reassuring. Remembering her own early heartbreaks she knew there was nothing she could say that would help. She began to wonder should she make a few discreet enquiries. They did have a few friends in quite high places – like the police – but being as things were at the moment in Northern Ireland, it probably wasn't a great time to trust anyone. She would discuss it with Tom. He might be able to think of something they could do.

'We'll find out somehow, sweetheart. Now stop worrying. Dry those tears. I am sure there will be a perfectly reasonable explanation and he'll show up when you least expect him to.'

Carol dried her eyes and eventually went dolefully to bed.

'Are you off your trolley?' Tom said to Maddy later. 'If you contact Reggie, or even, Harold, they'll have the 'specials', MI6 and half the army looking for Sean. For goodness sake, Maddy, have a bit of wit!'

'They got rid of the B Specials ages ago.'

'I know – but you know what I mean – hell, I trusted and liked Sean too, we could get him into all sorts of trouble. There's bound to be a logical explanation, unless . . .' he tailed off.

'What?'

'He could have been abducted.'

'You mean kidnapped?'

'Stranger things have happened.'

'Are you suggesting the IRA have abducted a chef? Well, I suppose they need to eat too.'

'Look, we don't know where he is from. He could be anything. Maybe being a chef or an antique dealer is a cover. Let's face it, a good chef could go anywhere in the world and an antique dealer can go anywhere in Ireland at the moment – and they do – look at the tinkers – no number plates or anything.'

'Oh my god, Tom, you aren't saying Sean could be a tinker?'

'I just don't know, Maddy. He's extremely plausible and, let's face it, he could charm the birds off the trees – he could be anything. I think all we can do is wait and see.'

All Maddy could think of was Carol quietly crying herself to sleep and if she could lay her hands on Sean right now she would throttle him.

The following morning a small black car came into the yard with a young couple in it. The girl stayed in the car, the young man stepped out, opened the back door and lifted out three framed pictures.

Maddy could immediately see they were quality paintings, better than any they had been given before and in expensive frames. Again, as with so many things, she knew enough to know they were good but even on close inspection, couldn't decipher any of the signatures of the artists or had the faintest idea how to value them.

'These are really interesting,' she said to the young man who looked hardly old enough to drive, let alone be the possessor of such art.

He merely grunted as Maddy helped him take the paintings into the saleroom. They propped them up against the bar, Maddy took out a collection form and stood with pen poised.

'You will have to give me some idea of the prices you are expecting to get for them.'

He was almost monosyllabic and handed her a piece of cheap lined paper on which the paintings were listed: 'Picture of

Farm House', 'Old picture of a coach and horses', 'Picture of a house near a lake.'

No artists names, dates or provenance. No name, address or telephone number.

'Where did these come from?' asked a curious Maddy.

'An aunt – she died,' the young man replied before turning to go back to his car.

'But, I need an address, a name. Where do we send the cheque?' Maddy began to think this was extremely strange. 'Don't you want to put reserves on the paintings? And you will need a receipt.'

'Nah, just sell away and we'll collect the money – we'd prefer cash. We'll give you a ring before we come up again.'

Before Maddy could reply he had begun to drive off. She ran up as he was turning the car round.

'I must have a name and a telephone number,' she insisted, banging on the driver's window.

The young man lowered the window.

'Paul O'Donaghue, Rathmines 55962,' he said as he put the car into reverse and drove the car out of the yard leaving Maddy standing with her mouth open trying desperately to remember the telephone number.

Maddy and Tom were only beginning to come to grips with the art market and already art collectors and dealers were coming to the auctions in the hope of picking up something that nobody else had spotted. Maddy already knew of one she had let slip through in a box of assorted items. It had been a quirky little painting of cottages with white gable ends on a long strip of wood. She had taken it into the kitchen, propped it up and looked at it for ages thinking it had something but she didn't know what. A scrawled splodge of a signature was in one corner which she didn't recognise and, after deciding it wasn't worth making a lot on its own, put it back in with the rest of the junk the person had given them to sell. The lot sold for fifty pence.

A few weeks later she learned from a very pleased Belfast art dealer, Jackson Conway, who had bought it, that it was a painting by Markey Robinson, a Belfast artist whose early primitive paintings were often dashed off on pieces of scrap wood. Jackson didn't tell Maddy what he was hoping to sell it for but she knew it would be much more than fifty pence. She felt slightly bad for the seller but he was a dealer too who had admitted he was only using their auction to rid himself of rubbish he had been unable to sell on his market stall so she reckoned it was fair play in this case.

She hated her ignorance had been displayed but also knew for sure the art dealer who had found the 'sleeper', as they were called in the trade, would be a regular customer from now on. She also knew, having looked at that painting for some considerable time, she would never let another Markey Robinson escape her again. She also wondered if she should get Jackson's advice about the paintings that had just been delivered and suggested this to Tom.

'Oh, I meant to tell you, did you see that thing that came in the post yesterday?' he said in reply.

'No.'

'I think they must be targeting everyone who receives the Antiques Trade Gazette. It's called "The Art Sales Index". It is expensive but it consists of several volumes which list every painting that has sold at auction almost anywhere in the world over the past year. I think we will have to get it. I don't like the thought of discussing the art we are given to sell with anyone who might be coming to our sales – it might look like collusion – you know what people are like.'

She certainly did. Many people were still of the opinion that auction rooms were the dens of crooks and vagabonds, Killybane included.

'You mean, if we can decipher the name of the artist we can see what his work has sold for and work out what it may be worth?'

'Exactly, and we will also have to start going to exhibitions and gen up at the museum, yet another learning experience in store for us,' he chuckled, wild horses wouldn't have got him to the museum a year ago.

The museum! That was it. Maddy would take the paintings there and have them assessed. She had taken ceramics to the museum when she hadn't been too sure what they were and the head of the Department of Ceramics and Glass had been extremely informative and helpful. She knew it was against the policy of the museum to give valuations, but if they could tell her who the paintings were by and the dates they were painted then she would be able to make further enquiries from any one of the art galleries who advertised in the Antiques Trade Gazette. If Tom obtained this Art Sales Index thingy, they would be home and dry.

However, once again she was running out of time. She couldn't see how she could fit in a trip to the museum before the coming sale. The paintings would have to wait until the next one. She was glad she had, at least, obtained a telephone number for Mr O'Donaghue. At least she could contact him and let him know.

Life had become slightly easier for Maddy now Tom was working for Killybane Auctions full time. He'd even taken on the school runs. There weren't quite so many three o'clock in the morning typing sessions but it was getting busier and Tom was doing all he could to make the business grow.

Taking the advice from Dr Walker (who insisted now they call her Annie) he wrote to every solicitor in the yellow pages phone book explaining how Killybane Auctions worked, their speed of payment and personal input. He had a chat with their bank manager and asked him to put in a word for them with the Executor Department which, he knew, frequently used one of the dingier Belfast salerooms for the disposal of deceased estates. Again, they couldn't understand why. Rumours abounded about the integrity of this particular room, which, if it were possible, was more through-other than the others. Gossip and rumours, they had come to realise, were part of the business and paid them little attention, suspecting all sorts of terrible things were more than likely being said about them.

The number of people coming to the auctions was still increasing and they were beginning to get to know their regulars. Friday night viewing was becoming a social occasion with the newly added benefit of a coffee machine and a basket of biscuits. People could pay an extra fifty pence at the door and help themselves. While Emma was sweetness and light to everyone, she mentally had a little black book. The first person to go in it was the biscuit nicker.

'Mrs Daniels, I saw him, three times and he never paid at the door!' She was consumed with anger. 'See him? If he ever asks me for a favour, of any kind, I'll have his nuts for starters!'

View Day was then added to View Night. So many people had asked could they come to view the auction in their lunch hour or after they had dropped the children off to school that it seemed the right thing to do. Everything now had to be ready a day sooner, which meant the work was beginning to compound itself again.

They also now needed someone to answer the phone when they weren't there. People hated using answering machines and Tom knew theirs was losing them business. Frequently, all three of them had to go on calls to collect things leaving the yard empty which also wasn't good but they were not yet making enough money to pay another person full time.

Maddy and Tom were in the middle of discussing this problem when the phone rang.

'Hello Madelaine'. It was Sylvia Pentland, someone she didn't know very well but Tom knew her husband who had been a business associate and with whom he had massacred unsuspecting pheasants at the same shoot for many years. 'I hope you don't mind my ringing you out of the blue like this, but could you use some part-time help? A friend of mine was widowed recently and would love to get involved with something.'

'Are you clairvoyant, Sylvia?' asked Maddy and continued, 'Tom and I were just saying that we needed someone but couldn't afford full time help. Would she be happy to answer the phone and deal with people delivering stuff – things like that?'

'Oh absolutely, Maddy. She is a very capable person – I wouldn't be ringing you if I didn't think she could.'

'Do you think she would mind a sort of 'as and when we needed her' job?'

'I think that would be just what she would love.'

'Brilliant, Sylvia. Tell her she can start on Monday.'

'Now you are interviewing by proxy, Mads,' Tom said on over-hearing. 'Your technique is improving…'

And that's how Pam Bigland came into their lives. Tall and slender, with slate grey hair piled on top of her head she walked with the grace of a ballet dancer. Maddy felt calm in her presence and knew instinctively this woman was a coper. She had a gentle, infectious laugh of the kind that could dilute tension if there was any and as soon as Maddy heard her answer the phone with her reassuring, modulated, distinctive voice, she could tell at once Pam was going to be just what they needed.

Twenty-Three

Returning home from the school run Tom found he was humming as he bounced gently on the sprung seat in the cab of Killybane Auctions' first proper van. Not since his days driving three tonners in the Territorial Army had he so enjoyed himself.

The younger kids from next door had enjoyed it too. James and Harry had tucked them up on the cushions and blankets used for packing around furniture and they had chirped like happy chicks in their nest all the way to school. It was probably highly illegal but Tom didn't think a treat would hurt for once in a while.

The sun shone and from the high cab he could see over hedges filled now with fragrant clumps of wild honeysuckle and roses, surrounding fields that were beginning to sprout with lush new grass, early potatoes and barley, rolling all the way to the mountains in the distance. He no longer thought wistfully of his long gone Porsche, from which he had never even tried to see over a hedge, and decided he hadn't been so happy for years. He was answerable to no one else – except Maddy and Emma, of course (and that could be tricky enough sometimes) and he was getting the hang of being an auctioneer. He'd even cracked the professional incremental raising of the bidding. This had taken several nights of practice with Maddy, James and Fizz standing in as bidders but he'd finally got the hang of it and the business was beginning to make some money at last. Not a lot but enough to afford this, albeit second hand, gorgeous big truck with 'Killybane Auctions' painted on the side and his name underneath. At that moment Tom was unable think of anything more he could want.

He knew too that auctioneering was his 'thing'. He'd had no interest in antiques at all until he had to sell them. Now he was gaining knowledge about them at the same rate he had gained knowledge about textiles. When he had something to sell he made himself learn about it as if his life depended on it which, of course, now he thought about it, it did. Maddy had been brought up with them, he hadn't. Thus he had a different view-point. He was not 'in love' with them, she was. He was dispassionate and could see things she was unable to. Fine, she might be able to date a piece with more accuracy but he could see the construction, the style and, what was more important, the people who wanted to sell them, with a finer 'eye'.

He knew though that he and Maddy made a pretty indomitable team.

He also reckoned they owed a huge debt of gratitude to the reporter, Maeve Furley, who wrote the 'Round the Auction Rooms' article every week.

When she rang to say she was coming to interview them for an article they went into a frantic spin to get the saleroom looking good. Minutes before she arrived they were desperately moving furniture, lighting the fire (praying it wouldn't belch smoke which it periodically did) and trying to find a comfortable chair to put beside it for her to sit in. Emma had made some of her tray bakes and she and Pam were poised to bring them in with tea.

Maeve arrived minutes after he and Maddy had changed into decent clothes, hoping they would give the impression that this was the way they always looked and, gosh, wasn't it all jolly fun! Whether Maeve guessed they had put on a show especially for her, she never said but she wrote a glowing, full page article which told the tale of how and why Killybane Auctions had started and how quickly it had become established. There was a photograph of them in the middle of the article holding a vase with the saleroom in the background that sent Maddy into peals of laughter.

'We both look so well dressed and serious! We are going to get our legs pulled by everyone who knows us!'

167

It turned out to be quite the contrary. A few days after the article appeared, the phone began to ring non-stop, with people wanting to sell and others to buy. The power of the Press, thought Tom. It was the shot in the arm they had so badly needed. He was more than thankful too they had taken on Pam who could now hold the fort while he, Maddy and Emma went on furniture collections that were beginning to take them all over the country.

The one thing they still dreamed of was being asked to do a house sale. They read about these each week in The Antiques Trade Gazette and the prices always seemed to be phenomenal compared with regular sales. They happened all the time in England but in Northern Ireland they were rare. Not so many grand houses, not so many people. Still, they occurred from time to time and he and Maddy kept hoping.

The only blot on the landscape was the disappearance of Sean. It was nearing time for Carol to go to University and Tom hated the thought of her going away from home in her sad state without resolving the mystery. He too missed Sean, not only for the frequent help he gave lifting furniture and generous sharing of his knowledge of antiques and paintings but they got on well, the fellow was good 'craic'.

Twenty-Four

The night was pitch black and light from the saleroom windows poured bright trapezoid patterns onto the dark yard. There was another hour and a half of viewing to go and Maddy was walking from the saleroom to the house to get Tom a badly needed coffee in a mug, not a paper cup.

As the evening wore on, after a day of being nice to people and with the auction looming next morning, his demeanour was languishing and she knew he would not be talkable to until tomorrow night when the auction was over.

Smiling to herself, she realised she was becoming accustomed to this part of the proceedings. She reached the back door when an unfamiliar sound emanated from the shadows.

'Psst! Psst!'

Maddy stopped and a figure moved slightly into the light. There were so many people only a few yards away, she was more surprised than frightened and, anyway, she knew at once who the person was.

'Sean! What the hell are you doing? And where on earth have you been and what...'

He grabbed her by her shoulders and steered her towards the back door. He was 'disguised' in a low brimmed hat, dark glasses, a thick muffler and – yes (she almost laughed when she saw it) – a trench coat.

'Please, Maddy, don't yell or anything – I'll explain everything – PLEASE don't yell.'

'Of course I won't yell!' she yelled. 'You have a LOT of explaining to do! Why did you ...'

Again he cut her short. 'Can we go inside? I really don't want to be seen here – is Carol in?'

'No, she has gone to the cinema with some friends.'

'Good. Okay – innnn.'

He propelled her through the door and into the kitchen. Fizz leapt out of her chair and flung herself upon him, piddling in ecstasy. He bent down briefly to fondle her ears but he didn't take his eyes off Maddy.

'Look, Maddy, I don't have much time. Where are the paintings that should have been in this sale?'

'What paintings, Sean? I don't know what you are talking about. There are lots of paintings in the sale.'

Sean, agitated, took a deep breath. 'The ones that were delivered last Tuesday by a young couple, a painting of a farmhouse, a .....'

It was Maddy's turn to interrupt.

'Oh those – what on earth have they got to do with you? And what have you done to our daughter – she is heartbroken and I know if Tom came in right now he would kill you.'

'God! Maddy – I am broken hearted too, but I couldn't tell her and I wouldn't be telling you if you had just put those pictures in the sale. This whole thing has to be kept as quiet as possible. Anyway,' he looked almost embarrassed, 'I am sworn to secrecy.'

'Oh Sean, you aren't involved in, in...' She couldn't bring herself to say, 'The IRA', but he knew what she meant.

'In a way, I am.'

'No, NO! I don't believe it. You can't be. Carol would have more sense than to fall for a, a ...'

'I'm in the CID.'

'The what?'

'I am in the police – Criminal Investigation Department – drugs, money laundering, and the passing of stolen goods.'

'They could have taught you more about disguise – I recognised you immediately.'

'Well, I might be able to get you a job there! But, please,

Maddy, please, what about those paintings?'

'How do I know you are telling me the truth?' She turned to put the kettle on and prepare Tom's coffee. Sean's patience was wearing thin.

'Och Maddy, I know that you know I am. But here -' He reached inside his coat, pulled out his I.D. and showed it to her.

Maddy barely glanced at it.

'That could be a forgery – and I haven't a clue what those things should look like anyway.' Then she couldn't resist taking a closer look. 'Crikey, that's an awful photograph; it doesn't do you any favours. You look like one of the Kray brothers – why did you not...'

'Look, Maddy, I am being picked up in five minutes will you PLEASE LISTEN!'

'Funny, that's what Tom is always saying to me.'

'Those paintings – where are they?'

'In the sitting room – I haven't had time yet to take them to the museum.'

'The WHERE?'

As they left the kitchen and walked into the hall towards the sitting room, Maddy explained to Sean that she had made an appointment to take them to the museum next Tuesday where a Mr. Pringle was going to have a look at them and tell her what they were.

'Oh God, Maddy, PLEASE don't do that!'

'Why not? I know they are good – I sat and looked at that one of the farmhouse for ages and I just know it is a fantastic painting. I have got to find out about it before we sell it.'

Sean raised his eyes. 'The Van Velsen,' he sighed deeply.

'The WHAT?'

'Velsen'

Maddy's mouth opened and shut and opened again. 'A Willem Van Velsen?' She stared at the painting which was propped up against the sofa. 'Sean, if that's a Velsen it's worth thousands and thousands....' She put her hands up to her face cupping it as if, almost, to keep her head on her shoulders. Her eyes closed in disbelief. 'I don't understand any of this!'

'It's horribly simple, Maddy. Now,' he said, putting a hand up defensively, 'without being rude or detrimental in any way about your business, you have to admit that, at the moment, it can only be described as a 'wee country auction house' – okay?'

'Okay,' grudgingly came from Maddy.

'Now, if stolen goods come into say, Cork, from the Channel Islands ...'

'The Channel Islands? Cork?'

'Yes, please let me finish.' Maddy kept quiet. 'When one and all here are concerned with nothing but guns and explosives, who is going to look at a few old paintings as they move gradually north and end up in an auction house that is hardly yet on the map?'

'Oh my God, are you saying we are being used to pass on stolen goods?'

'In a nutshell, yes.'

Maddy's narrowed eyes glared at Sean. Anger boiled over.

'You - YOU! You have planned all this. You have wormed your way into our family and you have broken our daughter's heart. You are going to ruin our reputation before it has even got going! To hell with Tom, *I* am going to kill you!'

She looked round for something to throw at him but the sound of the back door opening made them both freeze.

'Hi Mum!' Carol called and Sean became frantic.

'Maddy, she mustn't know I am here.' He looked round the room, dashed to one of the windows, threw it open and began to clamber out. Over his shoulder he whispered to Maddy. 'Those paintings have to be in the next sale. I have to know who buys them. It will all be discreet – no reflection on Killybane – I promise and I will explain everything to Carol and you guys as soon as I can.' Seconds before Carol came into the sitting room, he had disappeared into the blackness.

'Mum! What are you doing? Why have you got the window open?'

'Just letting Spike out. He was yowling his head off.'

'Oh. I thought I heard you talking to someone.'

'I was talking to Spike.'

'Do you know, Mum, I had this irrational, silly feeling it

might have been Sean. I suppose that was daft.'

Maddy had never felt so duplicitous in her life and could say nothing. She was still in shock and knew if she said anything it could maybe raise false hopes and make things worse.

'I am making your dad a cup of coffee – would you like one?'

'No thanks, Mum. Think I'll just go to bed.'

As Maddy slammed the window shut she wanted to cry, scream and kick something all at the same time.

She brought Tom his coffee but instead of staying and talking to viewers, couldn't resist going back into the house to have another look at the painting of the farmhouse. She knew a little bit about the Fauve painters and although not as well known as Derain, Cezanne, Matisse, or Dufy, Willem Van Velsen had been very much part of their group sharing a preference for brilliant colours and simplified forms. Their work had shocked the critics at first, hence their nickname meaning 'Wild Beasts'. They had excited her at school where she had been taught by Miss Spooner, an imaginative, scatty and fun art teacher who had trained at The Slade.

In those days there were few books with coloured illustrations so Miss Spooner would demonstrate to the class, sloshing colour about as if it had just been invented.

Later, at a visit to the National Gallery with her mother, they had been bowled over by an exhibition dedicated to the Fauvist movement. It made Maddy realise how little she knew and now, thinking about the Velsen in her sitting room, her craving for more knowledge about painting and art in general began to gnaw away at her like a dog trying to reach marrow in a bone.

The Velsen was still there, leaning against the sofa. Maddy curled up on the floor with her back against an arm chair and gazed at it, willing herself to look at it in an analytical way. It appeared to have been swiftly painted with long dramatic brush strokes thick with paint. She even wondered had some of the paint been squeezed straight from the tube, the colours were so vibrant and pure. The windows of the farmhouse were mere daubs and their reflections in the pond in front of the house were not strictly where they should have been. The fields around were brilliant oranges, yellows and ochres; the sky angry with dark, grey, stormy clouds. A scene Maddy had seen many times on her walks with Fizz when a rain cloud covered half the sky and the sun shone on everything in front of it making trees and hills glow as if lit from within. Her photographs could never capture those moments. This painting did. It was like a light in the room, enrapturing Maddy with its luminescence. But she could not envisage many of the people who came to their auctions at the moment being drawn to it. Most of the art collectors and dealers were interested in Irish Art of a more conventional, representational kind. Colour, she knew, was approached with great caution in Northern Ireland, remembering her mother telling her the problem she had had when she first came to live there getting a decorator to paint a wall red. 'All they want to put on their walls is magnolia!' she had railed. 'And when it comes to the outside – every bloody house in the country is painted cream and green!'

The other two paintings were good, too, watercolours but probably much older. One was of a horse drawn shiny black carriage with a crest on the side door and the other a two story cottage with roses round the door overlooking a river. Maddy had yet to decipher the signatures of these. The Velsen's was a large V with a squiggly line. Only an expert would know what it was.

She wanted to sit in front of it all night. *Blooming heck a Velsen!* she thought to herself. *I know, God, I have asked you to send us better stuff but sending us this seems slightly- and literally, come to think of it - off the wall.*

She also reluctantly remembered a brief promise to Jonathan to refer anything 'London-worthy' to Westbury's. She hoped to goodness he wasn't going to come to the next auction and if he did, his knowledge didn't run to Velsens.

Twenty-Five

Conscious of Tom entering his usual, pre-auction screwed-up-ness that was probably akin to stage fright, Maddy knew it would be unwise to tell him about Sean's visit and the paintings until the sale was over. There was no time to do anything about it anyway, so she kept it to herself. She too was suffering from pre-auction nerves and along with worrying about stolen goods and smugglers, she felt like an over tightened guitar string about to break.

At breakfast next morning she saw James shaking an empty Cherios packet over an empty bowl.

'Mum, we've run out of Cheerios – again,' he wailed.

'Well, what's to stop you getting on your bike, going up to the petrol station and getting SOME MORE?' she shouted from the sink, becoming horribly aware she was about to throw a mug she was rinsing at him.

James could see 'signs' and quickly said, 'Weetabix will be fine, Mum.'

Maddy knew he hated it and realised she was dangerously near exploding point. The children teased her constantly about her keenness for everybody to have a healthy breakfast – especially Weetabix which was sugarless and, as far as they were concerned, tasteless and, when milk was poured over it, had the texture of sodden cardboard.

'I have another box of Cheerios in the pantry, silly,' she said, coming down three notches from lift off and went to find it.

'Sorry, Mum. I should have looked,' said James, sensing he had narrowly missed a major incident. 'Um, anything wrong, Mum?'

'Oh, just pre-auction nerves, darling. Sorry. I didn't mean to snap. Before an auction I know something is going to go wrong and I never seem to be able to stop it or cope with it when it does. I was wondering what it was going to be this time,' she sighed because that was, in fact, the truth.

'Doesn't matter, Mum. It's always alright in the end. You and Dad will sort it out, whatever it is, and by the time next auction comes along you will have forgotten all about it.'

Oh Jesus Christ and Holy Mary, I hope so, Maddy prayed, and would have offered up pleas to as many other deities as she could think of if Tom hadn't come in for breakfast. Emma also arrived to gather up the auction lists and the registration book.

After the incident of the piano being sold four times in one auction because a bidder had used an old number, it had been decided they should keep a register of bidders for each sale. When someone acquired a bidding number either with or without a catalogue they were asked to give their name and telephone number. Surprisingly, there were no objections and some people even asked if they could have the same number for every sale. Emma kept a list and the 'reserved' catalogues increased with each sale. This was something they found deeply satisfying; an affirmation that they were getting some things right at last.

With this system it was not necessary for anyone to buy a catalogue if they didn't want one so long as Killybane had a name and telephone number for each bidding number. There was also the added advantage of being able to contact buyers if they left anything behind after an auction, as happened frequently. All Maddy or Emma had to do was track the lot number on the auction sheets, find out the buying number and the register would tell them the phone number of the bidder. Provided, of course, the bidder had given the correct number...

Venturing out into the gathering auction crowd on this particular morning was more than usually fraught with anxieties and foreboding for Maddy. Everyone she looked at was a baddie. They were all smugglers, crooks and bandits. The memory of Hennessey Bergman and his cryptic remark about 'corrupting' Killybane 'like all the other auction rooms' kept popping into her mind. He hadn't been around recently and she had been hoping this was a good sign. She even kept looking at dark corners for a badly disguised Sean. When, even the gentle twin sisters, Anne and Penelope Winters who, clad in hats and gloves, came to Killybane to buy boxes of 'assorted items' to sell for charity, became suspect criminals, she realised she had to get things in perspective.

These two quiet, well spoken ladies, who had been coming to the auctions for some time, hadn't at first seemed like auction-goers at all. They eventually explained to Maddy that Anne's son and his girlfriend had gone to Rio for a holiday and had been so shocked by the number of homeless children living on the streets they made the decision to stay there and see what they could do to help.

After a few months they had acquired a number of dwellings with a 'parent' placed in each where the children could be taken care of.

Anne and Penelope were raising money for them in a number of ways one of which was buying boxes of bric a brac, books and kitchenware from Killybane. The contents of these they would then sell from empty shops landlords were persuaded to give them the use of, free of charge, for a day or two at a time. They poured their lives and souls into the enterprise and Maddy felt ashamed of her misguided thoughts.

She took a deep breath, told herself to lighten up and managed to greet everyone with her usual cheerful friendliness. So many people were now coming on a regular basis, including the antique dealers who had begun to come in force. They were not hard to spot as they mostly arrived in Volvo Estate cars with roof racks.

Big Heck seemed to be the main man towering above them all, usually wearing a voluminous black jacket or coat that made him look even bigger. He had a full time job with an electricity company but seemed to be able to work for it and go to every auction in Ireland at the same time.

There was Willie O'Hanlon who chewed anti-smoking gum and spat it out onto Maddy's clean, swept yard with monotonous regularity. He was charm itself to Maddy but she wouldn't have trusted him as far as she could throw him. He was never still, shuffling from foot to foot, even when standing waiting to bid or drinking a coffee. He had an antique shop somewhere in the wilds of Fermanagh but drove a brand new Mercedes van so she reckoned he must be running a successful business of some kind or other.

Toddy Brandon considered himself a cut above the others thinking he was classy and debonair in a tweed sports jacket two sizes too small for him and a cap inherited from his father. He had a shop in Helen's Bay with a fine selection of antique furniture, paintings and porcelain which was doing very well, according to Big Heck.

Then there was 'Wee Dan' Dougan. He was tall, taller even than Big Heck but skinny as a rake. He had a long, solemn face and a shock of red hair. He had beautiful hands and Maddy wasn't surprised when Big Heck told her he was a well known fiddle player. He made his living supplying antiques to shops and travelled round Ireland with his fiddle and a load of antiques in his ancient van. He was kind and gentle and Maddy liked him a lot.

Sammy Redmond, it was obvious, came at the bottom of the pecking order as he was always running errands and lifting things for the others. He was a jovial young man but gave the impression of being slightly out of his depth, never too sure if he had said or was saying the right thing.

These were the dealers who came to every auction but others joined them from time to time depending on what was of interest in the sale and they constituted the 'ring'.

Maddy and Tom had become aware of this auction phenomenon a while ago but had never seen it in action. Maddy was searching for a client's list one day, immediately after a sale, when she glanced out of the kitchen window overlooking the garden at the back of the saleroom. For the first time she witnessed Big Heck, Willie and the others gathered in a circle (a ring no less) where they thought they could not be seen. Each was clutching a catalogue and a pen. She couldn't hear what they were saying but their expressions and gestures made it pretty clear what each one was thinking about the proceedings.

Big Heck, clad in his voluminous anorak was conducting his own post sale auction like some kind of demon king from a pantomime.

When two or more antique dealers come to a sale they usually agree that only one of them will bid for items they both want. What would be the point of bidding against each other? It would make the prices too high for them to be able to sell the items on at a profit. So, before the sale, they get together and agree who will bid for what. After the sale they have their own auction, money changes hands, the spoils are divided and they go home happy – mostly. This is known in the trade as 'ringing'. However, when there are more than two dealers it becomes complicated. Tempers can get frayed or lost, as Maddy was witnessing. This practice is also illegal but nobody seems to worry about that.

Wee Dan didn't have the aggressive stance of the others and would occasionally acquiesce with an almost imperceptible rise and fall of his hand. Willie, spitting his anti smoking gum onto Tom's neatly trimmed lawn, was hopping from foot to foot and shaking his head violently whenever Big Heck pointed his pen at him. Toddy Brandon kept looking nervously over his shoulder as if the law was about to come round the corner and pounce. Sammy Redmond looked worried and confused.

They never quite came to blows but it was patently clear it was serious. At that moment Maddy hated them with a fury as pure as a woman's fury could be. How dare they do this? These creatures had manipulated the sale to their advantage. She was planning her revenge when she heard a chuckle and turned to see Tom standing behind her also taking in the scene.

'Oh Tom,' she sighed, 'just when people have begun to trust us and we are getting really good stuff.'

'Don't worry, Mads. It is okay. I have their measure now.'

'How do you mean? How can you do a thing about it?' Tom grinned and tapped the side of his nose to indicate a big secret.

'I can tell, when they are bidding, how much further they are prepared to go before reaching their limit and I can push them pretty far even though other people in the room have stopped bidding.'

'How do you mean, you can tell?'

'I just have to watch their body language. Have you never noticed how Big Heck's neck begins to go red when he's bidding? When the redness reaches his ears I know he's only got a few more bids to go. Willie begins to twitch when it's his turn. His shoulder goes a mile a minute and as soon as that starts I know I can't push him much further.'

'Hang on a minute, Tom. Are you telling me you bid them up – on your own?'

'Yes.' Tom was still grinning. 'It hasn't failed so far. What else can I do? They would be getting everything for far too little and it wouldn't be fair to the people who put the stuff in.'

'What does Toddy Brandon do?'

'He starts pulling at his ear. As soon as he does that I know I have two bids left, maybe three, depending of course on what the increment is. Sometimes it's only one.'

Maddy's anger subsided and she began to laugh. Her admiration for Tom went up several points, especially when she observed the escalating aggravation on the lawn. The Ring was not having a good day – prices had been high.

'But, y'know, Mads,' Tom added, 'I have to be careful. I can't take them too far. We need those guys. Let's face it, they buy a lot of things the privates would never go for – that awful moth-eaten stuffed badger, for instance, or that massive, hideous, Art Deco wardrobe. They buy for retailers all over the country who have specialities that only they know about. It's how they make their living. But I now know they need us as much as we need them – but if Willie O'Hanlon spits chewing gum on my lawn one more time I will go and get my twelve bore and shoot him.'

On another level there were the posh shop owners. Those who took part in antique fairs gave public valuations, talks to the Women's Institute and were in with the right people. Like luvvies in the acting world, they were always telling stories of who had bought what from them, what grand houses they had been to, what they had

180

bought and how it was 'sold already'. They viewed the auctions but never had time to come to them. The truth was that they knew if they were seen to bid, every other dealer would bid for whatever it was and the price would shoot up. This was because it would be assumed the item they were bidding for was something precious no one else had noticed (there was never any doubt they knew their stuff) or it would be done sometimes out of sheer competitive badness.

The women in this division were usually tall, elegant and imperious. They had their followers, clientele who hung on their every word. Decor was decreed by them. They became everybody's mother and when they placed a piece of furniture, a painting or a vase in a home and declared it to be just right it was a serendipitous moment.

Then there were the privates, people who were not dealers but keen enough to come to auctions to buy furniture or collectables because they knew they would never pay what they would have to in a shop. They also loved the excitement and the buzz of an auction and, once they learned that the majority of dealers were not quite the ogres they had come to believe they were, began to relax and enjoy the day. There was one exception and he was approaching Maddy now as she walked over to the saleroom.

Mr McCurdle was making a determined bee line for her. His life's mission, Maddy was convinced, was to cause trouble or a row wherever or whenever he could.

He approached her clutching a large serving spoon that was quivering, echoing his entire, diminutive, badly be-stripe-suited body, with rage. Even his black hair was bristling, making him look like an irate lavatory brush.

'You said in your catalogue this was silver,' he snarled when he was up close, and he added, 'but when I got it home after the last auction, I discovered it was silver plate!'

He spat this through clenched teeth and Maddy could tell he was on the verge of one of his temper tantrums. She was determined to calm him down.

'I am so sorry, Mr McCurdle. It came in at the last minute and I didn't have time to check it. I'm afraid I wrote down what the seller told me.' She smiled as sweetly as she could and continued, 'I'll know not to do that again.'

'Well, I want my money back!'

'Of course, Mr McCurdle. You can go up to the office and tell Mr Daniels senior that I said it was okay and he will give it to you. Do you have your receipt?'

'It's downright DISHONESTY!' he shouted, totally ignoring Maddy's request for the receipt. 'You auctioneers, you just try to fool people into thinking something is what it ISN'T!'

'It was a mistake, Mr McCurdle. I am sorry.'

An audience was now gathering.

'DOWNRIGHT DISHONESTY!' Mr McCurdle shrieked, playing to the crowd waving the spoon aloft like a Damocleian sword.

Maddy's string broke.

'Tell me, Mr McCurdle,' she said as loudly as she could above his ranting and resisting the urge to grab him by his scruff, 'if we had described that spoon as "silver plate" and you had taken it home and discovered it was actually solid silver, would you have brought it back and complained?'

The crowd began to laugh, which was something Mr McCurdle frequently invited but hated. He whirled round and, muttering to himself, stumped up the steps to the office. Maddy knew from the glance of abject hatred he threw her before he opened the door that this was a pyrrhic victory for her and wished she'd had time to read the latest book she'd ordered entitled 'How to Cope with Difficult People'.

None of the other auction rooms provided catalogues for their regular sales and sometimes Maddy and Tom wondered if all the extra trouble was worth it. Complaints on view days were numerous.

'That chair over there has woodworm and you didn't say "damaged" in the catalogue.'

'There are only three ornaments in that lot and the catalogue says there are four.'

'The catalogue says that table is Victorian and it's no more Victorian than I am.'

Try as they would, fault was always found somewhere. Then someone suggested estimated prices should be put beside the descriptions. Maddy's heart sank to its lowest level and she could see herself typing in her sleep. Tom, however, thought it was a good idea that could save him considerable time on view days. Sometimes his patience wore extremely thin when lengthy queues of people formed waiting to ask him what prices he thought lots were going to go for. So estimates were now included in the catalogue and they did, indeed, make view days a lot easier – for Tom.

He also had the idea of attaching bidding cards to the buying numbers for people wanting to leave bids. These he could enter on his auction sheets in his own time rather than have the person dictate them to him.

Paddy and Cait Fitzgerald were, without doubt, Maddy's favourite dealers. Husband and wife with a family of seven, they ran a second hand furniture store in Dublin and lived more or less over the shop. Paddy also had a furniture removal business and they arrived at each auction in their huge van. Cait stepped down from it as gracefully as if it were a winged chariot landing her in the yard. She dressed smartly and yet was able to help Paddy lift and load anything they might have bought that day without dislodging a hair of her beautifully coiffed head or going over on her high heeled shoes.

She could also talk for Ireland, even when bidding, paying her bill or drinking coffee. She always had a tale to tell either about one of her children in dire trouble of one kind or another or the outrageous behaviour of her arch enemy and shop-owning competitor, Dymphna, who also sometimes came to the auctions. They had once been great friends but now would stand as far away from each other as possible while trying not to let either see what they were bidding for. Invariably, they would want the same thing and much subterfuge, huffing and umbrage took place.

'Did I tell you about Aiden's penis?' Cait shouted at Maddy one auction morning across a yard full of people. Maddy indicated that she had not been apprised of this information so Cait continued, 'Yes, he was climbing over a fence and got a bit of a scratch from some barbed wire while we were away in Majorca which was fantastic. We got it cheap from the travel agent, a real bargain and one of the best hotels. The food wasn't bad, but there was a great supermarket nearby and Paddy could buy his beer and they had great fruit, but Aiden didn't want to tell anyone about his little accident until we came home. By that time his poor penis was infected and he had to get circumcised.'

Maddy was deprived of further details as the auction had begun and Cait ran off to bid for an early lot.

Cait never failed to enliven each auction with similar anecdotes, somehow putting the world in perspective and invariably relieving any tension Maddy might be suffering from. She could do with a bit of Cait's craic right now, but the big van had not yet appeared.

Then, to her further dismay, she spied Hennessey Bergman strutting into the saleroom. A small, dark haired man accompanied him in a navy blue coat with big shoulders hunched round his ears that made him look a bit like a tortoise, as if he might slither down into it and hide at any moment. With hands in his pockets, his eyes slid from side to side as he walked.

Hennessey dismissed the proffered catalogue at the door and strode about looking at the furniture in his usual sneery way. Maddy wondered could he be involved in the picture thing but she kind of knew furniture was his speciality and today she could see he didn't give the pictures a glance. Having told her he never attended auctions she wondered what he was doing there.

The other dealers looked nervous as he approached them where they were gathered in their usual huddle at the end of the Saleroom near the coffee bar. All seemed to be well as they chatted and the auction began.

There were one or two pieces of quality antique furniture in the sale and the dealers had made it clear they were interested in them. A mild gentleman, a private, began to bid for one of them. Hennessey at once moved to stand near him and bid so aggressively he almost knocked over the man who immediately ceased bidding and backed away. Having disposed of this bidder, Hennessey began to stride up the room shouting his bids louder and louder as

184

he approached the rostrum with his creepy crony slinking behind him. The other dealers remained huddled and silent. Maddy noticed Tom's hand begin to shake but he glared fixedly at Hennessey who was quelling every bidder in his advance up the room. Was this what he meant by 'corrupting' the sale?

He hadn't taken into account Edwina Turkington who had been a sister in the army nursing corps and was afraid of no one. She appeared from nowhere and, thrusting a catalogue in front of Hennessey, almost slapping him in the face, bid against him.

On seeing this, Tom Wilson (who normally came to buy golfing memorabilia) took courage and bid as well. Before long all the privates, the regulars and the so called after-tea dealers - Annie Walker, Jake Wright, With a bit of Luck, and even the Rat Catcher were one and all bidding like crazy and Hennessey, having probably bid way beyond his intended limit for the interesting, but not outstanding, chair, opened and shut his mouth a couple of times and retreated.

Tom finally knocked down the chair to number 45, but it was attached to a catalogue in a sea of catalogues and he couldn't see the bidder.

There were triumphant grins all round and Maddy tried hard not to cry with relief and gratitude. Clearly, Mr Bergman was not going to control their auction room, nor was he going to corrupt it.

She could see Tom had a following. She didn't dare to describe it to herself as 'loyal' but it certainly wasn't going to allow him to be bullied and what was more encouraging, she could see the other dealers smirking at each other with something like satisfaction at the failure of Hennessey's attempt to rule Killybane's roost.

Contrary to his aggressive, bombastic bluster, Hennessey took the whole affair in his stride, gave the auctioneer a bon homie wave and departed in his car, but not before drowning out Tom's announcement of the next lot with ear-splitting decibels of Wagner.

Twenty-Six

That night, Maddy bided her time and waited until they'd had a meal and everyone had gone home before telling Tom about the paintings and Sean's visit. He was always exhausted after a sale and it had not been easy.

As expected, his euphoria at the defeat of the dreaded Bergman was rapidly replaced by indignation and anger. He was furious and wanted to contact the police immediately to get rid of the blasted things and not get involved. The risk of losing their steadily growing reputation was enormous. If it ever got out they had received stolen goods let alone sold them, they may as well say goodbye to Killybane Auctions for ever. He was adamant he was having nothing whatsoever to do with any of it and, clutching his glass and a bottle of wine, marched out to sit in the garage. In the absence of a shed it was the next best thing.

Yet Maddy had seen the desperation on Sean's face. This was obviously a vital part of something he had been investigating for a long time but she knew Tom also had a valid point. She was frantically trying to think of someone they could go to for advice when Sean appeared again. Dressed as himself this time and with an ecstatic Carol on his arm they came into the kitchen.

'Mum, Sean has told me everything. I just knew there would be a rational explanation.' She gazed up at him with adoration.

Maddy couldn't share her joy, tried, and failed not to show it and was dreading Tom's reaction when he came in to see Sean there. Sean was looking more than worried as he could guess how angry Tom was going to be.

'I had to get permission to explain it all to you,' Sean said. 'I am really sorry things happened the way they did but it was out of my control and all I could do was go along with what was happening. I did not deliberately involve Killybane Auctions, in fact I tried very hard to avoid them sending anything to you, but if I had they would have become suspicious and I would have lost my contacts.'

'Look, Sean, save your explanations for when Tom comes in – I'll go and tell him you're here and then you can begin at the beginning and we can all be put in the picture together. Oh dear, I didn't mean that, what a dreadful pun.'

At least it gave them something to laugh at, which they were doing when Tom came through the door, stopping abruptly when he saw Sean.

'Oh, it's you,' he said. 'I heard someone come into the yard. And what have you got to say for yourself?'

'Dad, don't be cross,' Carol pleaded. 'Sean couldn't help it – it's his job and he...'

Tom cut her short, saying, 'Carol, I am sure Sean can speak for himself.'

'I will begin by saying how very sorry I am, Tom,' Sean said, 'for the fact that you have been involved but please believe me, if I hadn't become friends with you, things would have been a lot worse. You would have taken those pictures in and sold them in good faith, then the police would have swooped in a big drama, with the press probably on their heels, and you would have been in serious trouble.

"Now they know you are totally innocent of any connection with the people who are running this "activity" for want of a better word, you will NOT be implicated in any way. All we want you to do is what you would have done anyway – just go ahead and sell the paintings and we will do the rest.'

'Are we allowed to know exactly what is going on and why?' Tom said.

'It's a long story,' Sean began. 'Do you remember a big

robbery some years ago in county Liesford, Lord Lamphreigh's collection of antiques, paintings and silver?'

'Yes, I think I do.'

'Well, hardly any of the stolen paintings have turned up. That's because, like many robberies of really important paintings, the perpetrators find them hard to sell on. Unless the thieves are robbing to order or are going to demand a ransom from the insurance companies, they find it difficult to source the right people who will give them the kind of money they are worth. Then the provenance has to be covered up. Some paintings remain hidden for years before re-appearing because the idiots just don't know how to get rid of them. Putting them into auctions is a good way of muddying the waters of ownership. Some people put them into a sale under an assumed name and buy them back themselves. This way they can say they genuinely acquired the painting at auction. If it is by a painter who is increasing in value, such as Jackson Pollack, Andy Warhol, say, or Howard Hodgkins, all they have to do is hang on to it for a year or so and they will recoup the money the auction sale cost them plus a lot more. If they place it in a small auction room without the prestige and expertise of, for example, Westbury's, it will more than likely be undervalued or assumed to be a fake if anyone notices it at all and will make a fraction of its genuine value. The only snag in this case is that it is not just about stolen paintings – which, let's face it, is not usually life threatening – this is about money laundering and financing terrorism.'

Tom was now listening intently. 'Oh.'

'We have been looking out for the Lamphreigh loot for a long time and have finally got a definite lead on who might be holding what's left of it, but he has been very clever to date, typically even sending some of it to America and France. Those paintings you have in your drawing room have been to Germany where they failed to find a buyer and have now come back. That's why I had to disappear as I have been following them. If we can find out who buys them here I think we will have a good enough lead to the main villain of this particular heist.'

All the talk about perpetrators, villains, loot and heists was making Maddy feel she was in an episode of 'The Sweeny' and was finding it hard not to giggle, although she knew it was all extremely serious. Carol was gazing at Sean as if he were Dennis Waterman and John Thaw all rolled into one.

'What about the young couple who left the paintings with us?' asked Maddy. 'I tried to phone them to tell them when the pictures were going to be sold but the exchange told me there was no such number.'

'Of course there wasn't, Maddy. They were just runners for whoever is organising everything. If it all goes according to our plan they will realise they have been rumbled and you won't hear from them again.' Sean looked pleadingly at Tom. 'I know this is all hard to take in. Am I forgiven?'

'Yes, Sean. Of course you are, but you can't blame us for feeling like we did.'

'I certainly don't and, once again, I am really sorry I wasn't able to explain it all long ago.'

He then continued with exactly what he wanted them to do at the coming sale. It sounded simple enough but Maddy knew it wasn't going to be. Where auctions were concerned nothing ever was.

Twenty-Seven

'I have just had an awful thought,' Maddy said as she was finishing the washing up. Tom was sitting at the cleared dining table working out the auction receipts prior to writing the cheques to vendors. Sean and Carol had gone and James and Harry were watching television.

'Mmm?' he said, only half listening.

'What if that couple thought those paintings were going to be in today's sale? What are we going to do if they come for their money on Monday or what if the person coming to buy them was at the sale today? I wonder if Sean had thought of that.'

'What, Mads? Say that again?'

So she did.

'Well, yes, Sean must have thought of that. Don't forget he knew the pictures weren't in this sale when he came here on view night dressed up, according to you, like a poor man's Sherlock Holmes.'

'Oh yes, of course.' Maddy put a saucepan away. 'I don't suppose you saw anyone on view night that looked, you know, suspicious?'

'Christ, Maddy, all the art dealers look suspicious. They go cross-eyed trying not to look at the pictures they are interested in. You know what they are like. No, I didn't see anyone I didn't know – well, I don't think I did.'

'Tom, do you really believe no-one will notice those paintings? We have a pretty savvy lot of arty people coming now.'

'Not if we do what Sean tells us to do. We won't hide them, we'll put them in pride of place, make non-committal descriptions of them in the catalogue like 'after the style of' and 'in the manner of' and people will assume they are reproductions or copies. If we were to put them in the Restorers Room in a dark corner they will be discovered as sleepers and the world will go mad for them. I think Sean's right – for what that's worth.'

'Okay, but I can't help thinking it won't be as simple as that...'

'Please shut up and let me get on with these – or I won't have the cheques ready tomorrow.'

'Sorry, but I am beginning to feel we are involved in something really scary.'

'Stop fussing, for God's sake. Sean has it all sorted.' Tom turned back to his sheets of paper. Maddy knew he wasn't as confident as he sounded but said no more, finished the bottle of wine, took Fizz for her night-time walk and went to bed. For once, she left Tom working into the small hours and fell asleep deciding that being scared had to wait until later. They had another auction to organise.

The Sunday morning after the Saturday sale was the best time of all in the auction cycle for Maddy. It began with her getting up quietly so as not to wake Tom and slipping down to the kitchen. She made herself a huge cup of tea, sat at the table with the auction sheets in front of her and began to go through them. Having sorted everything in the auction from beginning to end, she knew each lot. She had valued every lot and typed an estimate beside each lot, so finding out how much each one had actually made was like prospecting for gold. She would also find out how they had done for each seller: how well she had lotted their items, if she had she put them in the right place, if she had estimated them correctly. Then, finally, the total amount of their cheque.

Inevitably some things made more than the estimate and others less. Sometimes there were surprises like the Wedgwood china 'Fairyland' lustre bowl in the last auction making ten times the estimated value a London auction house had given her. Four or five people really wanted it and the bidding had been furious. Auctions were unpredictable which is why most people found them exciting and fun.

Maddy had given up guessing which vendors would be pleased with what Killybane Auctions had done for them and those who would be disappointed. Everybody had their own agendas as far as auctions were concerned and, of course, everyone secretly hoped their stuff would make more than it was worth.

The sheets would tell her all. Almost like Tarot cards, she would learn what she had done right in the past, what had gone wrong in the present and what she could put right in the future. This was her moment and she relished it.

Then the real day began with the children and Tom coming down for breakfast and afterwards taking off for their Sundays; sailing, fishing or just going back to bed.

Tom continued with the paper work that would take him most of the morning. Maddy had to face the saleroom and yard – Willie's chewing gum, cigarette butts, sandwich wrappers, sweetie papers, discarded catalogues and torn up bidding cards. A dustpan and brush was the answer and she invented a massive, remote controlled, exterior vacuum cleaner in her head as she bent to sweep up the public dross.

By lunch time the place was tidy and at two o'clock people came to collect things for which they had left successful bids. Others came for their cheques and pieces that had not reached reserve prices in the auction. Trailers and cars once again filled the yard.

One Sunday an art buyer appeared with a tape measure. He asked if he could 'size' an un-sold painting that was still hanging on the wall. Measurements of all paintings were in the catalogue but Tom acquiesced while the buyer measured the painting for himself.

'Hah!' he said after doing some calculations on a notepad. 'As I thought, the reserve price on this painting works out as £11.50 per square inch and the artist normally only sells for £10.00 per square inch.'

Tom had never heard of paintings being valued by the square inch and could think of no rejoinder except to extol the virtue of the rather large frame which probably had a greater collective volume than the picture itself.

There was a long pause and he began to think he had overstepped the surreal parameter of the conversation when the gentleman decided this was good reasoning and bought the painting. Tom, astonished, wondered if he was going to have to advise the Arts Sales Index of this extraordinary new method of art valuation.

Collections, deliveries and telephone calls over the next two weeks pushed their thoughts of the stolen paintings and what was going to happen at the next sale to the backs of their minds. Their days became fuller than ever.

An ex heavyweight boxer, rejoicing in the name of 'Slam' Duncan, had booked their first call. On his retirement he had decided that the antiques business was the thing to be in and had bought a large emporium on 'The Pass' (as Donegal Pass is known to antiques hounds) being where most of the antiques shops were in Belfast.

The previous owner was languishing in Crumlin Road jail. Rumour had it he'd combined his retail activities with a considerable amount of breaking and entering in association with active agents from as far away as Dublin, Derry, Galway and Cork. The police had retrieved as much from the premises as they could identify but Slam had explained to Maddy on the phone there was a lot left and it needed a 'wee bit of a redding out'. Would Killybane Auctions come and take what they thought they could sell and give him a bit of space?

The exterior of the emporium looked impressive. A typical Belfast turn-of-the-century building made of red bricks (more than likely fired on site) with two bow fronted shop windows flanking either side of a mahogany panelled and carved double doorway with stained glass panels.

Maddy, Tom and Emma stepped through these into a wide foyer that stretched to the back of the building. Four individual antique shops each with its own speciality, oil lamps, jewellery, glass and silver, ran down one side. They looked pretty and interesting. Mr Duncan's domain on the other side gave the appearance of having been charged through by a large bull looking for a mate. Furniture of every period and style in conditions ranging from rotten to the not-so-bad was piled everywhere in shambolic disarray and smalls were scattered on and under every conceivable surface.

Among these Maddy spied a Moorcroft Pottery vase with a ridiculously high price stuck on it lying on the floor under a chair and another sitting precariously on top of a pile of books. A tiny lady materialised from behind a wobbly stack of drawers from a chest that must have been sitting empty somewhere. She wore a pastel coloured caftan over a thick, purple, polo necked sweater, long gold triangle earrings and fairisle gloves with no fingers. She weaved her way towards them between the jumble of furniture and effects as if she were struggling through a jungle and told them her name was Lily. She complained of the cold but told them not to worry as she was wearing her thermals.

'Oh dear,' she said, shaking her head of blonde/silver curls in a distracted fashion and waving her gloved hands. 'I know it's a terrible mess but it is always like this and as soon as it gets sorted out, in comes more mess.'

Whether she had been acquired with the building by Mr Duncan or if she was his assistant or wife or mistress was anyone's guess.

She smiled over Tom's shoulder and said, 'Ah! Slam, there you are. The auction people are here to see you.'

Mr D filled the door frame, his large battered face beaming with delight and friendliness. He reached over the pile of books and ornaments to shake Tom's hand and knocked over the vase in the process.

'Not my kind of thing,' he chuckled as he swept the broken pieces into a pile.

Lily started looking for a brush and a bin and they wondered what on earth his 'kind of thing' could possibly be.

'Nice to meet you Mr Daniels,' he said, 'heard a lot of good things about you. I'm Slam Duncan – call me Slam. I'm sorry I couldn't have been here earlier to get organised for you.'

Maddy and Emma exchanged glances of incredulity knowing this place would take several months, if not years, to get 'organised'.

Lily pointed to three pieces of furniture near the door, a dresser, a desk and a blanket box and suggested to Slam they could go for auction. The smile left Slam's face and his brow furrowed.

'D' y' think they'll make much?' he asked Tom anxiously.

Tom began to examine the pieces and gave what he thought were reasonable estimates.

'Oh my goodness, umm. I don't know, I mean I would have to...' and his sentence trailed off.

'Slam, for goodness sake,' Lily said. 'We need the space and Mr. Daniels will do his best for you.'

She smiled sweetly at Tom who smiled back his knock 'em dead smile much to Maddy's disgust.

'Oh alright,' Slam said, 'take them – yer right Lily we'll not get set up if we don't have a bit of a clear out.'

He still looked worried. Making decisions was obviously no easy task for him.

Maddy began to make a list while Tom unscrewed the plate-rack top of the dresser prior to loading it into the van. This seemed to un-nerve Slam who looked horrified as Emma and Tom lifted it off.

'Makes it easier to lift,' Tom explained, seeing his consternation, 'kinder to us and also to it!'

'Oh, yes. Yes, I can see that. Yes, of course.' Slam still didn't look happy.

People were drifting in and out of the foyer now where a gentleman, wearing a black bowler hat and a navy blue boiler suit, had placed a composite set of twelve Edwardian dining chairs. If anyone stopped to make enquiries about the chairs he would produce a little note book into which he peered with much concentration and pencil licking. The place seemed to be surprisingly busy for a Monday morning.

After they had loaded the dresser, Tom and Emma put the blanket-box in the van and were carrying out the desk when Slam ran after them. Indecision was written all over his face again.

'Maybe that should stay. What did you say it would make?'

'Taking into account it needs a new leather skiver on the top,' said Tom, 'and one of the legs has woodworm, I think about £100 - £150.'

'Is that really all it will make?' Slam asked. It had begun to dawn on Tom and the others that he hadn't a clue about antiques or their values.

'But, you know auctions, Slam, it could make more. I don't like to value things too highly in case people are disappointed.'

'Ah, yes, of course..... ummm.'

It was clear the man didn't know about auctions. Emma and Tom were standing on the road balancing the desk on the edge of the floor at the back of the van waiting patiently for his decision and their arms were beginning to ache. Emma was wondering how on earth he had ever, in the heat of the moment in a boxing ring, been able to decide when to thump an opponent and thought it was a miracle he was still alive. Maybe he wouldn't be by the time they had finished this call as she could tell Mr Daniel's fuse was getting shorter by the minute. Maddy was making a note to order replacement leather for the desk. It would make a big difference to its sale price. She then wondered why Slam couldn't have had the desk done up himself. The leg was no big deal either. But she was not there to question his motives and stood patiently with the others as he made up his mind.

'Ah, go on, take it,' he finally said and then, after more deliberation, added, 'I think I had better show you upstairs before you take any more from down here.'

He declared they would go up in the lift. Behind a pile of rusty stacking chairs and some old curtains at the end of the Foyer reposed an aged lift with metal mesh concertina-style doors. Slam placed a beefy finger on a red button on the wall beside it and pressed firmly. The lift door slid open a few inches and promptly shut again. They heard grating, grinding sounds and a heap of quivering furniture and junk began to appear from the basement.

It was about halfway up the height of the door when it stopped. Slam resolutely refused to take his finger off the red button and after some minutes they noticed him begin to sniff in an enquiring fashion. The smell of burned out lift motor began to waft from below and permeate the foyer.

'Well, that's that then,' Slam said, finally taking his finger off the button. 'Motor's probably gone!' He didn't seem overly upset at the prospect of having to invest in costly lift repairs.

Tom was becoming infuriated with the man but Emma was looking mightily relieved she wouldn't have to get into that cranky old lift. This made Maddy remember a comment she had made when they were driving through Belfast past a fun fair with a large wheel. She had gazed at it for a few moments, gave a sort of 'hmmf' and said, 'All you'd need would be one loose nut!' Maddy could see the lift, to Emma, was a pile of loose nuts.

'What about the stairs?' said Maddy and received a kick on the ankle from her loving husband who had seen the stairs - nasty, narrow, steep, mean, ancient things. Getting anything larger than a handbag down those was going to be tough.

They climbed them and the sight at the top took their breath away, even drew an 'Oh my God and granny's socks!' from Emma. A huge room, the length of the whole building, was piled to the ceiling with brass bed ends, fireplaces, architectural mouldings, pillars, architraves, unidentifiable grot and even more grot. They couldn't believe it.

'Where do we start, Mr Duncan – Slam?' said Tom.

'Oh, just take what you think you can sell.'

Maddy's eyes lit up and she went into 'hoking' mode. This was grist to her mill and she began by unearthing a set of eight Victorian balloon back chairs, badly in need of restoration, but eight was a good number and she knew they would sell well. She dug out two matching fancy corbels and all the pieces of plaster for a ceiling rose.

She asked Slam if he would let them sell these and he said that anything from upstairs could go. He knew it was all rubbish and, anyway, those were only bits of old plaster out of a house, weren't they?

He laughed when he saw the chairs and couldn't believe they were worth selling. Maddy hoped he would be pleasantly surprised when he saw what his 'rubbish' would make. Ideal stuff for the Restorers' Room, she knew for sure, as she plundered the pile.

As expected, it was back-breaking to manoeuvre anything down those stairs. The frame of a chaise longue nearly got stuck as fast as the velvet sofa in Holywood but was fortunately missing its castors so no holes were dug in the walls and it was light so they could lift it over the banisters.

On one of their journeys trooping down the stairs, through the foyer and to the van they noticed three or four policemen and two others who could have only been 'plainclothesmen' (Maddy was, of course, now experienced in this sort of thing) removing the Edwardian dining chairs in a kind of Royal Ulster Constabulary human chain down the Pass and into a waiting police Land Rover.

The gentleman in the bowler hat and boiler suit had disappeared as had Slam Duncan. Lily smiled in a strange way when Maddy enquired as to his whereabouts and said he'd gone for lunch.

A kind man from one of the little shops in the foyer took pity on 'the ladies', as he referred to Maddy and Emma, and began to help with lifting and carrying. Emma suspected nosiness rather than chivalry but he was able to explain that the lift had been used by the previous incumbent as a kind of refuse pit down which to throw rubbish and a broken shovel had become wedged between it and the wall.

He said he'd tried to tell Slam about it, but he didn't think he had taken it in...

After some time Slam returned through a back door looking warily round the foyer. Tom had just struggled down the stairs with a cast iron fireplace complete with back plate and begged Maddy to stop 'hoking'. Anyway, he said, the van was full and it was time for lunch.

Tom told Slam they were going home and wondered if he wanted them to come back for more. After checking with Lily, Slam said they would see how things went.

'Sure, we've a bit of space now. You've done a great clear out and we can see what is what.'

Tom couldn't see the place looked any different from when

they had arrived. Slam said he would discuss it with his advisors and let Tom know. Tom wondered who his advisors could be. How could anyone possibly expect this extremely pleasant but inexperienced man to turn this chaotic mess into a business?

Maddy asked Slam to sign the collection form and gave him a copy.

'I hope you can make sense out of it, Slam. I am afraid there are lots of crossings out (she was too polite to say it was because he kept changing his mind). I will re-write it all when I get home and type it out clearly for you.'

'That would be great, love. Hector and Willie will want to see what I've given you.'

'Who? Do you mean Big Heck Livingstone and Willie O'Hanlon?' She hoped the horror didn't show on her face but Emma said later it had done.

'Yes, Sir! They are helping me get started. They say they are going to keep me right – going to sell me stuff for next to nothing to stock me up and all that.' He gazed around at his shambles of a shop and beamed at the ethereal Lily. 'Sure it's going to be great.'

'It's goin' to be a disaster,' Emma said on the way home. 'Y' see those two – they'll run rings round that poor man. I'll give him two weeks an' he'll be wishin' he was back at the boxin'.'

Twenty-Eight

When they returned home Pam came out to help unload and label the van's contents regaling them at the same time with a somewhat puzzling telephone call she'd received that morning from a Mrs Jansen from Dromore.

'She said she was bringing us some things to sell including some "turracatta pats" that were big and 'rure' and she wanted 'serious' money for them. Forgive me, but what exactly are they?'

'Ah, Pam,' Tom said, realising English-born Pam's grasp of the local accent was good, having lived in Northern Ireland for over forty years, but did not run to that of the misty hills of Dromore. 'You mean, Mrs Johnstone and her terracotta pots! She imports them from China where they are made in their thousands and for 'rure' read 'rare' which they certainly are not, but they are big.

'Well, she is delivering them this afternoon.'

'She'd better not put reserves on them,' said Tom. 'I had to withdraw all the last lot – made me feel a right idiot.' He added weakly, 'Do you think we could have some lunch? It is two thirty.'

Maddy recalled she had soup somewhere and bread and cheese and was glad Pam could cope with the new arrival coming into the yard that would give them time to wolf it down. Everything happened at once these days.

Muffled barking was emanating from the (mostly) blue painted van driving through the gates. A large German shepherd dog could be seen charging about the interior, barking fiercely whenever its fang-baring face came close to the windscreen and windows which were thickly misted and covered with slavers of dog spit. The driver, Maddy knew, was William Rose. The dog was called Prince. As soon as the engine was turned off Prince ceased barking and sat like an angel on the passenger seat, no more threatening than a King Charles spaniel.

'It's alright,' Maddy assured the concerned looking Pam. 'That's Prince and he is a big softee – he'll even give you his paw if you ask him.'

Pam didn't look too sure as she went round to the back of the van to meet William who was now opening the doors to reveal his latest offerings for Killybane Auctions.

William had been delivering things to them for some time but never came to the auctions. He was a true scavenger from the large land reclamation dumps in Belfast. A licence was required for this activity, he'd explained a while ago, and there was a definite pecking order. Like the allotment system, one had to wait for a vacancy. William had made the mistake of ignoring this procedure when he started going to search the dump and ended up being prosecuted.

'I ended 'up the Crum',' he told Maddy.

'Goodness, William – Crumlin Road jail?'

'Yes! Three months.'

Maddy realised that she hadn't seen him for quite a while and also noticed he looked a bit pale and was sporting a pretty dreadful, extremely short, hair cut.

'Oh dear, William. Was it awful? What was the food like?'

'Nah, it was alright. Lot of me mates was in at the same time and the food was great. Better than the wife's - and it arrived on time.'

The contents of William's van never failed to astonish them. The first two loads he brought had been plan cabinets and partners desks that, according to William, were being hurled out of upper story windows of various vacated offices at the shipyard. They had been so well made this treatment had taken little toll on them, apart from a few chips and splinters.

Shades of the RMS Titanic's cabinet makers' work, they were akin to other pieces Maddy and Tom collected from the shipyard area from time to time. Ancient 'homers' made from solid mahogany (and weighing a ton – no wonder the ship sank so quickly) such as dressing tables, 'captain's' arm chairs and, sometimes, ship's washing cabinets fitted with concealed drop down ceramic basins and brass taps. Never things of great beauty, but wonderfully well made.

By the time Tom, Maddy and Emma came out to the yard again after lunch, Pam was busy saying goodbye to Prince, holding his paw and stroking his ears. From William she had taken two mantel clocks, a Victorian wicker bassinette, a carved oak hall settle and a magnificent pottery chamber pot printed with hunting scenes. As soon as William was ready to leave and started the engine of the van, Prince became the snarling vicious Hound of the Baskervilles again.

Laughing, Maddy explained to Pam that William worked in a rather insalubrious area and acquired Prince when he'd become concerned for the contents of his van if he had to leave it parked. He had tried to train Prince to be snarly and horrible when the van was stationary but the dog had got it into his head that he had to be really nasty when William was with him and the engine was turned on.

While in 'savage' mode Prince never tried to bite William who had eventually come to the conclusion he didn't have it in him. It was all a bit of an act.

'Sure, what can I do now, Mrs. Daniels?' William said. 'At least at road blocks, as long as I keep the engine runnin', the police don't dare to ask me to wind down the window, let alone ask me to show them my licence!'

Maddy could see this might have some advantages in certain circumstances.

The following morning Maddy and Tom found themselves walking down the long sun-lit colonnade in Drumbandon House near the village of Drumbandon in County Tyrone. Lady Alice Bandon had asked them to come and value the contents of the attics of her and Lord Bandon's magnificent residence built in 1875, designed by the Architect, John Nash.

Beautiful and vivacious, the new Lady Bandon was redecorating and had sent a substantial amount of what she described as dreary brown furniture to Westbury's in London who had suggested Killybane Auctions might be a more suitable auction room for the contents of the attics.

For that read 'the dross,' Maddy thought, with a silent, doleful sigh.

They passed several splendid pairs of marbled, ionic columns that flanked alcoves in which she noticed matching bright red amaryllis in ancient blue and white Chinese porcelain cache-pots. All at exactly the same stage of flowering, she marvelled, how on earth had Lady Bandon managed that?

Through one of the floor-to-ceiling Palladian windows that gave on to views of the surrounding countryside and immaculate lawns and gardens, she spied a gardener.

I wonder if he grows masses at the same time in order to get five that match? He's probably got something else 'coming on' in a heated greenhouse to replace them when they are finished. Ahh, how some people live...

Maddy's musings had taken her up the exquisite flying staircase across a landing and now through a discreet panelled door behind which a steep staircase led to the top floor under the eaves. These were not the cramped, draughty rooms she had been expecting. They were cosy, with their low tongue-and-groove wooden ceilings affording insulation. Each apartment led into another either side of the staircase – obviously one side for females and the other for the male members of the staff. No longer used, they were empty now save for the furniture.

Maddy's and Tom's hearts lifted as they walked from room to room which were filled with Irish pine furniture that must have been there since the day it was made; dainty little dressing tables with free-standing swing mirrors, chests of drawers, small occasional tables, chairs with spindle and ladder backs and any amount of brass and iron bedsteads.

There were two huge feather filled mattresses and masses of patchwork quilts – the 'country' kind that were beginning to be sought after – even the worn and tatty ones.

Maddy stopped to lift the corner of a mattress on one of the beds. 'Great!' she said. 'These are horse hair mattresses, Lady Bandon. We have a client for these. She is an upholsterer and is desperate for horse hair!'

'Do you really think she would want these old things?'

'Absolutely. We don't put them in the auction as they are hard to display – they flop all over the place and look awful. As no one else wants them we sell them to her for fifteen pounds each. She actually washes the horse hair in her back yard in an old tin bath.'

'Good God! Who would believe it!'

'Please don't get the wrong idea. They are the only thing we sell out of auction and we don't charge commission.'

'What about the rest of the furniture? Will you be able to sell that?'

'We certainly will, Lady Bandon,' Tom said. 'Vernacular pine furniture is very popular at the moment.'

'Brilliant! Now come and have lunch and we will arrange when you can collect the furniture after that.' She turned again to Maddy. 'This upholsterer lady, she actually washes the horsehair? How does she dry it?'

'I'm sorry, I don't know. With some difficulty I would imagine. I can't imagine her hanging it on a line!'

Laughing, they trooped downstairs again and Lady B ushered them into an enormous dining room where a long refectory table was laid for lunch.

'It was like a cartoon,' Maddy told Mary later, who was agog to hear about the house. 'Lady B sat at one end and Lord B sat at the other. If they each hadn't had their own salt and pepper they would have needed a conveyor belt to pass it to one another. Tom and I sat opposite each other in the middle. It was surreal! But they were lovely and we had a gorgeous lunch. They were fascinated with what we are doing – or pretended to be anyway and Lady Bandon couldn't get over Mrs Wilson wanting the horsehair mattresses or anyone in the world buying one of those quilts!'

Thinking of her own tiny attic at home full of cobwebs and dead spiders, Maddy couldn't help commenting on how tidy, clean and spotless the attics in Bandon house were and wondered did staff still live up there.

'Oh goodness no!' said Lady Bandon. 'There is much better accommodation for the staff in the new wing – well, when I say 'new', it was built in 1945. It's all ship-shape up in the attics because of Mrs Tiggywinkle.'

'Who?'

Lady Bandon giggled.

'Elish O'Mahony, I nicknamed her that poor thing - she is such a wonderful house-keeper. As soon as I phoned her to say I was getting Westbury's to look over the contents of the house she went into super cleaning action and by the time we came back from Australia – we go there every year for a few months – she'd not only cleared up the attics but the basement as well which was full of the most extraordinary amount of rubbish. I was going to ask you about that. I am hoping you can come and collect the few things she left there.'

Maddy's heart sank as it always did when she heard a lay person had cleared somewhere out. She could never help wondering what had been thrown out that might have been valuable. She had heard so many stories of relatives filling skips with priceless memorabilia and artefacts in the throes of clearing a house after an uncle, an aunt or a cousin had died.

She sighed inwardly and told herself she couldn't win them all.

'Lots of broken stuff,' Lady Bandon said, 'put down there waiting to be repaired – old plates, copper pots, pans, masses of old pictures and frames. I simply couldn't have faced it and blessed old Tiggywinkle when she said "just you have a great time in Australia, Lady B, I'll get it all sorted out for you." And she did.' Lady Bandon sighed and smiled, 'She is like gold dust. It's so hard to find people like that nowadays. And her nephew, Brendan, works tirelessly in the garden.'

'Oh, I think I saw him, Lady Bandon. Is he the one who grows the wonderful amaryllis you have in the hall?'

'He certainly is, and he does a lot in the house as well – even waits at table when we have a party. They more or less turned up out of the blue a year or so ago and are a godsend.'

If lunch was anything to go by, Lord and Lady Bandon were very lucky to have found such treasures, Maddy thought as she nodded off on the way home.

'Can I come and help collect it?' Mary asked.

'Of course you can – I am dreading manhandling those mattresses - it's a long way and lots of stairs from the top of the house to the yard where we'll have to park the van.'

She knew Mary wouldn't mind. Her passion for houses and interior decor meant she would plod through bogs heaving stuff if she had to.

Twenty-Nine

By the end of the following week they were once again full to the gills with furniture, paintings and smalls. More and more people were bringing things for valuation. 'I know this vase is very, very, very old because it belonged to my granny.' A girl plonked a box down on the bar and continued, 'My neighbour said she saw one identical on the Antiques Road Show and it was worth five hundred pounds.' She stared defiantly at Maddy.

As the young lady couldn't have been much more than eighteen, her grandmother couldn't possibly have been as old as she was implying and could have bought the vase last week.

When unwrapped, it was much as Maddy expected, a transfer-printed monstrosity of no age or value whatsoever, something one might receive as a prize at a fun fair. She also saw, thankfully, it was cracked.

'Well, I can honestly tell you it is not as old as you thought and it is, unfortunately, cracked, Miss Scott.'

'It's only a wee crack.'

'I know, but when a pot is damaged its value is greatly diminished. The collectors only want perfect pieces, unless, of course, they are exceptionally old or rare.'

'Well, that vase is rare – my neighbour said so.'

Resisting the urge to advise her to tell her neighbour to sell it for her, Maddy wrapped it up again and put it back in its box.

This kind of exchange was becoming familiar and she had

learned that telling the truth at the start was the only way to go. As soon as one began to admire something, which some appraisers do, in order to soften the blow that it is worth very little, the value, in the enquirer's mind, shoots up and no amount of explaining can reduce their expectation or make the disappointment any less.

The time to say something like 'but it is a nice piece, madam, and if you like it, that's the important thing,' is after the blow has been delivered. The response is usually a tight smile and they are off to find another auctioneer who will tell them what they want to hear.

Those she dreaded most were amateur painters. Usually retired and gentle but convinced they had an emerging talent hitherto hidden from the world (by a selfless existence, working tirelessly in a tax office or looking after a demanding parent), and which was now going to make them a killing at Killybane Auctions.

Maddy reckoned their teachers, probably struggling artists, scraping a living by giving classes, were to blame, as they had assured all these ancient hopefuls they were wonderfully gifted - all they needed was a bit more practice – and more lessons.

Tom absented himself when he saw them approaching and left them to Maddy. She hated having to tell people their work was un-saleable but eventually hit upon a polite way of explaining that the market just wasn't quite ready for them yet and most of the art sold at auction was by artists who were, actually, dead.

Pretty pictures were all well and good but if they weren't painted by a known artist and, preferably, a dead one, they wouldn't make even the price of the frame at auction.

This candid approach seemed to work quite well and most of the hopefuls accepted it as they packed up their canvases of cottages and cows and trundled away.

Maddy hoped they would, at least, depart from her feeling glad they were still alive, even though she couldn't sell their paintings.

There were also people who drifted in for a chat, again, retired - usually male - with time to fill.

Their opening gambit would be something like, 'I was having a look round and was thinking about bringing you some really good paintings/books/jewellery/furniture to sell. Would you be interested?'

Maddy yearned to respond with, 'For goodness sake, what would we want with that sort of stuff?' But didn't. Then the person would either sit down or lean on the bar and, with a sinking heart, she knew she would be stuck for at least an hour listening to reminiscences of auctions they'd been to and tales of their youth.

Some of them would have been interesting if she didn't have so much work to get through before the day was done. She could see her bed-time becoming later and later as she sat or leaned on something herself, politely listening, more than ever convinced she had a face like a bar maid, silently praying for Tom or Emma to come in and take over, but no, they had things to do, too, and left her to get on with it.

'You're much better at it than us,' Emma said when accused of conniving with Tom to leave her lumbered with the time wasters. 'Sure, you know rightly we'd only tell them to boggle off.'

Maddy knew that was absolutely true and thus resigned herself to the status quo.

Then, there were the gypsies or the 'travellers', as some preferred to be called.

On her own one morning in the saleroom Maddy was sticking numbers on lots. She heard a noise behind her and looked round to see a gentleman in a grey shiny suit. He had red hair, cut short, above a body and face that looked like they had been fed on fried food since he was born.

'Good morning, missus. How are y'doin today?' he said.

'Good morning.' Maddy said, feeling, at first surprised then slightly apprehensive. She didn't like his walking into the room unannounced and his weird assumption that he knew her.

He was walking towards her when she heard another sound and turned to see an almost duplicate person had entered from the door at the other end of the saleroom. He, too, had begun to walk towards her, and she became aware of being really on her own. Emma had gone to the dentist and Tom was away doing a valuation. Fizz was being her usual friendly self to the first one that came in.

Blast, thought Maddy, *I could do with Prince right now.*

'Would you be sellin' us some stuff, lady?' asked Number One.

'I'm sorry, but we don't sell anything out of auction.'

'Ah now,' said Number Two, and Maddy whirled round. 'Sure, we'd give you good money for that chest over there.'

He was walking closer to her. She was really frightened now, and they kept talking all the time, each one over the other.

'Sure, we'll give you a great proice for that clock and that table. We'll pay you tree times what you'd get for it in the sale.'

'Sure, you would be mad not to take what we could give you.'

They were closing in on her and Maddy, in desperation, grabbed a tall vase with a bulbous body and a slender neck that was the nearest thing she felt she could use as a weapon.

'I will not tell you again, we do not sell out of auction. If you want anything here you will have to come to the auction and bid for it.' She held the vase upside down and shook it as they continued their approach. 'I must warn both of you, I am a pretty good shot and if I throw this vase, one of you is going to be clobbered good and proper. I then will have no compunction in calling for an ambulance and - the police.'

Their look of horror was quite satisfying until she realised she was threatening to throw a quite valuable cloisonné vase that they'd probably 'clocked' in the first place. They began to back off.

'Ah now, missus, we didn't mean no harm, now put the vase down. Sure, it's of no consequence, is it?'

Maddy looked at the vase, realised what she had grabbed and knew she had them. Threatening to let it go like a fancy shot put at any minute, she got them to back out of the saleroom and into their brand new non-registered Volvos.

She knew they would be back and that was how the Shaughnessy brothers, Sammy and Gerry, came into their lives.

It came as a revelation to learn that these travelling folk knew more about antiques and had more money to spend on them than anyone else in the land. Seemingly a large container ship travelled to America once a month full of antiques they obtained by going round the country 'knocking', that is, literally, going up to people's front doors, knocking on them and offering money for anything of value they could spy when let in. A common trick was to offer a ridiculously high price for a mediocre piece – a hall table perhaps or a hat stand, and then virtually nothing for the most valuable piece. They belonged to a nation-wide network and each worked their own patch. Should one family of tinkers try to impinge on another's area, it was war.

Sammy and Gerry lived in state-of-the-art caravans in a number of halting sites at various times in Belfast. The clan gathered from time to time in a village in Kerry where every second house was an antique shop and this was probably where they had gained their extensive knowledge. Few of them seemed to be able to read but their numeracy skills could not have been sharper.

Tom discovered there is a strange sort of decency with the tinkers. They don't expect, or want, your version of it. They have their own. It takes some understanding but, after his dealings with textile merchants in Hong Kong, Korea and, even the Gorbels in Glasgow, he appreciated they had their own way of going and one had to consider that. And he knew they admired courage.

The fact that he came back alive from a confrontation with them on one of their halts over an overdue bill proved that a strange sort of mutual understanding had set in and a general respect for each other came into being.

Not for Maddy, of course. She was a woman and, after the cloisonné incident, one to be avoided. They didn't even look at her after that.

'Mornin', missus,' they would say, fixing their eyes on some distant planet over her head if she ever met them in the yard.

Thirty

DDay Minus One was upon them. View Day. The Velsen and the two watercolours, which they now knew were by Samuel Prout and Frank Walton, and had not been part of Lord Lamphreigh's estate robbery but belonged to some other unfortunate victim, had been hung along with fifty or so other prints and pictures.

The Velsen was on the wall near the fireplace and the other two were nearer to the rostrum. The pictures at each auction were now being sold consecutively and the time they were due to come up for sale was printed in the catalogue.

Tom, finally having reached his goal of selling approximately one hundred lots an hour, was now able to work out the times various lots would come up for sale. This meant buyers solely interested in art would know roughly what time to be there to bid for the pictures they wanted. This was appreciated by those who had their own galleries to run as they could little afford the time to spend a whole day at an auction. Dealers who bought on spec for various galleries and private collectors were also glad of this new arrangement.

Tom was sitting, as usual, on the rostrum available for viewers to chat to about lots they fancied and leave bids with. He could see the whole room and everyone who came in and went out. Today he kept saying to himself, 'don't look at that blasted painting. Don't look at that blasted thing.' But his eyes seemed to be dragged back to it time after time. No matter how he looked at it he couldn't see the importance of it and could quite understand the possibility of it going through a general sale unacknowledged. Give him a Maserati any day.

Maddy spent view day walking round as usual, catching up with viewers she knew and fixing muddled lots. She took Tom's place from time to time so he could eat and take a break. It was a long day for him from nine in the morning until nine at night – mostly making small talk which he found as boring as hell. He did, however, enjoy taking absent bids and, at the end of the day, found it reassuring to see them on a goodly portion of the auction.

Maddy found it very pleasing when people made remarks like 'you have a great show this time' and particularly when they came from Annie Walker who remained an avid fan. 'You are getting there girl, keep it up. You really are beginning to worry the town auctions!' Now that was progress, Maddy thought with glee.

Molly Watson, another collector, who knew more about antique kitchenware and sewing memorabilia than anyone else, never actually said anything if she found the sale interesting. She whistled. Tom and Maddy would watch her with bated breath as she bought a catalogue and began to browse round the auction. When she began to whistle, they heaved a collective sigh of relief knowing she had seen things she liked and would be back to bid the next day.

Poor Fizz had to stay in the house. There were too many cars coming and going, but Maddy took her for walks during the day. Spike, their cat, on the other hand felt it was his bounden duty to supervise.

He usually began the day by sitting on the gatepost. If Maddy went over to him he would acknowledge her by reaching out a paw to pat her face. At the same time he would rise, arch his back and stretch his head over to butt her forehead. He would receive a stroke in return. His aquamarine eyes, with narrow black marquise shaped pupils, would gaze at her briefly before he settled again on his 'podium'. Being an auction cat had its responsibilities and he took them seriously.

From this position he could observe everyone who came and went on view days, right from the bottom of the lane, into the car park, then into the yard. From here he would move to his 'I am an ornament' duty, which involved placing himself on a table amid a 'lot' of ornaments and staying very still.

Maddy became aware of this particular stratagem one view day when she was standing in the yard. A piercing scream rent the air and a lady came running out of the saleroom and up to Maddy clutching a bleeding hand.

'There was this strange rabbity looking thing sitting on a table,' she said, 'and when I leant over to lift it, it suddenly moved and scratched me!'

Maddy commiserated and went to get some disinfectant to dab on the wound.

Spike, a 'rabbity' looking 'thing'? He was her beautiful tabby cat! Maddy thought the woman deserved to be scratched. But he shouldn't have done it. She would have to have a severe word with him.

She remembered his arrival. It was the evening before their first 'proper' auction and they were up to their eyes trying to get ready when Mrs Shortall from next door appeared clutching a sack that looked as if it had a very small potato at the bottom of it.

'Mrs Daniels, I heard about you losing your last cat and I was wondering would you like another one? Mine has just had kittens and William is threatening to drown them if I don't find them homes.'

'Absolutely NO!' Tom called, overhearing from the dining room. 'We have more than enough to do tonight without a blasted kitten under our feet.'

A plaintive cry came from the sack and Maddy took it from Mrs Shortall. The kitten was indeed no bigger than a small potato and it sat on her hand bleating with hunger. She winked at Mrs Shortall who disappeared with the empty sack.

'I meant it,' said Tom appearing in the hall. 'We don't have the time or the – oh my God – it's tiny!'

The bleating stopped and the blue eyes gazed at him. And that was more or less that.

By the time Maddy returned from an emergency trip to the vet for special formula kitten milk, 'it' had a gender, a name and a make-shift bed. They crawled into theirs at about 3 am.

'You and your bloody animals,' grumbled Tom as he turned out the light. 'We needed this like a hole in the head!' But they both went to sleep smiling.

The first person to make an enquiry about the Velsen was Jackson Conway, the dealer who had spotted the Markey Robinson a few months ago. His speciality was Irish art – old and contemporary.

'Can you tell me anything about that painting?' he asked Tom, 'the one down there at the fireplace – the one of the house and the lake. You have it in the catalogue, described as "after the Impressionist style." What do you mean by that?'

Tom squirmed. He could tell this man knew a lot – and knew that he didn't. But he went along with what Sean had told him to do.

'I'm afraid that's all I can tell you, Jackson. We found it in an attic in a vacated house on the Antrim Road. Maddy thought it might be something and showed it to Westbury's but they weren't interested. They said it was just that: "after the style of the Impressionists".'

'Oh, right. There's something about it though, isn't there? I might just take a punt on it.'

'It's up to you, Jackson. I wouldn't give it house room myself. Do you want to leave a bid on it?'

Jackson said he would go home and think about it and departed. Tom hoped he'd managed to convey a disinterested demeanour.

Later, another dealer, Thomas McCreery, asked Tom if he could take it off the wall and have a look at the back. He also wanted to know about the other two paintings left in with the Velsen.

Tom was beginning to seriously wonder if their buyers were a good deal cleverer than Sean had imagined they were. God, how he wished it was all over.

He knew the back of the Velsen would only tell anyone it wasn't a recent painting but little else as there were no inscriptions or labels. They had all been removed.

215

Thomas gave a non committal 'hmmm', said he might come to the auction tomorrow and left with a thoughtful expression. Tom had a dark feeling that Thomas knew something.

As the day progressed it became busier with viewers chatting and leaving bids, but Tom couldn't help scrutinising anyone he wasn't familiar with.

Quite a few faces they hadn't seen before appeared, but that was usual now as more and more people were coming to each successive auction. The baddies could have been any one of them.

There was no sign of Sean unless he had finally perfected the art of disguise and any of the newcomers could have been plain-clothes police.

As Maddy checked the saleroom, she thought it looked good with all the pine furniture, the brass beds, now polished and gleaming, strewn with the quilts and the antique pieces collected from Slam Duncan and other people were well displayed. The glassware and china were shining and clean and the walls were covered with pictures.

It looked full and interesting.

With some surprise she saw Lady Bandon appear, accompanied by a slightly older, harder looking woman, stunning in her own way with a perfectly cut blonde bob and equally well cut tweed jacket and skirt. They were going over to talk to Tom so she decided to go to the fireplace and put another log on the fire. She would wait and say 'hello' when they came round the room to where she was.

The log she had placed on the fire began to spit and crackle and she was gazing at it, wondering if she should get the fireguard when she heard a sharp intake of breath not far behind her.

'My God, Amanda, that's my painting!'

Maddy froze but didn't turn round. Out of the corner of her eye she could see Lady Bandon's friend standing in front of the Velsen with her hand over her mouth gazing at the painting in astonishment. Luckily there were few people at that end of the room and Maddy had only just heard her shocked, whispered exclamation.

'Surely not,' said Lady Bandon. 'It's an awful thing – I

could never imagine you would have a thing like that – far too bright – a splodge if ever I saw one! It could have been done by a child!'

'No, you don't realise, my dear, it's a Velsen.' She paused with some drama, 'MY Velsen!'

'I never knew you'd had an affair with a Dutch man!' Lady Bandon said quietly with a slight aspersion on 'Dutch'

'No! Of course I didn't. The man I was having an affair with sort of gave me that picture. Well, he asked me to look after it for him. It's painted by an artist called Velsen. He came from Cork.'

'A painter called Velsen who came from Cork?'

'No, silly, the man I was having an affair with!'

'Christ, it wasn't that thief, Michael Curgeon, was it?'

'God! How on earth did you know – don't tell me – not YOU too?'

'Well, darling, I am not as green as that little shamrock that grows on our Isle! Are you sure that's your picture?'

'Of course, I'm sure. Oh gosh, I sooo enjoyed it.'

'Too much information, darling.'

'Not the affair, the picture – well - the affair too, I suppose. But it was jolly awkward when it was stolen along with all of our stuff – impossible to explain to the police that it had been stolen already, if you know what I mean, so I just sort of kept quiet.'

'Well, if that's the case, don't you think you should keep quiet now? What if they found out old Blinky had claimed the insurance money for it not realising it wasn't one he had bought?'

'Gosh, yes. I mean he acquires stuff all the time from all over the place. He never talks to me about it and I am sure he can't possibly remember everything he has. The insurance people come from time to time to make lists and things. I had that picture in my room hanging over my bed. They probably just assumed it was his. Oh God, I loved it, I really did.'

'Oh Christ, Lucy, you are impossible. I think you should calm down and keep a low profile. Why don't you come to the auction tomorrow and see what happens?'

Her friend thought about it briefly. 'Actually, that might be rather interesting,' she said, and they moved on without noticing Maddy staring rigidly at the fire, expecting MI5 to rise out of the walls.

Nothing happened. She then shot up to Emma who was at the door keeping the register and handing out catalogues.

'Emma, did that friend of Lady Bandon's get a catalogue? Did she give you her name?'

'Yes, she did.' Emma looked down the list. 'Another Lady, Mrs Daniels,' she replied and gave Maddy a satisfied grin. 'We are imminatin' in the world!'

'Yes, yes, Emma. What is her name?'

'Ermm – ah yes,' she pointed to her careful writing in the Register which read: *Lady Eleanor Lamphreigh*. Emma continued, 'She spelled it for me. I don't know how to say it.'

Maddy went white and gazed up at Tom on his rostrum. He was beaming happily at one and all, having been congratulated by Lady Bandon on how gorgeous everything looked and wasn't he wonderful.

He caught Maddy's gaze and gave her the thumbs up sign. She felt weak at the knees as she climbed the ladder.

'Oh! God,' Tom said, when Maddy told him it was Lady Lamphreigh of the stolen painting who was with Lady Bandon. 'What the hell are we going to do now? What if that woman comes back tomorrow and tries to bid for her picture?'

'Let's hope they will just keep quiet and stay out of it all. Tom, I think we should take those pictures off the wall after viewing and keep them in the house for tonight and switch all the outside lights on and.....'

'I think you are right, Mads.' Tom, for once, looked worried. 'And I think I had better ring Sean...'

Later, at about seven thirty in the evening, Slam Duncan appeared, accompanied by Lily. He clambered up the Slingsby ladder to speak to Tom.

'Hello, Slam. What can I do for you?'

'Just came up to see how you're gettin' on. Great place you have here. My stuff looks okay – didn't recognise the desk.'

'Good, Slam. Glad you are pleased.'

'I think I'll have to put more on that desk now.'

Tom's eyebrows shot up. 'I beg your pardon?'

'Well, I see in the catalogue you have it as £150 - £200. That's not enough. I would need at least £500 for it.'

Slam didn't realise that this was not a good time to be testing Tom's patience.

'Slam, we have a collection form signed by you with a reserve of £150.'

He did not say he was holding bids up to £300, which would not have happened if Maddy hadn't replaced the leather and Harry hadn't spent hours restoring the leg. Searching for words to explain that it was too late for Slam to change his mind about the reserve, he had to fight an almost overwhelming desire to shove him hard off the ladder. He then noticed Big Heck and Willie lurking at the end of the saleroom and knew they had put him up to it.

Lily was standing below the rostrum. He thought she looked a bit strange – was that rouge on her cheeks? A velvet hair band held her hair back with a silk rose attached, positioned coquettishly over one ear. Her low cut dress with puffed sleeves and full skirt in a floral print made her look as if she were about to audition for The Sound of Music. She gazed up at Tom with unabashed adoration and gave a fluttery little 'hello' in his direction with wiggling fingers on a raised hand. Tom wrenched his eyes from this apparition and swallowed hard. 'Slam, I don't think you understand. I can't change the reserve now.'

'Why not? It's my desk.'

'Yes, Slam, but we have repaired it, we have cleaned it, advertised it and it has been viewed all day by people who have seen the estimate at £150.'

'Have you been telling people that's the reserve?'

'No, of course not - we never do that - but people who come to auctions on a regular basis know that, if a thing is reserved, it is the lower figure of the estimate in the catalogue. How can I withdraw it tomorrow – and I do announce when things are withdrawn - if it doesn't make £500? I would rather you just removed it now altogether. I will be happy to deliver it back to you.' He made to get up and looked down at Emma. 'Emma, could you possibly find Mrs Daniels – we have to remove ...'

'No, No!' expostulated Slam. 'No! Please don't. I see what you mean. It's been seen now an' advertised an' all an' an' you lifted it an'all...'

He backed down the ladder looking defeated and Tom, knowing the poor man had been set up, felt mean for being so cross.

'Look, Slam, I'm pretty sure the desk will do better than the estimate and there has been interest in your other things. Don't worry. Please trust us. You'll do alright.'

Slam gave him an embarrassed smile and turned away to view the sale. Willie and Big Heck had disappeared.

Lily, in the meantime, was drifting around, turning to look at Tom from time to time over her shoulder, batting what Maddy swore were false eyelashes.

'Talk about glutton dressed as mutton,' Emma whispered to her as they marvelled at her seductive sashaying down the room.

Just when they thought viewing was ending and they could tidy up and take the pictures into the house, the door swung open and in stepped Hadwin Noble. A cashmere coat with a velvet collar was draped over the shoulders of his immaculate suit, his polished bald head echoing his shoes.

He lifted a catalogue from under Emma's nose and waved away her request for a name and one pound with a languid hand. She glared at him and then questioningly at Maddy who gave a slight shake of her head to indicate 'let him go'. She knew his minder was in the yard outside the door and another would be in the car park guarding his Rolls.

Turning to Maddy, his piercing grey eyes zoned in on hers, his mouth widened and opened slightly revealing expensive teeth but closed too soon for it to be called a smile. 'So what have you got here that will take my fancy?'

'It, ah, depends on what your "fancy" is, Mr. Noble.'

Her attempt at a smile had about as much success as his. He was walking down the room now and stopped in front of the Velsen.

'What's that going to go for?'

'Oh, that. A bit of a plaster, isn't it? We were estimating about £150 - £200.'

'Ah. Right.' His eyes seared into her again. She felt he could read her mind, smell her fear. What was she to do now? How much did he know? Was he involved?

'Would you like a cup of coffee?' She was sure each word came out as a squawk.

'Yes, that would be lovely,' he said while turning his eyes towards the painting and Maddy didn't think anything was going to be 'lovely' at all. *Oh my God, Oh my God! What have we got ourselves into? Please help me out of this.*

Maddy pleaded to as many 'On High' as she was wont to do, but none of them came to her assistance. She escaped to get him a coffee wondering if one of the henchmen would have to taste it before she handed it to Hadwin. When she returned he was looking intently at one of the other, older paintings, the Samuel Prout.

'Did this come from the same place?' he asked.

'I am sorry, Mr Noble, but I am not at liberty to say where these paintings came from,' Maddy said, handing him his coffee.

He gave her a knowing look and walked on to view the rest of the sale. What his game was she couldn't even guess at. Sean had said there would be no obvious purchaser, things would just be 'normal' and not to worry.

'He's just a bit of a poseur, that's all,' Tom said after the Rolls departed, trying to comfort Maddy. 'If he was involved, this is the last place he would want to be seen. Wouldn't it?'

Maddy left the question hanging in the air as she cleared away the coffee machine. Then they bade goodnight to Emma, took the pictures into the house and stacked them against a wall in their bedroom.

'Leave *The Farmhouse* on the outside,' Maddy said to her more than tired husband. 'I want to go to sleep looking at the best picture we are ever likely to have to sell.'

'You are quite the battiest person in the whole world,' Tom said as he propped it up on a chair facing her side of the bed. He had seen all he ever wanted to see of that bloody farm house.

Thirty-One

The door bell was ringing and Fizz was barking her head off. 'What the hell?' said Tom, as he leapt out of bed.

Maddy sleepily picked up her alarm clock which said 6.15. 'Who on earth could that be? Oh dear, do you think it's Sean?' She too rose quickly and put on her dressing gown.

'Mads – go and answer that. I need a pee.'

'How can I go to the door looking like this?'

Tom slammed the bathroom door in reply and Maddy, much to her fury, had to go to see to the persistent ringing without her makeup. Who should be standing on the doorstep but Hennessey Bergman.

'Christ, you look good without all that muck on your face,' he commented and, uninvited, walked straight into the kitchen demanding coffee. 'No milk and two sugars please.'

Speechless, Maddy picked up the kettle and turned to the sink. 'To what do we owe this – ah – pleasure?' she finally asked after filling the kettle with water and putting it on the Aga.

'I've come to do you a favour. I've heard a rumour – just a rumour but I have come to warn you that you are going to be asked to shift some stolen goods. I don't know when but I felt you should be told.'

Maddy nearly dropped the sugar bowl she was lifting from a cupboard and tried to compose her addled brain. How on earth could he have known about what was happening or was he referring to something else? Did he have connections with the police?

'Have you any idea what these stolen goods are?' she asked as he sat at the kitchen table to wait for his coffee.

'Paintings, probably. Jewellery and silver can usually be shifted by other routes. Of course, it might be furniture but more than likely paintings.'

'And just what are we supposed to do about it?' Maddy was beginning to get annoyed with all this vaguely threatening, non-specific stuff. Before Hennessy could answer, Tom, dressed now, came down stairs and glared at him.

'This is a bit early to call on people!'

'I have heard a rumour and have come to warn you of dangers ahead, Mr Auctioneer. I know you want to be squeaky clean but it's not going to be as easy as all that!'

Maddy couldn't bear any more of it, handed them both a coffee and went upstairs to get dressed. And, in spite of Hennessy's comments, she was going put her face on. A big brave face to cope with the day! The children would be down soon for breakfast and there was an auction to run...

'Hennessy wasn't able to elaborate any more on what he had already told you,' Tom told Maddy later. 'He insinuated he was in with "certain people" and wouldn't say if they were police or villains. I got the feeling he didn't know anything about today's little affair and, of course, I said nothing. I don't think I will mention anything to Sean about him yet. It could be he's playing some kind of silly game with us. He's a strange chap. It's hard to work out what he's up to. Crikey! We didn't need this today of all days!'

'You've said it,' Maddy agreed as they went out into the yard to greet early arrivals and get ready for this more than scary Sale day.

'Mrs Daniels, do you have a plug handy anywhere?' Larry Bingham, a dealer from Derry had his Volvo backed up to the bottom door of the saleroom with the boot open revealing a huge television set.

'Larry, what on earth are you doing?'

'It's The Grand National today, Mrs D. Did you not know? We want to be able to watch it. Sure, Mr Daniels, you'll take a wee break when it's on, won't you? Surely, you'll want to see it too?'

'It never occurred to us, Larry, but yes, I think I can do that. I'll have to get you an extension lead for your TV,' said Tom grinning. 'And I'll have to ring the bookies and put a bet on – any tips?'

Tom was giving the impression that he hadn't a care in the world and Maddy really didn't know how he did it

'Weather Warning has a fair chance.'

Hmm, that's kind of apt, Maddy thought.

'Or Tomorrow's Dancer. But you know The National, Mr D. It's anybody's guess.'

Tom disappeared to find the extension lead and Maddy walked over to chat to Jennifer and Helen who were setting up their catering equipment on the bar. They had an electric boiler for the teas and coffees and they would probably have to share the plug for that with Larry's TV. She suggested it would be best for them not to be switched on at the same time as the 'electrics' were temperamental in the saleroom.

Emma and Pam had arrived. Pam was busy helping Tom's dad get ready in the office and Emma was having a conversation with Mr Shortall from next door. He was making sure the lane would be kept clear for him and his wife to drive up and down. At the last auction people kept parking so he couldn't get past on his tractor. If they did it again there would, he promised, be trouble.

Maddy found James and put him in charge of the lane. She instructed him not to let any cars park there and to make sure it remained clear at all times. The last people in the world they wanted to offend were the Shortalls who shared their lane and had been kind enough to give permission for Killybane Auctions to go ahead in the first place.

The dealers were huddled together in a corner of the yard, no doubt plotting who and for what each of them was going to bid. Cait and Paddy's van had arrived and they were preoccupied with viewing. There seemed to be a larger number of people than ever before making Carol extremely busy at the door selling catalogues and explaining to newcomers how the auction worked. Emma's job was to 'float' and see to anything that might need sorting out during the sale. James and the porters were organising their duties for the day and Maddy and Tom eventually made their way to the rostrum. From there they could see Slam appear with Lily who settled herself on a chair from where she could fix her obsessive eyes on Tom for the duration of the sale. The hair band she wore today was turquoise velvet, bedecked with sequins and sparkly bits.

'Oooh, your girlfriend is looking stunning this morning,' Maddy whispered to Tom who narrowed his eyes and grimaced at her in reply.

At ten o'clock precisely the crowd quietened down and he began the auction. The paintings weren't due to come up for sale until 12.30 so none of the art buyers were there yet. The sales always began with the items in the yard, followed by those in the china cabinet: jewellery, trinkets, watches, small pieces of silver and such. After these, the lots ranged from modern furniture, collectables, lamps, ornaments, clocks, linens and so on that increased in value as the auction progressed. The best lots, such as quality antiques, large pieces of silver, silver plate, collectable china and often a dinner service laid out on the end table and, indeed, the end table itself, were kept as the last lots in the hope of keeping bidders until then. It usually worked. Curiosity, if nothing else, kept them there. But there was also the hope that at the end of the Sale they just might get a bargain...

Everything was going well until about half an hour into the auction when Mr McCurdle rushed in and began to bid for something. Shortly afterwards James came into the room, grabbed Emma and they disappeared. Then James appeared again and whispered something to Mr McCurdle who turned and ran out of the door. Two minutes later shouts and yells could be heard coming from outside and Maddy didn't need two guesses as to who that might be. Emma then materialised beneath the rostrum and mouthed something to Maddy. Maddy couldn't make it out and Tom had to stop selling to allow Emma to climb up onto the rostrum and talk to them directly. She could hardly speak she was laughing so much.

'Oh, Mr Daniels, sorry to stop the sale, but Mr McCurdle parked his car on the lane. James asked him to move it and he refused, said he was in a hurry to get to bid for something. James said he was blocking the lane and he had to move it. Mr McCurdle just ran off into the saleroom – what could poor James do? Mr Shortall then came up on his tractor, couldn't get past and went away again. Then he came back with a load of ...' At this stage Emma exploded with laughter and eventually got out the word *manure*. 'Now Mr McCurdle's car is well and truly fertilised!'

All three of them and half the auction crowd went out to look and sure enough the McCurdle car was totally buried under a brown steaming mass. Its two headlights were just peeking through the car-shaped heap and Mr McCurdle, a considerable way from it, was hopping from foot to foot, clenching his fists with rage. Emma fetched a yard brush, handed it to him and then she and the Daniels went back to resume the auction. It was a few minutes before Tom was able to switch on the microphone and begin selling again with a straight face.

The time for the paintings was approaching and sure enough all the art dealers had appeared, even those who normally left absent bids. Maddy was now certain they instinctively knew there was 'something' about the Velsen.

Anyway. What's going to happen is going to happen and there is nothing we can do about it. We just have to do what we were told to do. Sell the darned thing, she thought quietly to herself.

She could tell Tom was tense, his voice was becoming clipped and his hands were beginning to shake. There was no sign of Sean but a couple of strangers had appeared.

One was a small, stout, middle-aged lady in a buttoned up red Macintosh who wore a head scarf and large tinted glasses and the other a tall chap wearing a brown leather jacket. He had a trimmed beard and long black hair in a pony tail. He looked familiar and she thought she had seen him somewhere before but knew it hadn't been at the auctions.

Maybe men with pony tails all had something similar about them. Her thoughts were interrupted when she spotted Lady Lamphreigh wearing a hat with the brim pulled down low over her eyes and the deep collar of her coat turned up. Did she think she was unrecognisable?

'Lot number 243,' announced Tom. 'An oil painting, unattributed, in "the Impressionist style". Twenty-six inches by thirty-six inches. Will someone bid me twenty five pounds?'

One of the dealers bid and Tom was soon taking the bids up in increments of one hundred pounds and they kept rising. Lady Lamphreigh was in there pitching too with a determined look on her face.

When the bidding reached a thousand pounds, Pony Tail held up his catalogue and said, 'Two thousand.'

The other bidders looked shocked and there was a pause for a while. Tom was hoping this was the end, but Lady Lamphreigh suddenly came in with a bid of three thousand and gave Pony Tail a vicious glare. He remained impassive and bid four. Lady Lamphreigh seemed to crumble then and turned away.

'The painting is at four thousand now. Any more bids?' said Tom. His voice had lost its nervousness and confidence was exuding from him.

'Four thousand, I am selling at four thousand.'

'Five,' said a calm voice in the crowd. It was Red Macintosh. Pony Tail shook his head and walked away.

'The painting is now at five thousand,' Tom continued. 'Any more bids? None? Five thousand. I am selling at five thousand...' Tom paused, everyone seemed to be holding their breath and a pin falling on the floor would have burst their ear drums. Lily was in a kind of swoon. Tom finally brought his hammer down on the most expensive thing he'd ever sold and he'd loved every minute of it.

Red Macintosh went over to Carol who directed her where to go to pay and the atmosphere gradually returned to normal. The crowd began to move up the room their attention now focusing on the succeeding paintings.

Maddy was about to slip one of the porters a note to tell them to take the Velsen and put it somewhere safe when she noticed a pair of gloved hands reach up and remove it from the wall. It was Lady Lamphreigh. What was she doing? Taking one last look? No! With everyone's attention on the continuing sale, she was walking away with it.

Maddy tried to catch Carol's eye to no avail and couldn't see Emma anywhere. She waved to Jennifer who was standing at the bar as Lady Lamphreigh walked past and all Jennifer did was smile and wave back. As bold as brass, the woman was walking off with the Velsen!

Maddy knew there was only one thing she could do. She left her chair, clambered off the rostrum, leaving a startled Tom, and dived into the throng trying to spot where Lady L had gone. She couldn't see her anywhere. How the hell had she got past Carol? Then she noticed the bottom door had been left open for the lead for the TV and realised Lady L had slipped away through that.

She tore into the yard and round to the car park just in time to see the 'lady' in her car moving out towards the lane. Some bloody Lady, she thought, as she ran after her for all she was worth. Fortunately Lady L had to stop her car to let another come up the lane. Maddy got to her and, yanking open the driver's door said, 'I think I would like to take that painting back, please.'

'What painting dear? I think you must be mistaken.' Lady Lamphreigh didn't make a very good job of appearing innocent. Maddy looked on the back seat and it was empty.

'Would you mind opening your boot, Lady Lamphreigh? I saw you take that painting.'

Lady L saw a chance and put her foot down, knocking over Maddy, but another car coming up the lane forced Lady L to stop again. Maddy struggled back to her feet, anger helping her to ignore the pain she felt down her side, and ran over to open the car door once more.

'What on earth are you trying to do? For God's sake, stop the car!' Maddy begged. 'You'll have to back up and let that person through. You won't be able to get away now.'

Tears began to roll down Lady Lamphreigh's face.

'It's all I have left of him,' she whimpered, 'the love of my life'.

'Lady Lamphreigh, back this car up NOW,' Maddy shouted. 'Let that other car through, go back to the car park and we can . . .' she took a deep breath, 'talk about this.'

Lady Lamphreigh did as requested and they sat side by side

in the car while she told Maddy about her love affair, its final, heart-wrenching end and her departure back to her loveless marriage. Her only souvenir was the Velsen painting. She hadn't intended to take it from the saleroom but when she saw the unattended open door, total madness had overcome her. She was really, really sorry... and then there were more tears.

Maddy did, actually, feel for her but could waste no more time as the buyer would now be looking for the painting that was no longer hanging on the wall. The whole operation was on the verge of being completely undermined by this crazy woman.

'Look, Lady Lamphreigh, just give me the painting and we'll say no more about it. I have got to have it back - please.'

Lady L stepped out of the car, opened the boot and lifted out the painting.

'Oh my goodness!' she gasped as she handed it over to Maddy. 'I've just remembered that man, the one in the hat. He said I would shortly be parting with something very precious.'

'What man? Oh, heavens, you don't mean Francis?'

'Yes,' Lady L said. 'I think that was his name.' She began to cry again. 'And he said.....said...I would have a... a broken heart. How could he have known?'

'Maybe he can read faces, Lady Lamphreigh. Please try to forget about him. He's just a mischief maker.'

Lady L looked so forlorn that Maddy was tempted to tell her she would be getting the painting back, eventually, but decided that would be unwise and let her go on her sad, lonely way. And, yes, she decided, she was going to have (in Emma's Parlance) Francis Maloney's nuts for starters!

Maddy returned with the painting in time to hand it to Red Macintosh who was coming down the steps from the office after paying for it. Maddy was struck that such an innocuous looking little woman could be involved in all this skulduggery.

She offered to wrap up the painting for her but it was taken firmly and swiftly with assurances of a blanket in the car. Maddy then realised that she had forgotten Tom. She had to get back to clerking. Goodness knows what mistakes were going on with his auction lists. She had missed twenty lots. Gosh. So much can happen in twenty lots, she thought, climbing back up the Slingsby ladder to her seat on the rostrum. It was only then she became aware of her whole left side beginning to ache.

Tom was announcing the break for the Grand National and everyone went to gather round Larry's car. Someone produced some beer and one solitary man cheered when his horse, a rank outsider, 'Laramee Lad', came romping home at 15 to 1.

'What the hell happened to you?' Tom asked Maddy.

Maddy was busy taking the opportunity of the break to catch up with the clerk's lists.

'I'll tell you later – let me do this.'

When finished, she handed them to James to take up to Pam who had been helping Geoffrey in the office throughout the sale. Maddy had noticed they got on really well and frequently came upon them laughing at some obscure monetary joke or other. She also noticed that Pam came dressed to kill on sale days and Geoffrey's shoes were suddenly polished to Fred Astaire's standards.

Tom was getting back into auction mode and muttered to Maddy that he was having problems with Willie and Big Heck bidding up the pieces from Slam's shop.

'Thank God I am holding some good bids on all of it and can bid against them. They are getting annoyed but they can't get away with it! I am running this auction – not them.'

Slam was looking confused as usual and Lily was continuing to give Tom her 'My Hero' look. He was glad the crowd mostly obliterated her from his view. It was all getting a bit much.

Maddy got through the rest of the sale in a daze. She felt a bit sick and wondered if she had concussion. The other two stolen paintings had been sold for twelve hundred pounds and two thousand pounds respectively while she had been dealing with Lady Lamphreigh.

They had been bought by Pony Tail.

Tom had thoroughly enjoyed selling those, so much so, in fact, he didn't give a damn they wouldn't be getting the money for them.

Maddy was crossing the yard to get to the house when a

230

vice-like grip took hold of her whole body. Slam Duncan had appeared and had enveloped her in his massive arms.

'Slam. Ah. Hello,' was all she could think of to say in between bouts of excruciating pain.

'You, Maddy, are a wee treasure,' he said, squeezing her, hard. 'I had no idea what you were goin' to do with all that rubbish you took away and you have done a fantastic job.' He hugged her again and she thought she was going to faint. 'The wee desk made a great price in the end and those rotten chairs and that load of plaster – well, there's no accountin' for it is there?'

'It was a pleasure, Slam,' she said between gasps of agony while trying to get free, politely, from his friendly grasp.

'You can come and take whatever you want next week, love. I'm thinkin' I might even get that lift fixed.'

'That would be great, Slam,' she said. 'We'll get in touch with you – I have your number. I think I had better go and...'

'Ah yes, you would be tired now.' His kind eyes wrinkled at the corners and Maddy would have stayed talking to him for much longer had she not felt so sore and sick. He was a good natured soul and she was glad they had done well for him. Bidding him farewell she got to the house in time to sink into a chair, forbidding Fizz to jump up. She was feeling really odd.

It had been some day. Their relief when it was over was massive, but they were dying to know how it had finished. They had done their bit, but had to know what had happened to the pictures after the auction.

Maddy was wilting but managed to dish out the stew. Carol, after taking Fizz for a walk and giving her and Spike supper, was just about to sit down and eat when Sean arrived. He was brandishing a bottle of champagne and beaming from ear to ear.

Thirty-Two

For once, Geoffrey had to go home immediately after the sale. Emma had a date with Wallace Gillanders and was not staying for a meal and Pam had grandchildren coming to stay the next day so had to get home quickly to prepare for the onslaught.

James and Harry, who were still laughing about the 'manuring' of Mr McCurdle's car, had not been privy to the drama of the stolen paintings, so were swiftly enlightened and sworn to secrecy. They sat spellbound, looking at Sean with more respect than usual, as he regaled the assembled family with what had happened next.

'Now, d'you see when that wee lady in the red Mac drove her Austin Mini to the end of your lane? Well, she stopped, got out, took the Velsen out of the back of her car and hid it in the hedge!'

Maddy gasped 'She WHAT?'

'Tucked it into that bunch of brambles you have at the end of your lane.'

'Oh how awful!' said Maddy fearful for the painting.

'Maddy, don't fret – she had it wrapped in a rug. We had a man on the other side of the road watching her every movement. The poor fellow was in a bunch of brambles himself.'

'What happened then?' James asked.

'We had a guy on a motorbike hidden further up the road who took off to follow the lady in the Mini, but the guy in the brambles stayed watching the painting and within a few minutes,

232

the chap with the pony tail, driving a Ford Fiesta, came down the lane and put the two pictures he bought in the same place. Then he took off with one of us following him. An insignificant little white Peugeot van then came up and parked right beside where the paintings were. A man got out, searched the hedge and pulled them out. He wrapped them up in another kind of a blanket, put them in the back of the van, put more folded blankets on top of them and drove off. Our man in the brambles fished his motorbike out of a ditch and took off after him. And, would you believe it, those paintings were subsequently hidden in ditches, hedges, and even behind a stone wall, before they were finally picked up by the person who led us eventually to the headquarters of the whole thing – well, the whole thing in Ireland, that is. It is huge, you know, worldwide. We can only do so much – but we did it today.'

'Sean, you haven't told us WHO it was!' Maddy said.

'Ah no, I am sorry, I can't.'

'But why the hell not?' said Tom.

'Because we are not too sure yet. It's complicated and very hush hush.' Sean was looking awkward. 'I am a bit like yourselves. I am only part of – like, a link in a chain. Maybe it's just as well you don't know who it is. Anyway, have some more bubbly. You all did a fantastic job.'

Maddy started to giggle and decided that champagne was frightfully good for concussion.

'What is so funny?' demanded Tom.

'Because I know exactly who it is,' she said, just before she slid off her chair and passed out.

'Bloody hell, Sean, I didn't realise how bruised she is,' Tom said when he noticed her arms, as they carried her to the sofa in the drawing room. 'What the hell happened to her? She was only gone for about twenty lots. And she looked okay when she came back up onto the rostrum. She was going to tell me but we haven't had a minute'

'I wouldn't have a clue, Tom. I was only monitoring the saleroom cameras. Look, she seems to be coming round. I don't think we need to call an ambulance. I think she's exhausted as well as bruised. If I can get a word of sense out of her and we can keep her awake for a while she'll be okay. I know a little bit about these things.'

Tom wasn't too sure but was exhausted himself so conceded to Sean's superior knowledge.

Maddy felt better now she was lying down and the awful about-to-be-sick feeling had left her. Tom and Sean came into focus with the anxious faces of the children behind them.

'Sorry. I didn't mean to spoil the party. Stop looking at me like that, I'm fine now. Just a bit groggy. It was a pretty difficult day. Guess I am not as tough as I thought I was.'

She wished they would all go away and she could sink into oblivion again.

Fizz had snuck in and was putting her paw up, prior to levering herself onto the sofa. Sean was talking and asking questions, something about prime ministers and the day of the week. She answered as best she could, put her arm round Fizz, who had somehow wormed her way up beside her, and they both fell into a deep, blissful sleep.

The following morning was not so blissful. Maddy woke up feeling like she had been kicked around a football field. Bruised ribs have a way of creeping up on you and hers felt like they were being tightened slowly by an Allen key every time she moved. She prayed she wouldn't have to sneeze. Breathing was hard enough. Tom appeared with a cup of tea.

'What did you mean, you knew exactly who had done it?' There was no such thing as a free cup of tea with Tom.

'What on earth are you talking about? Do you mean Lady Blooming Lamphreigh? She was the one "wot done me in". The car wasn't going all that fast but blimey I was lucky all I got was a few bruises.'

'No, not that. You told Sean you knew who the big 'ring leader' of all the money laundering and art thefts was.

'Golly? Did I really?'

Maddy sank into her pillows. It was late and she hoped someone had had the sense to take Fizz out. She was also wondering what she had worked out last night. The only thing she could remember was struggling up to her bed in the early hours of the morning. Her thoughts were interrupted by Fizz who, soaking wet from the morning walk with James, bounded into the bedroom and jumped onto the bed. She settled herself damply on Maddy's chest, ignoring the protests, sticking her nose in her face as much as to say, 'Come on – you should be up by now. The day has begun. Time to be up and running.'

Springers, thought Maddy, *they don't let you away with anything.*

She reluctantly decided Fizz was probably right and it was best to be up and moving. She levered herself out of bed and hobbled to the bathroom. A shower would make her feel better.

She had just shampooed her hair, finding it quite painful to reach up, and was languishing in the warm flowing water when she remembered.

Pony Tail!

She knew where she had seen him before. She leapt out of the shower and, wrapping herself in a bath towel, ran to the top of the stairs and shouted down to Tom who was sitting at the kitchen table working at the receipts.

'I've remembered what I forgot, Tom.'

'Oh, that makes a change.'

'I have remembered who it was that I saw. It was Pony Tail!'

'Yes, well, we all saw him.'

'No! I saw him at Bandon House, the first time we went there. I distinctly remember thinking I had never seen a gardener with a pony tail before.'

Tom had now come to the bottom of the stairs and was staring up at Maddy in disbelief. 'You don't seriously believe the Bandons are, what did Sean call it, the perpetrators? That's absurd. He's a peer of the realm!'

Maddy had now made the carpet soggy and was wiping shampoo out of her eyes as she continued, 'What's more, I only saw the wonderful Mrs Tiggywinkle at a distance when we went to collect the furniture, but I would swear she was the woman in the red Mac. God! It's almost impossible to believe the Bandons could be involved in anything like stealing paintings – but, you never know! Hah! Look at Lord Lucan!'

'Maddy, are you absolutely sure? You did have a hell of a clobber yesterday.'

'What are you shouting about, Mum?' asked Carol, appearing from her bedroom, looking bleary eyed.

'Are you seeing Sean today? I think I have remembered something important about the painting fiasco.'

'Yes, Mum. He's coming up shortly. He thought you and Dad could do with a hand, you being beaten up and everything.'

'I was not beaten up! Just a bit bruised. But that is kind of him. We can have a word with him then.'

'He won't be able to stay for very long. He has to go to a de-briefing thing about the pictures. Did you know there was over ten thousand pounds worth of cocaine concealed in the frame of the Samuel Prout? It's so complicated. I don't really understand what it's all about.'

'I don't think any of us do, Carol. I am just relieved it's all over. I never want to be involved in anything like that again.'

Maddy felt better once she was dressed. Not having eaten the night before she could have devoured a horse. Sean appeared and cooked her bacon and eggs. The aroma of grilling bacon roused the boys and soon they were all round the table. Maddy told Sean what she had remembered.

'Ah, Maddy,' he replied, 'I was hoping in a way you wouldn't remember because, if you did, I knew your assumption would be that maybe Lord Bandon was the ring leader. We – the chaps - followed the man you called "Pony Tail", Brendan O'Mahony, and his aunt, "Red Mackintosh" Elish, back to Bandon House yesterday where they played all innocent. Hadn't they just been to an auction on their day off? Of course, by this time we knew the pair of them had form and they are now in custody for questioning. Lord and Lady Bandon were genuinely horrified to have the police descend on them and utterly shocked to learn their attics and basement (now, as clean as a whistle) had been used for god knows how long to store stolen paintings and drugs. It was the perfect place. Who on earth would think of looking there? Lord

Bandon lived in London after his first wife died and had little interest in the house over here. He and his new wife are abroad most of the time now so, "when the cat's away" as they say. I feel really sorry for them and I am hoping to hell we can keep all this out of the papers.' Sean looked at James and Harry. 'I hope I can trust you two to keep quiet about it – it's in all our interests to tell no-one.'

The boys nodded in assurance and Maddy hoped they wouldn't blurt it all out to their friends. They hadn't had so much excitement in years.

'So what happened to the paintings?' asked Tom.

'Hah!' Sean said. 'The string of people handling them eventually led us to a private air field in Donegal. We managed to grab most of them, as well as the paintings before they were loaded onto a waiting plane, but the darned thing took off before we could find out who was flying it. Its registration number is being traced as I speak.'

Sean looked crestfallen. His quest was not over yet.

'At least the owners will get their pictures back,' he said and Maddy felt glad for Lady Lamphreigh but sad for Lady Bandon who was going to lose her gem of a house-keeper and a great gardener.

Later in the day Maddy was sorting out paper work and asked 'Tom, what are we going to do in the accounts about the sold /unsold paintings from the Lamphreigh robbery? Sean did say it all had to be kept quiet so I suppose we can't include them in our list of interesting things sold we send to the newspapers. Sean said we wouldn't hear a thing from the police and to go ahead and send a notice to Round the Auction Rooms column. I have put them down in the books as 'unsolds' to account for the money not being taken by us, but people saw them being sold at the auction so there is no reason why we can't mention them.'

A faraway look came into his eyes.

'Oh Mads, if only we had stuff like that to sell every auction. I really did enjoy selling at that level – even though I didn't!'

'Yes, I know Tom, but I think it will be a while yet! And I could do without all the aristocratic melodrama that goes with it!' Maddy replied. 'I wonder does that sort of thing go on at Westbury's in London?'

'Probably not,' Tom said, 'but I'll bet they are not having half as much fun! God, Maddy, did you ever see such a mess as McCurdle's car? We probably won't see him again.'

'I wouldn't bet on it,' Maddy said. 'I have a feeling it's going to take a lot more than a pile of manure to get rid of him. And I will thank you for not referring to my aching ribs as 'fun'. That woman could have killed me – do you realise that? She was quite barmy. See what 'love' does! Hah! Talking of that - you will have to look out for Lily!'

'I am not going to even acknowledge that remark with a reply,' Tom said and threw a screwed up piece of paper at her. Maddy laughed for the briefest of moments and clutched her ribs again. Laughing was painful.

'Serves you right!' was the only sympathy she received from her husband.

'Did you ask Sean about Hennessey Bergman last night?'

'Yes, as a matter of fact I did. Sean has known him for a few years. He has been on the antiques scene here for a long time. He came over from England and scoured the country for grandfather clocks in the 1950s. They were ten a penny then. He got to know everyone in Ireland, seemingly. He has friends in extremely high places and extremely low ones and, when it suits him, can be of invaluable help to the police. Sean, while acknowledging he is a rough diamond seems to have a great deal of time for him, says he taught him a lot.'

'Hmf! Rough is right, don't know about the 'diamond'. Yet it was kind of him to come and warn us. Oh heavens, I hope he was referring to what has just happened and not another stolen goods fiasco. I don't think I could stand another day like yesterday. And, by the way, where was Sean lurking during the sale? I didn't see him.'

'He was in a surveillance van in the Shortall's field behind the hedge at the bottom of the garden. He showed me inside it.

They are just like the ones on the telly. He could see all the saleroom activity on little screens and could hear everything on ear phones. They have to sit scrunched up for hours waiting for what they think might happen. It must be ninety five percent totally boring. I couldn't stand it. But, hey, I forgot to tell you, he also mentioned there might – just might – be a reward from the company that insured the Lamphreigh estate.'

'Or we could just run off with the money!'

'Sorry, Mads. Sean took it away – fingerprints and so on.'

'Actually, when you think about it, that amount of money wouldn't get us very far!' Maddy was pensive and would have sighed if it wasn't going to hurt. 'Five thousand pounds for a painting that is worth hundreds of thousands. It's a bizarre old world, but I can see now how that laundering thing works. None of those so-called art dealers had the knowledge or probably the money to risk going with their instincts. However, those other two paintings, which of course were signed quite clearly, the Samuel Prout and the Frank Walton watercolours, they made their market value. People must have been bidding against Pony Tail, which just goes to show – we have the buyers now – you know, for that range of paintings. So, scary as it was, it looks like yesterday has done us no harm. In fact, I think it has given us both a lot more confidence. I wonder, do you think . . ?'

'Mads, will you just shut up and let me get on with these receipts.'

They were running late. They had to be ready for people coming after lunch to collect purchases and some, even, to collect their cheques for lots sold.

Maddy put her thoughts to one side and went to check Carol and Sean had cleared up properly. They had vacuumed, for which she was grateful, and had cleared the yard of Willie's chewing gum, torn bidding cards and general gunge that littered it after the sale. There were always bits and pieces left behind that only she and Emma would know which lots they had come from and the purchasers would be phoned in the morning.

As she went from room to room, various things that had happened the previous day came to mind. Like palm reader Francis.

She could see him now, homing in on Lady Lamphreigh who was waiting for 'her' painting to come up for sale. Francis knew instinctively when he saw a damsel in distress. He was standing beside her when she bid. He had probably been stroking her hand and telling her fortune before that. In her present state she would have been easy prey for him.

Wicked and wily as he was though, she remembered him finding a bundle of twenty pound notes in the yard after a previous sale which he had handed over to Tom. Twelve hundred pounds and nobody had claimed it yet. Dealers generally had money in rolls secured with rubber bands in various pockets about their persons so it could have belonged to any of them.

One, a highly nervous individual rejoicing in the name of Aloysius Wilde, had entered a pressure cooker in the last sale and the lady who bought it (for the vast sum of twelve pounds) let out a scream when she lifted the lid. A neat roll of fifty pound notes was nestling inside. Aloysius dropped a chair he'd bought that he was taking to his car and ran over to her spluttering with anxiety. The money was now legally hers! Everyone knew that and Maddy was wondering why neither she nor Emma had checked the inside of the pressure cooker before putting it on display - probably because it was brand new and still in its box. Ah! They would know the next time.

Everyone knew Aloysius and liked him. His energetic enthusiasm for anything to do with auctions was infectious. He loved postcards and would sell his soul for old albums of them but his fancy could be caught by anything if it was going cheaply enough.

He lived in an immaculate bungalow with his wife and young daughter in the grounds of an old house which was the store for his auction purchases. The pressure cooker may have been surplus to his wife's requirements or he could have bought it at another auction. He had obviously used it as a cache for one of his bundles of money.

'That's my – er – money!' he said to the lady who was standing holding it with a look of amazement on her face.

Maddy held her breath to see what would happen next. The

lady, who regularly attended the auctions, fortunately knew Aloysius and had maybe even had dealings with him, smiled and with a twinkle in her eye handed the money to him. The relief on his face was obvious and without hesitation, he peeled off a fifty pound note and handed it to her. With a sigh of gratitude and relief Maddy went over to the lady and thanked her from the bottom of her heart for avoiding what could have been a tricky problem.

'Sure, we all know Ally,' she said. 'He would have done the same for me - although I don't have enough money to leave it lying around and about like that!'

She laughed and trundled home with a good tale to tell.

Thirty-Three

That was the trouble with auctioneering, Maddy was thinking. One never knew the whole story. Sending stuff to auction is only a tiny bit of any story. After all, 'stuff' is merely part of people's lives, never a huge or important part, unless, of course, they fall out.

Maddy would never forget the first divorce they had to accommodate. An auctioneer has to value things. He has to estimate what they would make at auction. If he is a recognised auctioneer in Northern Ireland he is qualified to write these down on a piece of paper and print it and it can be accepted by law.

The client's monstrous purple backside squished next to Maddy's as she settled herself with folded arms supporting her heaving bosom clad in a vermilian home-knitted sweater. They had picked her up at a bus stop somewhere near her home, the whereabouts of same she was not going to divulge.

'Ye'll not tell him where I live?' she said as she got into the truck.

'Of course not,' said Maddy. 'We don't even know where it is anyway – do we?'

'Suppose not. D'y know what that bastard done to me – AND – his bloody mother?'

'Don't think we need to know that kind of thing,' Tom said, trying to manoeuvre the van into a container storage yard off the Lisburn Road.

'Well, I can tell you. He is one hateful wee bit of ...'

'Think we can park here,' Tom said, reversing the van into a marked space.

The client's thighs began to quiver as she looked out of the windscreen of the van and spied her 'ex' standing on a ramp leading to an opened storage compartment that held all their previous prized possessions. Everything was wrapped in padded brown paper bound with sticky tape.

She climbed out of the truck and walked up the other side of the ramp. She glared at him and they stood like figures in an Austrian animated mechanical automaton, poised to come out and jerk their arms and be carried in again after the hour had struck.

Or like something out of High Noon, Maddy thought, as they squared each other up.

'Jesus,' Tom said aside to Maddy, 'what the dickens am I supposed to do now? They look like they are ready to start a war.' Tom, bravely, marched up the slope between them and said, 'Now, what do you want me to value?'

'You could start with this clock,' Ex said, ripping some of the brown paper off a large wall hanging time piece that was nearest to hand.

'Oh, ha, ha, ha!' Purple Bottom sneered. 'He thought he'd bought an antique clock and brought it back and showed it to me like it was Big Bloody Ben. Why is it not tickin'? says I. Because the battery has run out, he says. The money he wasted at auctions! Knew nothin'.' She folded her arms under her bust again and with eyes raised heavenwards, gave a disgusted grunt.

Ex picked up the clock and showed it to Tom. 'It's got Latin an all on it – look,' he said, pointing to the words "Tempus Fugit" written in Olde English lettering over the top of the face.

'Ah! Yes,' Tom said. 'That doesn't necessarily mean it is old. It seems to be a reproduction of an old one. I can't see it making much more than ten to fifteen pounds.'

Ex looked furious and Purple Bottom cackled with delight. He'd obviously paid considerably more for it. They moved further back into the container and the next item they wanted a valuation for was a chaise longue.

'That's MINE!' Purple Bottom expostulated. 'My mother

gave me that and he…' She paused and pointed an angry finger at Ex. 'He restored it. Wud ye look at it! Rooned!'

Maddy could only agree. She had always regarded the chaise longue as a preposterous piece of furniture suitable only as an artist's prop for painting imagined scenes of Victorian romantic propriety or, conversely, uncomfortable impropriety.

The restoration of this one was verging on the lunatic. The turned legs had been cut to short stumps and sported castors twice the size they should have been. The brown and dark green, sculptured moquette upholstery looked as if it had been salvaged from a 1930s 'club' sofa and the decorative turned wood spindles on the back and exposed wood on the front of the arm had been varnished with something similar to dark brown, waterproof, fence-post paint.

Ex looked at it with pride. 'It was a wreck when she giv it to ya,' he muttered. 'It took me ages to fix it up.' He clenched his fists and took a step towards Purple Bottom.

'Ah Hemmm!' Tom intervened, cutting short what looked like the beginning of a nasty incident. 'I think the price that it would make at auction would be forty to fifty pounds.'

'REDICULOUS!' they both retaliated together, glaring at Tom who was now instinctively holding his plywood clipboard firmly over his chest.

Maddy was beginning to wish she had brought her wooden spoon and stepped in now with her infamous 'Right!' She knew she would have to sort these two out otherwise they would be here all day or end up being taken to A&E by ambulance.

'The best way to get through this is if you leave it to us.' They were glaring at her now but she carried on as firmly as she could. 'We, Mr Daniels and I, will go through it and send you a list. If you have no faith in our valuations – no harm done. You can find another auctioneer and that will be that!'

To her amazement, they agreed. Tom ran Purple Bottom home and returned to help Maddy with the unwrapping and valuations. Ex departed in his restored 1950s Buick that defied description - having similar characteristics to the chaise longue.

Two weeks later Killybane Auctions received instructions

to sell all the 'possessions and artefacts' of the estranged couple without reserve, the proceeds to be sent to Purple Bottom's solicitor.

Tom's and Maddy's mouths fell open when, on the day of the sale, both protagonists appeared – side by side. As the sale progressed they checked their list together as their items came up for sale and didn't appear to be too concerned when some were sold for very little. Ex later bought Purple Bottom a coffee. Maddy couldn't believe her eyes and kept making mistakes with her clerking.

At the end of the auction Purple Bottom (who was now wearing a mustard coloured suit) came up and thanked her and Tom very much for 'everything' then she and Ex walked out of the yard with their arms round each other. Last seen, they were driving down the lane in the Buick into the sunset. . .

Thirty-Four

There were no repercussions from the Velsen episode except that Maddy received a huge bunch of flowers from Lady Lamphreigh with a little card saying, 'Truly sorry, please forgive me, Lucy L'. They didn't hear anything from any insurance company and never saw Red Macintosh or Pony Tail again.

Carol was now at Newcastle University reading history so they didn't see quite so much of Sean even though he still came to Killybane's sales and was always on hand if they needed extra help.

Although Maddy missed her dreadfully, she was glad Carol had made the break. There was a while when she thought she and Sean might have decided to make their relationship more permanent, but they had been incredibly sensible and had decided to put it on hold for a while. Sean accepted that Carol needed to get away and see a bit of the world and study her beloved history but it didn't stop him frequently making visits to Newcastle and it didn't stop Carol coming home for as many weekends as she could manage.

The number of people attending the auctions was still increasing and the salerooms had now extended into another out-building across the yard from the existing saleroom.

Harry, now seventeen, had decided he would like to try his hand at auctioneering, so instead of using the space for storage it made sense to use it to sell from. Maddy stepped down from clerking for Tom and let Harry take over to get the feel of being on a rostrum.

After a few sales, Tom allowed him to sell the first few lots of each sale until he felt confident enough to climb up onto his own rostrum in saleroom Number Two.

Harry began his auction an hour before Tom's which included the lots in Room 2, those in the Restorers' Room and any lots there might be in the yard such as the 'turacatta pats' which were still being delivered in their various forms.

Not to be outdone completely James opted to be his clerk. He was no longer required to park cars as children from all around the area of Killybane were queuing up for jobs on sale days. They began when they were about twelve or large enough to help lift things. Being 'old stagers' John and Richard became head porters and supervised the newcomers.

Tom had a found a new clerk in Wendy, the wife of piano tuner Tim, from down the road and Emma had taken over from Carol at the door. Maddy decided she was more use on the floor during the sales, directing the porters, sorting out mixed lots, confused bidders and more often than not, Mr McCurdle.

Emma went into peals of laughter when Maddy read her a page from the book she had acquired about coping with difficult people, particularly those who were prone to temper tantrums.

'The person throwing a tantrum has been allowed to get away with this kind of behaviour since childhood so it is advisable to regard them as a small child. Imagine them with no clothes, wearing nothing but a diaper (the book was American). You will find this will help dissipate your own anger and you will cope with the situation more calmly. Look at the person with a dispassionate, expressionless face and allow them to have their say.'

At this stage Emma interrupted.

'Mrs Daniels, you could never do that.'

'Why not?'

'Because the look on your face…' she giggled.

'I beg your pardon?'

'I can tell from your face exactly what you are thinking whenever anything happens.'

'Oh dear. Then I haven't a hope of coping with Mr McCurdle.'

'Not a chance.'

'Well, listen to what the book says next and maybe you'll be able to do it,' she said, and began reading again, 'After they have paused for breath and you have a chance to get a word in, say something like "I hear what you are saying Mr Jones. Leave it with me and I will see what I can do". The tantrum-thrower will usually retreat and the chances are they will not return or, if they do, they will have calmed down.'

'With Mr McCurdle?' Emma said, 'Not a hope in Hebrides.' Emma always pronounced this 'Hee-brides' for reasons Maddy and Tom never plumbed.

'Mind you, Emma, imagining him stark naked in a nappy rather appeals to me. I think it might help, especially if it has a large safety pin that is about to come undone!'

'Now you are talking!'

Since the manure incident, Mr McCurdle had been absent from one or two auctions but had returned, not to Maddy's surprise but much to her chagrin. He had behaved himself extremely well until one day, during a sale, Cait came up to the office in high good humour. Maddy was helping Geoffrey as Pam had flu.

'My God, Maddy,' Cait said. 'That son of yours is a great auctioneer! There is WAR going on in that saleroom and he is selling away as if nothing is happening and I got a beautiful coffee table for a POUND!'

'Cait - what on earth?' Maddy stood up to leave. 'I had better get down there.'

'Och, it's probably all over now. What happened was Harry was sorting out two people bidding against each other directly in front of him and there was a woman at the back bidding as well but he was ignoring her. She must be new because she should have known Harry would get to her once he had sorted out the two in front of him. Anyway Jim McCurdle went up to her and tried to explain what was happening and she hit him and told him to shut up.'

'So, what did he do?'

'He hit her back!'

'Oh my God.'

'Precisely! But when he hit her, she fell backwards into the woman behind her who fell over too into the man behind her and half the room went down like a pile of dominoes! But Harry was brilliant – he just went on selling.'

Maddy flew down to Room 2 expecting to witness scenes of utter destruction but it had more or less calmed down. Harry glanced down at her with a big smile - he'd obviously taken it all in his stride. She was immensely proud of him.

Mr McCurdle, looking slightly scuffed, scuttled past her to go to the main saleroom and she tried the 'nappy' thing but he'd disappeared before the picture could fully form itself in her mind. And anyway he wasn't throwing a tantrum. It would keep.

Winter was approaching again and the buildings/salerooms were beginning to feel damp and cold. Emma accepted the oncoming hardships because, as her uncle had explained, she had been 'reared in the yard' and the rigours of life on a farm.

Not so for Maddy who, used to central heating and hot and cold running water without thinking about it, found working in winter extremely difficult.

One morning she put Emma in the car and drove into Belfast to the Outdoor Shop. She equipped both of them with ski trousers, jackets and waterproof thermal boots.

'Right Emma,' she announced on the way home, 'we can now survive the winter!'

'Nnnth snthzzth,' replied Emma from inside her down-filled hood.

'Sorry?' Maddy replied.

'Nnth snthzzth,' Emma replied again.

'Emma will you please undo that zip and talk properly.'

'Nnth snthzzth,' Emma reiterated.

Maddy finally stopped the car and discovered Emma couldn't unzip her hood. She was entirely encased in feather down and, unused to such luxury, was about to expire.

'We should have maybe let them put them in bags instead of wearing them home.' Maddy said. 'But they were so warm and comfy I didn't want to take them off.'

'Nth snthzzth,' Emma said now, getting fainter, as Maddy frantically tried to unzip the zip.

'The bloody thing will have to go back. It's ridiculous. Imagine if you were stuck in an avalanche or something. What were the designers thinking of?'

'Nth snthzzth,' came even more faintly from the hood.

Eventually after much tugging and swearing Maddy got the zip to undo and exposed a gasping Emma.

'Oh Mrs Daniels, I thought I was going to suffocate in there. I just pulled the zip up to see where it went and it got caught up with the price tag and a bit of my hair. Did you not hear me screaming?'

'No, Emma,' Maddy said. 'Inside a ski suit – no one can hear you scream. . .'

Emma didn't get the joke and picked bits of hair and label out of her zip. She was beginning to wonder if her female boss was, maybe, a wee bit, as they say lacking?

The unsympathetic weather continued and the thought of another three or even four months of it was more than Maddy could stand.

'I swear, Tom, it's like working under a waterfall in a cold, damp, drippy cave – without that sense of wonder one would normally feel in such circumstances!'

The rain had been falling in sheets off the ancient gutterless roof and negotiating the door was akin to one of those unavoidable showers you had to go through in old fashioned swimming pools. Maddy and Emma were not only clad in their full ski gear but sou'westers as well. They looked like two diminutive Michelin men about to tackle the high seas. Emma, as usual, was taking it all in her stride but Maddy had nearly had enough.

Now the full Irish winter had set in, working in this shed/store that had been a wonderful idea in the summer, was proving to be little better than working in the car park.

The small add-on building at the back of the saleroom had once been used for livestock and Tom had reared pheasants in there for a local shoot. Its stone walls wept with damp, the single, ill fitting mesh covered window rattled in the wind and, after a particularly long day of rain, a small spring emerged from the hardened earth floor in a corner and flowed gently towards the door. Their waterproof thermal boots were requisite as well.

Smalls had been piling up in the house to such an extent it was becoming impossible to move from room to room without stepping over a box or walking round piles of china, books, linen and myriad other items. Although housework was never Maddy's forte she almost yearned to be able to use her vacuum cleaner again.

They had decided that, if they put a padlock on the door and some shelving round the walls, this little building would make an ideal place to store the smalls from now on. A table in the middle served for unpacking and numerous trays were acquired for their final move to the saleroom. The fact that things needed to be washed occasionally meant Maddy and Emma had quite a trek to and from the kitchen in the house - the only place where there was hot running water.

'Tom,' Maddy said after trudging in with another tray of dirty glass and china, 'if we can afford a big posh van, could we not afford a decent workshop, with a sink? We could build one out at the .....'

'For goodness sake, Mads. Stop talking rubbish. Have you any idea how much that would cost.' This was not a question it was a final statement.

'Tom – come here – look at Emma.' She pointed through the kitchen window into the yard. Emma was walking round from the back of the buildings towards the door of the saleroom. She was being pelted with rain, the tray she was carrying had a bin bag over it to protect the things on it and she was walking backwards to avoid the wind blowing her and the contents of the tray all over the yard.

'Tom, we can't go on like this – it's ridiculous.'

'Oh, for goodness sake, you said it was a great idea a few weeks ago.'

'I know, but I had forgotten how awful the weather can be.'

Maddy knew she'd said enough for the moment. It was going to take time but the seed had been sown. What she didn't know was that, in a strange way, help was imminent and things were going to get better more quickly than she could have imagined.

Next view day, Tom found a letter propped up on the top step of the Slingsby ladder as he climbed up to the rostrum. It was addressed to him so he opened it:

For the Attention of Mr Daniels
Killybane Auctions

Dear Sir,
I am writing on behalf of several of your regular customers who wish to express their discomfort and concern regarding the lack of adequate heating in your sheds during auctions and viewing.

As you will appreciate, it is now the winter and temperatures have dropped considerably over the last few weeks. It is no pleasure going to auctions and viewing days and being expected to stand in the freezing cold in your various sheds and outbuildings which have little or no provision for warmth.

Many of your customers are elderly and feel the effects of cold and draughts to a greater extent than do younger ones; others have long distances to travel and would appreciate adequate heat and shelter when they arrive.

I would therefore ask, on their behalf, that you consider up-dating your heating arrangements for the benefit of your customers. After all, I assume that you would want them to put their hands in their pockets for money, not just to keep them warm!

Yours, etc
Ice Cube

'Hmph!' Tom said after showing the letter to Maddy. 'Doesn't that blasted person know how much it's going to cost to heat those rooms?' he exclaimed. 'Why can't they just wear warmer clothes?'

His gaze lit on Maddy and Emma in their ski gear. Even in the height of summer the barns were cold and damp and not pleasant places to work in at all. Tom never felt the cold and had no sympathy for those who did.

The letter lay on the kitchen table among the auction lists and other papers, its arguments shimmering off it like those of an accusatory wife. Tom tried hiding it under things but it kept floating to the surface to silently berate him. Maddy still said nothing. She didn't need to. She could see the signs. Tom began picking the letter up and putting it down again.

'It's quite well written,' he grudgingly acknowledged more to himself than anyone else. 'Obviously from someone who is fairly well educated. Did you see that semi colon? God! They're asking us to spend thousands!'

'Yes dear,' Maddy agreed.

'I mean – for two days, every three weeks. It's ridiculous!'

'Yes dear.'

'Just when we were beginning to make a profit,' he muttered and grumbled on for the rest of the day as the letter seemed to follow him around the house.

Then, silence.

Tom spent a day writing down numbers and thumping his calculator. He went to see the bank and then phoned their plumber/electrician/builder/friend, Michael Ashbourne.

Killybane Auction Rooms were going to be insulated and have oil fired heating installed. They never found out who 'Ice Cube' was, but Maddy and Emma knew they would be eternally grateful to him (or her), as, in their ski gear, they quietly 'high-fived' over the rising spring.

Thirty-Five

As the business grew so did the paperwork. Maddy had acquired another ironing board (bought at Killybane Auctions for the vast sum of fifty pence) on which to spread her lists for checking before each sale. This only lasted for a short time. When the number of clients increased she resorted to spreading them on the floor again.

It was usually about two o'clock in the morning when each lot number had been matched to the correct owner, an incredibly boring job akin to filling in 'Os' and tiring, too. One minute she was stretching up to check the lists on the kitchen counter and ironing boards, and next she was grovelling on the floor.

'There must be a computer that could do this,' she moaned to an equally tired Tom who was checking his own lists.

'Don't be stupid,' he snapped. 'Computers don't grovel.'

By some weird quirk of fate a circular came through the door the very next morning extolling the advantages of an Apple computer.

Maddy was ecstatic. Her grovelling days were over. Help was at hand and with a mere press of a button or two, catalogues would appear like magic, everything would be allocated the correct lot number and all would be joy. *Hooray for the twentieth century*, they both thought. Little did they know what chaos awaited them.

A callow youth with forty seven 'A' levels and a degree in computer science placed the new computer on the kitchen table. Maddy was instantly terrified of it, remembering the time her college introduced the brand new, innovative, electric typewriter. Nervous breakdowns and hysteria had reigned for some weeks as they had struggled to learn how to use it. Instead of thumping keys they now had to develop a much softer touch otherwise the device went off like a machine gun typing rows and rows of the same letter. Tom's attitude was infinitely superior to Maddy's. All you had to do was tap a few bloody keys, wasn't it? Now, which ones?

The salesman was eager and keen to explain that Maddy was quite correct in assuming a computer would get rid of unnecessary time consuming, repetitive paper work and leave them free to get on with the more important aspects of their daily toil. But, knowing nothing about how auctions functioned was of little help in working out how a computer could be applied to their particular business. He showed Tom how to type lists and print them out. And then he went home.

At five o'clock the following morning Maddy woke and noticed Tom hadn't come to bed. She went downstairs to find he was still sitting staring at the Apple, bleary eyed and surrounded with mounds of continuous wide, printed paper with perforated edges.

'Got the hang of it yet?'

'No!'

'Coffee?'

'Yes, please.'

Maddy knew desperation when she saw it.

'Don't you think you should get some sleep? It may help.'

Tom didn't answer, maintaining a hunched, intense concentration, glowering at the machine. 'Oh Christ!'

'What's wrong?'

'It says "Invalid Entry Please re-key" for the hundredth time.'

'What the hell does that mean?'

'Haven't a clue.'

'Can't you ask it?'

'It can't bloody talk!'

'I know, but can't you type in "please explain" or something like that?'

'Okay, here goes.' Tom typed in "please" and before he could get in "explain", "please?" came up on the screen.

'What do I do now?'

'Can you erase that and just put up "explain"?'

'Okay.' Tom complied then "explain?" came up on the screen.

'Maddy, this machine is CRAP! I have wasted all these hours when I could have done the lists manually in a fraction of the time. It's going OUT.'

'Where?'

'Into the YARD! I don't want to have anything more to do with it. And that's that.'

Tom rose, kicking aside the pile of paper and put a hand either side of the computer to lift it up.

'Tom – no! It cost a huge amount of money. Just ring McClellands and get them to come and collect it. Or get them to send someone else who can show you how to use it.'

A force ten gale was blowing outside and rain was battering the windows. Tom was determined.

'Bloody crap con job,' he muttered as he unplugged the computer. 'It is going OUT!'

'Tom, please. Leave it and go to bed. You are knackered.'

He finally gave in, ran his hand through his hair, rubbed his tired eyes and did as he was told.

The computer sat on the kitchen table for several days like an unwanted dinner guest. They ate round it and Tom gave it an occasional glare. A twelve year old was sent by McClellands to show Tom how to use it. The young man was obviously conversant with the intricacies of the world of Apple but unable to convey its marvels to uninitiated dumbos such as Tom who could only follow his instructions for a few seconds after which they dissolved into high tech gobbledigoop delivered at the speed of light.

The computer company then decided a computer programmer had better visit to create a special programme to run the auctions. He did his best but with no knowledge of auction administration it was like asking a good plain British cook to make a foreign dish with unfamiliar ingredients without a recipe. It was almost impossible to explain the self made, convoluted system Killybane Auctions had evolved over two years and the man went away, defeated.

Maddy was dejected. They were working seven days a week, sometimes twelve hours a day, so having the time and patience to master computer arts as well was totally out of the question.

A week or so went by and they continued to organise the sales without the aid of modern technology. Then another circular was slipped through the letter box from a firm of computer programmers who specialised in auctions.

'Now these people sound as if they know what they are doing. I am going to give them a ring,' Tom said and thus began a lifelong telephone friendship with Jenny and Angus who had both worked in well known auctions rooms in England for many years and now ran their own business designing programmes specifically for auctioneers.

Jenny was available on the telephone round the clock and, over the next few months, was able to introduce Tom to the skills required to work the programme. It was not plain sailing as this technology was new to everyone, but Tom had faith that it was going to make a big difference to how things were run. There were other nights of anguish over the Apple, but between the three of them, Jenny, Angus and Tom, particularly using Tom's accounting skills, a programme was developed and would be continually improved upon.

Maddy's ironing boards were placed in a cupboard and rarely seen again. She and Emma's system was turned on its head but became much faster and even more efficient than before. Emma's affiliation with numbers meant she took to using the computer with ease, delighting in her new found ability, frequently being able to tell Maddy where she was going wrong.

Maddy was more than happy to leave it all to Emma as she was still terrified of the thing, but the Apple gradually took over more and more and the Roneo duplicator became obsolete, meaning Maddy could say goodbye to months of churning out auction sheets, catalogues and great globs of sticky ink.

The duplicator had been particularly cranky in the winter time, when the ink froze, and they'd had to surround it with Super Ser gas heaters to persuade it to print. It continued to behave like a huge cosseted Dalek, frequently exterminating her painfully typed stencils, scrunching them up and splatting them out in ink-sodden bits. It took malicious pleasure in feeding the paper through in great chunks rather than one sheet at a time and once managed to grab one of the rubber gloves she wore when using it. She'd pulled her hand out just in time.

Now that the salerooms were insulated and central heating had been installed, 'Ice Cube' no longer had reason for complaint. The heating, of course, was only used for viewing and sale days but Emma and Maddy were now in heaven with a brand new workroom adjoining the back of the main saleroom. It had a sink with hot and cold running water, special shelving for paintings and smalls and two huge work tables for unpacking and sorting. It even had a fridge and an electric kettle. What more could they want?

'Tom?'

'Yes.'

'Would it be possible for us to have a telephone in the saleroom? When Pam isn't here I am going to fall flat on my face one day running into the house.'

'We have the radio phone,' Tom said, lifting up a brick-sized cordless telephone with a large antennae sticking out of it.

'Yes, I know, Tom, but you usually have it in the house, reception is lousy sometimes with our old stone walls and there are so many times when I can't find it. It surely wouldn't cost too much to have an extension from the house phone?'

'For goodness sake! We have just spent an entire year's profit on central heating and a work-room and now you want a bloody phone.'

'Tom, you know it would make sense. Also a phone up in the office during sale day would mean people could phone in with bids while you were auctioneering. A lot of people have complained they can't get through when we are having auctions. They like to know if they have got what they have left bids on.'

Of course, once installed, they wondered how on earth they had managed without them. Maddy even managed to fall flat on her face running to answer the saleroom phone one morning but hid her bruises and embarrassment from everybody, having won her case.

People did indeed phone Geoffrey and Pam in the office and leave bids during the sales so often that a porter had to be detailed to do the running up and down to the saleroom to the clerks with notes of the bids to slip to the auctioneer at the appropriate time.

Killybane Auctions were still making it up as they went along but it was turning into a fairly efficient operation. Eight local teenagers were now portering and they were each given a special jacket with Killybane Auctions and the logo embroidered on the pocket.

They started off with the sleeves having to be rolled up, but as most of them were at the sprouting age it wasn't long before they were bursting out of them and they would have to move on to a larger size.

Much better things were coming in for sale now and they were clearing whole houses but they still hadn't been asked to do a House Sale on site. When they heard of other auctioneers getting them Maddy and Tom ground their teeth with envy and listened with forced smiles to excited reports from the dealers and others.

One view day Maddy was near the phone when it rang and she picked it up. A voice with an American twang said, 'You have a diamond ring for sale in your auction tomorrow – lot 365.' Maddy checked the catalogue.

'That's correct. Do you want to leave a bid on it?'

'I want it but I want to know, what grade are the diamonds?'

'Ah. I will have to be honest and say I don't know.'

'So, you don't know your job.'

'I don't know about diamond grades but I can find out by this evening. If you come to view the ring I will tell you then.'

'I am in New York.'

'Oh. Maybe then, if you would give me your name and telephone number I can call you back when I have the information.'

'My name is Flora Dupont – Mrs – and my number is ...' and she reeled off a long distance number. 'Bear in mind the time difference but you can leave a message,' she added before hanging up.

'Clarity, carats and cut are the first things you have to know about diamonds,' Maddy's helpful jeweller friend, David, said. 'But you have to be a trained gemmologist to say for certain what grade they are. The grades D to M describe colour, D being the best and the whitest.'

He disappeared into the back of his shop for a while and, on reappearing, declared the diamonds to be of J colour. About middle of the range.

Maddy called the New York number. 'The diamonds are J colour, have minor inclusions and medium to faint fluorescence, Mrs Dupont. I hope this answers your questions?' Maddy knew more about diamonds now.

'I want that ring.'

'Okay, would you like to leave a bid with me?'

'No, I will bid for it myself – by phone.'

'Oh.' Maddy's head began to reel. She hadn't reckoned on this when the phones went in and the phone in the saleroom had to be switched off on sale days. They did, however, still have the radio phone which was flex free but didn't always work if it was too far away from a land line. She would think about it later.

'I will call you about two minutes before the ring comes up for sale, Mrs Dupont. Will that be convenient? It will be around 11.30 a.m. our time – about 5.30 yours.'

Hah, I'll get the cow out of bed, thought Maddy with relish and, after replacing the receiver, began to wonder, how the woman had known about the ring.

Was it a family ring an Irish cousin had appropriated? Had she hankered after it for years? It wasn't a startling piece and of no great value as diamond rings went. Surely she could buy something much better in New York?

Auction day came and the radio phone had been tried and tested; it seemed to be working. At 11.30, amid the bidders on the floor, Maddy punched in the number Mrs Dupont had given her, aware of stares from the assembled crowd. Most of them had only seen telephone bids at auction on the telly and it was all rather exciting.

Sharp as ever Mrs Dupont answered and Tom began to sell the ring. It had been estimated at five to seven hundred pounds – roughly a third of the insurance valuation – and the bidding began at one hundred.

'Two hundred', said Mrs Dupont immediately and Maddy felt a rush of adrenaline as the bidding rocketed up to five hundred. She began to imagine dramatic headlines in the newspapers, describing jewellery being sold at Killybane for record prices to bidders from across the world! Then someone in the room bid six hundred and when Maddy told Mrs Dupont she would have to go to seven, all she heard in reply was a sigh and, 'Nah, I don't think I'll go any further. Goodbye.'

The line went dead and the look on Maddy's face caused much amusement as she stared in bewilderment at the disconnected 'brick'.

Thirty-Six

With the advent of the computer, the dynamic of Killybane Auctions changed yet again. The lot numbers, the prices and the buying numbers of each lot could be entered into the computer as the auction went along and, as before, buyers could come up to the office and pay for what they had bought, but now they would receive a beautifully printed receipt with details of each lot purchased. The computer would also digest these details and later print out the vendors' lists, saving Maddy hours of typing on a Sunday after the sale.

Being a typist, it was Maddy's job to enter the information into the computer that was moved up to the office for sale days. Emma sat beside her at the counter to check the sheets as they came up and to take in buying numbers.

Pam and Geoffrey were still needed to keep a manual record of the proceedings as the computer went down with infuriating regularity.

They sprang into action when this happened with not a little alacrity and a 'I told you this modern technology was a load of rubbish' look from Geoffrey.

A slight blip in the electricity grid and the computer screen went blank. If there was lightning about or high winds it threw a complete wobbly and Maddy would feel like doing the same. Knowing more about it than anyone else, Tom was often called upon to stop his auction to come and fix it. It would have all been chaotic without Pam's and Geoffrey's back up.

This was happening one day when Maddy noticed a gentleman leaning against the back wall of the office observing her panic over yet another glitch. He walked over to her and said, 'How would you like to have a battery pack that would take over when your electricity went off?'

'Are you joking? Is there really such a thing?'

'Yes, because I have invented it.'

'Wow,' said Maddy. 'That would be fantastic.'

A few days later, Craig Mitchell appeared towing a trailer with a pile of batteries that would have powered a moon landing. Maddy wouldn't have cared if they had been the size of Mount Everest, as long as they would take away the constant fear of computer melt down.

Along with working the computer during sale days Maddy was still the one person anyone sought out if anything went wrong at the auction, which it frequently did. Her concentration was constantly interrupted by people wanting to ask her things or complain. Emma did her utmost to intervene but it was always Maddy who ended up mediating or sorting out the problem.

She hit on the idea of putting a large vase of flowers on the counter in front of the computer round which anyone trying to get to her had to negotiate. It made little difference though, because they knew where she was.

'Missus Dannnyells!' Nellie Kelly bellowed from the door of the office requiring the instant attention of everyone in the well populated queue. 'Your husband missed my bid – an' he done it DELIBERATE!'

With a determined tread belying her eighty two years and brandishing her blue and white spotted, furled umbrella to make way like an ice-breaker through the throng, she arrived in front of Maddy.

'WHAT are you going to do about it?'

Maddy's fingers went to jelly over the key board and her brain followed suit. Nellie's lantern jaw was resolute as a rock beneath a pair of thin, determined lips. Her defiant, rheumy eyes declared she was having none of this, never had and never would!

'Now, Mrs Kelly,' Maddy croaked, hoping she was smiling. 'I am sure my husband wouldn't have ...'

'Oh yes he did! AND he done it DELIBERATE! And everyone here will agree with me what saw it.'

She glared around at the crowd who suddenly found something absolutely amazing about the ceiling and directed their eyes thence.

A hush descended and Maddy was aware every ear in the room was pointed in her direction. Nellie had both fists resting on the counter, one still clutching the umbrella which was now sticking out behind her like a rudder. The gold Albert and other watch chains which perpetually hung around her amphibian neck dangled like anchor chains.

At the same moment the youngest, smallest porter burst through the door with the latest auction sheets. Like the Artful Dodger he wove through the crowd and, coming up beside Nellie, plonked the sheets on the counter in front of her.

She remained oblivious until, in his haste and smarting from a ticking off he'd had earlier for not coming up to the office with the sheets quickly enough, he whirled round to speed on his way downstairs again. However, the rolled up cuff of his too long sleeve caught the ferule of Nellie's umbrella and with one blissful stroke she was spun round.

As luck would have it there was an artfully placed branch sticking out of the flower arrangement on the counter that suddenly acquired the properties of a hook which caught Nellie's swinging gold chains as she rotated. This had the effect of jerking her quickly back again to face the way she had begun but not before the momentum had knocked her hat over one eye, spilled the flowers and poured water and bits of foliage all over her purple and green silk two piece suit. She would have fallen over had not Jake Wright, who was standing nearby, caught her in his arms.

Thus, now, before Maddy was not only an angry lady but a soaking wet, angry lady in the arms of the quick-witted Jake who immediately said, 'We've got to stop meeting like this, Nellie love, they'll all be talking about us.' At that point, the fascinated bystanders dissolved into fits of laughter.

This was too much for Nellie who must have been suffering from various emotions, not least the one caused by the unfamiliar and long forgotten feel of a man's arms around her.

Confused, wet and perhaps a little starry eyed, she straightened herself and her hat and, wielding her brolly, departed.

Thirty-Seven

The tinkers, Sammy and Gerry Shaughnessy, were now viewing the sales regularly. They rarely stayed for the actual auctions preferring to leave bids with Big Heck or other dealers in the Ring, but there was one occasion when Gerry thought he would have to be there in person.

A well known and long established dealer, Phil O'Neill, from Omagh discovered he had cancer and would have to sort out his affairs. He did not want to leave his wife with the responsibility of the numerous stores he had around the country full of furniture he now needed to get rid of. He'd also accommodated the gypsies for a long time, allowing them to use space in these stores for some of their acquisitions as they never lived in one place long enough nor had the premises to store anything.

Phil called Tom, explained his situation and it was agreed that Killybane Auctions would sell whatever he was unable to sell himself. They weren't particularly looking forward to doing the job because, as Tom pointed out, if Phil hadn't been able to sell it in the first place it probably wasn't tremendous. Still, Phil was a great character, much respected by the trade in general and they wanted to do what they could for him.

Their joints were stiff getting out of the truck after a two hour drive and their enthusiasm had dwindled to zilch by the time they arrived at Phil's warehouse on a remote and windy hill.

Tom had been right about the quality of the furniture. It was all a bit tired, like poor old Phil who gave them a cup of coffee and

266

showed them around. He would have replaced that table leg, or put a new drawer in that chest. He meant to get a replacement pediment for that wardrobe and a new mirror for this dressing table but. . . he didn't need to continue, they understood.

However, Tom could see that a lot of the furniture had what some people might describe as 'relics of auld decency' and would do well in the Restorers' Room so they began to load up the truck.

After removing several wardrobes, a chest of drawers and two sideboards, a whole new room was revealed, which was also full of furniture, including a fine set of six Victorian mahogany 'balloon' back dining chairs with unusual carved ribbon decoration.

'I am surprised you haven't been able to sell these, Phil.' Tom said.

'What?' said Phil, who rose from a battered old arm chair and walked over to see what Tom was talking about. 'Glad you mentioned those. They aren't mine. I was storing them for Gerry Shaughnessy. I have asked him over and over again to come and get them. He would drive you to drink! (Tom knew that Phil was a lifelong teetotaller) You'd better not take them. I'll have one more go at asking him.'

It took about another hour to fill the truck.

'That's nearly it, Phil,' Tom said. 'I am afraid we'll have to come back for the rest if you want us to.'

'Och, you've done a great job, all of you. Look, I've been thinking. Take those chairs of Gerry's and sell away at them. Never a penny does he pay for storage and I have had those and other stuff for years. Those guys get so much gear I think they forget what they have and where!'

Although they were delighted to get the prettiest set of balloon backs they had ever seen, they drove home with sad hearts, almost certain they wouldn't see Phil again.

Most of Phil's furniture went into the Restorers' Room as they had expected but Maddy and Emma had a good old clean at some of it and Harry glued and fixed a few parts that had come loose, so quite a few pieces made the saleroom. The dining chairs were in pride of place at the end of the sale and were much admired on view day.

Gerry and Sammy came to view as usual and Tom watched, fascinated, as Gerry did a double take when he saw the chairs. He picked one up, examined it in the usual way, replaced it and looked up at the rostrum at Tom.

'Dem's a great set o chairs,' he said. 'What d'you reckon they'll make?'

Tom had been expecting him to claim them as his own and, to avoid trouble, decided to plead ignorance.

'Hi Gerry,' he said. 'Yes, they are nice aren't they? Probably in the region of twelve hundred – no reserve, by the way, we just have to sell them.'

'Roight! I'll be here tomorrow.' And with that he disappeared.

The sale cracked on next day and Harry did a good job of selling the things from Phil in the Restorers' Room. Emma had decided to have a go at entering the auction into the computer and Maddy found herself rushing about in the yard getting boxes for people who had bought tea sets. She paused for a while to discuss some prices with Aloyisious. It was then she could have sworn she saw Phil chatting to a gaggle of dealers at the coffee bar.

She went back and peered in for another look and sure enough it was Phil, wearing dark glasses and a duncher cap pulled down low.

It was nearing the end of the sale and people were everywhere, packing and loading their cars. The balloon back chairs were the last lot and it was nearly time for them to be sold. Gerry appeared out of nowhere and stood half in and half out of the door. He could not from that angle see who was at the other end of the room. A porter held one of the chairs up high.

'Lot 607,' announced Tom. 'A set of six mahogany Victorian Balloon back dining chairs. I have bids on the book (his language for absent bids) the lowest of which is eight hundred.'

'Noine,' said Gerry from the door.

Someone at the back of the room bid and Tom said, 'Ten' and pointed his gavel at the far bidder. Then he looked down at Gerry.

'Eleven,' said Gerry.

'It's now on the floor,' said Tom, indicating that the absent bids had been out-bid. 'Twelve,' he said now, taking a bid from the back of the room.

'Tirteen,' said Gerry.

And so the bidding continued until it reached two thousand pounds. The person at the back did not raise his bidding number again and the chairs were knocked down to Gerry who punched the air with delight as he slipped back out of the door into the yard.

Maddy overheard another dealer say to him, 'My God, Gerry, that was some price you paid for those chairs.'

'They were for nothin'!' Gerry replied. 'Sure, haven't I got another six identical at Phil O'Neill's, so I will now have a fabulous set of twelve!' And he went back to his car chortling with glee.

'Who was bidding against Gerry?' Maddy asked Tom later. He replied that the room was so crowded all he could see was a waving catalogue and the bidding number, but the bidder was a man wearing dark glasses and a large duncher. Phil was obviously in remission.

Thirty-Eight

At school Maddy had won prizes for her neat handwriting, so precisely when it began to deteriorate was anybody's guess. Because Tom was the one having to announce descriptions of lots from the rostrum, he had now taken it upon himself to enter them into the computer. For this he was reliant on legible writing on the collection forms and Maddy's drove him to distraction.

'You should have been a bloody doctor!' he declared one day as he strode out of the office and across the yard for the umpteenth time to ask her to decipher what she had written.

'Sorry, Tom – I was in a hurry.'

She always had some excuse, quietly fumed Tom, ranging from, 'my hands were freezing,' to, 'it was pouring with rain!'

Early one view day, Big Heck came up to Tom and, looking keen and eager, said, 'Where's the Beaumier?'

'Over there,' Tom said, pointing to a fairly hideous pale oak Shipyard piece a keen cabinet maker had poured his all into. It had a bookcase with four stained glass doors above an open shelf over a fall-front bureau with two long drawers underneath. It was made in what some people called 'good solid wood' (Maddy's mother would have called it coffin oak) and was large and heavy in the extreme.

As the day wore on other dealers and some privates made enquiries about the Beaumier. Tom had obviously listed it in the advertisement details. One and all seemed to be impressed with the piece and Maddy kept meaning to ask Tom about it as she had never heard of Beaumier furniture.

Biedermeier, yes, but not Beaumier. Tom must know something she didn't. It wasn't until she was going through the sheets on the Sunday after the sale and saw the price it had made – eight hundred and fifty pounds – that she remembered to ask him about it. It certainly hadn't been a thing of beauty in her eyes.

'Tom, what's Beaumier?'

'Oh yes, that. I meant to ask you. It made a great price, the dealers all went mad for it – did you find a label on it or what?'

Maddy checked the collection form she had filled in when she had taken delivery of the bookcase and saw what she considered to be clearly written: 'Bureau Bookcase'.

'Oh dear,' Maddy began to giggle.

'What?' Tom demanded.

'What's in a name, Tom?'

'A rose by any ... No! Don't tell me. There's no such thing as Beaumier, is there? It was your damned writing! And I was just about to put it in the list of items of interest to send to the papers.'

'Big Heck bought it. He's probably trying to flog it to his London dealers as we speak! I wonder what he's going to say to you when he finds out.'

'I feel like giving you a hundred lines: "Maddy must write more legibly in future."'

Some days later Tom came into the new workroom with an odd expression on his face, saying, 'I've just been talking to Conor.'

'Conor McWilliams, our solicitor?'

'Yes.'

Maddy knew something was up and for a moment she was terrified there might be legal repercussions about the Beaumier!

"Tom, for goodness sake, what?'

'We've got a house sale.' Tom was smiling now.

Maddy put down the silver jug she was polishing and squeaked, 'Where? Who? How? Why? When? Is it a big house? Oh! Bless Conor. I want to go and hug him.'

'Calm down,' said Tom. 'It sounds big – a big house, I

271

mean. It's in Rostrevor. The owner has died and has left everything - except some of her jewellery - to be auctioned and the proceeds to go to the Cats Protection League. Conor wants to meet us there tomorrow morning at ten. He says the house is large and full of stuff.'

Emma and Maddy could hardly hold their excitement and spent the rest of the day planning in anticipation. 'We'll not fill the place with dealers' pieces, like the other auction rooms do,' Emma declared. 'They'll want to do that – Big Heck and all of them. Let's hope there's enough in there to be able to say "no" to them.'

'You are right, Emma. Do you remember the last house sale Burrows did? It was full of things the dealers couldn't get rid of. And you could see from the pale squares on the walls that the original pictures had been taken off and the ones the dealers had put in didn't look right at all. Oh, Emma, I want to do a house sale that the owners would have been proud of. Wouldn't it be lovely if we could make it look good, flowers in vases and fires in the grates . . .'

'You're dreamin' again, Mrs Daniels – it'll probably be a filthy old mess of a place and we'll have to work miracles.'

The following morning Tom and Maddy drove through an imposing gateway. Maddy noticed 'Old Fort House' carved into one of the entrance pillars before they crunched up the curving, pebbled drive, lined with mature oak trees. Even though it was nearly the end of autumn the garden was still full of colour from blooms in the shrubs that surrounded the neatly mown lawns. The grey stone house was indeed large and imposing, built perhaps by a prosperous Edwardian gentleman.

They rang the bell and a lady opened the door introducing herself as Georgie, the housekeeper.

'I kept the heat on for you,' she said. 'And I will bring you a cup of tea in a wee while.'

Conor was standing in front of a fireplace in the large square hall to greet them and showed them into an immense drawing room graced by tall windows that looked out onto the garden and the sea beyond. Maddy loved the house immediately and couldn't believe that their dream was maybe, possibly, please God (any God), about to come true.

Conor could see her excitement and grinned. They had known each other since childhood and she knew he'd always thought of her as being a bit wild. She sensed this and was glad that he now realised she'd grown up and could cope with the opportunity he was about to give them.

'I will show you round the house in a minute but I think it would be ideal for a house sale. I want to know what you think – you both know more about these things than I do now. By the way, there is quite a lot of jewellery. Some has been bequeathed to a niece but there is quite an amount left. Could you handle that?'

'Oh yes,' Maddy said, nodding her head and smiling in what she was sure was a completely goofy way. She could already see view day with fires lit, flowers in vases everywhere, brass, silver and furniture polished to the nines.

She dragged her concentration back to the issue and asked Conor if there were insurance valuations for the jewellery. He assured her that he had those and they were relatively up to date. Maddy was glad of this as it would be professionally and adequately described on the insurance forms, saving her the time it would have taken to go through it with David, her jeweller friend.

'You know you can only expect about a third of the insurance valuation, Conor. People find selling jewellery at auction quite disappointing.'

'I am aware of that, Maddy, but I don't think the cats will make a fuss! Mrs Carrington was a lovely lady and she adored her cats. She had ten or eleven when I was here last. She married an extremely wealthy Canadian chap late in life and he died a few years ago. They didn't have any children, hence her bequest.'

Georgie brought in tea and, as she poured it, said although she lived in the village, she intended to look after the house until the auction and she would keep it warm for them to work in. If there was anything she could do they only had to ask. What a lucky lady the deceased had been, Maddy thought, to have had such a thoughtful and kind person looking after her and she hoped Georgie had received a decent bequest as well as the cats.

Tom and Conor discussed commission and logistics as Maddy's mind spun with how they would display the jewellery and all the lovely silver pieces and ornaments she could see scattered about. On view day they would have to have a security person in each room, but the porters would be able to cope with that; it would be a change for them. There were so many things coming into her head she had never thought of before when it had only been a dream.

Conor rose to show them round the house and Georgie carried out the tea tray. Her scones had been delicious and Maddy wondered if she might like to help provide some of the food for the auction. She would ask her later and made a mental note to get herself a big fat notebook for ideas and lists.

The rest of the house didn't disappoint. The bedrooms were all spacious and not one but two dressing rooms led off the master bedroom which had a pale yellow tiled glamorous 1930s period bathroom en-suite. All the clothes were going to The Distressed Gentlewomens Association which Maddy thought was a shame as, after a surreptitious peek into one of the wardrobes, she spied some gorgeous silk flapper dresses. If any were left behind she could always borrow a few mannequins from a local dress shop, couldn't she?

She was belting way ahead of herself again and knew she must slow down and concentrate on thinking about how long it was going to take to sort everything, and get it catalogued. There were some lovely paintings too. They would all have to be assessed and listed properly.

A massive grizzly bear skin, its glass eyes staring blankly at the cornice, was displayed on a wall in a back upstairs corridor along with various moose heads and some American Indian memorabilia. Mementos of the wealthy Canadian gentleman, Maddy reckoned. The animal-loving lady of the house had obviously relegated them to the nether regions of her abode.

There were chests of drawers everywhere, upstairs as well as down, and a quick glance in some of these made her realise going through them could take a long time. On returning downstairs they walked past several pantries full of china and another room with ten empty cat baskets. Maddy was reassured by Georgie that the incumbents were all now with the Cats Protection League waiting for new homes. She didn't want to think about the poor things being uprooted. They must all be missing their mistress and this lovely house with acres of grounds to hunt in. She was glad she had never known the lady or her cats as it would have been unbearably sad.

Maddy was continuing to tot up the time it was all going to take. She reckoned a couple of hours at least to go through each pantry and was silently grateful to Georgie that everything seemed to be spotless. Some of the vases looked interesting and she was sure she had spotted one by Clarice Cliff.

Rostrevor was an hour and a half away from Killybane and she had a day job – remember? Hmmm. A considerable amount of midnight oil was going to be burnt, but she didn't care. She was going to give this auction all she'd got and couldn't wait to get started.

When they came to the back door Conor produced a key and said, with a smile and a crinkled-eyed glance at Tom, 'Now come with me.'

He stepped out into the yard and they followed him round a corner where they came to a garage. Conor put the key in a padlock and slid back an old slatted sliding door. There, glinting in the gloom sat a large black car. Its distinctive radiator grille gave the game away.

'Oh Conor,' Tom said, 'a Bentley Continental.' And on walking round its stunning, flowing form, he whispered in awe, 'An R type fast back.'

'Yes,' Conor said, obviously equally enamoured. 'Isn't she wonderful? 1953 – only two hundred and eight of that model ever made.'

Tom was finding it hard to speak. 'Have they owned this from new?' he managed to ask.

'No, actually,' Conor replied. 'Her husband bought it from that actor – you know the one who was crazy about cars – Stewart Wheatfield – in 1972. He had it from new.'

Maddy gulped. She and her best friend Helen had fallen in love with Stewart Wheatfield when they were twelve, spending most of their early teenage years lusting after him in the local

Odeon cinema. Now she was standing in front of his actual car – one he had SAT in! She couldn't wait to get home to phone Helen to tell her even though she now lived in New Zealand and Stewart Whitfield had died of old age.

'Do you want us to sell that too?' Tom asked. He was trying to sound casual but not succeeding.

'Don't see why not,' Conor said. 'You seem to be able to sell most things, so why not a car?'

Emma was all agog when they returned and Maddy tried to pretend it was a big disappointment but she didn't kid Emma for a minute; together, they did a little dance round the kitchen.

'I hope you're not going to mind going without sleep for a month, Emma.'

'Not if it's as good as you say it is. You'll have to ring Pam. You're going to need her much more if we are going to be away down there all the time.'

'Yes, Emma. And Mary, too. I'm sure she'll want to lend a hand. It's a beautiful house. She'll love it.'

Tom appeared with the diary. 'I reckon it will take us at least four or five weeks to organise. What do you think?'

'At least, Tom. What with things going on here too.' Maddy said.

'Okay,' said Tom. 'Let's make it the 10th of December. It can take the place of the auction we would have had here. People can come and buy Christmas presents!'

He walked over to the wine rack and said, 'For goodness sake, let's all have a drink to celebrate.'

And they jolly well did.

Thirty-Nine

*C*hristmas! thought Maddy. *Oh no!* She had totally forgotten it was so near; it was going to happen almost immediately after the house sale and her parents were coming to stay from the U.S.

Emma found her the next morning with her head in her hands at the dining room table.

'A wee hangover, Mrs Daniels? Would you like me to make you a wee cup of coffee?'

'No, Emma. I would like you to make me a big one.'

Why does everything in Northern Ireland have to be 'wee'? Maddy wondered. Even the postman that morning had asked her for her *wee* signature for a *wee* (huge) parcel delivery. However, she was glad of the coffee and didn't really mind the *wee* thing. On thinking about it she realised she found it quite endearing.

'Emma, I had totally forgotten about Christmas and you know my mother and father are coming. How on earth am I going to cope with all that and the house sale as well?'

'It will all be over by then, Mrs Daniels, and I will help all I can. Sure as soon as the auction is finished we can get stuck in and, if I know your father, he'll only be too happy to help you with anything.'

Emma and her father had bonded the last time her parents had visited. Despite the years that separated them they had recognised each other as downright doers. Emma had helped him chop logs and fix fence posts.

'Why don't you ask him to do the cooking?'

Maddy knew her dad loved to cook and was good at it but he did, at the same time, need a slave following behind him clearing up. He managed to use every pot, pan and implement in her kitchen, even when he was making scrambled eggs. She wondered how he would get on with Sean. But, she decided Emma was right. She had to learn to give in a little, delegate, not be in total control, just calm down, take it a day at a time, manage her time, take Fizz out for a walk, go behind a hedge and scream.

'I know you will, Emma. Please forgive me. You are so good. Thank you for all your support. Now I will take Fizz for her walk and we'll talk about it later.'

She needed that *wee* scream and hoped her dog would be a few fields away when she did it.

Emma, Tom and Maddy plus James and Harry, who were desperate to see the Bentley, drove down to Rostrevor the following Sunday to have a calmer think about what exactly needed to be done.

Conor had taken most of the silver back to his office for safekeeping and they had yet to collect it along with the jewellery. Tom and James were also going to measure up for a rostrum they were intending to build; it was going to be situated at one end of the drawing room.

'Just make sure you'll be able to get it through the front door,' Maddy said, knowing Tom's propensity to build big.

She received a sour look in reply and a wink and a nod from James that meant he would keep an eye on his father – he knew what his dad's constructions tended to be like. Then the three of them disappeared to have a look at the Bentley.

Maddy and Emma walked slowly from room to room trying to decide where the best place was to start. The drawing room, they agreed, would have to be left as it was for viewing, but when view day was over it needed to be completely cleared and the rostrum put in. There was probably going to be enough room to move everything into the dining room.

It was at this stage it dawned on them that, unlike their regular auctions in the saleroom, it was not going to be possible to hold up or point to most of the items being sold. The crowd would not be able to move round with the sale. Bidders would have to view and mark their catalogues and bid from those. If they had two porters working together they could maybe hold up some of the smaller pieces but that would take some planning.

They would need at least four or five locking display cabinets somewhere for the jewellery and silver and each one would need a person to look after them during viewing. The smalls couldn't be left lying about the house as they were at the moment.

They were beginning to see a house sale had its problems alright. They wondered how crowded it would get and how they were going to cope with possible shop lifting. They knew now, from experience, there were some people who wouldn't dream of stealing anything from a shop but considered auctions fair game for nicking the odd piece. It was a continual worry. The best thing was to remove temptation as much as possible.

They soon discovered Mrs Carrington never threw anything out. She had been of that era of the Second World War when everything from brown paper and string to metal hair pins (known as kirby grips) was precious and had to be conserved. Polythene bags from the year they were invented took up entire drawers and shelves, all labelled – 'large bags', 'very large bags', 'small bags' and so on. Pieces of fabric in bundles were everywhere and lavender bags, eucalyptus seeds and leaves were tucked in every nook and cranny. Cat ornaments and calendars were on any free surface and Maddy found herself becoming fond of Mrs Carrington.

She had obviously loved make up, too. Bottles and jars filled the drawers of her dressing table and lined all the shelves in her bathroom. A large linen cupboard on the landing was chock a block with Elastoplast tins on one side and on the other, every Christmas card she had ever received alongside old pill boxes filled with broken stocking suspenders. One of the two drawers underneath was full of corks and the other with cardboard inners of toilet paper rolls.

Later, when Maddy, with not a little sadness, was taking most of these to the dump, a man pounced on the corks and asked was it alright if he took them. When she enquired what he was intending to do with them he said he didn't know but he'd think of something. She wondered if he'd fancy the suspenders...

Tom appeared clutching a gun. It looked like something James Bond would have brandished in one of the earlier movies. He'd found it at the bottom of a filing cabinet in the study.

'I am going to have to take this to my friend, Inspector Hill, tomorrow. I know we wouldn't be able to offer it for sale here.'

'Well, not at the auction anyway,' Maddy laughed. 'Maybe Mr Turnbull would give you a few quid for it – he could send it to London via Westbury's.'

Tom and Maddy planned to come down again the following night to start cataloguing the furniture and paintings. Emma decided she would join them to sort out the linens upstairs that filled ottomans in every bedroom and the large airing cupboard. They too were stored in an efficient and orderly way tied in bundles with ribbon and labelled: 'Mother's double bed sheets – Irish linen', 'Granny's embroidered pillow cases x 4. Egyptian cotton', 'Elizabeth's bedthrow. Sculptured Cotton', 'Two pairs Irish Linen double bed sheets with Oxford hems' and so on.

'It's almost as if she knew we would be cataloguing them someday,' Emma said. 'It's kind of - a bit spooky!'

'Not at all, Emma,' Maddy said, knowing where Emma's fondness for drama could lead. 'She was just a really efficient lady and old fashioned in her way of housekeeping. God bless her – at least we won't have to unfold everything to see if the sheets are double or single. You know how cross people can be when we get it wrong.'

'Don't I know it. D'you remember Mrs Hawthorne when she bought those king size sheets and discovered they were just single ones with a bumpy seam down the middle! I thought she was going to expedite!'

The next morning Tom took the gun to Inspector Hill after phoning Westbury's weapons department with a description. They had told him it was an Artillery Lugar and, depending on condition, was probably worth about four to five hundred pounds.

Inspector Hill explained to Tom that, as it was still an

offensive weapon, there were four options: a) The police could 'buy' it for £20.00. b) It could go to Westbury's in England for sale. c) It could be sold to a person here in Northern Ireland if they could get a legitimate licence for it, which they both knew was virtually impossible, or d) He could just leave it at the Police Station and forget about it.

Tom was tempted to leave it. With all the trouble involving guns that was going on at the moment, just holding it made him feel uncomfortable. It was, however, a collectable piece and, as such, had a value and the cats had to come first so he decided to send it to Westbury's.

Maddy had also found a gun, only smaller. In one of the Elastoplasts tins she had found an exquisitely made silver revolver about an inch and a half long. Wrapped up with it, in a bandage, was a tiny box of percussion caps. It worked perfectly and made an astonishing noise when the trigger was pulled.

In the other tins she had also found broken gold watches, single earrings, broken chains and loose pearls. Every box and tin had to be opened just in case something other than the suspenders was secreted inside.

Maddy eventually began to wonder, was Emma right, had Mrs Carrington known they would be here one day? She had, without doubt, left a fascinating treasure hunt.

It couldn't have been a worse time of the year for driving at night. The road to Rostrevor, winding round the Mourne mountains, was busy with few places to overtake and, after a day's work at Killybane, it was a tiring slog. Still, the house was always warm and welcoming with coffee and shortbread left in the kitchen by Georgie.

They were progressing quite well but it was all taking a lot longer than they anticipated. Maddy couldn't expect Emma to go with her every time she went to the house. Things were really busy during the day at Killybane and the girl was working her socks off. With Fizz for company, Maddy was content to go and work on her own.

One night she began to empty Mrs Carrington's bureau which was full of fascinating old photographs of her from the time she was a young child posing dutifully in lace trimmed dresses. She must have been a good lacrosse player in her youth as there were pictures of smiling teams of girls clutching their sticks beaming at the camera with a large cup or trophy of some kind in front of them. There were others of a handsome young man in full hunting regalia on a huge horse.

Time always disappeared for Maddy when she was doing things like this. Questions, unbidden, came into her mind about all these unknown people whose pictures were fanned out on the floor. What a lovely happy child Mrs C seemed to have been and what a beautiful mother.

The man on the horse, had he been the rich Canadian or a previous 'beau'? Where had she played lacrosse? There were no clues in the pictures. Why had she married so late? How had they come to live in Rostrevor?

She was years and miles away when an unusual sound came from the hall dragging her attention back to the present. It was Fizz – growling. She had never heard her dog growl – ever. She wasn't a growly dog. Barky, yes, sometimes enough to madden. And squeaky, especially when she was chasing a rabbit, but growly, no.

Maddy rose and went into the hall. Fizz was standing with her back to her, every hackle erect (Maddy was not aware she had hackles), staring fixedly at a corner near the kitchen door. Her teeth were bared and she was snarling. The growl was a low rumbling sound coming from somewhere deep inside her trembling form. Going goose-pimply cold in a few seconds, Maddy was unable to move.

'Fizz,' she whispered. 'What is it?'

Fizz turned her head slightly in Maddy's direction then whipped it back again to stare, snarl and growl at a totally empty corner of the hall.

'Think it's time to go home, Fizz.'

Maddy began to gather her coat and bag. At the word 'home' Fizz stopped growling, the hackles subsided and she came over to Maddy wagging her tail, a normal dog again.

Turning off the lights was something Maddy didn't want to

do but she screwed up as much courage as she could and went round the house and did so. Her hand shook as she tried to get the key into the door to lock it which seemed to take forever before she could run to her car with Fizz at her heels.

She shivered as they drove home through the darkness until they reached Newcastle where the bright lights of the promenade made her feel better. Fizz, of course, was curled up on the seat beside her sound asleep, oblivious of the fact that she had given Maddy the biggest fright of her life.

Forty

Tom had gone to bed by the time Maddy came home and she decided not to tell him what had happened. She knew he would put it down to her over-active imagination but she was darned sure she wouldn't go there again without a human companion and certainly not alone again with the psychic Fizz.

In the morning Tom told her that the trade had finally got to hear Killybane Auctions were going to have a house sale. How the word had got out was a mystery but it had. Over the next week, one by one each dealer approached either Tom or Maddy with offers of stuff to help fill the sale.

'I would give you great pieces,' Big Heck said to Tom. 'Now, it would be really good stuff. You could just slip it in and sure who would be to know? And I wouldn't put big prices on them.'

'Sorry, Hector, but we have enough lots already and they are all unreserved. If we had any more the sale would go on until midnight.' Then Tom had an idea. 'And, actually, the lady of the house said in her will that it was only her things that were to be sold in the auction. We can't go against that now, can we? The solicitor wouldn't allow it. It would probably be against the law.'

At the mention of the law Big Heck gave up, but Tom knew he would leave no stone unturned attempting to find out the location.

The excitement and the rumours had begun.

Emma was having the time of her life with dealers chatting

her up, bringing her boxes of chocolates and trying to winkle the address out of her.

'Big Heck has even offered to take me out for fish and chips!' she told Maddy. 'Shall I tell him it's Belfast Castle? What d'you think?'

'Lord! Emma. He'd probably have a heart attack and I am sure you don't fancy giving him mouth to mouth!'

'No, he'd have to take me somewhere grander than the chippie for that!'

Maddy decided not to ask what her idea of cardiopulmonary resuscitation was and returned to cataloguing the silver. She was sure Emma had come with her on that last First Aid course.

Tom had done some investigating for display cases and had come up trumps with Benson Travers and Julian Carter. They ran antiques and book fairs, had regularly attended Killybane Auctions since the beginning and knew everything that could possibly be known about the antique trade in Northern Ireland. Benson had more degrees in history than you could shake a stick at and Julian's knowledge of coins, medals, postcards and memorabilia was vast. They had been partners for years and lived in an amazing house where all the walls were lined with books.

'Not only do books decorate a room,' Benson was fond of saying, 'but they insulate it!'

They had kindly offered to lend their various display cases for the auction and gave lots of advice about the duplicity of determined nickers of stuff.

'How could someone nick anything out of a display case if one is standing over it?' Maddy asked when they went to pick them up.

'I am afraid, dear,' said Benson, 'you will find out.'

'Oh' said Maddy, looking worried.

'When it does, just accept that there are very clever people about and you would have to be as devious as they are to prevent it happening.'

Maddy took this philosophical advice with trepidation but had to get on with things and was soon down at the house again.

The auction was a week away and there was still much more to do.

There had been a huge amount of crockery, glass and china. Displaying this was a problem Tom solved by removing the doors of the kitchen units. Maddy and Emma were able to place lots in the cupboards, separated by the shelves, making it clear where one lot ended and the other began. There was also the added advantage that no-one was going to get bashed on the head by an open door.

Maddy had been correct and she discovered not only one, but two Clarice Cliff pottery vases. One had the rare 'Dahlia' design and the other was from the famous 'Bizarre' range decorated with a bright and cheerful 'Sunrise' pattern.

She knew several collectors who would like to know about those!

A moulded glass rose bowl embossed with parrots, which she found sitting upside down on a draining board, turned out to be made by Lalique. One similar in Millers' Price Guide was valued at five hundred pounds.

Georgie was shocked when Maddy told her about the estimated values, remembering how many times she had tipped dead flowers out of the vases into a bin, then casually rinsed them under the tap. She was even more horrified when she heard about the Lalique bowl from which Mrs Carringston's cats had supped their milk!

Tom took a photograph of the house which was featured atop the advertisements he placed in the newspapers. Another one of the Bentley was placed below. He also put an ad in the Antiques Trade Gazette with little hope that dealers would come over from England but he felt it was worth a try.

Northern Ireland was not getting a good press abroad and the people living there mostly had it to themselves – apart, of course, from the British Army.

Quite a number of officers and their wives stationed with the Army in Northern Ireland, were keen auction goers. Killybane, because it had a single car lane leading up to it, had been deemed by those on high as a safe auction room to go to.

One of these wives, Adrienne Hay-Thompson, had even

ended up working for them, part-time, during her stay. She had worked for Westbury's arch rivals in London, loved the auction world and wanted to keep her hand in. She was, in fact going to help with the house sale as a porter and was desperately hoping her husband and, more importantly, his commanding officer, General Andy Trueman, wouldn't find out. She knew they would have preferred her to keep a low profile. Getting involved in a highly public auction was not low profile.

The general and his wife usually viewed the Killybane's regular sales. He would stride casually into the saleroom as if half his troops weren't hiding in the hedges and lurking behind parked cars ready to leap to protect him should trouble arise. His wife, too, wandered in as if she were dropping in for a casual chat. They were charming, particularly the general who was the most outrageous flirt.

'Hello, Sweetie,' he would say to Maddy, almost nuzzling her with his eyes, gazing at her as if she was the most attractive woman in the world. 'And how are you today?'

His wife at this stage would more than likely be chatting to the auctioneer with equal doses of charisma. Knowing in her heart of hearts the two of them worked their charm all over the world, Maddy still couldn't help looking forward to his visits. He was a kind of pick-me-up who re-asserted a part of her that had long since disappeared with late night typing, heaving and hauling furniture, early morning preparations of the evening meals and the irritable Mr McCurdle.

A few months previously, when the general had been on his way to an exercise, he'd literally dropped in - by helicopter. It had caused great excitement when it landed on the lawn at the back of the house. The pilot told Maddy it was the perfect place for landing, provided she didn't put the clothes line up. From then on she had to leave a note in the kitchen on viewing mornings: 'NO CLOTHES LINE'. Did no-one realise how much else she had to do on sale days?

Now I am an air traffic controller, she said to herself as she cut the sinews out of the kidneys for that night's pie. But then, the general was worth it!

Maddy was beginning to realise she was glad they hadn't had a house sale any sooner without the experience of the past two years. She now had a long list of people she could call on for extra help, as and when she needed them. She knew very well there were pitfalls ahead and they would, once again, learn the hard way, but she was confident they had covered most eventualities and she had a great team behind her. Even her cleaning lady, Angela, who had just started coming once a week, demanded to be involved and turned out to have the neatest writing of all when it came to the door duty, selling catalogues and filling in the register.

Maddy and Fizz were in the hall, Emma was in the dining room arranging cutlery, tying on labels with lot numbers when there was a commotion at the front door. Tom, James and Harry had arrived with the rostrum in the open trailer. They had offered it to the door and yes, it was slightly too big. Tom decided the double doors had to be removed which would give them the extra inch or two they needed. Maddy wondered if they had thought about how they would then get it through the door to the drawing room.

'Morning boys,' Maddy said. 'Ahemmm. Before you remove those doors, have you thought about getting this thing into the drawing room once you have got it through here?' All three looked like they had left their school satchels at home. 'I have some good news for you,' Maddy smiled. 'What about the French windows? Once both of them are open I think the space will be a little bit bigger than the front door and I have a key here labelled 'French Windows – Drawing Room'.'

Maddy couldn't work out if Tom hated her or loved her more at this moment, but James smiled with relief as they trundled round to the front of the house with the thing. She wondered if 'rostrum' was an anagram of 'monster' but there was so much else to do she didn't have time to work it out.

There were enough flowers in the garden and more than enough vases to make Maddy's dream came true. She was able to make an arrangement for every room and put a lot number on each one. The beds were bedecked with gorgeous linens - and lavender bags and eucalyptus seeds. The dining table was laid with a Limoges dinner service and dainty engraved Edwardian glasses but the silver flatware was being sold in its canteen. It was under lock and key with a porter designated to guard it with his life. The room looked splendid as if it were ready for a fine dinner party.

The jewellery was displayed in a long coffin-type glass case on trestles in the hall and the small silver ornaments, including a Boson's Whistle and the miniature revolver (not classed as an offensive weapon) were in another. There was a considerable amount of costume jewellery, some Christian Dior, mostly of the Art Deco period, and it was in two smaller cases, again with a porter instructed to help people view but only one person at a time was allowed to lift a piece out to examine it as per Benson's advice.

There was one ring Maddy had fallen in love with. She rarely thought of jewellery and hadn't craved a massive engagement ring so Tom had bought an antique ring set with chrysoberyls and promised that one day, when he could afford it, he'd buy her one with diamonds.

The ring Maddy fancied was set with a ruby in a cluster of diamonds with a tiny diamond encrusted butterfly on each shank. There were others with whopping great diamonds in them and a beautiful sapphire and diamond necklace but the ruby ring spoke to her. When she thought no one was looking she tried it on and it fitted her finger perfectly. She sighed and put it back in its box.

Too soon, she thought. Killybane Auctions would have to be going for a few more years before she could start asking for diamond rings!

Forty-One

'Right guys,' Tom said to the assembled crew of porters (which included three girls) on view morning. 'This is it! Keep your eyes peeled, be polite – any problems come to me, Emma or Maddy. And don't go hungry. Georgie has sandwiches and stuff for you in the kitchen. Good luck.'

They all went to their allotted posts not a little anxious but excited as well. It was a change from Killybane and everyone had been talking about it. They felt proud to be part of it.

The longcase clock in the hall chimed ten as the eager viewers began to arrive. Emma was doing the first stint with the register, selling catalogues and greeting everyone with her impish smile. She was good at remembering names which made people feel important.

Fires were burning in all the fireplaces and everything *was* polished to the nines. The house looked wonderful and the viewers, Maddy could see, were impressed. The aroma of fresh coffee was wafting from the kitchen where Georgie had set up a coffee station and for a few hours everything looked as if it was going to be a problem free day.

Tom was, as usual, perched on the rostrum talking to folk and taking bids. Quite a few enquiries were coming from England as a result of the advertisement in the Trade Gazette, mostly about the Bentley. Pam was on phone duty and John and Richard were organising the rota for the porters to do guard duty in various rooms. Carol wasn't arriving from Newcastle until the evening and

Sean was going to pick her up from the airport. They would come and help on sale day. Carol wouldn't have missed it for the world. Maddy was lending a hand with the display cases when anyone needed a break, and permanently checking the lots that could conceivably have something taken from them. It was nearing lunch time and the number of people coming through the door began to increase.

At one stage there was a queue down the drive. The catalogues were selling rapidly and were about to run out. Harry, who was now driving, was summoned to go to The Copy Shop in Belfast and get more. They would be ready to be collected by the time Harry got there.

First lesson learned: with a house sale you order ten times more catalogues than you think you will need. Harry wanted to know could they spare Tilda, one of the girl porters, to go with him? She could run in and get the catalogues without him having to park. It would be quicker.

Ho ho, thought Maddy as she agreed, having suspected there was something going on between them for some time.

Once again, she thanked her lucky stars they had given up on the duplicating machine otherwise she might have been heading home to do battle with that.

The stream of people was growing and it became so crowded Maddy knew things were going to go missing. And she was right. Only little things but they made nonsense of the catalogue. Six cat ornaments were now only five cat ornaments. Three glass bud vases were now only one. If only the hateful people doing it knew how much it hurts! Maddy muttered to herself.

Tom would have to announce from the rostrum the next day that lots had been 'altered'. It was infuriating. Then she was reminded of Benson's warning.

She was on duty with the costume jewellery at one of the small display cabinets filled with Art Deco jewellery. Benson had told her to keep it locked all the time even when there was a queue of people waiting to view the contents, to lock it after each person had looked at what they were interested in. Just holding down the lid wasn't a secure enough procedure. Maddy was sure she had her hand on the lid as she was talking to someone about the sale. She looked down and a pair of marcasite earrings had gone. She couldn't believe it – literally from under her nose. It was becoming serious.

She asked Adrienne, the army lady, to take over from her, found Richard and John and told them what was happening. They spread the word to the other porters who went into super observation mode and made themselves as conspicuous as possible.

Then, over the general hubbub of people chattering she heard a low thudding noise that was becoming louder and louder. A helicopter was hovering overhead making the chandeliers rattle. Everyone rushed to the windows to see it settle on the lower part of the lawn.

'My God!' gasped Adrienne and looked frantically at Maddy. 'It's the general! I've got to hide. David is probably with him. He'll give me hell if he sees me here.'

'There's a broom cupboard in the kitchen,' Maddy said, 'Go and ask Georgie – she'll protect you!'

Adrienne sped away. With everyone's attention on the helicopter Maddy was terrified the nickers would take advantage of the diversion and searched out the porters to make sure they were on the alert and not peering out of the windows.

The crowd was getting denser and Maddy's anxiety level was rising by the minute. She then felt an arm round her waist and hot breath on her neck.

'Hello Sweetie!'

It was the general. She whirled round trying to be polite.

'Ah! Good afternoon, Andrew.' She needed this like a hole in the head.

'You are looking gorgeous as usual,' he murmured in her ear. 'I couldn't resist popping in to see how you are getting on.'

'Well, actually, I could do with about a hundred of your men at the moment to keep this lot under control.'

She really meant his wandering hands that had somehow entwined themselves round her bottom.

'Mrs Daniels – Mrs Daniels!' Maddy could see Emma's hand frantically waving from the porch just above the impossible crush of people and she extracted herself from the general's adhesive grip.

'What is it Emma?' she shouted over the heads of several people and saw what Emma was trying to point out to her.

About twenty horses were milling about the drive and one was approaching the front door. It looked as if the local hunt had decided to divert from their usual route to take in viewing the auction.

'Sorry about this,' said the huntsman leaning over and talking to Maddy, 'we need the key for the bottom gate – we usually collect it from Georgie – is she about?'

Maddy heaved a sigh of relief, having envisaged the horses tied up 'ranch' style all over the garden while the riders wandered round the house. She battled her way to the kitchen where Georgie produced the key.

'I am sorry Mrs Daniels – I clean forgot this is hunt day. I should have run round with the key last night. And, by the way, wee Adrienne is in the cupboard next to the toilet. I've locked the door so no-one can open it. She'll be alright there.'

'Horses and helicopters and ladies hiding, Georgie – what do you think we'll have next?'

'Don't know Mrs Daniels, but I heard last night the Womens Institute in Newry is hiring a bus. It's great isn't it? I'm near out of shortbread and the scones have all gone. I gave Adrienne some in with her so she'll not starve! I'll be cooking all night if it is as busy tomorrow.'

Georgie was clearly making a fortune. Maddy went back into the fray hoping she could avoid the general's advances. Couldn't he see she was frantic and trying to handle a chaotic situation? She wondered how he would cope with a war....would he know it was going on? All Maddy could do was pray nothing else would be taken but the crowd was so packed she knew she wouldn't know until viewing was over.

Some while later, having heard the general taking off again, she released Adrienne from the broom cupboard and was battling her way to the drawing room to talk to Tom when out of the front door she saw snowflakes as large as soup plates beginning to fall and lie on the ground. That was all they needed – snow on auction day.

Tom, perched on his rostrum, oblivious of the chaos, was chatting animatedly to a tall, interesting looking gentleman with an (almost) handlebar moustache.

'Maddy, this is Gerald Cartwright. He has come all the way from Huddersfield to look at the Bentley.'

'Gosh, Mr Cartwright, how brave of you to venture over here!' Maddy said. 'Have you got somewhere to stay?'

'My wife is from here,' he said. 'I am staying with her aunt just down the road. I do know it's not quite as terrible a place as the newspapers make it sound.'

Tom asked Maddy if she would mind taking over from him while he showed the Bentley to Mr Cartwright. Maddy climbed up to Tom's perch and was glad of an opportunity to sit down. All their Killybane regulars had come to view and probably the entire population of Rostrevor and surrounding areas, curious to see inside Mrs Carrington's house if nothing else.

At about five minutes before viewing was supposed to end, just when she was beginning to think this frantic day was coming to a close, a loud clanking noise emanated from the front drive. Maddy was wondering what on earth was going to happen next when Hennessey Bergman came staggering through the door looking extremely pale and not his usual blustering self.

His car had skidded in the snow. It had done a monumental spin and crashed into a wall just before Fort House. This wasn't going to stop him viewing though, and with headlights, a wing and a rear view mirror hanging off and a bumper trailing on the ground, he had made it up the drive.

Big Heck, who had been driving behind him, had witnessed the whole thing. Maddy could see he was finding it hard not to laugh as he described the incident to other dealers who were there but he did offer to drive Hennessy home and suggested he called for a removal truck.

When viewing was over it took a while to clear the drawing room, set the computer up in one of the pantries that was going to be the sale office and generally tidy up.

Much to Maddy's surprise nothing else appeared to have gone missing. Lots needed to be straightened up and re-assembled, fire guards were placed in front of the damped down fires, Georgie set up the coffee bar for the following day and Tom, Emma, Maddy, the boys, the porters and Fizz made their way home through the falling snow.

Forty-Two

Sale day dawned in a clear sky with bright sunshine. The snow had lain but it was not too deep. It sparkled and twinkled, making Old Fort House and garden look like a Christmas card.

Maddy decided when the porters arrived as many lots as possible should be packed and made ready for the buyers to lift and take home when they had been paid for. She was terrified the nicking would start again if it became crowded. It was chaotic enough after an auction at Killybane but in this house it would be bedlam. The porters understood and were busy packing, labelling and putting the smalls in a safe place.

Fizz had been shut in the car on view day but Maddy put her bed and a bowl of water in a corner of the pantry/office and she settled quite happily. Jennifer and Helen joined forces with Georgie in the kitchen where they were busy setting up what looked like a spread to end all spreads.

By ten o'clock the house was filled with people again. They were jammed like sardines in the drawing room, chatting quietly, staring from time to time at the rostrum and waiting patiently for the auction to begin. Snow had not put anyone off at all and the sun had melted most of it from the roads.

Tom was holding some good bids on the Bentley, some of the furniture and most of the paintings, but Maddy noticed his hands were shaking like those of an old man as he climbed up onto his rostrum. With seven hundred and fifty lots ahead of him, it was the longest and most important performance of his life but she knew he was ready for it and he'd do it well. The fact that there were no reserves and he could just sell away to the highest bidders would make it easier for him.

Emma and Maddy were ensconced with the computer and Pam and Geoffrey in another pantry next door to do their manual back-up system. James was organising the car parking with Harry, which was mostly on the road, as the driveway had filled almost immediately with hardly any passing or turning space. Hennessey's car had thankfully been towed away earlier.

Maddy was delighted to see Sean arrive with Carol and immediately put them on the alert to watch out for light fingered people. Adrienne and two of the porters had worked out a routine to show the silver, jewellery and ornaments as they were being auctioned so Maddy in the meantime acted as sheet runner.

The sale began with Tom selling the outside lots, garden tools, furniture and lawnmowers. The first sheet of fifteen lots totted up to three hundred pounds.

As Maddy ran with it to the office she realised this was the total sum of their first auction!

As the sale moved on, the totals began to rise and when one sheet added up to three thousand, three hundred pounds it began to dawn on her they were going to make an amazing amount of money. She hoped the cats would be pleased.

Now he'd got going, Tom was having the time of his life, even cracking the occasional joke which everyone laughed at. There was much bantering between the dealers, particularly Big Heck who couldn't resist making fun of Mr McCurdle who, unable to face the crush, was standing on the windowsill outside clutching the open top light of a window with one hand and bidding with the other.

Slam Duncan was there too with Lily who had excelled in her attire. She was clad in a white fur lined cape over a black satin trouser suit. Scarlet thigh-high boots completed the outfit but the overwhelming crowd of people curtailed her attempts at a vamp-like entrance and her diminutive form was obliterated.

After two and a half hours of selling Tom declared a break.

Georgie had made Pavlovas, apple pies, sausage rolls, Victoria sponge cakes and all manner of goodies. Along with Jennifer's and Helen's sandwiches and soup, a party atmosphere developed and most people drifted out into the sunshine to eat and relax in the garden in spite of the snow. There was a sheltered paved area tucked into the sloping lawn like a small amphitheatre which soon filled with auction-goers perched on the surrounding wall all enjoying their lunch.

Maddy and Tom were standing on the terrace just outside the French Windows of the sitting room taking in the spectacular view when a lilting Irish melody began to fill the air. 'Do you hear that?' said Tom. 'Someone must have brought a radio.'

'I don't think so, Tom,' said Maddy. 'It sounds like real music to me.'

And, sure enough, Wee Dan had produced his fiddle and was entertaining everyone with 'She Moved Through the Fair'.

Lily threw caution to the wind and began to sing. She didn't have a bad voice and neither did Big Heck, of all people, who began to sing along with her.

Then Wee Dan moved on to 'The Fields of Athenry' and everyone joined in with that, although most of them only knew the last line.

It soon wasn't long before the tempo changed and a reel was making everyone clap in time and stamp their feet with Wee Dan fiddling away for all he was worth. The strains of his music on that windless, still day were carried way up the mountains behind him and down to the little waves softly breaking on the shores of Carlingford Lough below.

'Gosh, Tom,' said Maddy. 'It's kind of magic, isn't it? Do you realise if my mum's neighbour hadn't had a garage sale the last time I was in California, we wouldn't be standing here now with all this going on.'

'I am not too sure about that, Mads, but if that's what you want to believe...'

A heavy, dark gray snow cloud rolled over the mountain and took away the heat of the sun and the party was over. One and all scurried back to the house and Tom to his rostrum.

'Bet they don't have live intermission entertainment at Westbury's in London,' Pam said as she passed Maddy on the way back to her office.

'I am sure they don't,' said Maddy. 'And I bet they don't have apple pie and pavlova either!'

Fizz had been notable by her absence and was soon discovered being given titbits by one and all. She would return to have a drink of water from time to time and by the end of the day her stomach was so distended she could hardly waddle.

The rest of the day seemed to go in a flash for Maddy. She and Emma took it in turns to enter the lots into the computer and neither of them had a chance to see what the actual auctioneering was like.

Tom said Adrienne had held up the silver and jewellery like a true professional which spurred the Killybane porters to do likewise and they all looked very impressive. The diamond and sapphire necklace made twice the estimate at two thousand and twenty five pounds.

As at many house sales, the private bidders gave the dealers a run for their money. Perhaps it was a desire to have something that belonged to Mrs Carrington or maybe it was sheer rivalry between two neighbours.

Maddy was filled with relief as it had gone so well with no major hiccups and was astonished at some of the prices which had gone way above their estimates. The Clarice Cliff 'Dahlia' vase had made £1,800 and the other with the 'Sunrise' pattern went for £950. The Lalique glass bowl shocked everyone by reaching the grand price of £1,500.

At this, Maddy had a sudden vision of the cats cheering and clapping.

The porters had done an amazing job keeping track of the lots, making sure they were safe and nobody complained about anything! Well, not to her anyway.

The final lot of the auction was the Bentley. Maddy and Emma couldn't bear not to see it being sold so deserted the computer to go to watch. Carol, Sean, James and Harry were watching too.

Tom opened the bidding at ten thousand pounds which was the lowest of the bids he was holding. Maddy looked around for Mr Cartwright, but he was nowhere to be seen. She thought that was odd because Tom had said he seemed really keen to have the car.

Tom took the bidding up from his 'book' to eighteen thousand and then it was 'in the room'. Big Heck bid nineteen. Then, as if from nowhere, Mr Cartwright appeared and bid twenty. Tom was as calm as a cucumber but Maddy, on the verge of hyperventilation, forgot to breathe. Big Heck bid twenty one. Then someone at the back bid twenty two. Maddy couldn't see who it was. She was conscious that Emma, standing beside her, was also afraid to breathe. Mr Cartwright bid twenty three. There was a total silence. Even Mr McCurdle at the window seemed to have frozen solid.

The person at the back slowly raised his bidding number and said 'twenty four.'

Mr Cartwright, who was leaning against the wall with his arms folded as if he did this sort of thing every day of the week, lifted a finger and said 'twenty five'.

Silence reigned again until Tom said, 'I am selling now at twenty five thousand pounds are there any more bids?' Nothing. 'No more bids?' and he brought the hammer down.

Everyone clapped and Maddy searched for the under-bidder in the crowd but didn't ever find out who it was. Mr Cartwright went up to Tom and, smiling, shook his hand.

'Would you have gone any further?' Tom asked him.

'That would be telling!' he said with a grin. 'All I will tell you is Stuart Whitfield was my father and I have wanted that car for a very long time.'

The fact that the porters had packed things up helped greatly in the aftermath. Big Heck told Emma he had been holding a bid on the Bentley for a car dealer in Belfast but it had gone way past his limit. He had bought quite a lot of the bedroom furniture and went upstairs to see what size of a van he would need to collect it.

It took Adrienne and Maddy quite a while to check out the jewellery and silverware. Buyers were everywhere. Flower arrangements were being carried out in their vases, furniture and boxes of smalls seemed to be moving of their own volition through the masses of people coming and going, making their way up and down the stairs.

Maddy and Tom were dying to know what the grand total of the sale was. Nobody seemed to want to go home and an hour after the sale had finished, people were still wandering about with plates of apple pie or munching sandwiches.

A roar and a piercing shriek rent the air, making everyone jump. Emma came scurrying down the stairs in terror being chased by Big Heck in the grizzly bear skin followed closely by Willie with the moose head.

Everything became quite hysterical for some time until they all collapsed laughing.

Benson Travers then appeared. He'd left a bid on some books and had come to collect them. Maddy thanked him again profusely for the display cabinets and confessed to having not heeded his warnings with dire results. He smiled and sympathised and then said a rather surprising thing.

'You know, this house is supposed to be haunted, don't you?'

Maddy went goose-pimply again and said, 'What?'

'Old Fort House. It's on the site of a very old fort indeed. It goes back to Viking times. They say a bloody massacre happened here when the local king was savaged by a huge Viking dog. Probably just folklore but interesting don't you think?'

Maddy swallowed hard and looked round for Fizz who was gazing fondly at Willie finishing off yet another sausage roll.

'Yes, I am glad you didn't tell me that before we came to work here – might have put me off.'

She would maybe tell him the story – one day.

Maddy felt sad after everyone had gone. The house looked battered and tired and she wished she had the energy to clean it and leave it tidy that night but she was exhausted. She'd promised Georgie she and Emma would come back the next day to sort everything out. There were still things to be collected and some people had asked them to deliver some of the furniture. No rest for the wicked, Maddy thought. A hot bath beckoned and a good night's sleep.

Tom appeared from the office grinning like the Cheshire cat and put his arms round Maddy who was standing alone in the hall.

'How much?' she asked.

'Ninety eight thousand smackeroos.'

'Oh my God and Granny's socks!' Maddy said. She grinned up at Tom. 'I think we happen to have a bit of a business after all?'

'I think we certainly do,' Tom replied, grinning back and giving her a huge hug.

'Mind you, we haven't one single call booked for the New Year.'

'Actually we do.'

'Oh?'

'Yes. Did you notice that rather odd looking chap with a mass of curly hair wearing a corduroy jacket?'

'Yes, I did – he had a red cravat and a very expensive looking shirt.'

'Indeed. Well, he is Australian and has inherited a castle here from a distant uncle. He's convinced the troubles won't last forever and he wants to turn it into a hotel. He says it's full of old furniture and stuff he wants us to sell for him. He said he was mightily impressed with what we did today.'

'Gosh! Blimey! Where is it?'

Tom couldn't resist laughing. 'It's on an island - in Lough Erne.'

'You are joking? And he wants us to do a sale – there – in the castle – on the lake?'

'Yes, he does.'

'It'll be as damp as hell and everything will be riddled with woodworm.'

'Stop being a pessimist, Mads. I have agreed we'll go and have a look at it next week.'

Maddy's mind was going hell for leather again and she began to chuckle, imagining how the trade would respond to a sale on an island. She could see Big Heck rowing across to view it and, knowing him, he would swiftly set up a lucrative ferry system. Wee Dan could play his fiddle on the battlements. Tom, expanding on the theme, wondered if he could persuade the general to lend them the use of his helicopter.

'I wonder if Mr McCurdle can swim?' Maddy said, relishing the thought of him floundering in the water. 'I can see Lily arriving in a motor boat – every inch a James Bond girl.'

They ended up sitting on the stairs because all the chairs had gone, laughing until tears ran. It was all totally preposterous – and yet . . .

Fizz calmed them down by scratching at the front door and turning to glare, making it obvious she wanted to go home and Maddy stood up. Tom made her sit down again.

'Before we go, I want to give you something.'

He put his hand in his pocket and took out a small, rather scruffy, old box which he placed in Maddy's hand.

She opened it and there was the ruby and diamond ring, twinkling and sparkling up at her like the snow had been that morning. . .

About the Author

Felicity Graham was born to English parents who came to Northern Ireland in 1946 when she was five. While her parents subsequently moved to the USA in 1964, she married and remained in Ireland; she has two sons.

She and her husband Robin started Temple Auctions in 1980 in similar circumstances to the book's characters, Tom and Maddy, and it thrived for twenty years until they retired.

Over those years Felicity kept diaries and wrote about antiques and collectables for Northern Ireland Homes and Interiors Magazine on a monthly basis. After retirement she attended The University of Ulster, taking a degree in Fine and Applied Art (specialising in ceramics) where she discovered she enjoyed research and writing more than anything else.

Consequently, she also writes about ceramics for Ceramics Ireland Magazine from time to time and covers the University of Ulster Ceramics Degree Show.

Her husband died in 2013 and a few months later she was invited to join a writing group. "It lifted me out of a great slough of despondency and I have been writing, reading and gardening ever since."

'Days of Wine & Wardrobes' is Felicity's debut novel.

Under a Cold
White Moon

By Lynda E Tavakoli

A truly inspiring and often dark collection of short stories from the award winning writer, Lynda E Tavakoli, ranging widely in atmosphere and place but always linked by a common thread - that of human frailty, which the author is unafraid to take on.

These stories often offer insight into the hidden sides of the human condition as ordinary lives belie an underbelly of deception and immorality. A number of these stories have been published in anthologies and broadcast on BBC radio.

Lynda E Tavakoli facilitates adult writing classes and is the author of two highly acclaimed novels – **Attachment** and **Of Broken Things** - and has won several awards for her poetry and prose.

Her fictional and journalistic pieces have been widely published in Ireland, the UK and the Middle East, but this is her first short story collection.

Santa Fe
Sisters
By Colin McAlpin

It is the late 1880s. Sisters Georgina and Violet Sophia Devonshire live in the village of Glenscullion in the beautiful Glens of Antrim in Northern Ireland enjoying a life of good fortune, until misfortune befalls them and they are forced to leave for a new, yet uncertain, life in America.

On the voyage from Londonderry to Baltimore they befriend an elderly gentleman who unfortunately dies during the journey. It is an encounter that changes their lives forever. Along the way, the sisters meet a collection of weird and wonderful characters, including a deadly business rival, a colourful vaudeville singer and an enigmatic preacher man. And romance may be on the cards too. But will their dreams turn to reality in the face of opposition, danger and betrayal?

SANTA FE SISTERS is a carefully researched story featuring strong female characters who will keep you enthralled until the very last page; it's a tale that will linger long in the memory and leave you wanting more.

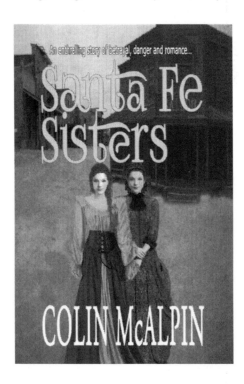

Our Ones
By Janice Donnelly

An insightful, revealing and heart-warming collection of memories about the joys and trials of growing up with family & friends - ***Our Ones*** - in Belfast in the 1960s and 1970s. Janice Donnelly, the author of *'Trying Times'* and *'Buying Time'*, doesn't hold back in expressing the mixed emotions involved in her reflection on a period when her hometown was changing from a city of love and peace to one of chaos and conflict.

"By mid to late seventies redevelopment dictated that we move on or stay put. Most of us moved on. The entire community was uprooted and over a period of time the houses were demolished. Many of us scattered to different areas across the city. We were still the same people, the same family but distance meant that the nucleus became fractured and fragmented. We were still connected but no longer in constant touch," she writes. *"These are true recollections that take me back to a simpler place and time when the streets of my childhood were alive with large extended families – a vibrant, thriving community – and a great place to grow up."*

93866925R00186

Made in the USA
Columbia, SC
20 April 2018